"LORD CASTLEBERRY, YOU ARE FORGETTING YOURSELF!"

A warm flush enveloped her body. His eyes were suddenly filled with warmth and longing. This would not do, she thought. She heard a guttural groan before his dark head bent toward her. Warm breath caressed her cheeks, and before she could jerk herself free, her husband was kissing her.

After that Lady Castleberry lost track of time. And of herself. Her body melted into his, her eyes closed, and her heart felt as if it would burst. Never had she felt such intense desire. There was no fight in her, but she knew for certain she must do something—else they would compromise their business arrangement.

He kissed her again. Pretending to relax, she caught him unawares and pushed him away with all her might. She had to stop this exquisite pleasure. . . .

A DETERMINED LADY

Irene Loyd Black

Zebra Books
Kensington Publishing Corp.

http://www.zebrabooks.com

ZEBRA BOOKS are published by

Kensington Publishing Corp.
850 Third Avenue
New York, NY 10022

Zebra and the Z logo Reg. U.S. Pat. & TM Off.

First Printing: November, 1996
10 9 8 7 6 5 4 3 2 1

Printed in the United States of America

One

James Evans Pembroke, J.E. to the upper five hundred Bostonians with whom he associated, looked at his firstborn and sighed deeply. Olivia, as usual, had her nose in a book. They were in the walnut-paneled library, where rich walnut shelves reached from the floor to the eighteen-foot ceiling, and were filled with leather-bound books, some with gold spines. He suspected that she had read every one of them.

When J.E. had inherited from his father the handsome house on Beacon Hill, the books had been there, and he hoped that when he died, they would still be there. The first editions alone were worth a fortune. The thought of selling them repelled him to the point of convulsions. He cleared his throat. "Uh . . . Olivia, may I have a word with you?"

She looked up. "Of course, Papa."

"Then put the book aside and give me your attention."

His voice was short, and he was sorry for that. But he could not help it. What man wanted his daughter to be a bookworm? And have no thought of her appearance? Obviously the large bun of hair wound onto the back of her head had not been combed and dressed since she had slept on it. Mayhap he should have sent her to a Swiss finishing school instead of to a university that excelled in academia.

Before the choice of schools had been made, many times he had broached the subject of a finishing school, only to have Olivia adamantly refuse, saying she wanted a real education, that her mother could teach her what she needed to know about manners and dress. Well, her mother had tried, but where Olivia's appearance was concerned, the girl just did not care, and she could not sew a delicate stitch, as girls were expected to do, if her life depended upon it.

He said to her now, "About the matter your mother has been discussing with you. She asked me to speak with you."

Olivia's loud groan drowned out his words. "Papa, I have no notion of making a high-society marriage with a man of good standing . . . which means he must have inherited his wealth. God forbid that he should dirty his hands by working." She drew herself up. "I have no interest in Bostonians with blue blood running through their veins. In truth, I have no interest in marriage."

"Then what do you wish to do with your life? You're twenty three . . . and there are no prospects."

"Twenty-three is young," she said defiantly. "And as far as what I want to do with my life, the answer is simple. I want to work for a publishing house, reading great pieces of literature for reprinting, and acquiring new works to be published."

And I want to see my own novel in print.

J. E. Pembroke was silent for a moment. He was small in stature, impeccably attired in gray trousers, a tight-fitting vest, and a white shirt with high collar points. This day he did not wear a coat. It was one of the few days he had taken time from his work at the bank to tend to business at home, and only now because it had been demanded of him by Alice, his wife of thirty years.

He rose from his chair and went to stand by the fire burning brightly in the marble fireplace. Propping his elbow on the mantel, he studied his daughter. He hated this chore, and if it were left up to him, he would forgo it altogether. God's truth, he thought, he did not hold out much hope of Olivia ever marrying. And any man who was unfortunate enough to wed her would certainly need sympathy.

J.E. remembered that when she was a small child, he

would attempt to hold her on his lap and converse with her on a child's level, and she would give him an obligatory kiss on the cheek, bounce down off his lap, and find a book to read to him. His second daughter, Alicia Rose, had not been like that. She had been soft and cuddly, Daddy's little girl. She would make a wonderful wife.

"Olivia," J.E. began again, and he continued, feeling as if some medieval torture were dragging words from his mouth: "Alice. . . . your . . . your mother and I do expect you to make a suitable marriage. She has asked that I tell you we cannot go on supporting you forever."

"Then let me go to work."

"That is out of the question," he countered, his voice suddenly forceful. "A proper Bostonian lady does not work. Nor does she write novels to sell. You are expected to marry, have children, and devote a certain amount of time to proper charities. As your mother has done."

Olivia did not answer. The book she had been reading was in her lap. She wanted to say that it was not her wont to marry and have children and devote time to charities, that she had only one focus for her life at the moment, and that was to get her beloved manuscript published. Turning her head, she stared out the window and was suddenly mute.

"Olivia, you are not listening to me. I need your attention."

"I'm sorry, Father. What were you saying?"

"I am attempting to explain to you that it is no longer your choice about marrying. The Pembroke coffers are near empty, and it is your duty to marry a man of considerable wealth who can, rather than be embarrassed by impoverished relatives, afford to help out with our creditors."

Olivia was appalled. Sell herself, that was what he was asking. "I suggest that you tell Mr. Nash at the bank that you can no longer afford to be a dollar-a-year man, that you need monetary compensation for your work."

J.E.'s brow shot up. Horrible pain showed in his pale blue

eyes. "I could never do that! Think of what it would do to your mother when word got out among her friends."

"Then I will do it for you, Father, and I'm sure Mama will survive."

With that, Olivia made to quit the grand library, walking across its great width, then turning back when she reached the doorway. "Another solution, Father, we can auction off these books. They would bring a small fortune."

Unintelligible words sputtered from J.E.'s mouth, and a muffled groan, but Olivia left quickly. She saw no sense in useless conversation, for she would never, never marry a man under the circumstances of which her father spoke.

Or under any circumstances. Marriage was not in her plans at all, she mused as she climbed the winding stairs to the second floor, where a small sitting room separated her bedchambers from Alicia Rose's. As she neared her destination, her steps slowed. She denied the pain that gripped her heart, and she angrily wiped the tears that had come unbidden to her eyes. But the pain was there; it always had been, since she could remember. J. E. and Alice Pembroke wanted her to be someone she wasn't. When she was a little girl, they would discuss her shortcomings within her hearing, most usually complaining about her love for books. Once inside the sitting room, she knocked on the wall of Alicia Rose's room.

The answer was immediate. "For what does my dear sister knock?" asked Alicia Rose. Seconds later she floated into the room and then bobbed a mock curtsy. "I am at your service, madam."

Alicia Rose, at seventeen, had not reached her potential beauty, Olivia thought. She could become a great actress . . . if only their staid parents would allow her full expression of her talents. Short blond curls framed a delicate, oval face, and dark brows and eyelashes framed laughing blue eyes. The gown she wore was one of perfection—light blue muslin with flowers embroidered around the hem. Puffed sleeves capped her small shoulders. A broad smile, as always, reached up to touch her twinkling eyes.

But the smile quickly vanished when she looked into Olivia's distraught face. "Are we going to a hanging? Or shall we burn someone at the stake this fair morning?"

"You must help me dress my hair."

"Dress your hair! I can't believe this. It must be more than a hanging . . . or a burning."

"Don't be smart, Alicia Rose. I need your help."

The words settled Alicia Rose. "Of course I'll help. I'll have you looking like the queen of England in no time."

"Please, not that. Did you know she's had thirteen children, and she has a mad husband?"

"Poor dear. Now, tell me what has you so worried, while I get the comb and brush."

"I'm going to call on Mr. Nash at the bank," Olivia said. She moved to sit in front of a gold-framed looking glass. "Should I wear my hair up or down?"

"Up if you're going to the bank. The sophisticated look would be proper. Why are you going to Papa's bank?" Alicia Rose asked as she proceeded to braid Olivia's long chestnut hair and then twine it into a delicate bun at her nape.

"To tell Mr. Nash that James Evans Pembroke can no longer donate his labor for one dollar a year, that the Pembrokes are in need of blunt to live on."

Alicia Rose dropped to her knees and looked up into Olivia's stricken face. "Oh, sister, do you mean that? I'd heard hints from the servants about bill collectors coming to the door, but I thought it rumor. The Pembrokes can't be broke."

"Oh, but we are." Again tears pushed at Olivia's eyes, and again she denied them. "They want me to make a suitable marriage, which means a blue blood with blunt. Oh, Alicia, I'm so angry, I could burst."

Alicia Rose patted her knee. "You should be angry," she

said sympathetically. "You should marry only if it is your wont. Why don't they look for a husband for me. I wouldn't mind."

"The oldest daughter must marry first, another antiquated rule."

"What is your wont for your life, Olivia? Besides selling your novel?"

"I guess that is why I've never thought of marriage. I so want to sell my writing, but I can't find an interested publisher in New York. I've written to all of them. So I've concluded that I should make my way to England and search out the anonymous English Lady who wrote *Sense and Sensibility* and *Pride and Prejudice.* She will surely help. As you know, I emulate her style, except my stories are set in the Colonies."

Alicia Rose looked at Olivia with incredulity. "But, sister, if the author is anonymous, how can you search her out?"

"Someone in England *has* to know who wrote those wonderful books. I'll simply go from publisher to publisher and ask."

Alicia Rose shook her head but did not argue. They were a long way from England. She felt sorry for Olivia. The manuscript in question was six hundred pages; soon she would not be able to carry it.

"How much does it cost to go to England?" asked Alicia Rose.

"More than we have. And we can't worry about that now. The most immediate concern is to get Papa properly employed so the Pembrokes won't starve."

Olivia carried herself well when she walked into Mr. Nash's bank. It was an expression of herself, and she had been told that she swept across a room. She had her mother to thank for that. Claiming that Olivia slumped—from bending over books—Alice Pembroke had made her walk with a book on her head every morning for two years. And she had kept a long, narrow pointer handy to swat Olivia across the shoulders when she did not hold her head high, her small chin up, and her shoulders back.

"A Pembroke has pride in her posture," Alice said with every swat. She herself was quite a beauty, with stately posture and a slender body, which she moved with confidence and authority. J.E. jumped when she said frog, and Olivia secretly thought him a cuckolded husband of the first water.

Even so, Olivia loved J.E. as any daughter loved her father; she just did not worship him, and oftentimes she wished she'd been born someone other than a Pembroke. And she abhorred being considered a proper Bostonian lady. How utterly boring.

Crossing the ornate lobby of the bank, Olivia was cognizant of the eyes that swiveled in her direction. She wore a fur-trimmed fitted coat that buttoned to her chin; fur at the hem touched the tops of her half-boots. The plume on her platter hat curled upward stylishly. But she was unchaperoned! Lifting her chin just slightly, she smiled and pretended that she owned the place, or at least was the daughter of the man who owned it. She had been there many times before, always with her mother, or with her father, and she knew exactly where to go.

She went to two huge oak doors, both deeply carved, over which was a plaque with ANTHONY CARL NASH, PRESIDENT, engraved into the brass. Removing her right hand from the fur muff she carried, she gave a curt knock before opening the door.

Mr. Nash looked up when she entered and then jumped to his feet. She proffered a hand, which he took and gave a courtly shake, bowing slightly and looking startled. "Olivia! What a wonderful surprise. Please sit, my dear. What brings you downtown? Not to tell me that J.E. is ill, I hope. I looked into his office and saw his chair vacant. Most unlike him . . . please . . . please sit."

Olivia lowered herself gracefully into a red leather chair. From across the magnificent desk inlaid with gold she kept her eyes leveled unflinchingly on the bank president's face as she said, "No, Father is not ill. There was family business to attend."

"Well, I'm sure he handled it with aplomb. A very efficient man, your father. He is invaluable to the bank. I would certainly hate to attempt to replace him." He gave a little laugh. "In truth, I don't think I could afford to replace him, if that were possible, so valuable is he to the bank."

"I'm glad to hear that, Mr. Nash, for 'tis my father's services to the bank I wish to discuss with you."

Nash's smile quickly vanished. "About your father's services? I don't take your meaning."

"Yes, I'm afraid that he can no longer be a dollar-a-year man for you, Mr. Nash. You must compensate him monetarily if you wish to keep him."

"Did . . . did J.E. send you here to tell me this? I don't believe it. Why, the Pembrokes are well known for their generous giving, and every year I've made a considerable contribution to your father's favorite charity for his work here. That has seemed to be enough for him, and now you are telling me he demands a salary."

"You are perfectly right about the contribution to charity—if you call a mere two-hundred-and-fifty-dollar contribution to buy soup for the indigent of the city a considerable contribution—and I'm terribly sorry that things have come to this end. But I fear it will be the Pembrokes who will be asking for charity if money does not come from somewhere. The family fortune is gone. Either you pay Father, or he will seek employment elsewhere. And no, he did not send me here to do this. In truth, he was horrified when I told him I was coming. I don't think he believed me. Father never could look adversity in the eye."

Nash's mottled double chin quivered. He was a portly man, with dark skin hooding his dark eyes, now a shade darker than when he had first asked Olivia to please sit. She watched him carefully. His demeanor did not bode well. What would she do if he refused, and her father returned to the bank over her protest? Then she would be back on the marriage mart to save the family from disgrace. A shiver danced up and down her spine.

Suddenly, Mr. Nash's demeanor changed, and he smiled broadly. His eyes locked with Olivia's, he said, "You are a very pretty girl, Olivia. I've admired you from afar since you were a little girl and coming to the bank with J.E. I remember that glossy auburn hair falling in waves down onto your shoulders. I'd like to see it that way again."

Why, he's flirting with me, thought Olivia, remaining silent and waiting.

"There should be admirers aplenty for you. A suitable marriage would relieve the strain on J.E., until he can get on his feet. I would be happy to advance money for a fashionable wedding."

Olivia rose so quickly that the red leather chair almost toppled backward. She spat out, "You're no different my parents. It seems I am the only commodity they have to offer."

"Oh, now, don't lose your temper. We want only what is best. If marriage is not a suitable alternative, then perhaps something else can be worked out. I'm very flexible." Leaning back in his chair, he winked at Olivia.

She knew what he was going to propose before he opened his filthy mouth, but she waited, never flinching, never averting her eyes from his, daring him to say it. She was very inexperienced with men, but she had read books that held veiled references to such arrangements.

"Do you not think we can come to an arrangement, Olivia?"

"What do you have in mind, Mr. Nash?" She hid her anger by speaking in a businesslike manner, and immediately Anthony Nash jumped to his feet and rounded the granatum desk. He stopped just short of reaching out for Olivia. She stepped back.

"Put it in words, Mr. Nash."

"Don't call me Mr. Nash." He grinned lecherously. Anthony will suffice. I will do as you ask, offer J.E. a salary, if you will promise to pleasure me on occasions when I see fit."

"In other words, be your mistress? Is that what you want?"

He gave a little laugh and reached to remove her platter hat. "I love the purple plume—"

She slapped his hand. "You despicable pig. I am going this instant to the *Boston Herald* and report this incident. Every proper Bostonian will know your disgraceful bent via the morning news."

"You can't do that, Miss Pembroke." His double chin was quivering again, his dark eyes the color of a freshly hulled black walnut, fright spewing from them.

"Oh, but I can. And since I have an impeccable reputation, I will be believed." She paused to let her words have full effect. "There is another alternative. You can put my father on salary with never a word to anyone about the Pembrokes' penury."

"That's . . . that's blackmail."

Olivia laughed. "So it is." Lifting her chin, she made to quit the room.

"Wait a minute. Mayhap we can bargain."

Olivia turned back. "There's no room for bargaining. I did not expect to be insulted when I came to your office, Mr. Nash. As you said, I've known you all my life. Your paying my father a salary for the work he does for your bank will keep my lips sealed, but you can never restore the high esteem in which you were held in my thoughts. I truly believed you to be a gentleman."

"I beg your forgiveness," he whimpered. "I will do as you ask. I'll inform J.E. tomorrow when he comes to work."

"And you will not reveal this to our friends? They can go on thinking we are living on inherited wealth?"

"That's agreeable, and I trust you will not tell J.E. what occurred in my moment of weakness."

"I promise, as long as you keep your end of the bargain. Should I tell him, he would most likely invite you to meet him on the field of honor."

Olivia knew this was not so, but she wanted to push her advantage while it was hers.

"Good God, duels went out with belief in ghosts."

"Oh, I don't know. Some people still believe in ghosts. Good day, Mr. Nash."

Olivia opened the huge doors and left before the bank president could move from his tracks, to which, at last notice, he appeared to be glued, the huge chandelier dangling from the high ceiling casting pallid light onto his unsmiling face. She let the doors close behind her and then hurried across the lobby and out into the street. Alicia Rose was waiting in the carriage.

"Is he going to pay Father?" she impatiently enquired.

"He is," Olivia answered, and when she had told Alicia Rose all that had transpired inside Mr. Anthony Nash's hallowed office, laughter filled the carriage, drowning out the sound of the horses' hooves hitting the cobbled street.

When the laughter had subsided, Alicia Rose said, "I'm really surprised at you, Olivia. I didn't realize you knew how to handle men. I would have never thought of blackmail."

"When you're faced with making a suitable Bostonian marriage or using blackmail, I'll take the latter," Olivia said, still smiling.

When they reached the house on Beacon Hill, the coachman drove around back and turned the carriage and horses over to a groom. The girls entered the big house through the back door.

Alice Pembroke was waiting for them.

"Where have you girls been? And why did you not enter

the house from the front? It is not proper for a lady to enter through the back door . . . like a servant. Alicia Rose, I depend on your doing the right thing. I gave up on Olivia a long time ago."

"Oh, Mama, let up on Olivia. She has done a most wonderful thing for the family," said Alicia Rose.

Alice Pembroke turned to Olivia. "I can't imagine what, unless you have decided to marry a suitable man."

"Nothing as drastic as that, Mama."

A big black woman wearing a white apron over a black, rustling dress came to take Olivia's and Alicia Rose's coats and hats, and Olivia patiently waited until she had quit the room before speaking. She had no notion of letting Mr. Nash break the wonderful news. "We've been to Papa's bank. Tomorrow Mr. Nash will put Father on salary, and the Pembrokes can pay their bills without my making a suitable marriage."

"P-put your father . . ."

That was all Alice Pembroke managed to say before she sank to the floor in a full-blown spell of the vapors, as ungraceful a swoon as Olivia had ever seen. "Oh, merciful heavens," she exclaimed with disgust. "I'm sure it's because she thinks that now people will know we're no longer rich. I can't abide such snobbery."

"But we can't just let her lie there, Olivia. Do something. Call Papa."

"And what good would that do? He would stand and stare while puffing his pipe. Get the vinaigrette from the kitchen. suppose we have to bring her out of it."

Alicia Rose giggled as she ran for the vinaigrette. "You sound so heartless, Olivia, when in truth I know you're not."

"Mama always swoons when she wants her way about something."

Two swings of the vinaigrette before Alice's nose brought her up coughing and sputtering. "I can't believe what you were saying, Olivia. I feel that I'll swoon again if I allow myself to think on it. Your father has never worked for a salary." Her hands flew to her chest, "Pray, tell me 'tis not so."

Alicia Rose spoke. "Beginning tomorrow he will be paid monthly, and the Pembrokes can stop hiding from the bill collectors. The servants can be paid."

"Servants paid? They aren't paid; we own them."

"You mean we own slaves, like in the South?" asked Alicia Rose.

Olivia was well aware that the Pembrokes owned slaves, except they were called servants in the North. She abhorred the very thought of it and had expressed her outraged opinion on more than one occasion. But Alicia Rose had never been told. Even the servants—slaves—had been ordered not to tell.

"They are servants, not slaves, and there's nothing wrong with it," said Alice Pembroke angrily. "We treat them well, and we never sell one off. We would never separate a family."

Jumping to her feet, she straightened her gown of royal blue silk trimmed with expensive lace. A bustle enhanced her slender hips. "Why are you wearing your Sunday gown?" asked Olivia.

"Because we are having a guest for dinner. That was why I was so worried about you girls being gone so long. Thoughtless, that's all I can say for you. Now you must make yourselves ready. And, Olivia, I implore you, pray try to look like something other than a street urchin."

Instinct told Olivia not to ask, but she did anyway. "Who is the guest, Mama?"

"Melvin Adams. A fine man from a fine family, a cousin to the Adams who signed the Declaration of Independence. I expect him shortly to become my son-in-law."

Two

"I can't believe she wants me to marry that fop," said Olivia when she and Alicia Rose were settled in the sitting room that separated their bedchambers.

"Speak with Papa about it," Alicia Rose offered. "Now that he'll be drawing a salary, there should be no need for you to marry someone who can help support the family."

"He would stand there and puff his pipe and acquiesce to anything Mama says, and she is not only adamant about not having a spinster in the Pembroke family, she wants the Pembroke name joined with another old Bostonian family. It's not just money she's after, 'tis status as well."

"I guess there's nothing we can do now that she has her mind made up," said Alicia Rose.

Alicia Rose was terribly close to her older sister; it had always been that way. As soon as she could walk she had followed her from room to room like a shadow, and cried when Olivia left each morning for school. And when Olivia went away to college, Alicia Rose beat her fists against the bed and screamed for hours. Finally, a physician had been called to calm her, not a small accomplishment.

Alicia Rose never used the personal pronoun *I*. It was always *we*. Olivia did not mind the unqualified devotion, for she was devoted to Alicia Rose as well, and she believed had their mother not been so cold and indifferent toward her daughters, it would not have been that way. She smiled at her sister. "Alicia Rose, I must find a way to go to England, where I will be out of Mama's reach, and, too, I am positive should I speak with this anonymous author, she can offer guidance. Selling my stories is the most important thing to me. Mama must accept that, whether she likes it or not."

For a moment she stopped and was thoughtful, and then she went on with her resolve. "Father's obsequiousness to Mama is not to my liking. No doubt he has a wonderful mind where figures are concerned. Mr. Nash said he was invaluable to the bank, but he should stand up to Mama. A man should take a strong hand where his wife is concerned. I've always been of that opinion. It is Mama who has unwisely spent the Pembroke fortune. Father has no backbone. He should have long ago pulled in the reins."

"I'm really surprised, Olivia," Alicia Rose laughed. "I didn't know you had given even one thought about what a husband should be like."

Olivia laughed, but her laughter held no mirth. "For sure it is not Melvin Adams." She pretended to swoon and the ambiance of the room lightened considerably. Alicia Rose was sitting in a chair with her bare feet—she had removed her half-boots and stockings—pulled up under her.

Olivia was sitting on the floor, her back against the short sofa. Smoldering coals in the grate sent warmth and a sliver of light out into the room. Neither noticed it was growing late until the door burst open and Alice Pembroke stood in the doorway, demanding they get dressed for dinner. And then she directed her angry words at Olivia. "You're a disgrace to the Pembroke family, Olivia, just because of your obstinate nature. Mr. Adams will be here momentarily, and you've made no effort to make yourself presentable. Look at that hair, the bun loose and hair hanging around your face. Which can't be pretty under the best of circumstances." Her face crumpled, as if she were about to cry. "I don't know why God gave me such a burden."

Olivia stood, taking a deep breath to hide the pain. Her

small shoulders squared, her eyes locked with those of her mother's, she said with unwavering calm, "God promised to never send more to one than that which one can bear, but obviously with you He did. So I will rid you of that burden, Mama. I will be leaving soon to go to England, where I expect to have my stories published. You may tell Mr. Adams that I am indisposed. Which I am. I will be writing another story . . . about a cruel mother who has no feeling for anyone other than herself."

Alice Pembroke's mouth flew open and her hands went to the sides of her face. "Why . . . why would you write that? Your own mother has been nothing but kind to you, looking out for your best interest. It was you who chose that awful school, your ruination. I knew that then, and I'll stand by it now."

"I know, Mama, everything I've ever done has been over your protest, and to your disgust," Olivia said.

As if Olivia had not spoken, Alice Pembroke continued with her diatribe. "I say again that extra schooling was your downfall. It made a bluestocking of you."

"What's a bluestocking?" asked Alicia Rose.

"It's the kind of woman no man wants for a wife," Alice retorted. Stepping back, she slammed the door. It quivered in its frame.

Olivia stood taut and straight for a moment, and then she felt her knees give way under her and she dropped to the floor. Sobs came, and she covered her face with her hands as copious tears so long denied surged up from her soul. Great gulping sobs tore at her throat. She was twenty-three; she shouldn't be crying, she told herself. But the tears were years old, saved from since she was a child.

Alicia Rose was immediately beside her sister, patting her shoulder, consoling her. "Oh, Olivia, I could strangle Mama. She didn't mean a word she was saying. She's just so used to having her way, and she gets so angry."

"Only where I'm concerned," Olivia managed to say.

Alicia Rose's words did not allay the tears, the sobs, the shaking shoulders. Not knowing what to do, she sat on the floor beside Olivia, their backs against the sofa, Alicia Rose's blond head resting on Olivia's shoulder, her small hand patting her in a comforting manner. Beyond the window, dusk gathered, and the room grew dark. Coals in the grate turned gray and no longer offered light. Alicia Rose secretly wanted to stuff a pillow into her mother's big mouth. "Please don't cry, Olivia," she said, her own voice breaking.

But Olivia did not try to stop the tears, nor would she, she decided, until built-up pain was expunged from her heart. The cleansing was long overdue. She had hidden herself in her writings, had denied that things were not right, had told herself she was doing what any good Bostonian daughter would do by obeying her mother. Except when it came to marriage.

Olivia was unaware when the crying stopped and thoughts began rumbling through her mind. It came to her that the four years at the small, obscure school, which had allowed only three women to attend from its inception, had been the happiest of her life. She also realized that when she had been ordered to return home—she knew now that it was so Alice Pembroke could see her properly married—she had obeyed because of Alicia Rose.

But the time had come when the tight bond had to be broken, or at least stretched, Olivia told herself. Alicia Rose must stop living vicariously through her older sister and plow her own field.

Olivia knew that it would not be easy to explain this to Alicia Rose, but she would try. She pulled away from her, gave her a hug, and then pushed herself up from the floor. In the gray darkness she struck a lucifer against the hearth and lit a kerosene lamp. Taking a deep breath, she began, "Alicia Rose, I cannot stay here. I must find work to support myself. That is what I should have done when I was graduated from school."

"Sister, you can't do that. What will become of me, left here with Mama? She'll run my life just as she has tried to run yours. And I simply cannot bear waking up in the morning and not having you to talk with. The years you were at school were just awful." The hurt in her voice was palpable.

Olivia, now sitting on the sofa, took the pins from her chestnut hair, let it fall to her shoulders, then combed it back from her face with her fingers. "Alicia Rose, you are seventeen, and I'm twenty-three. 'Tis time we separate."

"I'll go with you. I can work too. I've already decided against going to school another year."

"No, you may not come with me. You must listen to reason." Olivia was trying desperately to be firm, but the pleading look in Alicia Rose's blue eyes was devastating. "And don't look as if the world has come to an end. I fear I've done you an injustice by returning home after graduation. I'm going to New York to find employment. In time, I will sell my stories."

"I'm going with you."

"No, you're not."

Upon learning Olivia's plan to seek employment, Alice Pembroke took to her bed for a week, J.E. returned to the bank, and Alicia Rose spent hours on end moping about the house as if her last friend had died. It seemed to Olivia that she was the only one happy. Since the night of her pain, when her wounds had bled openly, she had determinedly taken charge of her life, and there was a good feeling about it. Two days hence she would leave for New York City to seek employment in a publishing house. J. E. Pembroke had reluctantly afforded her a small stipend, now that, thanks to her, he was gainfully employed.

Olivia thought it strange that he had never mentioned her going to Anthony Nash to ask for the money so the Pembrokes could live. Surely he was pleased. Thinking on it, she doubted that he was. And Alice Pembroke would never forgive her for refusing Melvin Adams's suit. She had to smile when she thought of the three of them dining together, when Mr. Adams had expected to dine with the Pembroke daughters.

"Look, Olivia," Alicia Rose said one day, holding out a copy of the morning paper joyously. For days she had combed the help wanted section of the daily newspapers for what she had just found. "Read this ad in the personal column. If you wouldn't mind being a wife in name only, here's your chance to go to England."

Olivia thought it another of Alicia Rose's tricks to keep her in Boston. All week she had come up with one ingenious idea after another to keep them together, one being that they would both go into a convent.

None of the schemes had worked.

"I don't believe you, Alicia Rose. What man would want a wife in name only? 'Tis another of your tricks."

"No, it is not! It just says a titled Englishman wants to marry a plain American girl if she will agree to be his wife in name only."

Olivia grabbed the paper. The pages were folded back, and there, boldly circled in ink, was the ad. Olivia couldn't believe her eyes. Her first thought was that the man must be as ugly as a mud fence to have to advertise for a wife, and a plain one at that.

"And why would he not expect to claim his marital rights?" she wondered aloud.

"It could mean the wife should not expect to claim her marital rights," offered Alicia Rose. "Does it not work both ways?"

Olivia was taken aback. How did her little sister know as much, and possibly more, than she did about marriage?

Because I've never given thought to it, Olivia mused, her eyes still glued to the paper. This could be the gateway to

England. God's truth, she thought giddily, it was perfect, and it did not matter that the man in question was ugly. He would not really be her husband. The ad said that one-way fare would be paid, and that Emry and Emry, a Boston law firm, would be taking applications from one until five o'clock in the afternoon.

"We must hurry," said Olivia, now believing.

"We'll ask that you take your personal maid and that fare be furnished," piped up Alicia Rose. "I will be your lady's maid, which will be a much better arrangement than having some stranger tend you. I understand every lady of the upper orders in England has her own abigail. That would be terrible, being tended by someone you don't even know. How would she know that you like to be awakened early so that you can work on your stories?"

"I will tell her," answered Olivia.

"Please, Olivia, take me with you."

"Don't be a goose," Olivia said, ignoring the tears in Alicia Rose's eyes. "I don't have the position yet. Do you think I'm as plain as his lordships wants? I know I'm not particularly pretty."

"You are too," countered Alicia Rose. "Your eyes . . . wide-set and gray-green. Why, I've even heard Mama remark about your eyes being pleasing to look at. And you have a pretty mouth, and a pretty smile, and when your hair is freshly washed, it shines like molasses."

Olivia laughed. "The ad said a plain American girl. You're making me out to be a beauty, and that is just not so." She took from the chiffonier a faded gray dress with a white collar. Tiny buttons closed the bodice from waist to throat.

"If I dress dowdily, mayhap that will impress this mysterious solicitor representing his lordship. I've never heard of Emry and Emry."

"Nor I," said Alicia Rose. "I think I should bind your bosom so it will be flat," Alicia Rose said. Jumping to her feet, she went to scramble through the linen closet until she found a worn sheet. Quickly she ripped strips of cloth and wrapped them around Olivia so tightly that Olivia cried, "Ouch," and then, "Stop it. I don't have to be *that* flat."

When she slipped into the dress, the hem was two inches above her boot tops.

"That ought to do it," said Alicia Rose. "That is double ugly. I can't believe you ever wore that rag. Now, let me do something with your hair."

"I'll wear the bun. Mama thinks that makes me as homely as a girl can get."

"Olivia, Mama didn't mean that. She's just always mad at you because you won't be the proper Bostonian lady she wants you to be and make a proper marriage. So she says ugly things. I asked her not to do it, but she does anyway. It's just her way."

A lump swelled in Olivia's throat as she hugged Alicia Rose. "You tried, dear, but the truth is I have never measured up to Mama's expectations. Finally, and I don't know just when, I gave up trying."

"Just wait until she hears you are going to marry a Lord somebody."

"I don't have the job yet. I'm sure there will be a line of women waiting to apply, just wanting to get married. Sometimes I worry that I'm different, that my writing means more to me than marriage. Perchance Mama is right, mayhap I am a little strange."

It even struck Olivia as odd that she thought of marrying Lord somebody as a job, a position, not as a marriage. She wondered if she would apply if the ad had not read "Wife in Name Only," and she thought she most likely would, so great was her desire to meet with the English writer. Just recently she had learned of another book, *Mansfield Park,* by the same author. Had she missed other of her writings?

"You're not strange; you're sweet and kind," said Alicia Rose. She brushed Olivia's long hair back from her face and then wound it into a huge bun on the back of her head. Not at her nape, as she had when they were going to see Mr. Nash. "We'll cover your head with a scarf. For sure if Solicitor Emry sees your beautiful chestnut hair, you won't pass as being plain. I think a few freckles made with iodine will help, and a birthmark on your neck."

The job of making Olivia a plain Jane completed, they spoke on how to escape the house without Alice's notice. Servants were about. Olivia looked out the window. A familiar sight. Cascading down the hill were red roofs, with brick chimneys, from which gray smoke curled up into the flakes of snow that had begun to fall. She had seen the rooftops thousands of times, but had never really noticed the symmetry, the sameness. Even so, for a moment she was filled with nostalgia. She had wanted so much to leave home, to be on her own, but she had never thought of going across the ocean. The white snow fell softly to cover more of the rooftops.

They would need the covered carriage, and a driver. And then she thought of how much she would miss Alicia Rose. Shaking herself, she laughed lightly. She did not have the job yet.

"Would you see where Mama is," she asked of her sister. "If she is not napping, just mention casually that we are going for a drive in the snow. I'll wear my black mantle so that she can't see the awful gown I'm wearing."

Alicia Rose returned shortly and reported luck was with them. Alice Pembroke was having tea with two ladies in the front parlor. "She'll never know we are gone. I sent Jessup to the stables to order a covered carriage and a driver."

"You're very efficient," said Olivia.

"I know. That's why you need me to go with you to England."

Olivia's voice was stern. "Don't mention it again, Alicia Rose. I explained to you that it is time you stop your dependency on me." And then she said something she did not mean, telling herself it was for Alicia Rose's own good. "I want to live my own life, without a younger sister hanging to my coattail." Then, refusing to look into Alicia Rose's blue eyes, Olivia swept from the room, and Alicia Rose followed, mumbling unintelligibly. They were near the same size, with Olivia only an inch taller than Alicia's Rose's five feet four inches. It seemed to Olivia that in the past two years her "little" sister had grown by leaps and bounds, her legs long and shapely for a seventeen-year-old. Stealthily, they slipped from the house.

It did not take long for the carriage to tool its way to the solicitor's office, a plain brick building located behind Mr. Nash's bank, with an alley entrance. Alicia Rose alighted first and then reached a hand back to help Olivia. "Soon you'll be royalty and have all sorts of people helping you. I hear that in England, an abigail wipes her lady's nose."

"Oh, Alicia Rose, your imagination is positively wild. What woman would want someone to wipe her nose? I've never even wanted a personal maid."

There was no receptionist to take their names. Ladder-back chairs with woven cane seats, some occupied by women of tolerable looks, lined the walls, and in no time at all, so it seemed to Olivia, Jade Emry was saying, "Come in, ladies." They had waited for only five applicants to be greeted in the same manner and then to quickly leave. Olivia felt foolish. What chance did she have if he had turned away five plain American women before her? And why did he call her before the other ladies who had been waiting longer?

Alicia Rose jumped to her feet, and Olivia immediately yanked her back to her chair. Standing, Olivia held out a hand. "I'm Olivia Pembroke, Mr. Emry. I've come to apply for the position of wife in name only for the English gentleman."

He gave a ready smile, shook her hand, and, with a flourish, waved her into his austere office and closed the door. He was a handsome man, middle-aged, his dark hair gray at the temples. His stiff white shirt collar made his dark skin appear even darker. He was part Indian, not a true Bostonian, Olivia quickly surmised. He stared into her face.

"Shall I sit?" she asked, at once uncomfortable and fully expecting him to say she would not do and send her away as fast as he had the other hopefuls. His dark eyes did not give a clue as to his thinking. She prayed he did not recognize the iodine spots as being what they truly were and not freckles. She had been foolish to let Alicia Rose concoct such a ruse.

"You'll do," he said, smiling.

Olivia's mouth flew open. "Just like that? No questions asked, no . . . no nothing. Why am I more acceptable than the five women you've just turned away? And why did you take me before the other women who were waiting?"

"I don't need to ask questions about you. I know you are J. E. Pembroke's oldest daughter, that you've been away to school, and that your mother has been trying to marry you off to a true Bostonian since you passed puberty. And that tells me a lot."

"I can't imagine—"

"It tells me that you are not interested in marriage, so you will live up to the bargain of wife in name only. My cousin is adamant about that."

"Your cousin? How can that be? 'Tis plain that you have Indian blood."

Jade Emry laughed. "Just a smidgen Iroquois. My great-grandfather, a rebellious rake, came to the Colonies when he was a strapping youth and married a beautiful Indian princess. So, you see, I have a little royal Indian blood, as well as a little blue English blood, running through my veins. The old man was of the nobility when he was in England, a third son of an earl, or some such rot. Somehow Fitzgerald Castleberry is my cousin, fourth removed."

"Fitzgerald Castleberry?" Olivia's words tried to stick in her throat.

"Lord Fitzgerald Castleberry, fifth earl of Robinbrook, your future husband. That is, if you agree to the contract."

"I have some questions," Olivia said. She really would like to know if this Lord Castleberry was an honorable man, and *why* he would send to America for a wife. Now that her ridiculous plan to get to England, even if it meant marrying a man she did not know, in truth, had never heard of, was about to reach fruition, she was beginning to feel a little afraid.

At last Jade Emry asked her to sit. Behind a scarred desk piled high with papers, he leaned back in his chair and once again leveled his gaze onto Olivia's face. She stared back at him.

"Ask away, Miss Pembroke," he said, "but I warn you, I know nothing of my cousin except that he is of the nobility. I suppose he didn't think it important the lady who was to become his wife know about him. His seat is in Kent, and the manor house he calls home is Robinbrook. It is near the sea and not far from the small village of Hythe. I understand the English name their homes as if they were one of their children. Robinbrook has been in the Castleberry family for over a hundred years."

"That is all you know?"

"That's all. Lord Castleberry said that since the marriage would never be consummated, that after a certain length of time it would be set aside and the lady can return to America if she so wishes. A monetary settlement will be made to compensate for her time."

"How did he know to contact you . . . if the two of you have never met?"

"A few years back I was researching my English ancestors, and I came across his name as a distant relative still living. I contacted him through a London solicitor. This is the first missive since those exchanged at that time, establishing our places on the family tree."

"Wh-what if he's a little mad?"

Emry laughed, a joyful, happy laugh that buoyed Olivia's confidence in him. Obviously he was not worried a whit, and his demeanor exuded honesty. "Will you give me the name of the solicitor so that if I need assistance, I will know someone to whom I can turn? Will you apprise the solicitor of the condition under which I'm going to Lord Castleberry?"

Taking the parchment on which the contract had been written, Jade Emry dipped a quill into ink and added the name of the London solicitor. He also noted his intent to contact such solicitor, and then he held it out for Olivia to read. After reading it carefully, she signed it with her excellent penmanship, then handed it back and stood.

Before she could ask, the solicitor reached across the desk to shake Olivia's hand again, giving his pleasant smile and saying, "The ship sails on Thursday, this week. I will have a copy of the contract and a one-way ticket delivered to your home on the morrow. I wish you a pleasant voyage, and I pray you find England to your liking."

Jade Emry stood by the window and watched as the Pembroke sisters were helped into the elegant carriage by a highly liveried driver who then climbed to the box and cracked the whip over the horses' backs. Soon they were tooling down the alley, back to the part of Boston where the elite lived. He smiled and wondered why Olivia Pembroke would accept such an offer from an unknown man. She had asked that the terms of the agreement be kept secret, so that she would not prove an embarrassment to her parents. Later, they could announce that she had met and married a man of the nobility. He had liked that about her, her concern for others' feelings.

Turning from the window, he returned to his desk and once again took up his quill, this time penning a message to Lord Fitzgerald Castleberry: "I think I've made an excellent choice for your bride. She has no curves; in truth, she resembles a broomstick, so flat-chested is she, and she is made homely by a face covered with freckles, and by a horrendous birthmark on an otherwise long, lovely neck . . ."

Emry did not tell his distant cousin the choice had not been made on Miss Pembroke's looks alone, but on her erudite mind as well. Whatever the reason for this strange request from the English lord, Olivia Pembroke could take care of herself.

Three

"You are what?" screamed Alice Pembroke when Olivia broke the news that she was departing on Thursday to marry an English lord who had advertised for a wife. Olivia had not told her mother the marriage would be in name only.

"I'm going, Mama. My one-way fare will be delivered tomorrow."

"What will my friends say? How can you embarrass me this way? Oh, don't tell me. A mail-order bride is what they'll be saying. It is not bearable."

"Your friends don't have to know, Mama. I swore the solicitor to secrecy. Tell them I have decided to go abroad, and then later you can announce that I have married the fifth earl of Robinbrook. That should impress the busybodies. I feel it is a chance of a lifetime."

"What if you can't bear the man?"

"I assure you he will be more bearable than Melvin Adams, the man you invited to dinner in hopes of making a match."

Olivia could see that the word *nobility* was working magic on her mother. Status, that was it. This had always disgusted Olivia, but society was the way society was, and that was that. At last Alice Pembroke sighed theatrically, then said, "Well, if you have your mind made up."

"I do, Mama." Olivia turned to J.E., who had been puffing on his pipe, a frown furrowing his brow. "What do you think, Father?"

"I'm not sure England is a safe place to live."

Olivia was taken aback. "Safe? What do you mean?"

He did not say more, and the look on his face mystified Olivia. She had always known that generations back the Pembrokes had migrated to America from England, but that was all she knew. When curiosity had prompted her to ask, her father had demanded that she not pry. Now the ambiance of the room had turned strange. She asked, "Do we have skeletons in our closet, Father? Were the English Pembrokes caught stealing horses?"

She was trying for levity. Even Alice Pembroke was looking at J.E. quizzically. Whatever was on his mind, it had not been discussed with his wife of thirty years, Olivia thought. And then he startled her by saying, "I'll give my permission for you to go, Olivia, only if Alicia Rose goes with you . . . for protection."

"For protection! Father, I'm nearing being a spinster. Why should I need protection?"

"Those are my words. Either Alicia Rose accompanies you, or you will not go." They were in the family parlor. He rose from his well-worn but comfortable chair and went to stand near the fire, his elbow resting on the mantel. He always did that, and she would always remember him so.

Olivia knew she did not need her father's permission to go to England, but she preferred that he be happy for her. Alicia Rose was, and always had been, the apple of his eye. So for him to now insist that Alicia Rose leave home at seventeen and go all the way across the ocean was puzzling indeed.

"Father, there's no money for ship fare for Alicia Rose. And, too, I feel strongly that she is too dependent upon me. She'll never grow up if we don't make the break, and the sooner the better."

"I will send some of my first editions into New York for the money. And as far as putting miles and miles between two sisters who love each other, I have no desire to do that.

Love is a precious thing, and I pray the two of you will hold on to what you have. Alicia Rose will grow up in her own time. You need not consider her a burden."

"Oh, no. I want only what is best for her. My heart ached when I thought of leaving her." After a pause, she added, "So I guess 'tis settled, then. You and Mama will be rambling around in this big old house all by yourselves after Thursday."

"Alice will keep it filled with her society friends." His words were tinged with bitterness. "She always has been more interested in that than in being a mother, except to get you girls married off. I don't want Alice choosing a husband for my Alicia Rose. You, Olivia, can give her guidance."

A strange feeling, a portent, or was it a frisson of fear, she wondered, came over Olivia, dancing up and down her spine. Why was she not afraid for herself but suddenly strangely afraid for Alicia Rose? "Oh, stuff! Papa's always been the strange one when it came to the Pembrokes," she said to herself.

Dismissing J.E.'s concern from her thoughts, Olivia went to tell Alicia Rose about the change of plans. Their father was deadly serious, she was sure, or he would never have offered to sell his precious first editions. She found Alicia Rose in her bedchamber, packing a huge trunk with everything she owned, so it seemed.

"I knew I was going if I had to stow away on the ship," she said when Olivia told her about J.E.'s firm decision.

"At first Father said you should go to protect me, and then he implied that should you stay here, Mama would be trying to marry you off to some Bostonian dandy. He thinks I can give you guidance when that time comes. Don't you think that odd, since it has been my bent not to marry at all?"

"When I'm ready to marry, I shall do my own choosing," said Alicia Rose emphatically. "But that's a long way down the road. We're going to England to see a mysterious author, are we not? Where does this Lord Castleberry live?"

"In Sussex."

After that they talked and planned for the trip, both trying to visualize what Lord Castleberry would look like, and it surprised Olivia that she even cared. "Alicia Rose, mayhap something will happen before we arrive that will make him change his mind about marrying. Going to a strange place doesn't scare me, but marrying a stranger does."

"We can tell him you've changed your mind and then offer to work as indentured servants."

"Surely he won't insist on marrying right away. I will tell him I would like him to pay his addresses for a short time, and during that time I can manage to seek out this author—"

"Olivia! That would be cheating. But I guess we could repay him for his expenses in getting you over there . . . after your stories sell."

When Olivia did not answer, Alicia Rose put forth another plan: "We'll make you so ugly that when he sees you, he will refuse to marry you. His ad said homely, not ugly."

Olivia laughed. "The truth is, Alicia Rose, I made a bargain, and I will stand by my word, but that does not mean I'm not a little frightened."

Before going to sleep that night, Olivia thought for a long time about Lord castleberry. What would he be like? And she asked herself why it should matter; their marriage would not be a true marriage. She wanted to sleep and not think about it, but the more she tried, the wider her eyes opened. Bewigged earls danced on the ceiling, and mad King George was looking for his chamber pot. After tossing and turning for what seemed an interminable time, sleep came, and a very old man with a hunched back and gnarled fingers with which he stroked her hair and caressed her face danced through her dreams. And those rough, gnarled hands felt cold against her naked flesh when he grabbed her and locked her in a dark closet, laughing loudly and saying she would be released when he returned to the castle.

She awoke frightened and in a cold sweat.

Thursday came quickly. Olivia hid her concern as best she could. Alice and J.E. went to the ship to see their daughters off, Alice now exuberant that her daughter would be marrying nobility, and J.E. with a worried look on his face. Olivia cried when they parted, not because she felt pain from saying good-bye, but because she had been such a disappointment to them. She kissed her mother on her cheek and then turned to her father, who, for the first time ever, gathered her into his arms and hugged her.

I guess that all I ever wanted was for them to love me, she thought as she waved from the ship, realizing for the first time that the wall she had built around her heart was not as impenetrable as she had thought.

Alicia Rose waved too, and thinking the tears in Olivia's eyes were because she was frightened about her upcoming marriage, she calmly assured her older sister the two of them could outsmart two earls.

And so the planning began, all the way across the Atlantic, first one plan and then another, finally hitting on one Alicia Rose swore could not fail: Olivia would pretend illness and ask for a delay in the wedding plans. No man, noble or not, would want a sick bride.

"Since it's in name only, why would he care?" asked Olivia. "We'll tell him it's catching, and he should not get near you until you are well," offered Alicia Rose.

Olivia remembered her dream of the man with a hunched back and gnarled hands, and shivered. "What if he's so ugly I cannot bear him?"

"Then, we'll tell him that whatever disease you caught on that dreadful ship is terminal, and we'll run away. I'll wager he won't be trying to find us."

"Alicia Rose, you are such a pea-goose. Where would we run?"

"We'll find Papa's relatives. Even if they are smugglers or horse thieves, they would surely put two lonely Americans up for a fortnight, which would be time enough for us to find this mysterious author."

Olivia sighed deeply. "Alicia Rose, you should be the writer in the family, your imagination is beyond the pale. What makes you think Papa's relatives would be smugglers or horse thieves?"

"Well, I certainly would not want them to be ordinary people. After all, Papa sent me along to protect you, and what if there's nothing to protect you from?"

Olivia laughed at last, glad Alicia Rose was along to quiet her fears. They were on their way to eat breakfast, their last meal before the ship was due to dock. The food was good, and they enjoyed the quietness that had come between them. There was nothing else to plan, and, besides, it was too late to plan. Then later, when Olivia saw a tall, dark man who was dressed to the nines walking across the East India dock, she immediately grabbed Alicia Rose's arm and asked that she find a place for them to sit for a spell.

Underneath her dark mantle, Olivia was wearing the same buttoned-to-the-neck, faded dress she had worn to visit the Boston solicitor. Her bosom was bound flat, and her hair was twisted into the tacky bun, with wild strands hanging untidily around her face. Even with all their careful packing, they had forgotten the iodine for the freckles and birthmark, and the ship's dispensary did not have any of the brown liquid.

"No matter," Alicia Rose said, "his lordship won't be expecting a lady with freckles."

The tall man bowed before them. "I beg your forgiveness, did you just disembark from the *Gloria*?"

"Why, yes, we did. We are to meet Lord Fitzgerald Castleberry," said Alicia Rose.

"I am Lord Castleberry. But I was expecting only one passenger. We are to be married."

Alicia Rose stepped forward. "I'm afraid the wedding must be postponed, your lordship. I am Miss Pembroke's personal maid, and, as you can see, she has taken quite ill."

Olivia looked her future husband up and down, seeing a hard, masklike face, which, seemingly, would break should he smile. He had thick black hair that grew to touch the collar of his superbly tailored coat, and smoldering blue eyes. He stood over six feet and had broad shoulders and long arms. The name Lucifer immediately came to Olivia's creative mind.

He was saying, "The wedding will not be postponed."

Olivia's hand tightened around Alicia Rose's arm. In a weak, almost inaudible voice, she said, "But, your lordship, I am too ill to—"

"You can stand, and if need be, your maid can hold you up. Come, the vicar is waiting." He reached for the satchel Olivia was holding with her free hand. She attempted to jerk it from his grasp, but he was too quick. "Gad's wallop, what do you have in this thing?"

"That is my business," Olivia said, her voice no longer weak. The satchel held Olivia's writings, all of them.

"Oh, but I'm afraid 'tis my business. As my wife you will be expected to share everything with me."

Her feigned illness forgotten, Olivia glared at Lord Castleberry. "The contract calls for wife in name only. I will not be your property."

"The contract pertains to the marriage bed, which I do not expect to share with you. After the vicar has said his words to make you my wife, you may go to bed and stay a week, with your personal maid tending you."

Carrying the satchel and taking long strides, Lord Castleberry headed toward a crested carriage in which a small man sat buried in one of the squabs.

"What do you think, Olivia," asked Alicia Rose as they

trudged along behind him. "Should we tell him your illness is terminal?"

"I've already named him Lucifer. That should tell you my opinion. But he's not the ogre I was expecting; that is, his looks are passable."

"Passable? Are you dim-witted? He's the most gorgeous specimen of the male species one would ever expect to encounter. And you're going to marry him."

"There has to be something wrong. Maybe he's the one who is dim-witted. Why would he want to marry a homely American? In my opinion, he's downright cruel. Look into those smoldering eyes and you'll glimpse the devil himself."

Alicia Rose giggled. "Put that way, it sounds most exciting."

By now they were at the carriage. Lord Castleberry was holding the door open, and when the footman jumped down from the boot and attempted to let down the step, he was told by his lordship that he would take care of the matter. But he didn't, not in the way one would expect, observed Olivia. His big hands simply spanned her waist and he effortlessly lifted her up into the carriage and deposited her on the squab opposite the little man. And then he did the same for Alicia Rose, placing her beside the little man, whom he later introduced as the vicar.

The black satchel was on the ground, at his lordship's feet.

"Don't forget my satchel," Olivia said.

When his lordship climbed into the carriage, he placed the satchel between himself and Olivia. If he had ever looked directly at her, she had not noticed. Mayhap his first glance had told him she was a homely American, and that was enough.

Silence ensued. It was not until they had stopped in front of a small white clapboard church not far from the dock

and had gone inside that his lordship addressed her again.
"Would you like to remove your cloak for the ceremony?"

Olivia felt herself pale. Dear God, they were going to be
married. And when she removed her mantle, revealing her
flat bosom, the faded gown buttoned to the neck, the hem
which stopped two inches above her half-boots, his lordship,
as if in supplication to his Maker, rolled his eyes toward
the ceiling and blurted out, "Dear God."

"Are you sure we can't wait until I am well, your lordship?" Olivia asked plaintively.

"The ceremony will take place," he said, and then he
stared directly into Olivia's face, his own filled with per-
plexity. He said to the vicar, "I beg your forgiveness, Vicar,
but this is not Olivia Pembroke. My cousin's missive spoke
plainly about Miss Pembroke's freckles, and about a terribly
ugly birthmark. fear this is an impostor. Please call the
authorities."

Four

The little vicar grabbed his quizzing glass dangling from the lapel of his long-tailed coat and glared through it at Olivia.

"You must pray so, your lordship. But who could this woman be?"

Lord Castleberry regarded Olivia with troubled eyes, which were also shooting sparks of anger, and then said, "An impostor."

Olivia found herself frightened, while wanting to giggle at the same time. "I'm Olivia pembroke." She looked at Alicia Rose, who was holding her hand over her mouth to smother laughter.

"You couldn't be Miss Pembroke," said Lord Castleberry. "The missive plainly stated she had freckles."

"Well, the missive was mistaken. What your cousin thought were freckles were beauty marks. 'Tis done in Boston all the time. When a girl goes out and does not want to be bothered by the opposite sex, she uses iodine and makes little dots on her face to resemble freckles. American men view freckles with total abhorrence. Mayhap I went a little overboard when I called on Mr. Emry, adding the birthmark."

Olivia was surprised that she was glibly lying about something she and Alicia Rose had schemed all the way across the ocean to accomplish—to delay the wedding vows. And this would certainly do that. By the look on his lordship's face, no wedding at all would take place. She began to worry. What if Lord Castleberry turned them out into the countryside? She looked at him again, studied his face, and decided that he would, mayhap, even kill them.

"I don't like subterfuge, Miss Pembroke," his lordship said.

"Nor do I, your lordship, and I wore freckles in America only because it was customary. Here I would not think of doing so, and I assure you I am not an impostor. And I'm glad to report that I am feeling better. Most likely it was the movement of the ship that threatened to bring me down with something."

As if speaking to himself, his lordship said, "Even with the round face and green—or are they gray—eyes, she's homely enough for my purpose."

"What is that purpose, Lord Castleberry?" Olivia asked. *Why does he want a homely wife, a homely American wife?* A vision of Lucifer danced before her eyes. Perhaps that was not fair to the devil, she thought, careful not to look at his lordship again for fear of finding horns sprouting from his frowning forehead. He did not bother to answer her question, mayhap because the poor vicar was waving his Bible around and practically shouting, "Would someone tell me what is going on? What do looks have to do with love, honor, and obey?"

"I won't promise to obey."

Lord Castleberry grabbed her by the arm. "Oh, yes, you will. A bargain is a bargain, and you took my money to come here to marry me. And brought a lady's maid!" Taking Olivia's hand in a firm grip, he turned to the vicar. "Proceed with the vows. And you can leave out anything except the obey part."

Within two minutes Olivia was Lady Olivia Castleberry, and she'd promised to obey this devil incarnate.

"Make haste," his lordship said. "It will be dark by the time we reach Robinbrook." He quickly passed money to the vicar, took up the black satchel, and with huge steps strode toward the door of the church, planks creaking beneath his feet. Olivia had no choice but to follow. The jackanapes could have at least kissed her cheek, for appearance's sake. She looked at Alicia Rose, who was no longer hiding laughter.

"Don't worry, Olivia," Alicia Rose said, sidling close to Olivia. "We'll find your author post haste, and then we can move to London and live like ladies of quality."

"Help me keep an eye on my manuscript. 'Twould be like Lucifer to throw it in the river, should we pass one." They scrambled to keep up. When they reached the carriage, the step was already down, and they climbed aboard unassisted, pushing the bridegroom aside when he offered to help.

"Put them to the bits," he said to the driver before climbing aboard himself. He turned his head away as if he could not bear to look at either one of his passengers, and silence ensued for a long while.

The silence did not bother Olivia; she was used to long periods of quietness, during which time she meditated on her writing. But now she found herself staring at his long, muscular legs and imagining them wrapped around her. Shock washed over her. Had she fallen from grace in such a short time? She had never had a thought like that in her life. Never. "Oh, dear," she said sotto voce. "I'm quite scandalous this day." She looked around her, fearful someone could read her wicked thoughts, and she kept her gaze averted from her new husband.

They were soon out of London and had ridden in such haste that Olivia could not see as much as she would have liked. The smell she had read about was there, even with the windows of the carriage raised. Some of the streets were deeply rutted, and garbage was strewn in all directions. She was sure they had passed through London's infamous East

End. There were no fashionable shops as she had read the West End afforded.

When they reached the countryside, she noted that her knowledge of geography served her well. The Thames was to the north of Kent, which had the sea on the east and south, with Sussex and Surrey to the west. Cherry trees were in bloom, the pink blossoms glistening brightly in the warm April sun. The air was fresh and sweet. Out of the corner of her eye she surreptitiously stole a glance at Lord Castleberry, who was sitting on the opposite squab. He still had the demeanor of Lucifer. Anger surely seeped from his pores. Not one word had he said since they left the little church where the wedding ceremony had been performed. Plainly his thoughts were miles away. 'Tis strange, she thought, that she felt no different than she had felt before they had stopped at the church.

"Do you feel different?" she asked his lordship.

His head jerked around. He raised a quizzical brow and glared at her. "I don't take your meaning. Am I supposed to feel different?"

"Different now that you are married?"

"Oh, that! 'Tis a business arrangement, so I would not expect to feel any other way than the way I feel. I wanted a plain American wife, and I now I have one." He leaned slightly forward. "In name only. Remember that. No one must know. To society we shall be terribly happy, terribly devoted . . . very much in love."

"Isn't that subterfuge, m'lord?" offered Alicia Rose.

"So 'tis, but there's times when a little duplicity is required. And after a time the marriage will be set aside because it will not be consummated. That's one of the few conditions on which Parliament will allow annulment of a marriage. There will be a settlement, of course."

And then, as if he just realized he was talking with a maid, he asked of Olivia, "Do maids enter into the conversation in America?"

Olivia gouged Alicia Rose gingerly in the ribs. " 'Tis just that Alicia Rose has been with me so long, and we do converse on occasion, that she doesn't notice the intrusion. Pray forgive her, your lordship."

When Lord Castleberry did not answer and resumed his gloomy mood, Olivia, without compunction, asked, "Why are you so angry, Lord Castleberry? Is not God's gift of life satisfactory? You wanted an American wife, and now you have one. I'd appreciate a little more pleasantness."

Silence.

They passed verdant pastures, cattle with large, full udders grazing lazily, and on the hillocks, sheep in large groups were watched by a shepherd. The brown hedgerows were beginning to turn green. To their left was the sea, lapping rhythmically against the shore.

When it was nearing the end of the day, the carriage made a sharp turn onto a tree-lined lane that cut across flat land toward a manor house placed among acres and acres of meticulously cropped lawn. Smoke curled upward from chimney pots. Now that the sun was sighing its last sigh, the air was chilled and damp. Olivia leaned forward and stared. *That* could not be her new home.

She sucked in her breath. It was magnificent, the edifice, made of buff brick, towering skyward in a stately manner, lichen climbing up the walls and wrapping around the mullioned windows, at least a hundred across the front, giving an ancient look.

"It's old," his lordship said. "Been in the Castleberry family two centuries. Awarded to my great-great-great-grandfather for bravery in battle." He gave a little laugh. I hope I got in enough greats."

It was the first time he had appeared friendly, and the laughter landed pleasantly on Olivia's ears. She hated grumpy old men. Mayhap he was not so bad after all, she thought, and then she realized the reason for his becoming more pleasant. They were nearing home, and he wanted to give the appearance to the servants of being a happy bride-groom. Talk about subterfuge!

When they had been deposited at the door of the huge house, Olivia looked back over her shoulder and saw in the distance the great expanse of sea, the rays of the setting sun playing on its rippling blue-black water.

"The servants are expecting us," Lord Castleberry was saying, and Olivia made a feeble attempt to push the loose strands of hair back from her face.

As the footman who had met the carriage skittered up the steps and pounded on the door with the knocker, Alicia Rose moved closer to Olivia and whispered, "How does a lady's maid act?"

Olivia frowned. They had thought to cover everything, but this was one subject their fertile minds had neglected. "I don't know. Just remain quiet, and I'll think of something to ask you to do."

Inside the house, servants stood in a straight line in a handsome great hall. It was large enough to place their Boston home in its middle, Olivia thought as she let her eyes traverse the epitome of grandeur. Not even in Boston's finest homes was there anything like it. Round, carved columns reached to the ceiling, at least forty feet. On the walls of polished walnut, portraits of ancient-looking people hung from long cords. In the huge fireplace, an inviting fire burned. Wide, curving stairs, with balustrades of dark wood, rose to the next floor.

The servants were dressed to the nines, very English, at least they wore what she had seen in pictures of English servants. Black bombazine and platter caps set the maids apart, while footmen wore bright blue and gold livery, the cook a chef's tall round cap, pristine white, and the butler long black tails and a white shirt with high collar points.

He was old and had a kind face. Most likely he'd been butler at Robinbrook well past the last generation. Bowing from the waist, he gave a warm smile when he was introduced.

Olivia returned the smile, shaking his hand, and then she introduced Alicia Rose as her lady's maid and asked that someone take her to their quarters. "Take my satchel, and my cloak," she said to Alicia Rose, who did not look too happy about being dismissed in such a way. Olivia almost laughed; mayhap Alicia Rose only *thought* she wanted to play the role of a lady's maid.

Heading the long line of servants were what Olivia supposed were members of the household. She was taken aback, and then she asked herself why she thought his lordship would live in such a large manor house by himself. She felt every eye turned on her, all registering extreme disbelief, making her conscious of her bound bosom and the awful dress she was wearing. Not to mention the ugly way her hair was dressed. In the sea of faces, an old woman unabashedly stared at Olivia through her gold-rimmed lorgnette.

The old woman's gown was fashionable, panniered, of purple silk, with layers of white lace around the square neckline as well as on the huge puffed sleeves that stopped just below her elbows. She had sharp brown eyes and gray hair which held two silk roses.

"Aunt Evaline," said Lord Castleberry, "I present my wife, Lady Olivia Castleberry."

This was the matriarch, Olivia could tell. She bobbed and then took Olivia's hand with no enthusiasm whatsoever. A smile at last softened her stern face, making her look less formidable, but her hand remained lifeless and dead cold in Olivia's own sweaty palm.

"Welcome to Robinbrook, Lady Castleberry. I've lived here for the past thirty years, even before your husband was born."

Olivia looked at Lord Castleberry, who was obviously hiding a rare smile. "What Aunt Evaline is saying is that she does not want anyone, wife or not, invading her turf. 'Tis by her orders that Robinbrook runs so smoothly."

"Oh, Fitzgerald, I was saying no such thing," Aunt Evaline said.

"That's quite all right, Aunt Evaline," Olivia said. "I'm a writer, and I've never taken to running a household."

"A writer?" Aunt Evaline's hand shot to her mouth, and her dark eyes widened in disbelief.

Lord and Lady Castleberry moved on. A male cousin was introduced as Trevor Castleberry, and as the farm steward, and then a handsome lad who appeared to be ageless. Olivia recognized immediately that something was lacking; it showed in his pale blue eyes, which glowed with warmth and begged for recognition. He gave Olivia an enormous smile, and she smiled back at him.

"This strapping youth is Chester," said Lord Castleberry. "He's no relation. One day he came to Robinbrook, said he was hungry, and stayed. He helps the gardener, and is quite good at it. When told I was bringing a bride home, he could hardly wait to meet her."

Chester bowed politely. "Lord Castleberry takes good care of me, like a papa."

"I'm glad of that," Olivia answered, thinking that mayhap Lucifer had redeeming qualities after all. Looking back, she saw that the servants had dispersed, leaving only the five of them.

"Where's Fred" asked his lordship. "I would've thought he'd be heading the welcoming party. He's been after me since I was in leading strings to get myself a wife."

"I don't think he expected an American wife, not after we lost the Colonies as we did," said Trevor.

She quickly looked him over. A portent of a sinister nature came over her suddenly. She pushed it away. His eyes were dark, almost black, and his thick hair, streaked an indeterminate sandy color, was long to his shoulders. He was dressed to the nines, obviously cut from the best cloth by the best tailor. Far more fashionable than Lord Castleberry, Olivia thought, and the thought came to her that this was Trevor's goal, to outshine Lord Castleberry, who at that moment, whipped around and leveled his gaze on his cousin. He was saying, "That did not answer my question. Where's Fred?"

"He took the dogs for a walk, the same walk he takes every day," offered Aunt Evaline.

Dismissing Trevor, a small laugh escaped his lordship. By way of explanation, he said to Olivia, "Fred is my grandfather on my late mother's side. He's nearing eighty, and he's smitten with Lady Patience in the neighboring house. Together they have nine hounds."

At that moment Olivia thought her husband almost human. The feeling lasted only for a moment. "Come," he said, taking her arm in a firm grip. "I will show you to your quarters."

Olivia pulled her arm free, and once again shook hands with the family members, including Chester, and told them how happy she was to be a part of the Castleberry family.

Aunt Evaline smiled, but not happily. "Likewise," she said in a far from friendly tone.

Trevor bowed slightly, and Chester smiled broadly as he lifted his hand and waved good-bye.

They left then and climbed the stairs. From the landing they turned down a long hall. At the very end his lordship stopped and knocked on the door, which Alicia Rose opened.

As Olivia stepped into the room, Lord Castleberry gave a slight bow and said, "A footman, or a maid, will call for you to escort you to the dining room for supper. I won't be present, but tomorrow I shall talk with you about what is expected of you while you live here at Robinbrook."

Olivia found herself wanting to slap her husband's handsome face. She closed the door. Never before had she felt so vulnerable, and never before, that she could remember, had she uttered swear words. "Demme that Lucifer. Demme, demme, demme . . ." And then she burst into tears.

Five

"What's wrong?" asked Alicia Rose, going to embrace her sister. " 'Tis not like you to cry, Olivia."

"I'm very tired," Olivia answered. Then she tried for levity. " 'Tis not every day one arrives in a new country and is married the same day."

"Well now, let's just pretend the marriage did not happen and get on with our plans. Come, look at these fabulous rooms. At least we'll live in comfort while here, and then we'll move into London. His lordship promised a settlement when the marriage is annulled. So pray think of this as a job, a position, if you please, since you are working for nobility."

"Oh, Alicia Rose, please don't ramble on."

Big tears rolled from Olivia's gray-green eyes onto her cheeks. Alicia Rose wiped them away with a lace-trimmed handkerchief. "I have some delicious on-dits. If you would like to hear. And I want to hear all about those people you met. Did you ever see such a receiving line?"

Olivia smiled. How could she be crying with Alicia Rose trying so desperately to cheer her up. Rejection was not new to her, so why let the cold, cruel Lucifer disturb her? Her small chin lifted automatically into an obdurate line, and when she gave the large withdrawing room a quick perusal, she felt her spirits lift considerably.

The room held pink Regency sofas and chairs in silk brocade, marble-topped commodes, gilt-framed ceiling-to-

floor mirrors, and there was a black marble fireplace with
a mantel holding a Regency *cartonnier* clock. The wall covering was white silk; exquisite candelabra sat on the commodes. Plainly the room had been recently redecorated.
Everything reeked of newness.

"The bedchamber is just as elaborate," said Alicia Rose.
"With silk bedhangings and window coverings, everything
in pink, and carpet so thick that one's feet could become
lost in it."

"Do you suppose these quarters have been prepared for
his lordship's bride, but why a plain American for such finery?" mused Olivia aloud.

"According to Lizzie, the maid who came to help me
unpack your clothes, they were redone in preparation of
Lord Castleberry's approaching marriage. But not to you.
His affianced eloped with another man. She said he was
besotted with this woman, and it came as quite a shock to
the staff here at Robinbrook that he should marry someone
else so quickly."

Olivia frowned. "Most likely he's still carrying the willow, and that accounts for his mean behavior. Why would
he object to my plainness when supposedly that is what he
wanted?"

"You are not plain, Olivia," offered Alicia Rose, "just
careless about your dress. And one can't blame you for that,
since your bent is toward books more so than toward your
appearance."

Olivia walked through the bedchamber, the dressing
room, where there was a huge copper tub for bathing, then
another room with lots of healthy greenery. Here, there was
a small dining table and four chairs and a handsome sideboard. Olivia could imagine the room bathed by the morning sun. She liked that. Looking out the east window, she
saw green meadows and distant hillocks covered with bud-
ding trees.

"A place to dine when one does not want to go below

stairs," said Alicia Rose, and then she added, "My room is across the hall."

Olivia's brow shot up. "Across the hall? Did they give us separate quarters? There's room here for you. Look at that huge bed."

Alicia Rose laughed. "A lady's maid does not sleep with her mistress. The valet's room is also across the hall. Mayhap we can develop a tendre for each other."

"Alicia Rose! That's scandalous talk. When the household is quiet, you just steal back across the hall and sleep with me. We'll have so much to talk about."

When Olivia had finished her bath, she brushed her chestnut hair one hundred times, attempted to twist it into a bun, but gave up, letting it fall to her shoulders. Lord Castleberry had said he would not be at the supper table, so there was no need for her to make herself appear more homely than she was. She was totally disgusted, furious, in fact, with him for using something as sacred as marriage vows to get back at his ex-fiancée. Had she known this was his intent, she would not have married him.

But I am just as guilty. I promised to love, honor, and obey just for a chance to come to England.

Her thoughts turned to the life she would live while at Robinbrook. His lordship had said she would be expected to attend social affairs with him. But why would he want a *homely* wife, she asked herself. Shrugging her shoulders, she vowed not to worry overmuch about that; time would take her and Alicia Rose to London, where she would continue her writing and Alicia Rose would find a suitable husband.

Standing before the tall mirror, wearing a chemise and pantalettes, her long hair glowing in the light of the arm of lighted candles, Olivia studied the contour of her face, her small nose, and slender neck, and realized that she was not as unattractive as her self-image had led her to believe. With her bosom unbound, firm, full breasts, without a corset for support, pushed against her chemise, nipples forming two distinctive peaks. And her waist was that of a much younger girl's.

Quickly she donned a deep green gown, tied the darker green ribbons under her bosom, and then stared in disbelief. She turned to speak to Alicia Rose, who was looking at Olivia and smiling like a Cheshire cat.

"I always thought you dressed slovenly to spite Mama," offered Alicia Rose.

"You know, Alicia Rose, I believe you are right. I've never tried to analyze my indifference to my appearance. Mayhap I did hide behind books. Not that I don't love to read, and most of all write, but now that I'm away from Mama, I can be my true self."

"But you still have to appear homely when Lord Castleberry is near. At least until he explains his reason for wanting a homely wife."

"I had thought of that. For both our sakes. With all the anger bottled up inside of him, he would most likely turn us to starving animals I'm sure roam the countryside. But we're safe for this night; he said he would not be at the supper table. Someone, a footman, I think he said, will be coming to direct us to the dining room."

"Not us, you," said Alicia Rose. "A lady's maid eats with other lady's maids, or takes her meals in her room."

"I will not have it," exploded Olivia. "Oh, Alicia Rose, I wish we had never started this nonsense of your being my maid."

Alicia Rose's laughter spilled out into the room. "I love it, Olivia. You tell me what you learn, and I'll tell you what I learn. On-dits will fly. I've heard that servants in English households know more than the family members know about what is going on."

"But 'tis not always reliable," said Olivia.

Later, Lizzie came, a small, dark woman of near thirty, Olivia surmised, with a small face and braided brown hair twisted around her head, on top of which sat a white platter cap. Over her black bombazine dress she wore a white ruffled apron.

Bobbing to Olivia, Lizzie gave a big smile. "At your service, your ladyship."

Olivia immediately liked her, even if she did gossip.

"Anything you want to know about the household, just ask," the maid said, and Olivia immediately asked, "When Lord Castleberry doesn't eat in the dining room, where does he eat?"

"There's a small club in the village where he plays cards. And he spends time at his place in London. Lately, he's been moping around this big house, ever since *she* ran off with that old man."

"Why would she elope with an old man. Was it his lordship's mean disposition that caused it?"

The maid heaved a huge sigh and shook her head. "Oh, he's just developed that since she broke his heart. Before that he laughed a lot. And when she was his houseguest, he just plain walked on air, waiting for their wedding day. Now, oftentimes he's drunk as a wheelbarrow."

My, she is full of on-dits, thought Olivia, and decided not to delve deeper. She did not want to hear about how happy her husband had been when he was affianced to another woman.

Husband in name only, she reminded herself as she let Lizzie direct her to the dining room where supper would be served.

" 'Tis a long way," Lizzie said, and then the silence grew heavy while a question in Olivia's mind begged to be asked. She resisted until they had turned yet another corner and entered another wide and spacious hallway. Then the question just spilled out of her mouth, "Is she beautiful, Lizzie?"

"Oh, my yes. She could easily be on the stage. But of course her being nobility, society would never stand for that. God's truth, Lady Castleberry, she's the most selfish woman I've ever been near. But his lordship was blind to it, simply blind as a bat to it."

They did not descend the stairs into the great hall, but instead went toward the back of the house and walked down stairs that spilled into yet another elegantly appointed withdrawing room. Adjoining was a rather small dining room, seating no more than twelve.

"The family dining room," Lizzie so informed. "I see Mr. Fred is here, and Lady Patience, and their nine hounds. And there's Aunt Evaline. Be careful of her. She's an apeleader and will go to her grave mad about it."

Olivia thanked the maid and entered the dining room alone. She should feel strange, her first night married and without her husband, she thought, but she did not. She smiled when she espied the nine black and white hounds lying supine and overlapping in front of a fire that had died to graying embers.

Mr. Fred, her new husband's grandfather, obviously the host this night, stood and reached out both hands to greet her. He was a tall man with a great shock of white hair. There was a pleasant air about him, although as he looked her over, he was somber, and she was relieved when a smile softened the time-wrinkled, leathery face. Under spiky white eyebrows his gray eyes sparkled.

"Welcome to Robinbrook," he said, and then laughter shook his big frame. "No, my dear, I shall not castigate you for what America did to England, but my good friend King George would not be so generous, being that the Colonies stole their independence from grand old England, right from under His Majesty's nose."

"We'll argue that someday," Olivia said, smiling at him. His hand rested on the back of a chair, and she went to stand beside it and he introduced her to the lady who owned

the five visiting hounds. He called her his dog lady, who
happened to be Lady Patience Winslow.

Laughter, and then, "If I am his dog lady, he is my dog
man. He owns four of my bitches' pups."

Olivia could see they were happy with each other, seemingly near the same age, and they both loved the hounds.
Lady Patience was small in stature and very straight, with
a flat stomach most women over forty would envy. Her face
reminded Olivia of a porcelain doll's, one that had been left
in the rain and then dried by the sun. Tiny wrinkles
abounded, but took nothing from her beauty.

She said to Olivia: "I pray that you and Lord Castleberry
will be extremely happy together. He's a good man and
deserves a good helpmeet, even though he did not have the
courtesy to dine with you this night."

"I think he had a previous engagement," Olivia said.

"On his wedding night?"

Fred interrupted: "Now, Patience, Fitzgerald can take
care of his own business."

"I doubt that. Yes, I doubt that very much, or he would
have never been fooled by that selfish, self-centered chit
who trades solely on her beauty."

A stern look from Fred brought silence.

So far not a word from Aunt Evaline, who appeared completely vacuous. Was she even listening to what was being
said? Olivia wondered as she sat in the chair Fred held for
her, and then, when Fred had regained his chair, two white-
gloved footmen came to serve supper from the sideboard.

Olivia found that she was ravenous, so she ate heartily
of first pâté de foie gras, and then stewed kidneys and small
cabbages. She wondered about Alicia Rose and hoped that
she was eating as well. "Where's Chester?" she asked.
"Does he not dine with the family?"

"He has his own rooms on the premises, near the gardener's cottage," answered Fred. "He prefers it that way,
and when he wishes to dine with us, he merely informs

Cook. And that is only when Fitzgerald is to be present. Chester adores him, and Fitz is quite fond of the boy."

"He lives alone? He can't be more than twelve," said Olivia. She had taken an instant liking to the boy.

"He is much older than he appears," said Lady Patience. I think he's in his late teens."

"At last Aunt Evaline spoke. "You say you are a writer, your ladyship. Does that mean you're one of those bluestocking chits which society frowns upon?"

"I attended a small university in America, and I read extensively," Olivia said not defensively. She added, "If that makes me a bluestocking, then I suppose I am. My greatest interest is in my writing."

That plainly whetted Fred's interest. He raised a white, spiky eyebrow. "By the bye, that's outstanding. What do you write, Lady Castleberry?"

"I have finished one full-length novel. Now I write short stories, novellas, about life in Boston. I plan to seek out the English writer who wrote *Sense and Sensibility* and *Pride and Prejudice* and ask her advice on getting my works published."

"In my opinion, a woman is foolish to choose such a course," said Aunt Evaline. "A husband is preferred. Now, if Mr. Appleby hadn't up and died, I would have been like the other women of the upper orders, married with a house full of children." She looked as if any moment she would cry.

"I'm so sorry that that should happen to you," Olivia answered, and Fred cut in with, "Fustian, spare me hearing that sob story one more time, Evaline. You're probably lucky old Appleby died. I believe we were speaking of my new granddaughter. It appears she has been successful in getting herself a husband, and she also has a creative mind. I approve of that, and a pox on what the *ton* contends, that a woman can't be a suitable wife and be knowledgeable at the same time. I expect many grandchildren from this union. Smart ones at that."

He raised his wineglass. "I drink a toast to the heir to Robinbrook, and may it never be that scurrilous cousin Trevor Castleberry. God forbid that no heir comes along before he inherits." A big smile crinkled the lines around his sparkling eyes. "I expect an heir to Robinbrook exactly nine months from this night . . . if that foolish grandson of mine can make it home from his dallying."

"Brother, you're disgraceful," scolded Aunt Evaline. "A young bride should hardly know of such things."

A big snort of laughter rumbled out over the beautifully appointed table. "Of course she should know. Her mother should have told her. An heir, that is what I want."

Lady Patience Winslow was grinning at Fred adoringly. "Fred, you're incorrigible. You're embarrassing Olivia."

"I'm only speaking the truth," he countered. He turned to Olivia. "I beg your forgiveness, but I've never meant anything more than what I said about Trevor Castleberry becoming heir to Robinbrook. That would be blasphemy. 'Tis up to you to prevent that. It's entailed, you know."

"No, I didn't know." Olivia rose to go. Her face was hot to her touch, and she could imagine its redness in the flickering light. Plainly no one there knew she was Lord Castleberry's wife in name only, and if she said more, surely she would give up his lordship's secret. Nodding good night, she turned and quit the room with alacrity and made her way to the top of the stairs. There, she was lost in one big, long hallway, and she did not see whatever, or whomever, she bumped into.

"I beg your forgiveness," she uttered, and she would have kept going at great speed had not a large hand reached out and grabbed her arm. When she looked up, she was staring into Lucifer's devil eyes. "Unhand me," she said, and not kindly.

"Why should I? You're my wife."

"Then why did you leave me to go to supper alone . . . on our wedding night? Did you not think questions would be asked? And things said that should not have been said?" She did not seem to be able to stop, and she tried to think quickly of something else to add. His hand was still gripping her arm. She jerked, but to no avail.

Lucifer was laughing.

Feeling helpless, Olivia kicked his shin.

"I should turn you over my knee. No chit kicks her husband."

"I do when he detains me against my will. Mayhap in the future it would behoove you to remember that. I demand that you let me go."

Again laughter assaulted Olivia's ears. "Wives don't demand, they obey. Remember your vows before God."

"That was foolish of me. We should have been married by a magistrate, if at all. Nonetheless, I will not grovel, even if you hold me prisoner all night."

"That won't be necessary. I shall escort you to my quarters, where we will have a pleasant little coze."

"Your quarters! I will not be compromised by you. Our marriage is a farce. For some reason you wanted a homely American for a wife. God only knows for what reason."

"And I shall not tell you." In the dim light he was smiling down at her, and Olivia wished that he wouldn't. Her nerves were on edge, and her heart began to pound in an uncommon way.

"But we do have business to discuss, and I prefer not to do that standing here in the hall," his lordship said.

Reluctantly, Olivia let him guide her down the long hallway. He still held her arm, but not quite as tightly. After a while he stopped before double doors, deeply carved, and of the same rich walnut of which the balustrades on the stairway were made.

But that was not what drew Olivia's attention. Adjoining

was her own suite of rooms. She sucked in her breath, and her temper flared so much that words would not come.

But not his lordship. Smiling wickedly, he said, "For appearance's sake."

Then he bowed slightly and, with a flourish, waved her into the room. . . .

Six

Olivia stepped into Lord Castleberry's quarters fully expecting to see a large masculine bed and other pieces of heavy furniture suitable for a large gentleman such as his lordship. Instead, she saw dainty French chairs and sofas, all in pink and white, gilt-framed mirrors, glistening chandeliers, and pink silk brocade window coverings puddling on pink Persian carpet.

Pink for a gentleman's quarters?

Surely nothing in the prince regent's Carlton House equaled the grandness of the room, thought Olivia as she stood for a moment and stared. Flickering candles cast shadows, and the fire burning in the grate furnished a modicum of light.

Something caught her eye. Her hand quickly went to her mouth to smother a gasp. An almost life-size statue of a nude woman with beautiful curves and extended brown nipples on her two perfectly shaped breasts stood on a dais by the east window.

Moonlight danced on the abundance of curls cascading down the statue's back. Her small chin tilted upward, her lips were opened slightly, and she looked as if she might speak.

In a low, strangled voice, Olivia asked, "Who's that?"

Lord Castleberry smiled sardonically and answered in a cynical tone. "My former fiancée. Her likeness was a gift to me from her. As you can see, she's inordinately beautiful."

"And I suppose she decorated this room?"

"Why, yes. Since we were to be married, I gave her carte blanche in furnishing what was to be our quarters."

Even though Lizzie, the maid, had already afforded the answer, Olivia could not stop herself from asking, "What happened to her? Did she die, and are you keeping this as a shrine to her memory?"

"Absolutely not, and she did not die. You will meet her on your first social engagement, which will be as soon as the modiste can complete your wardrobe."

"My wardrobe? I brought ample clothing from Boston."

He looked her up and down. "They will not suit. You must be elegantly dressed when we appear in society."

"But I thought you wanted a homely wife. Mr. Emry specified that in his advertisement in the *Boston Herald.*"

"That is true enough, but I will not have my peers thinking I've been reduced to penury. Your wardrobe must be the best in all of England. The modiste will come tomorrow to begin her handiwork. I expect you to cooperate fully."

Feeling herself bristle, Olivia raised a quizzical brow. "Oh! Am I your chattel to order around? I would have expected you to consult with me about such personal things as the clothes I will be wearing."

His lordship's eyebrows went up perceptibly, and Olivia's words were the only sound in the room. She smiled inwardly. Had he never heard a woman express an opinion? As yet he had not asked her to sit, and that was just as well, she thought. The dainty chairs looked as if they might break under her one hundred and five pounds, and she wondered where in the world his lordship would rest his long frame.

"Won't you please sit for a spell?" he asked, looking foolish in the chair he chose.

"Could not this woman you were planning to marry have

chosen at least one chair suitable for your large stature. That one looks as if it might break."

"I assure you it won't. 'Tis made of sturdy materials. She spared no expense."

"I can see that. She even left her naked likeness for you to lust after when she was not here."

"Lady Castleberry!" he scolded. "Ladies of quality do not say such words as *lust,* and where did you learn to speak so?"

"I didn't. I read it in a book, and until now I'd never had reason to use it. 'Tis a perfectly acceptable term to be used between husband and wife."

"Oh, I beg your forgiveness. I keep forgetting that we are leg-shackled."

"We're what? *That* word is not in my dictionary."

"That means married." He raised his quizzing glass to his eye. "And by the bye, I wish to speak to you of your obvious subterfuge. You are far from homely with your hair down. I prefer it up in that ugly knot on the top of your head, with strands every which way. I will not have you tempting me."

Olivia laughed. "I will oblige when we are in society, your lordship, but there are times when I prefer to wear my hair down. Like this night. You were not supposed to be present, so I had no notion of tempting you."

"I went to call on the modiste. Time is of the essence. I will be presenting you to the *ton* just as soon as your wardrobe is finished."

Even after he had dropped his quizzing glass, his gaze dwelled on her face, his hard, cold eyes seeking her own. Olivia shivered. For sure Lucifer was searching out her soul. "I wish you would not look at me in that manner, your lordship . . . as if I've committed some unforgivable sin."

He jerked his gaze away. "As I said, I believe you have been deceitful, making yourself up as being homely when you are quite fetching. Your . . . your complexion is lovely, so when we are in the public eye, would you mind adding the freckles. My cousin wrote—"

"I know what he wrote, and I've explained that. But what if I'm caught in a spring shower? I would be a fright with the brown iodine in rivulets on my cheeks."

"You will carry a parasol. I'll have Madame Hazlitt, the modiste, make a matching one for each gown. Ladies of quality use them to shield their complexion from the sun."

"A capital idea," she said, still amused. What was wrong with his lordship? Did he have windmills in his head? Why was her being homely so important? And what about at night? Did she carry a parasol to protect her from the moonlight? It did rain at night, did it not?

"Shall I bind my bosom as well?" she asked.

"Oh, no. In truth, I asked the modiste to make the décolletage of your gowns considerably revealing." He surprised Olivia by giving a wry grin. "I suppose 'tis not against propriety for husband and wife to speak in such a manner."

"That sounds quite strange," she said. "This is our wedding night."

"It would be if you were not my wife in name only," his lordship answered quickly, his gaze resting with obvious longing on the naked woman on the dais. Olivia was suddenly angry, and she did not know why. Lord Castleberry offered sherry, and while he was pouring, she walked to a huge cabinet filled with books, the only masculine piece of furniture in the room. She wondered if *she* liked to read and quickly decided that most likely she did not. Most likely she was an empty-headed bit of muslin. The idea of having a naked likeness of herself installed in her future husband's withdrawing room spoke volumes about the woman.

"Does your former betrothed enjoy reading?" she asked over her shoulder.

Lord Castleberry gave a light, mirthless laugh. "I doubt that she's ever read a book through. And only the social section of the papers. But women of the upper orders do not feel it necessary to engage their minds in intellectual matters. And I must say, the gentlemen I know are happy the ladies spend their time learning to make dainty stitches, and how to go on in society. As long as she knows how to please a man."

"Do you mean in bed?"

"Miss Pembroke . . . Lady Castleberry . . . that's beyond the pale to talk in such a manner, even to your husband."

"Stuff! How can a woman please a man if 'tis forbidden to speak of how and where he wants to be pleased. That is what you meant, is it not?"

His lordship cleared his throat and coughed, and if he answered, Olivia did not hear him. She lovingly ran her fingers over the spines of the books, many old classics such as in the Boston library of her former home. "How deathly boring the English ladies of quality must be," she said. "My soul would starve should I not read."

When his lordship again did not reply, she thought that the cat must have gotten his tongue. Returning to her chair, she sat with her hands clasped demurely in her lap. As he strode across the room, balancing two glasses of sherry in his hands, she became acutely aware of the muscles in his thighs moving fluidly against his tight-fitting trousers. His splendidly tailored blue superfine coat hugged his broad shoulders provocatively. His white cravat touched his broad, sun-browned chin.

A rugged outdoorsman, he looked ridiculous in this pink and white room, Olivia decided.

"Thank you," she said when he handed her the small glass of sherry. She then sipped gingerly, liking the taste, but it burned as it went down her throat. In Boston she had not been allowed to imbibe spirits.

His lordship again sat in the pink chair. "I think we have an amicable understanding, do we not? I would like us to be friends."

Olivia measured her words. "Yes. I am to be presented to society looking homely but fashionably dressed."

"And don't forget that we are to appear totally devoted to each other. But when I am unduly attentive to you, it will be an act and should not be taken seriously by you."

Olivia's voice was sharp. "And if I act as if I adore you, you must recognize it as my keeping my end of a business deal. When you have decided you've had enough of the charade—for whatever reason you deem it necessary that you act devoted to a homely wife—our marriage will be set aside and I shall receive a fair settlement. I wish that part to be emphatically understood."

"As long as you keep this our secret. Even the servants must not know. They are terrible gossips. And pray, do caution your lady's maid to keep her lips sealed. Servants are notorious for blabbering."

"Her name is Alicia Rose, and I assure you she does not blabber. She's been with me all her life, and she has yet to tell a secret I do not wish told."

"This room will be our meeting place," his lordship said. "Each day we can discuss the progress of our plan."

Olivia lifted her glass. By now she'd had several sips, enough that the liquid did not burn her throat, and her head was beginning to feel light. "To *our* secret . . . or secrets. There may be others." The glass went higher. "To our wonderful plan of being leg-shackled but not leg-shackled."

Lord Castleberry looked at her strangely, and when he did not answer her toast, her voice became serious. "There's one other who must know that I am your wife in name only."

"No, that cannot be. No one must know. 'Twould ruin everything."

"Your grandfather. Dear, dear Fred. He embarrassed me tremendously at the supper table by suggesting we right away have an heir to your fortune."

His lordship laughed hugely. "Fred has been hounding

me for years to get leg-shackled and have an heir. Even though he disliked Lady Jacqueline with verve, he encouraged the alliance. She does come from good stock."

Olivia snorted. "Are you speaking of breeding cattle? Or horses? Sounds so to me. A baby should come from love between two people."

"I fear you're a little old-fashioned. In the upper orders, love is seldom a consideration in a suitable marriage. The convenience of joining two pure-blooded families, well connected and endowed with wealth, and then producing an heir to that wealth, is the purposes of most *ton* marriages." He paused, sighed deeply, and then continued. "I tend to agree with you. I felt that it would be wonderful to have a child with Jacqueline."

Lizzie is right, the poor man is besotted.

Olivia wanted to spit. She stood to go. "I'll leave you alone with your loving thoughts of your Lady Jacqueline." She made to quit the room by the same door through which she had entered.

"You may go this way," Lord Castleberry said, and when she looked around, he was holding open a door that had been completely concealed by one of the huge gold-framed mirrors.

"Oh, a hidden door! How perfectly romantic!"

"A husband would not want to go out into the hallway each time he visited his wife's bedchamber," his lordship said in way of explanation.

"That is true," said Olivia, tilting her chin upward in the manner of the naked lady. And then she asked, "Can the door be locked to prevent the husband visiting his wife's bedchamber?"

"I assure you that will not be necessary," his lordship said. He bowed deeply and then, lifting her hand, he brushed it with his lips in a totally indifferent manner. "Good night, Lady Castleberry."

Clearly his mind was on Lady Jacqueline, or on her naked

likeness behind him. Olivia closed the door between them with alacrity.

In the sitting room adjoining her bedchamber, Olivia found Alicia Rose supine on a pink sofa, contemplating her toes.

"What a day," Olivia said. "I'm totally exhausted."

Alicia Rose, her blond curls in total disarray, bounced upright and put her feet to the floor, hiking her white night-dress to her knees. "Where have you been? I've been waiting for hours."

"You should not have waited up for me." Olivia sought a chair, dropped into it, and stretched her feet toward the fire. A branch of lighted tapers flickered in the dim dark-ness, once again revealing to Olivia the elegance of the room meant for Lady Jacqueline.

"How could I go to sleep when I didn't know what had happened to you?" asked Alicia Rose. "Lizzie said you left the supper table plainly disturbed."

"Lizzie is a gossip."

"I know, and I love her for it. She came to light the tapers and to stoke the fire, even though that's usually a footman's chore. So she informed me."

Olivia gave a little laugh. "She really came to find out if I was with my husband."

"Of course she did, and I told her you were in his cham-bers and would most likely spend the night there."

"Alicia Rose, you must not lie. You knew that I would not be spending the night in Lord Castleberry's chambers. 'Tis not a true marriage."

"But the servants must not know."

The sisters talked for a long while about how to fool the servants about the false marriage. It was Olivia who decided that Alicia Rose should sleep in the room across the hall, for Lizzie was bound to spread the word that the new Lady

Castleberry's abigail was sleeping with her. The goal was to appease Lord Castleberry until the marriage was set aside and the settlement made.

And if luck were with them, a meeting with the English Authoress would be arranged and Olivia's manuscript would be sold. It seemed like a wonderful plan to both of them. The sherry had made Olivia quite sleepy, but when the manuscript was mentioned, she suddenly became alert and asked Alicia Rose to please repair to her room so that she could do her writing.

"Oh, Olivia, can't you let one day go by without writing? We've so much to talk about. This is your wedding night."

"Pray, do not remind me. I have no notion of not writing this day. Now, scoot, I need peace and quiet."

Reluctantly Alicia Rose left, after which Olivia donned a flannel nightdress and climbed up into the high bed and propped herself up with plump pink and white pillows. Pulling her knees up, she positioned her notebook on them and made ready for words to flow. Dipping her feather quill in ink on the bedside table, she waited. And waited.

But imagery of his lordship's handsome face, his hard, muscled body as it strode across the room, his cold blue eyes, and his hard demeanor kept dancing through her thoughts, making it impossible to write about the little boy of whom her story was about. Ted was his name, and he had quite mysteriously disappeared. When she had left him, he was sitting on a small hillock minding the sheep in the flat land below, while reading a book. Olivia could not even remember the name of the book.

To move the story, something should happen to Ted, but Olivia could not think what. She referred back to her writing of the day before. It was of no help. Her mind was simply totally blank. Finally, after several aborted starts, and several sheets of crumpled paper on the floor, she gave up. The world would not end should she not write this day.

And then the quill began to move and words poured

themselves out onto the paper. The words were not about Ted.

Lucifer's cold, penetrating eyes bore down onto the face of the frightened governess, who was unaccustomed to being stared at. Pushing her long hair back and trying to appear unaffected by his gaze, she felt herself shiver, and then her heart moved to her throat and began to pound. Then, like an out-of-control river ravaging its banks, hot blood rushed through her whole body, starting in her loins and moving upward. She stared into his face, equally as ruggedly handsome as it was bone-chilling.

A small, mocking smile reached his fire-lit eyes as his big hand moved to take hers, to kiss its back, a mere whisper against her taut skin. As suddenly as it had come, the fright went out of her. She wanted his devil eyes to search her soul; she wanted him to kiss her, to hold her, and, much more frightening, she wanted his lordship to take her as a husband would take his wife on their wedding night. . . .

Seven

Alicia Rose awoke with a start, jerked herself up, and looked about, finding the strange, square room held no significance for her. The narrow bed in which she was lying was pushed against the wall. A rocking chair and a footstool were nearby for someone's comfort, and a cracked mirror hung over a washstand that held a ewer, washpan, a bar of soap, and a washcloth. A braided rug, well-worn, covered a goodly portion of the plank floor. Through a small window, shafts of first light lent the stark room a deceptive mellowness. Her sleep-drugged mind screamed, "Where am I?" But then reality slowly returned. She was in the maid's room, across a wide hall from Lady Castleberry's opulent quarters.

A smile found its way to Alicia Rose's face. She wondered if Olivia felt as strange in the rooms meant for Lord Castleberry's former affianced as she, Alicia Rose, felt in a maid's room. What a bumble broth they had created for themselves. Throwing the coverlet back and bounding to the floor, she went to the window and looked out, seeing in the mist rising up from the sea white egrets fishing for their breakfast. She pushed the window up and felt the cold air hit her face and sucked it deeply into her lungs. Suddenly eager to leave this small room and look about Robinbrook, she decided to dress quickly and go knock on Olivia's door.

The water in the ewer was cold. After filling the washpan,

she splashed her face and then soaped the cloth to scrub her body, feeling rejuvenated as chill bumps popped up on her arms and legs. She closed the window before pulling on her pantalettes and donning a purple and blue riding dress. If she could locate the stables, she would go riding.

The rest of her toilette did not take long. Her blond curls were always in disarray about her face; a few strokes with the brush did not change that, and within a few minutes she was knocking on Olivia's door softly. If she were not already awake, she did not want to disturb her. Oftentimes Olivia worked on her stories until the wee hours of the morning.

When no answer came to her knock, Alicia Rose turned away and made her way down the long, wide hall, lighted only by an occasional wall sconce holding a candle. Not knowing which way to go, she decided to take the same route she had taken when she'd gone below stairs to eat supper with members of the household staff. Smiling to herself, she wondered how long she and Olivia could continue their duplicity. "I pray long enough for Olivia to locate her author," she said aloud to the strangers whose age-darkened portraits lined the walls, dangling from long cords of rope that used to be gold.

She thought about her mama and papa in Boston, wondered if they missed their daughters, knowing, or at least believing, they did not. But she would send them a missive anyway. Later in the day, after she had done her exploring.

Just then Alicia Rose saw Lizzie, the delightfully gossipy maid, coming to meet her. Smiling broadly under her white platter hat, Lizzie rustled black bombazine when she dropped into a deep curtsy. She held the look of the Gypsy blood she claimed.

"Lizzie, you know you are not to curtsy to me. 'Tis Miss Olivia who married nobility."

"I know that, but I thought I'd just make you feel important. Besides, you look nobility in that handsome riding dress. Where are you going?"

"I had thought to go riding, but first I would like to eat."

"Then I know just the place . . . as long as the ape-leader don't catch you. Servants ain't allowed, she says. Follow me."

Alicia Rose laughed. "Lizzie, you should be ashamed of yourself, calling Lord Castleberry's aunt an ape-leader."

"That's what she is. Even worse than that. I hope Lady Castleberry puts her in her place."

Alicia Rose felt it best to let Lizzie do the talking, for anything she, Alicia Rose, might say would surely come back to haunt her. Besides, she could not speak for Olivia. As far as she knew, Olivia had no interest in who did what at Robinbrook. They came to two huge double doors. Lizzie opened them and stepped inside.

"This is the loggia, the most heavenly room in all of Robinbrook. Just look, windows all across, and out there is the sea. I think when I get to heaven, I'll tell the Lord I want a room just like this."

Alicia Rose gasped. Indeed, it was a wonderful room, big, comfortable chairs and sofas, fresh flowers with delicious smells, the roar of the sea swirling about it all.

But first things first, thought Alicia Rose. She was hungry. "There can't be a kitchen nearby. Or can there?"

"Of course not, peagoose. I'll fetch a tray. A footman waited on Miss High-and-Mighty when she came to visit, before she broke his lordship's heart, but I'll wait on you."

"Did *she* eat in this room?"

"Every morning. And the master ate with her. She could not forbear the sunny breakfast room in his quarters. God's truth, the whore could not forbear anything Lord Castleberry loved. When she learned he was not fond of the color pink, she had everything in her future quarters, and in the sitting room of his lordship's quarters, covered in pink. The whore—"

"Lizzie!" Alicia Rose said, appalled. "You are incorrigible. What right do you have to call Lady Jacqueline a whore?"

Lizzie grinned. "Makes me feel good, and I know you won't tell."

"How do you know that? I arrived only last evening."

"I can tell things. I've got the gift. Second sight, they call it. I can see inside your head."

"Lizzie, I don't believe a word you are saying. No one can see inside my head."

"I can. And I can see what's going to happen to you. My grandmother was a Gypsy, and I got my gift from her, and she got it from her grandmother. They even talked to the other side."

Alicia Rose scoffed to herself. Lizzie was getting too wild for believing. "Well then, you can see that I'm starving. If you will show me the way, I will go eat where I ate last evening. I really would like to go for a ride."

"Who's going to tend Lady Castleberry?"

Alicia Rose had forgotten that she was Olivia's maid. "She'll most likely sleep until noon. Besides, she's on her honeymoon. I'm certain she doesn't want me around."

"I'll fetch your breakfast, and then I'll tend her. You're dressed too grand to be doing maid's work." And then the maid swished out of the room, leaving Alicia Rose with the roar of the sea for company. She sat for a while and looked out at the terraced gardens beneath the window, complete with blooming flowers and guarded by a low stone wall, from which the land fell gently to the azure sea. Lizzie had been right; this was as near to heaven as one could get here on earth. And then a strangeness filled the place, bringing a feeling of déjà vu. Attacked by the strangeness, Alicia Rose knew that something of great importance would happen here in this room. It was a room with a future, mayhap a past.

Having seen only seventeen summers, and being a he-

donist at heart, Alicia Rose Pembroke had thought the future
something that would eventually come, without planning on
her part. Her carefree spirit had long ago deemed that what
was to be would be. She would ask Lizzie what she thought
about predestination. Did God have one's life planned from
the day one was born?

Alicia Rose went to sit in a chair flanking the round,
marble-topped table that held the fresh flowers. The strange
feeling held her mesmerized as she saw in the dimness of
first light a man enter the room. He walked slowly, deliberately, until he reached a chair near her, where he sat as
if he were at home. Looking into her face, he gave a smile
that spoke of fondness and familiarity. He was ruggedly
handsome, with flowing golden hair, and there was an aura
of purple and gold about his body. She waited for him to
speak, but the deep silence lingered, and time dragged interminably.

Alicia Rose, trembling while frozen to her chair, her heart
pounding in her throat, felt joined to this strange apparition
by some mystical thread. And then he was gone; the feeling
was gone, and after awhile the trembling stopped. She could
once again see the terraced lawn, hear the roar of the sea,
smell the heady scent of clean salt air. Paying deference to
the sea, she watched as evanescent streaks of fluorescence
formed in the waves as they rose and fell, and then, sparked
by the early morning sun, turned a brilliant, quivering green.

Lizzie at last returned with a silver tray laden with food.
Steam and the smell of brewed coffee curled up from the
silver spout of the pot; the cup and saucer were of the finest
china. Alicia Rose straightened from her stupefied posture.
She did not want the maid to sense her fright, and she did
not want to hear one more word about the maid seeing
inside of her head.

"Lizzie, the help does not use such finery. If Lord Castleberry's Aunt Evaline learns of this, she will send you packing away from Robinbrook."

"She won't know. She's in the Hunt Room, eating breakfast and arguing with Mr. Fred."

Lizzie poured the coffee and handed the cup with a gold crest to Alicia Rose, whose quizzical gaze leveled on the maid. "Why would you bring my breakfast on a silver tray? And this is positively the finest china cup I've ever drunk from."

" 'Tis no more than you deserve. You're not of the lower orders . . . I told you I can read your mind. I don't know why you're pretending to be a maid."

"You have windmills in your head, Lizzie. Of course I'm Lady Castleberry's abigail. Don't all English women of the upper orders have at least one personal servant?"

"Yes, but a real maid. Look at your hands, smooth as a baby's behind. I don't know what you're up to, and I ain't going to be telling, but you ain't no lady's maid."

Alicia Rose decided not to argue with Lizzie. *The smart maid might read my mind.* By now the feeling of having seen a man wrapped in an aura had left, and she was sure that in this new environment she had quite simply developed a penchant for the mysterious. Mayhap it was all those ancient portraits she had passed in the hall. She did not believe in ghosts, or in fortune-tellers, not even in witches, and certainly she did not believe that someone could see into another's head. A wild imagination had momentarily taken hold of her, and she had only *thought* she saw a man with flowing yellow hair.

She ate hurriedly, hardly tasting her food, but it satisfied her hunger and at last she swallowed the last bite and touched her mouth with the pristine white serviette. And then she noticed Lizzie swiping at every nook and cranny with a feather duster, moving like a snail, while quietly humming "Rock of Ages." As if her thoughts were a million kilometers away. Alicia Rose called her name.

Lizzie turned quickly around. "Oh, so you're through eating. Hope you enjoyed it. I'll take the tray."

"Is that why you've been hanging around, pretending to be busy, just to take the tray?"

"I ain't dim-witted, Miss Pembroke. I don't want nobody knowing I'm serving you in this room."

Alicia Rose laughed. "Well, since you're bent on taking care of me, I hold you to your promise that you will go to Lady Castleberry's quarters and tend her while I go for a morning ride."

"That will be my pleasure." Lizzie smiled, showing white teeth against her dark skin, and then she added, "On your way out, go by the Hunt Room and put an ear to the door. You'll learn a lot from Mr. Fred and the ape-leader." She laughed a low laugh. "They'll give you an earful."

"What were they arguing about?" Alicia asked.

"About the hounds. The ape-leader hates them, says they should not be in the house, and she hates Lady Patience. That really sets Mr. Fred off. If you ask me, I think the ape-leader is in love with him herself."

"Aunt Evaline in love with Mr. Fred? Aren't they related?"

"No. She's Lord Castleberry's aunt, his father's sister, and Mr. Fred—his real name is Fredrick Weatherby—is his lordship's grandfather, his mother's papa."

Alicia thought it strange that such a divergent family should be living at Robinbrook, but she supposed that was another of the peculiar English ways. In America, Grandparents, when they were old, often lived with their children, but not aunts and cousins, and Robinbrook even had Chester, who, so Olivia had told her, had just come to Robinbrook and stayed.

Alicia Rose left. After taking many twists and turns, she found a stairway which she believed was used only by servants and made her way below stairs. Using logic, she headed toward what she thought would be the back of the huge house.

A hunt room, where hunters gathered to do a little imbibing, socializing, and stuffing themselves before leaving to chase the poor fox, would be to the back of the house, would it not? The country homes of America's rich often had such a room, especially those who held to English ways.

She heard voices before she reached where she was going. Even though she'd given no thought to Lizzie's suggestion that she eavesdrop, she stopped and listened. It was not difficult to discern the voices were those of a man and a woman. Edging forward, she found a screen to shield her, and through a crack saw a white-haired old man, tall and well formed, and a woman wearing a fashionable morning dress, her mousy gray hair adorned with two red silk roses frayed at the edges. She had seen the woman last evening, waiting to meet Olivia. She was wearing the same red roses.

"She's positively the homeliest chit I've ever seen. I think Fitzgerald has lost his senses." Aunt Evaline stopped, and Alicia Rose thought she heard her voice break, as if she were crying. And sure enough, she was. She took a lace handkerchief from her sleeve and covered her face, muffling her words. "Lady Jacqueline was the one for him. He's a handsome man, and to be leg-shackled to a nobody. A fortune hunter no doubt. He deserves better."

"Stop your blubbering, Evaline," the old man said. "Lady Jacqueline's beauty is only skin deep. She thinks only for herself, and besides that, she's a dimwit. This woman is smart. It shows in those green eyes. Sharp as a tack, she is, a writer, and that's what a man should look for when he's wanting a mother for his heir. I've no doubt the son of Fitz and his American wife will have the mind of a genius. Just watch and see."

"Fred Weatherby, how can you think of his mating with *her*. I thought you hated Americans."

A rich, warm laugh came from Fred's throat. "That's King George. He's the one who smarts, or he did before he became addle-brained about the Americans outsmarting him. He thought they owed him the same allegiance as the English did."

"You're changing the subject, Fred," said the ape-leader. "What are we going to do about this marriage of your grandson's? Imagine a man of the nobility married to a nobody. He's the one who's addle-brained. I'm sure he did something to that sweet Lady Jacqueline to make her marry that old man. Broke her heart, most likely, and she married for spite. If you ask me——"

"Well, I didn't ask you, and neither did Fitz. I could hardly sleep last night, thinking that nine months hence there'll be an heir to Robinbrook. That'll really set Cousin Trevor Castleberry off. He's so sure he will inherit the earldom and all that goes with it. I'll wager he petitions the good Lord every evening for Fitz's death. I can't imagine Robinbrook being in his hands!" He shook his white head. "It doesn't bear thinking on."

Alicia Rose had no idea who Trevor Castleberry was. While Olivia had been meeting these people, she, Alicia Rose, had been taken to their quarters and left there until time for supper, and then she had eaten with other servants. There had been no mention of a Trevor Castleberry.

This argument could go on all day, she thought. Plainly Fred did not know Lord Castleberry's marriage to Olivia was in name only, and she could imagine his disappointment when nine months hence there would be no little feet pattering around this big old house. And when and if there were a child, the poor little thing would get lost anyway, and they would never find him . . . or her.

Lizzie had been right, mused Alicia Rose. One could learn a lot by keeping an ear to the door, but she did not feel disturbed by what she had learned. It did not signify. Let the old woman think Olivia was a fortune hunter, and not highborn enough for Lord Castleberry. She and Olivia would be leaving Robinbrook as soon as a meeting with the mysterious writer could be arranged. By then Lord

Castleberry would be ready to end his charade and the settlement will have been made.

It did trouble Alicia Rose more than a little that the old woman thought Olivia terribly ugly, and she had to near restrain herself to keep from going in there and snatching those ugly roses out of her mousy hair. But after thinking on it, she decided that if Olivia were truly ugly—which she was not—it was like one kettle calling another kettle black. Aunt Evaline certainly was no beauty.

Alicia Rose looked around for a way to escape to the outside without going through the Hunt Room, but every door she turned to led to another room. "Stuff, I'll just go in and introduce myself."

When she stepped into the huge room, she felt lost in its enormity, it was larger than most entire houses. Large squares of black and white tile covered the floor, and in the far end, a stone fireplace, large enough to roast a cow, reached the high ceiling. The room held the smell of smoke and roasting meat. Red cloths covered tables flanked by chairs, enough to accommodate at least one hundred hungry hunters. And then there were cozy areas, like where Fred and Evaline were sitting, in front of a smaller fireplace, around which were wicker chairs and sofas. Tall windows of paned glass afforded a view of distant rolling meadow and undulating hillocks.

The hounds rested at Fred's feet. It appeared that he and the grumpy old woman had just finished breakfast. A maid appeared from nowhere, bobbed, and took away their trays.

Boldly, Alicia Rose made her way toward them, bobbing as the maid had done. "I'm Alicia Rose, Lady Castleberry's personal maid. I think in England one who takes care of a lady's personal needs is called a lady's maid, or her ladyship's abigail."

Aunt Evaline scowled, and Fred quickly jumped to his feet, a huge smile on his weathered face. "I'm Fitz's grandfather on his mother's side, and this is his aunt on his father's side. We're glad to make the acquaintance of Lady Castleberry's personal maid. I hope you find Robinbrook to your liking. I'm especially pleased my grandson has finally found himself a suitable mate."

"Suitable! Huh!" scorned Aunt Evaline. " 'Tis a disgrace to the Castleberry name. Fred, how can you be so blind?"

"Pay no attention to Lady Evaline," Fred said. "Just because she was not fortunate enough to land a husband, she resents every woman who does."

"Fred, that is not so. If Mr. Appleby had not died—"

"Most likely he died to escape marrying you."

There was a teasing look on Fred's face, and Alicia Rose quickly discerned a genuine fondness between these two, who seemingly did not agree on anything. Thinking it best to get off on the right foot, she decided to address the old woman. "Miss Evaline—"

"Lady Evaline to you. My papa was third earl of Robinbrook. The title passed to Fitzgerald's father, and then to Fitzgerald, who is the fifth earl of Robinbrook."

"I beg your forgiveness," said Alicia Rose, nearly choking on the words and bobbing again because she did not know what else to do. Suddenly she was just a little angry. "But Miss Olivia . . . Lady Castleberry, is a very nice lady. Lord Castleberry is fortunate to have her for his wife. In Boston she was pursued by every eligible bachelor in town, and had she not had such a craving to come to England, she would have been married long ago."

Aunt Evaline snorted, and Alicia Rose crossed her fingers behind her back for the part about Olivia being pursued by every eligible bachelor in Boston. So she had told only a part lie. But the woman had no right to speak disparagingly of Olivia. And the part about his lordship being lucky to have her as his wife, even if it was in name only, was certainly true.

A hound rose from its comfortable spot at Fred's feet and sauntered to Alicia Rose's side. She patted its head, smiling down into its big brown, dreamy eyes. "What's your name?" she asked.

"That's Millie," Fred offered, "and this one's Mildred, and then there's Milton and Melvin. They're all scoundrels, lazy to a fault, and wouldn't chase a fox if starvation were knocking on their door. They think a rabbit is something with which to romp." He laughed his warm laugh as the other three hounds followed Millie's lead and gathered around Alicia Rose. She patted all of them and wondered how in the world one could tell which one was which. The male dogs, Milton and Melvin, were slightly larger, but all had black spots on their white coats in exactly the same places, as far as she could discern.

"I think they sense you are going outside," said Fred. "Were you going for a morning ride?"

"That was my plan, if I can find the stables."

"Then the hounds and I will go to the stables with you. Come." He snapped his fingers at the dogs.

As Fred rose from his chair and the dogs gathered around him, jumping and vying for position, Alicia Rose looked at Aunt Evaline, whose scowl had grown deeper. Grabbing her embroidery hoop from a nearby table, she began stitching, while saying, "Fred, the upper orders do not fraternize with the lower orders. This brash young thing is a maid."

"So she is, and she wants to go riding. I'll help her find a horse. She'll need to know her way around Robinbrook. I want her to like it here."

Alicia Rose bobbed again to Lady Evaline and then turned to quit the huge room, glad to be rid of Lizzie's ape-leader. Outside, her spirits lifted. A gardener's paradise. A small bridge bulged upward to cross over a small pond, plainly man-made. A black goose and her gosling swam in single file on the dark water, the mama goose's head thrust proudly upward. Alicia Rose was sure that if the goose could have smiled, she would have.

"The garden's Capability Brown's handiwork," offered

Fred, and before Alicia Rose could think, she had spoken, embarrassing herself. "And who is Capability Brown?"

"The foremost landscape artist in England."

"I must learn more of England's history," said Alicia Rose. "Miss Pembroke . . . Lady Castleberry would have recognized Capability Brown's name right away. She's a well-read lady."

"I have no doubt that Fitz will find his new bride stimulating intellectually, especially after that dim-witted Lady Jacqueline. I pray there will be many children."

Alicia Rose shook her head and again spoke without thinking. "I fear it takes more than a stimulated mind to produce children. In my opinion, Lord Castleberry appears to have no interest at all in that area. At least where Lady Castleberry is concerned. When he looks at her, his eyes are like shards of ice, not at all like a man wanting to mate."

Fred gave her a startled look, and Alicia Rose wanted to bite her tongue. She must remember to be more careful if she wanted this charade to succeed.

Eight

Lizzie was brushing Olivia's long hair. "Your hair shines like a horse's tail," she said with a theatrical sigh.

Olivia laughed. "At least you don't think it looks like molasses."

"Oh, that too. Burnt sugar, that's the way molasses look part red, part brown. I'm certain as I can be his lordship saw that right off. Now, take that whore's hair, 'tis as yellow as sweet corn, and she's so pale 'tis most scary."

"Who are you calling a whore, Lizzie?" Olivia asked, although she already knew.

"That thing Lord Castleberry wanted to marry. When he looks at her, he reminds me of one of the bitch hounds in heat, and she just poured herself all over him. That is, before she left him. Tempting him, that was what she was doing. She got him all lathered up, and then she ran off with that old man. I swear she'll get her just due, hurting a kind man like Lord Castleberry that way."

"Lizzie, I'll hear no more of your gossip."

Olivia spoke more sharply than she had intended, but she was not in the best of humor. She had hardly slept the night before, and almost at first light Lizzie had come knocking on her door, saying that Miss Alicia Rose sent her to tend Lady Castleberry, that Alicia Rose had gone for a morning ride. *When I get my hands on that sister of mine, I will throttle her,* Olivia thought. She said aloud, "That will be enough brushing. And I can dress myself. In truth, I've been dressing myself all my life. Alicia Rose has never been worth a whit as a lady's maid."

"I could tell that the minute I laid eyes on her," offered Lizzie. "But that won't matter here at Robinbrook. I'll tend both of you. If you'll tell me which gown you prefer, I'll get it for you."

"Lizzie, I told you I can dress myself—"

Just then she heard a door open. Whipping around, she saw Lord Castleberry standing in the doorway, dressed all the crack, his large frame practically filling the doorway. And she was in her pantalettes. She lunged for an afghan from the foot of the bed to cover herself, while his lordship stood there and laughed like a young man hardly out of leading strings.

" 'Tis all right, my darling, for a husband to see his wife in her unmentionables," he said, coming toward her as if he meant to stroke her cheek, or mayhap take her into his arms and hug her, and she found that was exactly what she wanted him to do. She thought about the stooped man with gnarled hands she had imagined her future husband to be, and almost wished it were so.

Not hardly that bad, she thought, but why does his lordship have to be so demme handsome? she asked herself in bewilderment.

She forced a small laugh and stepped aside when his long arms reached for her. "You must understand, your lordship, that I'm not accustomed to having a man enter my room without knocking."

"And I daresay you are not used to having a husband. I came to invite you to share breakfast with me in my own private dining room. The sun is just at the right angle to brighten and warm us. The view is nothing short of spectacular."

He turned to Lizzie, whose eyes, Olivia quickly noted, were as big as saucers, and said, "Please have breakfast for

two brought immediately. And you may be excused. I shall
help my wife finish her toilette."

Olivia could not believe her ears. The audacity of this
man. As soon as the door closed behind the maid, Olivia
turned on him. "How dare you enter my room without
knocking. And you will not help me dress. Get out of my
room and stay out until I am presentable."

"I beg your forgiveness," he said.

It appeared to Olivia that at any moment he would burst
out laughing. "Don't you dare start laughing. There's nothing to laugh about."

Plainly her words did not sober him, but he offered in
way of explanation, "I was taken aback to find one of Robinbrook's maids tending you. I thought to find Alicia Rose,
who knows of our business arrangement. When I saw Lizzie, who seems to be all over the house at any given time,
I could not let her suspect that things were not as they
should be between a husband and wife. 'Twould ruin everything. Servants are notorious gossips. On-dits fly from
house to house."

Listening to his lordship. Olivia completely forgot that
she was not properly dressed. The afghan was now clutched
in her right hand, dangling down her side, while her left
hand was placed firmly on her left hip. If Lord Castleberry's
devil eyes had not been looking her up and down, she
doubted that she would have ever noticed the absurd situation. "Don't stare at me that way," she demanded.

Lord Castleberry averted his gaze, and he appeared to be
angry, taking on the appearance of Lucifer. Anger danced
in his words. "I suggest you bind yourself, as you were
when you disembarked the ship. You were homely enough
then, even without your freckles. And wear your hair up."

"Do you mean that I should wear a binding cloth here
at Robinbrook? I'll concede to doing that in society, but
'tis most uncomfortable, and as I told you, I will wear my
hair as I please while here at Robinbrook."

"No, no, you have it all wrong. 'Tis in public that I want your décolletage to show. Only your face is to be homely, and the way you dress your hair. But here at Robinbrook you are not to tempt me."

Olivia laughed heartily. "With your being so besotted with Lady Jacqueline, how could I tempt you? Is your heart so fickle that you can be tempted by one chit while you are longing for another?"

"What I am talking about has nothing to do with my heart." He sighed deeply. "I suppose you would have to be a man to understand such feelings as being tempted beyond endurance. Love doesn't enter into the picture. A man has physical needs."

"I cannot speak from experience, but I assure you I have read about the difference in unadulterated pass ion and being totally in love. And being a male does not offer a monopoly on such feelings. Females have the same desires. Mayhap they are more civilized about it . . . and maybe not. Have you ever seen a female cat squalling for the male cat to mount her?"

His lordship looked as if he might faint. "Lady Castleberry! I will not have my wife speak in such a manner. I'm . . . I'm totally agog."

"I'm your wife in name only, and I think it perfectly correct to discuss with you what I've learned in my years of studies. I have no desire to tempt you, or any man, but I shall not wear my bosom bound just to alleviate your discomfort. Now, if you will kindly leave me to my dressing, I shall do so quickly and join you for breakfast. Mayhap we can discuss England's politics. I have definite ideas on the regent's disastrous spending of England's tax money. . . ."

Olivia was almost positive she heard a smothered groan as Lord Castleberry quit the room with alacrity.

* * *

In the grand library on the second floor, Lord Castleberry sat with his feet resting on a leather ottoman. His tasseled Hessian boots shone like new money in the sunlight that cut a swath across the room. He was wearing the long trousers that had, in the past year, come into style. Only recently had his lordship purchased a pair to test their comfort. The cloth was fashionable doeskin, his waistcoat, above which protruded the V of a white ruffled shirt, was of embroidered broadcloth.

For years he had not taken notice of his dress, but now that he could afford the luxury, and had the time for it, his dress was very important to him. He was not foppish by any means, he told himself, but he did enjoy knowing he was dressed well. And he supposed he was vain, for he enjoyed being told by the opposite sex that he was handsome.

He wondered if Olivia thought him handsome. Certainly she had not told him so. His lordship found himself smiling. It had been a delightful breakfast with Olivia Pembroke, he thought, and then he corrected himself, calling his wife Lady Castleberry. He had not yet gotten used to her being Lady Castleberry, for he had never thought he would wed anyone except lovely, lovely Jacqueline. A huge ache filled his heart. Where had he gone wrong in his pursuit of her hand? He had given her everything she wanted, and he had loved her completely.

He could only think with a shudder how she had danced through his dreams, keeping him awake hours on end, wanting her, yet he had held himself back, allowing himself only a chaste kiss now and then. A gentleman treated his future wife with respect and kept her pure. Courtesans were used to satisfy raging libidos.

He laughed aloud. No doubt Olivia had read all about passion sending hot blood raging through a man's veins. Why, he had heard men make claim that their bride sought the fainting bench when first she saw his hard maleness, claiming she did not know the transformation from flaccid to hardness was possible. He did not doubt Olivia's innocence, but he was sure she had *read* about how a man's handle became engorged with blood, and how it became as hard as a brick when he was aroused.

They had steered clear of *that* subject at breakfast and had discussed England's politics instead. They had even argued the merits of being a Tory or a Whig. Olivia was an extraordinary woman.

His lordship had to admit, even though he had seen thirty summers, he had had very little experience with women. He had become the fifth earl of Robinbrook when he was only fifteen, and after his years at Cambridge, where he had thought he would be letting his late father down if he did not excel in every subject, there had been the war. He had fought as hard for his country against Napoleon as he had fought to be the best in his class in school. There had been discreet liaisons with courtesans, for he had never lacked passion, but it seemed he had never had time for love. Then, when he met Lady Jacqueline, he had been totally unprepared for the force of his feelings. If only, earlier in life, he had experienced what was considered puppy love, but he had not, and when he finally did fall in love, it was beyond reason.

His lordship searched his mind as to why Lady Jacqueline had cried off and married another man. Surely he had caused her to act in such a rash fashion. She was such a tender, sweet little thing. He tried to envision her reaction when she learned he had married an ugly American gel, which she, Lady Jacqueline, had suggested that he do. Anger at the turn of events took away some of the hurt. Since being jilted in such a fashion, he had allowed his anger to build a hard shield around his aching heart. Anger at Lady Jacqueline had been behind his advertising for a homely American wife.

Now, in only a fortnight, he would introduce Olivia to

society. He would pretend to be besotted with her, and she would turn those gray-green eyes on him adoringly.

His lordship leaned back in his chair. He could envision the bulging eyes, and hear the gasps of disbelief, when the *ton* women viewed them dancing across the polished floor, Olivia in a gown that would take any man's breath away, a gown so beautiful that it would send every woman of the upper ten thousand scrambling to her modiste.

But what he wanted more than that was to fill Lady Jacqueline with envy, to make her see the error of her rash behavior, to make her want him for herself . . . when she saw how happy he was with his American bride.

Nine

As Fred and Alicia Rose made their way to the stables, the hounds romped around them, running away and then coming back for a pat on the head. Alicia Rose found the old man anything but doddering. His steps were light and quick, his back ramrod straight, and he swung his cane with the effort of a much younger man. He called to the dogs, naming each one, but it was only when his voice became stern did they mind him.

"Don't you have a title, Mr. Fred?" Alicia Rose asked.

"No. My daughter, Fits's mother, married into the upper ten thousand. Even though I had wealth, I was not one of them." A pause, and then, "It was a love match, and even though Fitz's grandmother and grandfather on his mother's side objected strenuously to the match, Fitz's father married my Angeline anyway. And then they had Fitz."

Alicia Rose saw that he was smiling. Love and admiration laced his words as he spoke of his grandson. "Fitz is a fine boy." He laughed then, his warm, kindly laugh that made the beautiful morning more beautiful. Alicia Rose would like this old man, she decided.

He called to Millie to settle down and then said to Alicia Rose, "I call Fitz a boy even though he's seen thirty summers. He has the kindest heart of anyone I know, and he's very smart. That is why I cannot forbear Lady Jacqueline. She is such a dimwit. But now, take your mistress. She's educated, like Fitz. She's more to my liking."

For once Alicia Rose did not speak before thinking. She did not want to lie to Fred, and she was not about to tell this kind old man the whole of it, that his grandson did not want a true marriage with Olivia, and that Olivia had come to England with the hopes of getting her manuscript published. Let his lordship talk to his grandfather about the "business arrangement" he and Olivia had made.

She smelled the fresh air, still damp from the dew that glimmered on the grass, and from the rumbling sea behind them. They had left the manicured lawn and were walking along a footpath toward the stables, passing the gardener's cottage and a smaller dwelling where, Fred told her, Chester lived.

"Chester just came to Robinbrook and never left. He's wonderful with the flowers, especially roses."

They came then to a cluster of tall, white clapboard buildings surrounded by fenced yards holding a variety of fine horses. In the carriage houses, whose doors were open, grooms were shining already-gleaming carriages.

"Will you ride with me?" she asked of Fred.

" 'Twould be my pleasure," he answered, his eyes twinkling.

Alicia Rose sensed that he had not said all that he wanted to say. After all, she was a maid, and a maid told her mistress everything. A groom came, and Fred asked him to saddle a horse for Alicia Rose.

"Not too tame," he said, winking at her. "And, of course, I'll be riding Bonaparte."

"And, pray, do not expect me to ride sidesaddle," offered Alicia Rose. Her skirt was long and full, and in America she had, from the time she was nine, insisted upon riding in a saddle like Papa's. She knew in England it was against propriety, but she did not care a whit about propriety. Again her thoughts went back to her life in Boston, and she made a mental note to ask Fred if he had ever heard of the Pembroke family. Later, when she knew him better.

But not now, she told herself. Olivia had cautioned her about telling too much, and Papa had hinted that the Pembroke family had left England under unfavorable circumstances. He had even hinted that England was not a safe place for a Pembroke to live.

The groom delivered the saddled horses and offered Alicia Rose a hand up. Fred mounted Bonaparte with the agility of a twenty-year-old.

"I'll show you Fitz's estate," he said. "There's nothing like it in all of England. Fitz, even when he was at war, saw that crops were rotated, that the fields rested, and, in turn, the land made him a very rich man. That has not always been so. Fitz has had a hard life, and it's only in the past few years that he could afford to take a wife and produce an heir."

"I thought anyone of the nobility was rich beyond reason."

"Having a title does not always mean riches."

Alicia listened with interest. She would have a lot to tell Olivia when she returned to the manor house. A hound frightened her horse, which the groom had called Martha, but Alicia Rose quickly settled the mare. Neither horse was too tame. They had no more than left the stables, when Bonaparte threw his head back and snorted, and it took not too gentle a pull on the bridle reins by Fred to calm him. They rode for a long while in silence. Alicia Rose liked Martha. She was a gentle but spirited mare, and soon they were cantering down a farm road that wound over vast acres of rich soil. Alicia Rose caught her breath as one pastoral scene followed another. On the verdant hillsides, sheep grazed, watched over by shepherds. In the deep, wide valleys, crops sprouted in freshly plowed ground. Acres of cherry trees were in bloom.

They passed clusters of small cottages, and Fred said in way of explanation, "Farm help, managed by the farm steward. But not left entirely to him. Fitz sees that their needs are taken care of, and that the children go to school. He even had a schoolhouse built and hired a schoolmarm."

"You love your grandson very much, don't you, Fred," offered Alicia Rose. It showed in his eyes, the way he smiled when he said "Fitz," and in the gentle tone of his voice when he alluded to his grandson.

"I love Fitz, yes, enormously, and I love Robinbrook. That is why I cannot forbear there not being an heir." His white, spiky eyebrows drew together in a ferocious frown, and the gentleness in his voice suddenly approached full-blown anger. "Trevor Castleberry cannot inherit Robinbrook."

Now I know why he offered to ride with me.

Alicia Rose smiled, simultaneously feeling sympathy for the old man. What Lord Castleberry and Olivia were doing all at once did not seem fair to Alicia Rose. How disappointed this kind, gentle man would be when he learned of their charade. And she was part of it, pretending to be Olivia's lady's maid.

Again she was tempted to tell him the whole of it, but held her tongue. Olivia would have her head should she speak. So Alicia Rose changed the subject and told him about the ghost who visited her in the room that overlooked the sea. "There was an aura around him; his blond hair fell to his shoulders. . . ."

Fred laughed. "Every old house in England has a ghost at one time or another. I suspect 'tis the way the sun reflects off the water that forms the aura, but I suppose it is possible this apparition . . . or ghost . . . could be from another life, a restless spirit who refuses to leave Robinbrook. I believe in more than one life, don't you?"

Alicia Rose was startled. "I don't know. I've never thought about it." She gave a small laugh. "I've never given this life serious thought, much less a past life."

Just then they came up over a small hillock, and Alicia Rose saw on the side of a taller hillock smoke curling up from chimney pots atop a stone manor house, a near replica of Robinbrook, except much smaller in size. As they approached the house, it did not appear ancient, as Robinbrook did. Lichen did not grow up to frame the windows, which overlooked closely clipped lawns and terraced gardens where flowers bloomed profusely. Young trees swayed in the gentle wind. Looking back over her shoulder, she could see the shimmering waters of the sea. And even from there she could hear the muffled rumble of waves as they rose and fell, the sea gulls cawing, and she smelled its rich salt smell mingled with the scent of cherry blossoms.

They guided their horses closer to the house.

"That's Trevor's home. Fitz had it built for him."

"That should certainly keep him happy," said Alicia Rose.

Again vitriolic anger was in Fred's voice. "It doesn't. He wants Robinbrook."

Ten

Olivia draped a dark brown mantle around the naked statue of Lady Jacqueline and then stood back. "Naked in view of others is beyond the pale, your highness, especially in front of a rakehell such as my husband, Lord Castleberry." She was being flippant, enjoying it immensely. Fastening the wrap firmly at the neck with a brooch, she made sure the brown nipples on the statue were sufficiently covered. And then she laughed.

Olivia could not remember when she had laughed alone in a room, nor could she account for her good mood. Humming, she whirled herself around and began to dance, round and round, pirouetting, until she danced herself right into two long arms, which, rather like an octopus, gathered her into a tight grip, pulling her backside against a hard, lean body. A low laugh floated past her ear. Although she should have been frightened, she was not. The feeling of warmth and closeness sent a shiver up her spine. A man had never held her like this.

"Unhand me," she demanded in as firm a voice as she could muster. She attempted in vain to twist herself around to see the intruder who was taking such liberty with her body, sending it spiraling into a world of warmth she had never experienced before. The laughter again, matching her own good mood. When his grip tightened against her wriggling, she lifted a foot and gave a hard kick to his shin, heel striking bone. The soft slippers she was wearing protected her very little when the blow struck, and a sharp pain caused her to cry out. He gave no sign of pain, not even an "Oh."

But he loosened his grip just enough for her to turn so that when she lifted her head she was looking into the cold, devil eyes of Lord Castleberry, Lucifer himself. She had known, although he had never touched her before. He smelled clean and fresh, as if he had been just freshly shaved.

"Lord Castleberry, you are forgetting yourself," she said, as a warm flush enveloped her body and the shiver turned into a shudder. His eyes were suddenly filled with warmth and longing, and that longing manifested itself into her as well. This would not do, she thought. Her quick mind did not have time to form a plan of escape. She heard a guttural groan before his beautifully shaped, dark head bent toward her. Warm breath caressed her cheeks, and before she could jerk herself free, he was kissing her in a most suggestive way. Her husband was kissing her.

After that Lady Castleberry lost track of time. And of herself. Her body melted into his, her eyes closed, bells rang inside her head, and her heart felt as if it would burst. Never had she felt such euphoria, such intense desire, strange and deliciously frightening. There was no fight in her, but she found that her hands had curled into fists. She beat on his chest, and then she found herself kissing him back, and it was only after he had ravaged her lips, probed her mouth with his hot tongue, and pulled her body closer against his hardness that she knew for certain she must do something—else they would be on the fainting bench, compromising their business arrangement.

Her beloved manuscript came to mind, and she held the thought. Even thinking thus, the heat did not entirely leave her body. She called herself a disgraceful chit and likened herself to Lady Jacqueline. He kissed her again. Pretending to relax, she caught him unawares and put her curled fists on his broad shoulders and pushed with all her might. She had to stop this exquisite pleasure. He smiled down at her.

Olivia felt that she stood before him naked as Lady Jacqueline's stone body before she had covered it. And then, as if he had suddenly come to his senses, the smile was gone and the anger and the hardness returned to those cold blue devil eyes. A clock ticked heavily in the room. He entwined his fingers from her long hair and let his hand drop to his side. A long silence began, and held until he spoke in a tight and strangled voice. "I've warned you not to tempt me." It was an accusation.

Olivia forced a laugh. "How dare you accuse me. I was having a perfectly wonderful time, dressing your precious Lady Jacqueline and then dancing because I felt like dancing."

"You shouldn't have been dancing. The way your body moved, as light as a feather, and the way your hair, shimmering in the yellow sunlight, swirling around your face, was nothing less than an act of seduction. Any man would have felt as I felt. I couldn't stop myself from kissing you."

"And I did not know you were about. So how could my dancing be an act of seduction? And the kiss was nothing. I felt nothing, so 'tis best you remember that when next you are tempted to repeat the foolish act."

Biting her lip and praying the lie did not show on her flushed face, she took a deep breath and waited as another deep silence wrapped itself around the room. Although her heart still raced like a horse bound on winning a high-stake race, big hooves pounding her tight chest unmercifully and her knees threatening to give way and let her drop to the floor, she squared her shoulders and lifted her small chin, looking unflinchingly into his lordship's devil eyes, giving her most charming smile.

"Did you notice I dressed your Lady Jacqueline? The chit has no shame."

If Olivia's heretofore words had not jerked his lordship

back to reality, her mentioning Lady Jacqueline most certainly did. The sparks of passion left his eyes, and his proud face now held melancholy and pain, and it was as if he had never kissed Olivia. She felt betrayed. Even though she had pushed him away, she wanted him to remember, to want to kiss her again.

Olivia told herself that it was she who had no shame. How could she be a willing substitute for Lady Jacqueline?

Leaving her standing in the middle of the room, his lordship walked over to the statue and stared down into the stone-hard face. And then he laughed, but not the pleasant laughter that had earlier floated out into the room. The cynical sound ripped at Olivia's heart. His blue eyes were like glittering hard diamonds, his jaw clenched. For a man to suffer such unrequited love was painful to watch. She hated Lady Jacqueline; how could she not?

"I wonder what she would think should she suddenly come to life and witness my kissing you," his lordship said more to himself than to Olivia.

"I was under the impression that 'tis quite normal for a husband to kiss his wife. Most likely she would not feel a thing. Her husband most likely kisses her as often as he likes."

A stricken look, and then, "Don't say that! I cannot forbear his touching her. He's an old man and incapable of passion. No doubt she's still a virgin. I hear *that* leaves a man as he nears fifty."

Incredulously, Olivia looked at him. "Did a man of fifty tell you that? My sources tell me a man is capable of begetting children, with a great deal of passion, well into his seventies, mayhap longer if his thoughts are right, and if he's in love. Did you not know that the brain is the most powerful of the sex organs."

Lord Castleberry gasped and turned from the statue to glare at Olivia. "Have you made a survey of men past fifty?

I would not doubt that you would do such a thing. Tis against propriety to even discuss things of that nature."

His lordship was at a loss for words, and he knew before she spoke that she would say she had read about the reproduction organs in a book. He had not bargained for this; perhaps his advertisement in the Boston paper should have stipulated a *simple,* homely American for a nobleman's wife.

Now angry herself, and she did not know why, or could it be pain, Olivia lashed out. "I can see there's no use talking with you, so besotted are you with your Lady Jacqueline. I think 'tis time I tell you my main purpose in accepting your ridiculous business arrangement was to make my way to England to seek help in getting my manuscript published. My writings are similar in style to the author of *Sense and Sensibility* and *Pride and Prejudice;* the same publisher will be interested in my work, I am sure."

His lordship raised a quizzical brow. "Do you think Jane Austen would promote her competition?"

"Oh, do you know this Jane Austen?" Olivia's heart was pounding like a hammer against her chest wall. "I was made to understand she wished to remain anonymous."

"I'm acquainted with her brother, Henry Austen. He negotiates her contracts. But Miss Austen's friends know of her writing. I imagine it would be quite a feat for an author of her caliber to remain completely anonymous."

Lord Castleberry lowered his oversized frame into the undersized chair his Lady Jacqueline had provided for him.

"Please sit, Lady Castleberry. I came here in the middle of the day, when I am usually busy with the farm's books, to discuss with you the modiste's progress on your wardrobe. Your meeting with Miss Austen can be arranged after our business arrangement has been brought to a satisfactory completion and the settlement has been made."

Olivia sat. She really had no quarter, she told herself.

She had agreed to the business arrangement. But she had no interest in discussing her ostentatious wardrobe, which had taken three days of measuring, fingering materials, and looking at patterns. Such a ridiculous way to spend time and money. So she sat in silence, her hands resting demurely in her lap. Let his lordship talk; he would have the last word anyway.

"Was Madame Hazlitt to your liking?" he asked. "I'm most eager to introduce you to my friends. Even though I was trying to keep my mind on the figures, my thoughts kept straying to the wonderful ball I'm planning. I'm thinking I prefer to hold it in London, mayhap at Almack's. I favor the Argyle Rooms, but 'twill be good for you to meet Lady Jersey and the other patronesses at Almack's. I understand they hold the reins to society's—"

"I'm not interested in society," Olivia quickly interjected. *Demme the agreement. And demme Lord Castleberry for disturbing my staid, tranquil life.*

Olivia looked at the man to whom she was wife in name only, and tears filled her eyes. Could she be in love with him? When he was obviously besotted with someone else? Did she have no pride? She had never considered love for herself, but now, looking at the hard strength of muscled limbs showing explicitly through his skin-tight pantaloons, the strangest feelings moved over her body, and she knew the long-denied emotion had come to her, that she was in love with Lord Fitzgerald Castleberry. What a bumble broth. She swore under her breath. If only he had not kissed her. She battled tears and held them at bay. Later, when she was alone, she would cry, and the tears would cleanse her soul, but she must not let herself hope that Lord Castleberry would ever love her. She would write; the pen could be the outlet for the pain she felt.

"Of course I'll live up to our agreement," she said when she realized how much time had passed since either of them had spoken. "Even if it means I must move about in society."

"It will be for only a short while," he said. "And I did not mean to be cruel in regards to writing, and in my supposition that Miss Austen will not be willing to help in getting your manuscript published. I know nothing of writers, or of the publishing world. I was being very selfish, thinking my feelings were all that mattered. Pray forgive me. When our agreement has reached fruition, I'll see that a meeting between you and the distinguished author is arranged."

"Thank you, your lordship," Olivia said. She felt subdued and hurt, but pride made her avert her eyes to look through the window at the pastoral scene of sheep grazing on a hillock. Determinedly her mind returned to the business arrangement.

"You were inquiring about Madame Hazlitt. She's pleasant enough, but I feel the clothes far too elaborate, especially the gown for this ball you are planning. One would think me the queen, to be crowned beside my husband at his coronation."

This brought a huge smile to Lord Castleberry's face. "That is exactly what I ordered when I spoke with her. She's very astute. I told her pale green satin, with pearls, plenty of pearls. And does it have a low décolletage?"

"Many, many pearls, especially on the train, and the neckline is scandalous, showing more bosom than any lady should be comfortable with."

As best he could, Lord Castleberry leaned back in the small chair, a satisfied look on his face, as if he were visualizing the effect the gown would have on Lady Jacqueline. "And the rest of the wardrobe? Will it be adequate? I told Madame to spare no expense."

Olivia gave a small laugh. "Carriage dresses, dinner dresses, garden dresses, morning dresses, theater dresses, walking dresses, I've never seen the like. All showing a little ankle, as she said was the style in London. Will the business arrangement be so long that I will need *all* those gowns?"

"Possibly not. But they will serve you well when you launch your new life in London, after our marriage has been set aside." He paused for a moment, studying Olivia's face, and then, "Or do you plan to return to America after you've found a publisher?"

"No. It is not my wont to return to Boston. Alicia Rose and I will live in London, and I shall continue my writing."

"Then you will need the gowns, and possibly more. In addition to the settlement which I plan to make, and I assure you that if you cooperate fully it will be considerable, I'll arrange a clothing allowance, and mayhap living quarters. That is, until you are married to a gentleman with means."

"That will never be. I shall never marry," Olivia said quickly. Too quickly, she feared. She had involuntarily sat forward in her chair, and this embarrassed her tremendously. Not for anything in the world would she have his lordship know her true feelings. If it took her life, she would not reveal that she had foolishly fallen in love with him. To solidify the facade she wished to put forth, she added, "My life will be dedicated to my writing."

"You will be cheating some poor man, for I'm certain you will have many suitors, and I'm just as certain you have a lot to give a man in a true marriage."

Lord Castleberry, for an instant, remembered the kiss, the warmth of her lips, the longing in her body. Why would she deny herself such pleasure, choosing books instead? But it was her life, he told himself, and it was not up to him to explain the need of one human being for another.

Of course his wife had read all about such biological need in books. But the emotional need could be learned only by experience. Again his mind returned to the kiss. For a moment before she'd shoved him from her he had thought there was desire in the way her body responded to

his own need for her. He felt no guilt for this, for it was a
well-known fact, and he had not read this in a book, a man
was made so that he could feel passion for a woman when
he was desperately in love with another, as he was with
Lady Jacqueline. No doubt the men of the *ton* loved their
wives, after a fashion, while keeping mistresses. He rose to
leave. "I'm pleased with the report on your wardrobe. The
night of the ball we shall stay in my rooms at the Clarendon
a few days at least. After the ball I will show you the sights,
mayhap even take you to ride in Hyde Park at five o'clock.
Everyone will be there. They go to see and be seen."

With that he was gone, and Olivia sat for a long while
and fumed. Of course they would ride in Hyde Park and
be seen by Lady Jacqueline. Oh, how she wished she had
never signed that stupid agreement. Suddenly she wanted
to see Alicia Rose. Why was the girl not there when she
needed her? Lizzie, when she had come to tend her, had
said Alicia Rose had gone for a morning ride with Fred.
Olivia shook her head. Soon the whole family would know
that Alicia Rose was not her lady's maid.

Olivia quit the room and went to the Hunt Room. According to Lizzie, the gossipy maid, only when Aunt Evaline
Castleberry was receiving did she use the withdrawing room
on the first floor.

She found the old woman in the Hunt Room, dressed to
the nines in a blue morning dress and with the two frayed
red silk roses in her graying hair.

Olivia spoke cordially, ignoring the caustic tone in Aunt
Evaline's voice. "Fred, the hounds, and your lady's maid,
though I don't understand what you Americans consider a
lady's maid, have gone off riding. I told Fred 'twas not the
thing to ride with the help. But as usual he ignores my
advice, regardless of how much it insults propriety. Fred
listens to no one except his grandson."

"Mayhap that is how it should be," Olivia said.

"I should expect you to agree. Americans are such an

odd lot. That's why they left England, they could not force themselves to conform to what the Crown expected of them." She paused for a moment before adding, smiling slightly, "Mayhap Fred should have gone over there and joined the other barbarians. It would have been good riddance."

"I like Fred," countered Olivia. "He has been very kind, and very solicitous of me."

Aunt Evaline did not let her finish. "Oh, he wants you to produce a Robinbrook heir. Naturally he's kind and solicitous."

Olivia, not wanting to join the old woman in *that* kind of conversation, looked out and saw Chester working in the garden and decided to join him. At least he would not be talking of her having an heir to Robinbrook.

When she reached the garden, she found Chester repairing a water fountain on which two doves were perched, one with its head on the ground and broken into pieces. Before he saw her, she watched as he deftly spread the cement and rebuilt the bird's head, adding each intricate indentation and shaping its tiny bill with a lathe held in his big hands. She was amazed, and so intent was he on the job before him that she waited a long while before she spoke.

Even then she said his name twice before he turned. "Your skill is extraordinary, Chester," she said, and a huge smile spread across his boyish face. Dropping his lathe, he bowed from the waist. "I'm glad to see you, Lady Castleberry. Someone or something broke my poor Neva's head, and I had to make her a new one."

Olivia moved for a closer look. The doves seemed so lifelike that they might at any moment fly away. "Did you build the water fountain, and the doves?"

"I built all the statuary in this garden. Lord Castleberry gave this ground to me. I plant flowers, and every morning I carry water and put it in the fountain so the birds can drink."

Olivia looked around. Not a weed anywhere, and flowers blooming in profusion. In the rose garden the blooms still held morning dew. "I don't believe Capability Brown could have made a prettier garden, Chester. And you have a real talent for sculpturing."

"Lord Castleberry says that someday, should I want to, I can have my own business. And that would be wonderful, but I can't read or write or do figures. I went to the little schoolhouse his lordship built for the tenants' children, but they laughed because I didn't catch on right away, so I told his lordship I wouldn't go back."

Without thinking, Olivia said, "Would you let me teach you? When you learn, you can go back to school and show them how smart you are."

"Oh, would you, Lady Castleberry? I've never told anyone how much I long to read, and just to sign my name. I would sure try hard."

Pity filled Olivia's heart. "Of course I'll help you, Chester. I'll come every day, starting tomorrow."

"You'll find me in my garden," the gangly youth said, and just then Olivia saw the riders coming over a hillock. She bade Chester good-bye and made her way to the stables.

A third rider had joined Alicia Rose and Fred, and when they drew nearer, she recognized Lady Patience sitting astride a sleek bay and wearing a contrasting riding habit of brown stuff. A bonnet of the same material framed her round, wrinkled face.

The nine hounds were jealously vying for attention.

Olivia greeted them pleasantly, but it was Alicia Rose she wanted most to see. "Alicia Rose, I must speak with you. Alone."

"What is it? What has happened?"

Alicia Rose asked the groom to help her from her horse and immediately went to Olivia and embraced her.

"Let's walk," said Olivia, and they did. After saying good bye to Fred and Lady Patience, they rounded the huge manor house and meandered toward the sea. Neither spoke for a long while. The fresh sea air hit them in the face, and it was to Olivia as if they were back in Boston, sisters walking together as they had done all their life. At that moment she wished it were so. She could face Alice Pembroke's ridicule with more fortitude than she could face loving a man who desperately loved someone else.

At last Alicia Rose spoke. "Olivia, what is wrong? I've never seen you so deep in the desponds. It shows in your face."

"I never thought it would happen to me, Alicia Rose. How could I be such a slowtop?" Her voice dropped. "This time the answer is not in a book."

"What's not in a book?" She grabbed Olivia's hand and looked at her imploringly.

Olivia, not able to help herself, burst into tears. "Oh, sister, I've fallen in love with Lord Castleberry. How could this happen to me? A spinster falling in love. It does not bear thinking on . . . I let him kiss me, and I knew then . . ."

Alicia Rose gave a pleasant little laugh, and they were quiet for a while. Then, at last, she finally broke the heavy silence. "Mayhap it's your pride that is hurting. I remember how Mama used to hurt you and how hard you tried to please her. One always desperately wants something one cannot have."

"Oh, Alicia Rose, I pray you are right. If Lord Castleberry declared his love for me, I most likely would run away. Yes, yes, I'm sure you're right. You're so smart, Alicia Rose."

"I thought the world was coming to an end and you were the only one who knew it. But consider that you really are in love with his lordship. Being in love with one's husband is quite the thing, I should think."

"Please don't be flippant, Alicia Rose. You know very

well Lord Castleberry is not in love with me. He desperately
loves Lady Jacqueline, and that's the whole of it."

"The answer is really quite simple," said Alicia Rose,
speaking as if Olivia had not spoken. "Sister, you must
make your husband fall in love with you. Is there not a
love potion we can give him?"

Eleven

A week later Lord Castleberry sat behind his desk in the library at Robinbrook, the account books spread out in front of him. But he was not working on the books. He was listening to his grandfather, who, his white head bent, his gray eyes on the wide-planked floor, was crossing and re-crossing the library's length in his stately tread, his cane hooked over his long arm.

"Demmet, Fitz, it just won't do for Trevor Castleberry to inherit Robinbrook. And there's my estate in Guildford, which will be yours upon my death. I'll be demme if he gets a dime of what's mine. I'm thinking of leaving it to the Crown if you don't get busy and produce an heir."

Lord Castleberry had heard this argument before. He smiled at his old grandfather. "Fustian, Fredrick, relax. There'll be an heir in time. I've seen only thirty summers."

"There won't be an heir by this woman. I don't know what you're up to, young man, but you're not treating her as your wife. No man leaves his bride on their wedding night. He stays home and does his duty. I happen to know that every night since your wedding, after the house is asleep, you've left and gone God knows where. And she sleeps in her bedchamber and you in yours, when you finally make it home. 'Tis not the thing . . . if one wants to beget a child."

All this without a break in his treading. Then, suddenly, he stopped and glared at Lord Castleberry. His voice no longer scolding, he asked, "What's going on, Fitz?" Taking his gold-encrusted snuffbox from his pocket, he, like the prince regent, flipped it open with his thumb and then sucked in a deep whiff.

Lord Castleberry leaned back in his big leather chair and sighed. He never could fool the old man. Always, it had been as if the old man had been inside his head, knowing his thoughts, his plans, his pain. "I think you're rushing things, Fred. My marriage is little more than a fortnight old, and there's the ball I'm planning, when I'll be introducing Lady Castleberry to society. I've been preoccupied."

Fred looked at his grandson with incredulity, his voice regaining its sharpness. "A pox on society. Better you be about the business of getting your wife in the family way. If your mother were here, she could tell you that a woman is eager to learn what goes on between a man and a woman in the marital bed. She may turn against him later, but she wants to have the experience. 'Tis your duty to Lady Castleberry. And 'tis your duty to Robinbrook to produce an heir."

Lord Fitzgerald Castleberry was in a quandary. His deep blue eyes met Fred's gray ones. He had never lied to the old man. His new wife had suggested that he tell Fred about their "business arrangement," and mayhap she was right. Then the subject of his begetting an heir with her would be put to rest.

Lord Castleberry soon learned that he was wrong.

"Business arrangement?" Fred blurted out when Lord Castleberry was through explaining that on a lark, and in a moment of hurt anger, he had advertised for a homely American wife, a wife in name only. The old man exploded: "Demmet, Fitz, what made you do a fool thing like that? And your bride is not homely, not by a long shot." Then, as if his old legs would no longer support him, he sat in a chair, occasionally tapping the floor with his cane, and taking another whiff of snuff.

Guilt rode Lord Castleberry for causing the old man pain.

Several years ago, he, Lord Castleberry, after drinking wine poured for him by Trevor Castleberry, had become quite ill. Fred had been sure the wine had been poisoned, and had Lord Castleberry emptied the glass, he would have died, leaving the earldom and Robinbrook to his cousin—the man who had poured the wine. The present heir to Robinbrook and the earldom.

Fred had never liked Trevor, had never trusted him from the time he had appeared at Robinbrook with papers in hand to prove he was a distant cousin to Fitzgerald Castleberry, and from the time of the wine incident, the old man had hated Trevor with an unmatched fervor. Lord Castleberry had never believed his cousin would do such a dastardly deed, but he had been unsuccessful in convincing Fred, and the old man had thought of little else than that Fitzgerald marry and produce an heir other than Trevor for Robinbrook. Now his face was white, His eyes strained in a wretched, lost look.

"I'm sorry, Grandfather," Lord Castleberry said. He could not remember the last time he had called the old man Grandfather. Pushing his chair back, he stood and went to the window to look out, talking as he stared at the glimmering waters of the sea.

"In a moment of pique, Lady Jacqueline told me that I deserved nothing better than a homely American wife, and foolishly, as only a man in love can, I thought to prove to her that looks did not matter to me, that I could be a devoted husband to someone less beautiful than she."

Fred struck the floor with his cane. "That's the most demme foolish reason for getting leg-shackled I've heard in my eighty years. And I suppose you're going to appear to be that devoted husband at this ball you're planning. Well, I suggest you get the gel in the family way before you present her to society, and to that scapeskull Lady Jacqueline. It would take a drastic measure like that to get through to her, and besides, then I could die in peace."

A shudder went over Lord Castleberry. He had never heard Fred mention dying before, and he could not forbear it. Fred was all he had now that Lady Jacqueline had cried off and married Lord Sappington. What a coil, he thought, turning from the window and going to kneel by the old man's chair, taking his sun-blotched hand and holding it lovingly. "Don't mention dying, Grandfather. I could not SURVIVE losing you. You've been my pater since I was fifteen. You reared me."

"Fustian! You raised yourself, Fitz, and a demme good job you did. I've just been here to love you."

"That's the most important thing, being loved. Since Lady Jacqueline—"

"Forget that Jade. Give Olivia a chance. You can learn to love her."

Lord Castleberry shook his head. "No, Fred, I will never love anyone except Lady Jacqueline. I'm like my mother. You've told me many times about how she loved my father, and no one else, even though they came from different orders in society." A pause, and then, "But I'll confess to you that when I kissed Olivia, I felt an enormous amount of desire. Two men can speak on that subject without offending sensibilities, I take it."

"Well then, that's it. Put that desire to work and get me a great-grandchild. Do you think I can live forever, waiting around for you to do your duty to Robinbrook and to the earldom? And, I might add, to your wife."

"The business agreement with Olivia calls for me, after a time, to have our marriage set aside. By law, that can happen only if the marriage is not consummated. I will make a healthy settlement on her, and she can go on with her writing. I'm sure by then Lady Jacqueline will no longer be married to Lord Sappington."

Fred's eyebrows shot upward. "What makes you think that?"

"Their marriage will be set aside for the same reason as

mine and Olivia's—the fact that it has never been consummated, due to his age."

The cane came down hard on the floor. "Fitz, your naiveté is astonishing. That comes from having the burdens of the world thrust on your fifteen-year-old shoulders when you lost both parents within a year. Robbed you of your youth. What you feel for Lady Jacqueline is nothing more than puppy love. Of course her marriage to Lord Sappington—that name suits him well, for he's a sap to have married her—has been consummated. I hear he's a randy old goat, keeping two mistresses, in case one is out of sorts."

Lord Castleberry's heart dropped to the pit of his stomach. His grandfather would not lie to him. Pushing words past the lump in his throat, he said, "I want to be fair with Lady Castleberry."

"Let me ask you something, Fitz. When you kissed her, did she kiss you back?"

"I really can't remember. My need was so great, and later she said the kiss didn't mean a thing. I do know she's a bookworm, and she's read all about matters of the flesh."

"If she's read about it, she'll want to do it. So get busy and seduce her. No sin in a man seducing his wife."

Twelve

There was such a sense of fairness about Lord Castleberry that he refused to even think of his grandfather's suggestion. Lady Castleberry was his wife in name only, and he had no intention of infringing upon their business agreement. Even though, now, in the middle of the night, the thought of claiming marital rights appealed to him immensely. He vividly recalled the kiss in its most minute detail, and desire was ravaging his body. This prompted his decision to visit London and his former mistress.

When Lady Jacqueline had come into his life and his heart, he had pensioned Hattie Marie and gave her permission to take another protector. He had missed her. A comely gel with an abundance of well-coiffured hair and skin soft to the touch, she had striven hard to please. The relationship had been satisfactory until Lady Jacqueline had demanded that even though she had afforded him nothing more than a chaste kiss, he gave Hattie Marie. While she herself, Lady Jacqueline, pranced in front of him wearing a gown of transparent muslin that clung to her curves as if it were her skin. This night he regretted having acquiesced, for he was sure that should he still have a mistress, he would not be panting after this wife in name only.

A fair mess he had gotten himself into, thought his lordship as in his lonely bed he turned yet another time. He could not forget kissing Olivia. Had his imagination worked tricks on him, or had she really kissed him back? He distinctly remembered her body leaning into his, and he remembered her dancing like a sprite, her silky chestnut hair flowing out from her face. He remembered the quickness with which he felt desire when he held her close. Little wonder he could not remember her response, so great was his own. Lying in his bed, looking at the scrolled ceiling he had seen too many times when alone. Cherubs dancing, children laughing—he acknowledged that had he known he would be getting himself into this coil of desire for a homely American wife—just to spite Lady Jacqueline—he would have never contacted Emry and Emry in Boston for help. Another toss to the other side of the bed, while praying to the deity of lost lovers for guidance. Beyond the window a full moon ascended gold and green through the trees. In the silence of the lonely room he heard over and over Olivia's smart retort: The kiss didn't mean a thing, the kiss . . ."

Sleep came, and when he awoke at first light, he was laughing. Olivia had offered him a challenge, and it was disturbing. That was all. His ego was suffering, and that was the throes of death for a man. His resolve to visit Hattie Marie hardened into determination. If he could judge by past experience, his former courtesan would welcome him with open arms. Pulling the bell rope, he signaled his valet to his bedchamber.

"Henry, I have decided to go to London for a few days, and I shall need you to accompany me. But at this moment I need a shave, and I think a hair trim."

All this was said over his lordship's shoulder, and when he turned and saw Henry, he was forced to hide his laughter. The poor valet, wearing a red, rumpled robe that barely covered his knees and showed long, bony legs, was asleep on his feet, his pointed red nightcap askew on his head.

Henry, nearing forty-five summers, had been valet to the fourth earl of Robinbrook before his death fifteen years earlier. Having come from Scotland to improve his lot in life, Henry had always appeared appreciative of his position at Robinbrook, and had willingly gone through the war with the fifth earl of Robinbrook. A quiet man, he spoke little, and he never complained. Until now. It must have been my laughter, thought Lord Castleberry, when Henry's eyes suddenly opened and he stood glaring at his employer.

"Have you developed windmills in your head, your lordship?" he asked, his tone strident.

"Not at all, Henry. What's wrong with a man wanting a shave and hair trim at first light?"

"Not anything, but 'tis not first light. That's moonlight that's lighting up your room. The moon's in full, in case you haven't noticed. And I suspect you're howling. I suggest you pull the window coverings and go back to sleep." He turned and made to repair from the room.

Lord Castleberry looked at the mantel clock and saw that indeed it was only four o'clock. Just then the demme thing began striking, filling the room with its bonging. "Wait, Henry. Don't leave. I need your company," he said. "Mayhap we could have a cup of coffee together."

The familiarity with his valet was not unusual for Lord Castleberry. He and Henry had been together too long to stand on formality. They often drank coffee together, but never this early in the morning. Without a word Henry shuffled across the room and went into the outer chamber to prepare the requested coffee. Lord Castleberry decided to take a quick bath while Henry was thus occupied, and when Henry rejoined him, carrying a huge silver tray, he was back from his dressing room, wearing new fawn breeches and a white shirt, minus a cravat.

His lordship felt refreshed, rejuvenated, even though a glimpse in the mirror showed an abundance of uncombed, wet black hair and bloodshot eyes. White silk hose covered his big feet and long legs. He would wait about donning his boots, he decided, and went to sit in front of the fireplace, where gray coals lay lifeless on the grate.

"Have you not turned everything around, your lordship?" Henry asked.

"I don't take your meaning, Henry."

"Well, a bath and dressing usually comes *after* the shave and hair trim. And why are you going into town without your new missus?"

His lordship's voice was suddenly sharp. "Set the tray down, Henry. You look as if you might drop it."

When the tray was on the table, the coffee poured, Henry returned to the subject. "What is your problem, your lordship, and don't try lying to me." He gave a wry smile. "I've been with you too long not to know that something is wrong. Why is your missus not accompanying you to London? And one pillow on your bed appears unused, yet the bed looks as if it might have weathered a raging storm. Did you toss and turn all night?"

Lord Castleberry let out a deep sigh. The coffee was bitter to his tongue. "I did toss and turn all night." He paused, wanting to tell Henry only enough to stop the questions. He would not tell his valet that his bride was still a virgin, or that he was planning a visit to his mistress.

"Fustian, Henry, I have a lot on my mind. This ball I'm planning, to introduce Lady Castleberry to the *ton,* is an enormous undertaking. Something new for me. I'm going into town to confer with the patronesses of Almack's and request a voucher for my wife. If the patronesses are agreeable, the ball will be held there. I want it to be special . . . very special. I thought to use the Argyle Rooms, which are exceptionally beautiful, but the cyprians hold their annual ball there. I thought it might affect the atmosphere."

Henry's demeanor told Lord Castleberry that the valet knew and understood more than he was pretending. The question about the unused pillow, the rumpled bed, went unanswered. For a long while they drank coffee in the enveloping silence, until at last Lord Castleberry asked, "Henry, have you ever been in love?"

"Once," the valet said, and the heavy silence returned.

Outside, first light had at last pushed the moon off its perch. "Once? Why just once?" Lord Castleberry asked, looking at Henry over his cup's rim.

"If 'tis true love, once is all it can ever be," the valet said. "She, my Lily, died. Before I left Scotland."

Lord Castleberry was stunned. Henry had never once mentioned having been in love. Lily was a name the valet had never uttered. "So you believe a man loves only once."

"When 'tis true love. Another woman has never turned my head. Not the way Lily did. She'll fill my heart forever."

"Fred tells me my parents were like that, a true love match, and I believe that's the way God meant it to be. I believe He makes soulmeets."

Lord Castleberry placed his cup on the tray and then pushed himself up onto his feet. *Surely after I've seen Hattie Marie, this demon passion will subside to a manageable level.*

The shave and hair trim were quickly dispensed with, and his lordship told his valet to please prepare to leave as soon as possible. "Breakfast can be had at a posting inn," he said, noticing that the valet looked neither pleased nor displeased as he left to do as had been suggested.

Left alone, Lord Castleberry began to fight with himself about whether or not to tell Olivia he was going into London to tend business, and would be gone less than a fortnight. He had no notion that she would suggest she accompany him, but there was the possibility. Nonetheless, in the end he found himself knocking on the door that opened to her bedchamber, and just as he was beginning to think she was not going to answer, she opened the door and stood before him in a white wrapper pulled closely around her lithe frame, her thick chestnut hair in total disarray.

Quickly he noted that her beautiful gray-green eyes were smoky gray in the dimness. He wondered if he had romped through her dreams as she had his. He found himself wanting to comb her hair with his fingers. But more than that, he wanted to carry her to her bed and make love to her. His desire was no less than it had been in the night just passed. But desire was not love, he told himself. Love used in that connotation was a misnomer. How could he make love to her when he did not love her? He and Olivia had talked of the difference between the physical needs of the body and that of being in love.

With great effort his lordship thought of Hattie Marie. "I'm going to . . ." he began.

"I don't care what you are going to do, your lordship. I need my sleep. It was near first light before I closed my eyes."

That was not entirely true, Olivia silently admitted, for she had closed her eyes many times, only to open them again and again to see his devil eyes devouring her, his lips curled into a sinister smile, his cold laughter filling the room. No doubt laughing at her for having fallen in love with him. *Oh, dear Lord, pray don't let him know,* she prayed, as she had prayed many times before. More than once during the long night she had taken up her quill to add to her story. Now she found herself speechless as his hand touched her face, tracing the outline of her mouth, her nose, while smiling down at her.

The touch was like a flame licking at her skin, and when his eyes moved over her with warmth and longing she realized she'd loosened her grip on the wrapper and that her thin white nightgown did little to hide her body. Her breasts thrust forward, showing small brown nipples through the gown.

She grabbed the wrapper to again cover herself and heard him groan, a deep throaty sound.

"I . . ." he said, his words barely above a whisper.

"You what," she asked, sorry she had spoken before the words left her mouth. The tightness in her chest intensified.

Please, please, go away. I don't want you to know how I feel. She wanted to pound him with her fists, to scream at him to go away and leave her alone. Demme the business arrangement; she only wanted him out of her sight. She remembered the sweet taste of his mouth.

I do not love him . . . I do not love him.

She tried to avert her gaze, but his hands took her face, forcing her to look at him. His breathing was ragged. His bottomless blue eyes were glaring down at her. And then with a low moan his lips covered hers, and she felt her body grow pliant and warm, throbbing.

But she refused to lean into him. She had learned her lesson the other time he'd kissed her. She could only hold her resolve if they were not close.

That resolve melted into the dimness of the room when his tongue touched hers. She was suddenly drunk with desire, kissing him back while he caressed her hips with his big hands, and then moved to her throbbing breasts to squeeze and massage them gingerly. For a moment she thought his lips would follow his hand, and prayed they would not.

With utmost fortitude she pushed her husband from her, breaking the delicious euphoria, the unexplained longing. She reminded herself that he loved Lady Jacqueline, not her, and felt cheated and angry. Her fighting spirit returned as quickly as it had left her, and her tongue was once again sharp and cutting.

"I would thank you not to do that again, your lordship," she said, and then added, "I shall have a lock on this door before nightfall."

Stepping back, Olivia started to slam the door, but her effort was thwarted by a foot shooting out like a rapier in battle for one's life.

"You jackanapes. Our business arrangement, can't you hold to your word?"

Anger shot from his blue eyes. The longing was gone. " 'Tis

your right to have a lock placed on the door," he said, withdrawing his foot and closing the door.

Olivia stared at the door as a huge emptiness filled the room that separated her bedchamber from her husband's.

Lord Castleberry did not own a fashionable town house in London, nor did he want one. After the war, and when his fortune increased to allow some luxuries in his life, he leased a pied à terre at the Clarendon hotel. It was small by his peers' standards, five rooms, all large, with a small room for his valet. A handsome parlor afforded a marble fireplace, the dining room would seat eight, and there was a sitting room joining his bedchamber, and a huge dressing room that held a water closet and a copper tub for bathing. Food, when needed, was sent up from the hotel's restaurant, whose cook was Jacquiers, former cook of Louis XVIII.

Riding in a crested barouche with a fold-back top, his lordship and his valet arrived at the Clarendon late evening. The two men alighted with alacrity, and the coachman tooled away to take the carriage and horses to rented stables. A nearby room was kept for his convenience, and he would stay there until summoned by his lordship the carriage was needed.

Most often Lord Castleberry, as he moved about London, would hail a hackney or a sedan chair, claiming it more convenient as well as more expeditious.

From a lobby covered with large black and white squares of tile, a wide stairway curved upward to the hotel's first floor. Lord Castleberry's quarters were another three floors, and he was panting considerably when he put the key into the lock. "Demme, Henry, I seem to be drained of energy these days, or is it that those stairs are horribly steep?"

"Both," Henry said matter-of-factly. "The strain you've been under since Lady Jacqueline cried off shows in your face, especially in your eyes. No doubt it has sapped your energy, and your becoming leg-shackled seems not to have helped."

"You're too demme observant," Lord Castleberry replied, and then, stepping into the parlor of the apartment, he breathed a deep sigh of satisfaction. This small, unpretentious place seemed to open its arms to him. It smelled of soap, of having been freshly cleaned. Without being told, Henry bent to strike a lucifer to the wood on the grate.

"Henry, I'll be leaving after a while," Lord Castleberry said. "I can do for myself, if you would like a night on the town."

A big smile showed when Henry straightened. "I do thank you, Lord Castleberry. A game of whist is very appealing after that long ride." He gave a slight bow from the waist and left, going in the direction of his own room, separated from the main living quarters by a narrow hallway.

Left alone, Lord Castleberry stretched his booted feet to the fire and leaned back in a chair large enough to accommodate his large frame. He could not help thinking of the small chair Lady Jacqueline had provided for him in the withdrawing room they were to have shared after their marriage. In one of the few times he had said no to her, he had refused to let her have her way in his place at the Clarendon. Instead, he had engaged a little-known decorator, Sydney Heatherton, to fill the rooms with good, solid English furniture. Red silk covered the walls, and moss-green velvet had been used for window coverings, tied back by variegated colors of fashion rope.

A portrait of Lord and Lady Castleberry, his lordship's parents, in a touching pose, smiled down on him from above the marble mantel. He studied them for a while and then went to the sideboard and poured two fingers of straight whiskey into a glass, returning to his chair to sip. Suddenly the rooms were filled with aloneness. An empty chair flanked the other side of the fireplace. He truly would like to have a mate to sit with him, he mused, his thoughts turning painfully to Lady Jacqueline. He looked up at the portrait above the mantel and raised his glass. "To love," he said, feeling tears sting his eyes.

Realizing that last light was closing in on him, his lordship thought to light a branch of candles but then thought better of it. He sat in the semidarkness and made mental notes of things he needed to do while in town. Seeing Hattie Marie was not as urgent as it had been when he was in proximity to his wife. Olivia went out of her way to tempt him. No, that was not true, he scolded. It had been he who had knocked on the door of her bedchamber. Why could he not leave her alone, keep his hands off her? Passion did strange things to a man, caused him to act in uncharacteristic ways. He forced himself to think of the list of things he needed to do.

This night, he decided, he would go to White's, where he would relax with a good meal, and later he would have a go at the gaming tables. With good luck he would encounter his good friend, Lord Nigel Avery, third son of the Duke of Beckworth. Although Avery had had fewer summers, they had been Brothers of the Blade in the war together, and had become bosom bows. But after Lady Jacqueline had come into his life, he had neglected his good friend. Now he felt an urgency to see him. Avery would have lots of on-dits to pass on.

Tomorrow, Lord Castleberry planned, he would go to Almack's and arrange with Lady Jersey for the ball he planned in his wife's honor.

And when Fred had learned that Lord Castleberry was going into London, he had asked that he go to Windsor Castle and pay his respects to failing King George III. Since the king's madness had advanced to where he hardly recognized Fred, Fred had not been able to visit with him, saying it hurt too much.

"I don't want to go," Lord Castleberry declared to the lonely room, "but I will. I owe a lot to Fredrick. After

Mama and Papa died, he let me lean on him. Now, in his advanced years, I must let him lean on me."

A visit to Hattie Marie's house, which he had bought for her, was still on his lordship's list.

Thirteen

The highly liveried footman at White's, in St. James's Street, welcomed Lord Castleberry with a huge smile and a deep bow. " 'Tis good to see you, your lordship. We've missed you."

Lord Castleberry handed him his high-crowned silk hat and returned his smile. "I'm happy to see you, Raymond. I've missed the place."

That was as much familiarity with a servant as propriety would allow, but his lordship found he truly was glad to see Raymond, and suddenly he was glad to be at, in his opinion, the greatest gentleman's club in all of London. His father and his grandfather before him had belonged, and this, in an odd way, gave Lord Fitzgerald a sense of returning to the arms of his own family. He nodded to several acquaintances as he made his way to the betting book.

From the bow window, Beau Brummell and his cronies, the Duke of Argyll, Lords Alvanley, Sefton, Worcester, and Foley, "Poodle" Byng, "Ball" Hughes, and Sir Lumley Sheffington, were busy passing judgment on the pedestrians on the street. This inner circle of Brummell's could be seen by those who passed by the club, but his stringent ruling made the recognition or greeting to any passerby a dreadful breach of etiquette. The Beau reigned supreme in the bow window, even though on-dits had it that he was deep in dun territory due to his weakness for gambling. It had even been mentioned that he would soon be forced to leave England to escape debtor's prison.

"To each his own," said Castleberry under his breath. Brummell's feeling of superiority over those he considered his closest friends was not to his lordship's liking, but he did not stand in judgment. The club was a superb refuge for those who needed a home away from home, a place where one could bet at the betting book, write letters at grand mahogany desks, or read the morning paper in a room lined with gold-spined books. And he could dine at the white-clothed tables laid with gleaming silver and the finest china in the elegant dining room. A game of whist was always in progress in one of the card rooms.

The betting book held wagers on a vast array of subjects. Gentlemen of the *ton* more often than not held differences of opinion, and they bet on those opinions—during the war with Napoleon, how long he would last, what country would ultimately win, who would bring the little man down. Life-and-death matters were also argued, who would bear a child first, who would die first, would a gentleman become leg-shackled, and to whom. How long would the marriage last before he took a mistress, and she a lover?

Castleberry's eyes scanned the pages, looking for Lady Jacqueline's name. A huge lump formed in his throat. Would he never stop thinking of her, he asked himself, and he knew that he would not. She was lodged in his heart forever. He hoped those around him could not read his thoughts and see the pain that ripped him apart. Away from Olivia the pain was worse, and he did not seem to be able to rid himself of it for a moment. Pride was also a factor. He did not want it known that Lady Jacqueline was the reason he had stayed away from the club so long. A slap on his shoulder caused him to turn to a familiar, smiling face.

His friend Lord Nigel Avery was announcing in a loud voice, "Look, gentlemen, Castleberry has risen from the dead. But it took longer than three days for him. He's not favored this fine club with his presence for months."

Castleberry was extremely happy to see Avery, a handsome lad of twenty-six summers, tall, a good build, blond hair, and this night dressed to the nines. However, this was not always so. A lecturer at King's College in London, clothes were not of the utmost importance to him. But here at White's he takes more care, Lord Castleberry thought. Because those around him vied to outdress other gentlemen who frequented White's.

"I'll lift a drink with you, Castleberry," another friend said, and more than one gentleman declared happiness to see the man who had, without a word of warning, disappeared from their lives for six months.

"What are you betting on?" Sir Malvery Stone asked.

"I was only looking to see where other people are placing their bets," Lord Castleberry said.

Turning his attention back to the betting book, the name jumped out at him: *Countess Jacqueline Sappington,* under which was a series of bets on how long her marriage to Lord Sappington would last, and how long it would take the old scapegrace to get his wife *enceinte.*

One bet was for a guinea that the marriage would last three days, another three months, two guineas placed on the bet. Both gamblers had lost their money, for the marriage was now six months old. With a forced smile Castleberry took the feather quill to hand and, with a grand flourish, wrote his bet of two pounds that the marriage would last forever. He would gladly lose the two pounds if only it were not so. And then his heart made him place another bet—that there would never be a child.

Somehow he thought by writing the words on paper it would never be. He could not forbear his Lady Jacqueline giving a child to Lord Sappington. He could not forbear the old gaffer laying a hand on his precious Jacqueline. He turned from the book and went to the whist table to gamble, to drink, and to forget. And he stayed long into the night.

His lordship awoke next morning with his head swollen and throbbing from the drink he had ingested at White's. He could not remember whether or not he had lost at the gaming tables. He could remember that Lord Avery had told him Lady Jacqueline and her husband were in France for a short vacation.

"Now that Napoleon is exiled to St. Helena, thanks to Wellington and those who fought under him, it seems to be the thing to visit the Continent," he had said, and when Castleberry had asked when the Sappingtons would return, Avery shrugged and turned his palms up, gesturing he did not know.

Lord Castleberry had not pushed for more information, but now he was in a quandary. What if Lady Jacqueline did not return in time for the big ball he was planning? The business arrangement with Olivia will have been in vain, he thought, as clearly as he could think with his muddled brain.

Henry came into the room just then and flung the curtains back, letting brilliant shafts of sunlight stream across the room. Lord Castleberry groaned loudly, grabbed his head, and swore, all of which were ignored by his valet. "Good morning, your lordship," the valet said brightly. " 'Tis time for you to be up and about. If you can stop complaining like a stuck hog. Is your pain that great?"

"Out! Who are you to tell me when I'm to be up and about? My head is throbbing—"

"I know, you were as drunk as a wheelbarrow last night."

"How do you know that?"

"You came to my room and told me to awaken you this morning, that you had business needing your attention. Otherwise, do you think I would have come bounding into your room, opening the draperies? I've made coffee, and they are sending your breakfast up from downstairs. You'll feel better then."

Scowling, his lordship rolled over, dropped his long legs over the side of the bed, and reached for the blue robe Henry had placed on a nearby chair. "I don't think I shall ever feel better, Henry. I don't remember ever overimbibing like that. I apologize."

"Don't apologize to me. That young man who brought you home, he's the one who deserves your apology."

"Who brought me home?"

"Your friend, Lord Nigel Avery. He helped me tuck you in."

What a coil, thought his lordship, wishing he were back at Robinbrook. It was serene and peaceful there, and then he remembered he had a wife at Robinbrook, a wife in name only who tempted his passion beyond endurance, a wife who dared to threaten to have a lock installed on the door between their chambers. All because he could not keep his hands off her. He could not understand why her lips were so demme inviting.

He tried to recall whether or not a mention of his having become leg-shackled had been made when he was at White's. He frowned. Did Avery know? There had been no reading of the banns for his marriage; he'd asked for and had been granted special dispensation, but surely the issuance of the license had been puffed off by the newspapers. But mayhap not. Often there was an oversight, or possibly a delay.

He would have the ball and chance that his beloved Lady Jacqueline would be home from the Continent by that time. The look on her face when she learned of his marriage would be payment in full for the pain she had caused him.

After making short shrift of breakfast, and after dousing his throbbing head into cold water in the marble basin in his dressing room, he dressed quickly and was soon on the street, looking for transport. Taking a sedan chair seemed too ostentatious, so he hailed an empty hackney and told the driver to take him to Almack's on King Street, St. James's. Even though it was nearing midmorning, a heavy fog still clung to London like a blanket, and the unsavory smell assaulted Lord Castleberry's nostrils. Still, he enjoyed the ride, watching pedestrians darting in and out of places of business, or looking into the windows at fashionable garments, the latest crockery, and fabrics just arrived from France.

His lordship thought about the ball he would be having. Almack's, founded in 1765, would give it proper exclusivity. Lady Jacqueline had once told him that if London was the mecca the Polite World journeyed to each year, then Almack's was the shrine where they worshiped. His former affianced would be impressed.

The fourth earl of Robinbrook had obtained for his heir a voucher to Almack's, for when he reached majority. The carefully issued voucher entitled the chosen to purchase a ticket to the social affairs held there. Guests could be brought, but only after he or she had passed a rigid social test.

This thought brought his lordship upright. Would Lady Jersey, if he were so fortunate to negotiate with her—he had met her on several social occasions—ask questions about Olivia Pembroke? Would he be forced to tell Lady Jersey that he had married and had kept it from the *ton?* If so, he would be robbed of the surprise to Lady Jacqueline.

As it turned out, Lady Jersey was the patroness available to talk with his lordship. She had the reputation of being difficult, but Lord Castleberry found her very cooperative.

"Yes, I have heard rumors of a marriage, but I will not tell if you wish me not to," she said.

His lordship was greatly relieved. He did not tell her that Lady Castleberry was his wife in name only. For sure, the strict patroness of Almack's would have objected to such subterfuge. It was agreed that the ball would be grand, grander than that which London had known for years.

"With the war behind us, 'tis time for a great celebration," his lordship said, and Lady Jersey gave him a quizzical look, as if to say this was not like the Lord Castleberry she had known in the past.

"I wish you a long and successful marriage, your lordship," she said, and then, smiling fondly as she talked, she told him of her own dear mama's and papa's marriage: "Mama and Papa eloped to Gretna Green." And then she went on to tell him that she was the eldest daughter of the tenth earl of Westmoreland and Anne, sole heiress of Robert Child, an enormously wealthy banker.

"When Grandfather Child nearly overtook them at the border, Papa drew his pistol and shot the leading horse of the Child carriage." She gave a small laugh. "It was truly a love match. I came along soon after, the apple of Grandfather Child's eye. Eventually he forgave my parents for going against his wishes. But not completely, I guess, for, when he died, he bypassed my mother and left his great fortune to me. Nonetheless, my parents were extremely happy. It seems as if true love can win if those involved are determined."

"An interesting story," Lord Castleberry said, convinced more than ever that God made only one true love for each man he put on earth. "I thank you for sharing it with me. Now I must say good-bye, for I have other business to tend."

Lady Jersey's raised, questioning brow told Lord Castleberry she had hoped to learn more about this marriage he would be announcing to the *ton*. Smiling wryly, he stood, gave a courtly bow, then took his leave, knowing the ball would be as grand as he wanted it to be. But would his true love be there? Only time would tell. Being an expert gambler, he was willing to take the chance.

Fourteen

Trevor Castleberry, in his house on the Robinwood Estate, stood before the floor-to-ceiling looking glass in his opulent dressing room and admired his handsome physique. He was naked from his waist up, showing curly chest hair and broad, muscled shoulders. He was perfectly proportioned for a man of six feet, he thought, and his tight yellow pantaloons left little to one's imagination as to what was from his waist down. When he moved, his well-developed muscles moved with a smooth ease, a whisper in the wind. While in leading strings, he had aspired to be a dancer on the stage of Theatre Royal Drury Lane.

His handsome face held a self-satisfied smile as he combed his thick, sun-streaked brown hair, which waved back from his forehead and fell in long strands low on his neck, and his perfectly trimmed sideburns grew well below his ears. older now, twenty-nine summers, and much wiser, his ambitions were much higher than dancing. Turning to his valet, he stormed out at him, "Don't just stand there, Zeke, hand me my shirt."

Meekly, Zeke held up a white shirt with a collar long enough so that a bit of it would turn over Trevor Castleberry's cravat.

Zeke was a small man in his late forties, dark hair frosted with gray, a back bent from hard work and lack of food when he was in his formative years. He had started as a lowly houseboy in the home of Lord Selvridge of Maximillion Hall, and, with grit and determination, had worked his way up to valet. Three years earlier, Lord Selvridge had suddenly died. Because of the valet's advanced age, he had been forced to take whatever position he could find. That had been with Trevor Castleberry, who took his undermaids to bed and shouted obscenities at his valet. He helped Trevor shrug into the shirt and then fetched a stiffly starched purple lawn cravat and began creasing it into perfect folds. His hands shook, for any moment the cravat would be snatched from him, wadded into a ball, and thrown to the floor.

But this day luck was with him. Trevor Castleberry seemed to be in a great hurry. "Demmet, Zeke, did God give you ten thumbs? Tie the demme thing and have done with it."

The outburst only made the valet's hands shake more. "You're not usually in such a hurry, sir. I'll make haste." He wanted to ask Trevor Castleberry where he was going but did not dare. When the cravat was securely tied around Trevor's neck and the shirt collar turned just right, he held up a white waistcoat of embroidered silk, and then a superbly tailored coat of deep purple superfine, cut away to show his employer's slim waist.

"A dandy," murmured the valet quietly, very quietly.

"I'm going to the big house, Zeke. My source tells me that my cousin, the high-and-mighty Lord Fitzgerald Castleberry, has gone into London for a few days. While he's playing whist at White's, I suspect his new bride is lonely. I plan to ask her to accompany me to Hythe. There's much to see there."

"You like playing with fire, do you not? Best you join his lordship at White's to get your plow cleaned."

Zeke knew that Trevor Castleberry was not a member of White's, or of any other of London's clubs for gentlemen. He also knew that Trevor secretly frequented the hells, underground gaming places where very young girls were kept for the pleasure of unsavory men.

This knowledge gave Zeke a sense of power over the man who treated him as a servant who carried out chamber pots, and his subtle dig about Trevor Castleberry joining Lord Castleberry at White's lifted the valet's spirits considerably. He suppressed a giggle as he watched fury ignite in Trevor's dark eyes and his face turn to a hard mask.

"You know I'm not allowed to darken White's august doors." Trevor paused, and then, "Someday that will not be true. Someday I will be Lord Castleberry, Lord Trevor Castleberry, the sixth earl of Robinbrook. White's and Boodles and Brooks will all fling open their doors to me. The footmen will bow and take my hat and my coat. Mark my word, Zeke, mark my word."

Just because my plan to poison Cousin Fitzgerald failed doesn't mean that I will not find a way to become Lord Trevor Castleberry. And I can't wait an age for him to die.

Trevor savored the thought for a moment, even visualized standing over the casket, shedding copious tears for his dear, dear cousin. Smiling with the pleasure his thoughts brought him, he said aloud, "One learns from one's mistakes."

Zeke knew about Trevor's adding poison to Lord Castleberry's glass of wine. It had been he who had emptied a portion of the poisoned wine from the glass and added extra so that it would not be a deadly dose. He had hoped Lord Castleberry would be forewarned, but his lordship had blamed his sudden illness on tainted meat he had eaten earlier in the day.

After that Zeke had often thought of warning Lord Castleberry, and he would have had he not been too frightened of losing his position. The thought sent shivers down his spine. He might never find another position and would surely have to go to the poorhouse. Nothing would stop wicked Trevor Castleberry. Hoping Trevor would brag and tell him of his plan, Zeke, in a voice that masked his true feelings, said, "I don't know how that will be, sir, your becoming one of the upper orders. Lord Castleberry has only one summer on you. You're not likely to outlive him. Besides, now that he's married, most likely there'll soon be an heir."

Trevor, realizing he had said too much and hating the valet for reminding him of something he would like to forget—that Lord Castleberry had recently taken a bride, complicating things—whipped around and quickly added to his dress a diamond-encrusted cravat pin, a chatelaine which held his watch, and lastly, his quizzing glass, attaching it to his lapel with a black riband. His top boots shone like new money, having been bathed in champagne and then rubbed with a soft cloth by Zeke.

After one last look in the mirror, feeling well pleased with what met his eye, he quit the room and made his way to the stairs. The conversation was over as far as he was concerned, and he reminded himself to be more careful in the future. He had no illusions that his valet felt loyalty to him in any fashion.

"Nor I to him," Trevor said sotto voce, thinking that he would replace doddering Zeke if that were possible. Not having *Lord* or *Sir* before one's name made it most difficult to come by a young, well-trained valet. Those he had employed in the past had not stayed long. Zeke had lasted three years, a record.

As Trevor descended the stairs, he was suddenly gripped by anxiety. He prayed that old Fred would not be about when he reached the big house. The old man was blatant about his mistrust of the heir to Robinbrook. And those demme hounds acted as if they would like to tear him apart every time they smelled his presence. Someday . . . someday . . . thought Trevor when no one was looking, he would kick the heads of the whole of them. His thoughts turned back to his anxiety.

What if Castleberry's new bride refused his advances at friendship. Friendship first, and then . . .

He could not forbear failure. Too long he had lived on the edge of poverty, until he, by chance, discovered that his real name was Castleberry, not Nelson, as his stepfather claimed. And then came the best surprise of all: There was not an immediate heir, and by the primogeniture law, he stood to gain a title and entail Robinbrook. He remembered well the glee he had felt. But he had not acted quickly or without thought. He had waited two long years before coming to Robinbrook.

The two years had been torture, Trevor now recalled, but he had forced himself to wait until he had learned everything there was to know about farming the land, raising and shearing sheep, and gathering cherries to sell at market. He knew about drainage, fertilization, and the rotation of crops, and in learning, blisters had turned to calluses on his hands, not the hands of a gentleman at all. What he could not learn by doing, he had pored over books about agriculture to discover, anything to further his cause. He smiled sardonically. He'd even sheared sheep until his hands had swollen to a strut.

So when he made his appearance at Robinbrook, Trevor Castleberry had come not only as a distant cousin dressed to the nines, but as a man knowing about farming. And he had matched his mannerisms to those of the upper orders by tailing them on the streets, by engaging them at the gaming tables, for it was not unknown that the upper orders frequented the same hells he frequented when he had an extra sovereign to bet.

A cordial welcome had been extended to him when he arrived at Robinbrook, a fine house had been built for him, and for the past eight years he had made himself indispensable as an overseer of the estate that would someday be his. Lord Castleberry, quite knowledgeable in the latest trends in farming himself, had been most generous, sharing a percentage of the farm profits with him. In truth, Trevor thought, producing a huge smile, he was a man of means. With only one complaint. He craved desperately to be the sixth earl.

Trevor did not see how one could get anywhere in life without planning. His house was quite grand, with an excellent array of servants, but it had no status, not like Robinbrook. As he approached the stairway, he caught his breath.

The stairway emptied into an extremely large saloon in the rich lush French style of Louis XIV, with gilded paneling on the wall, twin pink and white marble fireplaces, and furniture upholstered in green velvet. Pausing for a moment, he drank in its loveliness, let the feeling of success seep into his bones, let his mind think and plan for the future. Then, with sharp, quick steps, he headed for the two huge front doors. Under his left arm he carried a small package wrapped in silver paper.

"Your carriage is waiting," said the butler as he handed Trevor his high-crowned beaver and his marble-headed cane.

Without a word Trevor put the hat atop his head, took the cane, and then strode through doors the butler held open. He saw no reason to thank a servant for doing something the servant was paid for doing. A footman let down the step and assisted him in gaining the plush squab of the curricle; a groom handed him the ribbons.

There was a reason for his choice of transport. A curricle, built for two passengers, was a two-wheeled carriage pulled by two horses, with a seat in the back for a groom. But this day Trevor did not order the service of a groom. Olivia's abigail would occupy the seat in the back. He much preferred that no one accompany them, but he knew it was the thing for a lady of the upper orders to take her personal maid with her wherever she went. The placement of the backseat would preclude the maid's hearing the conversation inside the carriage.

Trevor intended, in time, to have his way with Cousin Fitzgerald Castleberry's American wife. It should not be difficult, he told himself, since Fitzgerald was so besotted with Lady Jacqueline that he would hardly notice what was happening until it was too late. And then Fitz would call him out onto the field of honor, and he, Trevor, claiming he would elope, would aim for the head. He was an expert marksman.

Thinking of that wonderful moment when Fitzgerald Castleberry would be dead, and thinking of getting Olivia Castleberry into his bed, made hot blood pulse through Trevor's veins. Having had lots of practice in the art of seduction, he had great confidence in his prowess as a seducer. Smiling the smile of anticipated success, he looked at the silver package in the seat beside him. As he had done about farming before coming to Robinbrook, he'd taken great pains in learning about Olivia Pembroke from America. But he must bide his time with her, he silently cautioned himself. That had been evident from the moment he had first looked in those gray-green eyes, the day she arrived at Robinbrook as Fitzgerald's bride. The plan had formed that very night, and waiting went against his nature.

He could not help wishing she were not so homely. Well, mayhap he would get used to her unkempt hair, and her flat bosom. That was the hardest part, the flat bosom. He liked voluptuous women.

Robinbrook was three hillocks and three valleys away from Trevor's house, and as the curricle moved over a curving trail, Trevor pulled himself up straight, staring at but not seeing in the spring sunshine the growing crops that promised a tremendous yield. This day, thriving crops were not on his spinning mind. He sternly scolded himself for thinking of such a trivial thing as Olivia's looks. Whether or not he became used to her ladyship's homeliness mattered little. He would take her from old Fitz, before there was an heir to lovely and prosperous Robinbrook.

In the loggia overlooking the sea, Olivia twisted her hair into a bun on the back of her head, and then, not liking the feel of it, unwound the long strands and combed it back from her face with her fingers, while good-naturedly hissing at Alicia Rose, her voice low so that if a servant should have had an ear to the door, she, Olivia, would not be heard. "You're supposed to be my abigail and dress my hair. Instead, you sit there prim and proper and let me do for myself. Why, I even had to pour my own coffee when the footman brought our breakfast. I'll bet the household thinks I have the laziest abigail in all of England."

Laconically, Alicia Rose said, "Lizzie would do it for you if you would only let her."

"I told you the reason for that. I don't want her to know that I'm not really Lord Castleberry's wife. Lizzie is sweet and kind, but her mouth runs like an overcharged racehorse. Everyone at Robinbrook would know before nightfall."

"You are his legal wife. You said the vows before a vicar."

"Don't remind me. I had no idea what I was getting myself into."

"You mean you had no idea you were going to fall in love with his lordship." Alicia Rose sighed. She was lounging in a chair, her feet propped on a stool. "Love does complicate things, does it not? I gave you good advice. Simply let him make love to you as any normal wife would do. Then the marriage can't be set aside. I offered to find a potion that would work on his lib—"

"Alicia Rose," Olivia admonished strongly, "don't you dare say that word. 'Tis not discussed, even in private. And besides, Lord Castleberry doesn't need a potion, and besides that, he can't make love to me when he's in love with his precious Lady Jacqueline. It would be blasphemous, an insult to the word love, should he come to my bed."

Olivia had thought about her husband coming to her bed more than a little, had even let it creep into her writing. But there's nothing wrong with a husband and wife making love, she reasoned. And it was so against propriety that she and Alicia Rose should be talking about it. But if she did not have her sister to talk with, surely something inside her would burst. Love was such a huge, soul-filling emotion. For sure Lord Castleberry's love for Lady Jacqueline filled his soul.

A sharp pain ripped at Olivia. How could she be so addle-brained? Did one know when one was falling in love. She thought not. It just happened, and then, as in her case with Lord Castleberry, it was too late.

"I must ask that a lock be installed on that door," she said aloud to herself, remembering her threat to his lordship. She gained a chair and sat in proximity to her sister.

"What door?" chirped Alicia Rose, suddenly again very attentive, and when Olivia did not answer, she asked again, "What door are you talking about, Olivia?"

Olivia shushed her. "Not so loud, a servant might hear."

"I'm going to shout from the roof if you don't tell me which door you want locked. I can guess, and I think you are the biggest peagoose I've ever encountered. How can your husband come to your bed if the door is locked?"

Olivia gave a little laugh. "He could break the door."

She did not know where the idea came from, and right away she thought to add it to her story. How romantic, to have her husband come crashing into her bedroom, demanding his wife submit to him. Or better still, to have him take her in his strong arms, smother her with kisses, and whisper that he loved her dearly.

"I don't think 'tis a good idea, Olivia."

"What? The lock, or breaking down the door?"

The conversation was interrupted by a sharp rap on the

door, and then Lizzie pushed it open and entered, almost stumbling when she dipped into her bombazine. Other servants scratched on the door, then waited to be asked to enter. But not Lizzie. Olivia immediately noticed that instead of her usual smiling face, a scowl showed below the maid's white platter hat.

"The butler sent me. Mr. Trevor Castleberry is below stairs, in the receiving room, Lady Castleberry. He wishes to speak with you. I think he's bringing you a present, something wrapped in silver paper. But I don't trust that man, present or not. The only reason he came to the front of the house, to be let in by the butler, was because he's afraid of Mr. Fred. Mr. Fred hates him, and Trevor Castleberry knows it."

Olivia could not help but smile. As Lord Castleberry had said, Lizzie was everywhere at any given time and knowing everything all the time.

Turning her thoughts to Trevor Castleberry, Olivia recalled the night she'd come to Robinbrook as Fitzgerald Castleberry's bride. She had not liked her husband's cousin and had thought there was something sinister in his demeanor. Having not seen him since, she now wondered if her imagination had been on a rampage. Why would he be bringing her a present? How would he know whether or not she would like his selection?

It all seemed strange to Olivia, but there was nothing to do except to receive the farm steward. She would be cordial, as her Boston upbringing had taught her to be. Before quitting the room, she asked Lizzie to see that a lock was installed on the door between her bedchamber and the sitting room adjoining Lord Castleberry's bedchamber. " 'Tis silly, I know, but with his being away, I find that I sometimes awake during the night frightened out of my skin."

"I understand, your ladyship," said Lizzie, smiling like a Cheshire cat.

As for Olivia, this was not true at all. The big fat fib just rolled out of her mouth. But what could she do? For sure she did not want Lizzie to know she wanted the lock, not because she couldn't trust Lord Castleberry, but because she could not trust her own need for him to hold her and kiss her when she awakened in the night.

Bobbing, her eagerness to please showing, Lizzie promised the lock would be in place before the sun could sink into the sea. "You can count on me," she said to Olivia, who was by then making her way out of the room.

Olivia was wearing a dove-gray morning dress with delicate lace bordering the low décolletage, the high waist gathered under her bosom by an inch-wide blue ribbon tied in a small bow between her pointed breasts. She'd brought it from Boston, and it was the new style, showing just a little leg above her half-boots. Sensing a presence, she looked around and saw Alicia Rose coming along behind her.

"You can't go with me to receive a visitor, Alicia Rose. Remember, you are my lady's maid."

"I'm not staying in that room by myself. The smiling ghost might decide to pay another visit."

"Don't be silly. I'm sure it was your imagination, or, as Fred told you, the aura you supposedly saw was the bright sun reflecting off the dark water of the sea."

"Then where did the flowing hair, and the smile, and his twinkling blue eyes, come from? There's nothing in the sea that can account for that."

"Out of your imagination," Olivia said, laughing.

When she neared the receiving room on the first floor, she saw Trevor Castleberry through the doorway and was surprised that he was dressed all the crack, as if he were going to some grand party. Except that his cravat was colored, and one wore only white cravats to a grand party, so her source, which was a book about a gentleman's dress in Regency England, had stated. As she approached, he jumped to his feet and gave a fancy leg, smiling charmingly when his brown head lifted and his deep brown, almost black

eyes locked with hers, not flirtatious, just with the utmost
friendliness. Strange, she thought, for she could have sworn
that the first time she had seen him he'd had a surly manner.
Now he was as handsome a man as she had ever seen, and
he certainly exuded friendship as he held out the silver
package to her.

"A welcome gift for you, your ladyship," he said. "No
one could be happier than I for Fitzgerald that he's found
such a lovely wife. And an American. I have the greatest
admiration for the brave people who settled the Colonies."

Trevor Castleberry wanted to gag on his own words, except the part about Olivia being lovely. How could this be?
At first sight her heavy hair had made her appear top heavy,
and her bosom, which now bulged above her décolletage,
showing delicious white flesh, had been as flat as a board.
Now her rich red-brown hair fell in heavy folds onto her
shoulders, framing her anything but homely face. And
where were the freckles, and the hideous birthmark?
Strange, strange indeed, he thought, staring unbelieving at
Olivia. His cousin must be addle-brained to be off in London rutting after Lady Jacqueline when he had such a wife
at home. At least Fitz could have stayed homebound until
the newness wore off the bedding of his wife.

"Thank you for the present," Olivia said. "I shall open
it later, when I am in my chambers."

"Oh, no. Please. I'd want to see your face when the paper
is torn away. I was in quite a quandary when choosing it
for you. Knowing absolutely nothing of your wonts, I was
so afraid I could not please you." He reached to take her
hand, brushed its back with his lips, then let it drop, while
looking deeply into her eyes. "Won't you please open it
now?"

Olivia, giving a small laugh, went to sit on a short sofa.
Trevor took a chair opposite her. "So I can see if your
beautiful eyes light up. Good manners would force you to

say you like it when you really don't. I'm quite good at reading one's true thoughts."

"I'm sure I will adore it," Olivia said. " 'Tis a long time since I've received a present."

"One of your husband's shortcomings, I fear, not thinking of others."

Immediately Olivia was on the defensive. "Lord Castleberry is, I am sure, a very generous man. We haven't been married long, and no doubt he will come from his business trip to London loaded with presents."

She ripped at the silver paper and gasped, tears filling her eyes. It was the most wonderful gift ever, a copy of *Emma* by Jane Austen. She hugged it to her breast. "How did you know what book to buy for me? Why, I read her every day, so much so that my own writing tends to emulate hers."

Trevor's smile broadened, showing beautiful white teeth, and he wanted to strut around the room with his success. But he never left anything to chance, he told himself.

"What a thoughtful thing to do," Olivia exclaimed, still overwhelmed. "I shall tell my husband the moment he returns from London."

Trevor chuckled delicately. "Mayhap it would be best that you not do that. Men are funny creatures. His lordship, although the kindest, most generous man alive, might feel that he has been remiss in not thinking of buying the book for you."

"Most likely he will bring a copy when he returns home . . . if he is not too preoccupied with the business needing his attention."

If he's not too preoccupied with Lady Jacqueline, she thought before continuing. "But I take your meaning. He would not like being usurped by his farm steward."

Anger jingled every nerve in Trevor's body. "My being the farm steward would not enter into his feelings, I am sure. I am heir to Robinbrook, and Fitz treats me with the utmost respect."

"Oh, I didn't mean to imply—"

"I know you didn't, dear Olivia. May I call you Olivia? We're practically cousins." His smiled seemed to Olivia to come straight from the heart.

"Of course. I'm hardly used to Lady Castleberry." She laughed lightly. "In truth, sometimes when I'm addressed as Lady Castleberry, I look round to see to whom the person is speaking."

"I suppose being married also seems strange, Fitz being a stranger when you said your vows."

"Oh, no! It seems that I've known Lord Castleberry all my life," Olivia said, crossing her fingers behind her back for the fib. She stood. The visitor had been there ten minutes, and that was long enough, even if he had brought her the most wonderful present. She could hardly wait to return to her quarters, where she would devour the book in one sitting. She would tell Alicia Rose that she did not want to be disturbed, and if Lizzie came knocking on her door, she would simply tell her to go away.

"Thank you again, Cousin Trevor. It was most kind of you to make a welcome call, and to bring such a wonderful present." She proffered her hand for a farewell shake.

But Trevor Castleberry was not ready to be dismissed. He took her hand and held it. "I have a capital idea. I'm going into Hythe on business. Why don't you accompany me? With your abigail, of course. For propriety's sake. 'Twould be a wonderful outing for you, and it would take your mind from how much you miss your husband. I'm certain you miss him terribly."

"Oh, I do," Olivia said, and her first thought was to reject her husband's cousin's kind offer. Then the thought of getting away from Robinbrook for an outing took hold of her, and she found she desperately wanted to go. She had read that Hythe was an interesting seaport which smugglers frequented.

Without more thought than that, Olivia heard herself saying, "I would love to go with you, Cousin Trevor. Please excuse me while I return to my rooms for my reticule, and to leave my precious book. And, of course, I will fetch my abigail . . . if I can find her."

Fifteen

Alicia Rose was not difficult to find. She was in a small cubbyhole next to the receiving room, where a water closet had been installed for guests who could not wait when they came to call. In a loud, hissing whisper, the first words out of her mouth were, "Olivia, do you have windmills in your head? Fred hates that jackanapes, and Fred is old and wise. I think what brains you did possess have flown the coop. The on-dits will fly, and your husband will be furious."

By the time Alicia Rose paused for breath, Olivia was laughing. "You were eavesdropping. Shame on you. But whisper a little lower. He will hear you."

"And I don't care if he does hear me. I'm going now to tell Fred that the gel he thinks is so smart and so wonderful is really a scapeskull, that you're not smart enough to have a Robinbrook heir."

"My husband has never proposed that I have an heir to Robinbrook, our marriage is in name only, and I think if I should want to go on an outing with his cousin—while my husband's off panting after Lady Jacqueline—I should do so. Now, if you want to go as my lady's maid, go fetch my reticule. Trevor is waiting in the salon only next door."

"And what will you be doing while I'm *fetching* your reticule? And what was the present the farm steward had for you? You should not have accepted it. You're only inviting his advances."

"Not accept *Emma*! 'Tis the most wonderful of presents. I wonder how Trevor knew how much it would please me."

Alicia Rose showed her disgust by drawing a deep breath and glaring at her sister. "Of course he knew. Men like that make it their business to know what is dear to a woman's heart."

Olivia was surprised at Alicia Rose's words, and thought that mayhap her baby sister, since coming to England, had grown wise beyond her years.

"Stuff!" Olivia said aloud. She wanted more than anything to go on this outing, and there was no one else to take her. Bored and lonely without Lord Castleberry, tears filled her eyes. She had become a sniveling child. Where was that woman who would square her small shoulders and stare directly into her mother's eyes when she said hateful, disparaging things to her? She could visualize the wonderful time Lord Castleberry was having in London, and she could see no reason why she should stay home.

"While you are fetching my reticule, I shall tell Fred we will be gone for the day." She held out the book. "Will you take *Emma* with you? Place the book in my bedchamber, under my pillow. I can hardly wait to return and begin reading it. I know it's the most wonderful book."

Alicia Rose gave her sister a pitying look. "Better that you stay home and read her words today. But you're stubborn as a mule, I can see that. So be prepared for old Fred's wrath when you tell him your intent. There's no limit to his hatred for Trevor Castleberry. He talks of little else when we are taking our morning rides."

"Alicia Rose, what does a city-bred gel like you know about a mule's stubbornness? And I think you are exaggerating about Fred. He'll be gentle as a lamb when I tell him."

Olivia could not have been more wrong. Fred glared at her, so choked with anger that he could not utter a word.

Lady Patience was with him in the Hunt Room, as were the hounds and Aunt Evaline, who was stitching away as if nothing untoward were happening.

Lady Patience went to stand beside Fred's chair, and gently stroked his brow. "Now, precious, don't get in a fluster. You must control your temper. A ride into town won't hurt a thing."

"Won't hurt a thing! Most likely he will wreck the carriage and kill her. Can't anyone but me see that the evil Trevor Castleberry will stop at nothing to see that he remains heir to Robinbrook? I shall send for Fitzgerald this minute. He's a fool to be off in London, leaving his new bride alone. Trevor saw his chance and is moving in for the kill."

Olivia did not know what Fred was talking about, mentioning Trevor wanting to kill her, and she was beginning to think the old man was slightly deranged about an heir to Robinbrook. And he was wrong about Trevor, who had given no indication that he had anything in mind except a pleasant ride into town, to show his cousin's wife the sights. Alicia Rose would be with them, so what was there to worry about?

"I'm sorry, Fred, that my wanting to go into town with my husband's cousin disturbs you, but should Lord Castleberry be here to take me, I would be going with him. I think that is plain." She whipped around and quit the room and went to wait with Trevor for Alicia Rose to return with her reticule. She did not understand Fred, a lovable old man who was obsessed with her, or anybody, for that matter, having an heir to Robinbrook. It was as if tomorrow, or the next day, were the end of the world if an heir was not produced. Even if one were ordered today, and that was not likely, it would take nine months.

As if he could read her thoughts, Trevor said, "The old man had a fit when you told him you were going into town with me, but, pray, do not let him ruin our day. He's delusional, claims I tried to poison Fitzgerald so I could inherit Robinbrook. The old gaffer should be put away—"

"Oh, don't say that. Just because he's old and wants his way. All old people are like that. In truth, I quite like Fred, and I'm sure he'll be calmed down when we return."

Just then Alicia Rose came prancing into the room with Lizzie in tow. "Lizzie needs to go into town, so I asked her to come along."

"She can't go," said Trevor quickly, a terrible frown snapping his brows together. "There's only room for one in the seat reserved for a groom. I fear 'tis impossible. One lady's maid for Lady Castleberry is quite enough, I would think."

"Lizzie and I both are thin as rails, both together not as bulky as a groom, so we shall fit nicely in the one seat."

"I think that a capital idea, Alicia Rose," Olivia said. "You won't be lonely, and Lizzie can point out the sights along the way."

Trevor could see that he was bested by the three women. He did not like it, for it meant he would have to be very careful and not play his hand too blatantly. But he could manage that, he assured himself. He would go slowly and let Olivia get to know the side of him he wanted her to know, the charming, friendly, kind side of Trevor Castleberry. He chuckled to himself. His cousin Fitz should be there taking care of his wife if he did not want someone else to move in. "Well, shall we go?" he said, forcing a lightness into his words. "I hope you two maids don't feel too cramped. Mayhap I should change the transport, get the town coach."

The town coach was a large, impressive four-wheeled vehicle holding four passengers in an enclosed body, pulled by two, four, or six horses. Today, for show, there would be six. The last thing Trevor wanted was a carriage for four passengers, which would mean the two maids would be riding on the opposite squab from Lady Castleberry and himself, hearing every word said. Then back at Robinbrook the servants would know, Fred would know, and then Lord Castleberry would know.

That would be putting a noose around my own neck, he told himself, and was greatly relieved when he heard Olivia saying, "Oh, half the day would lost if you went for other equipage. We shall make do with the transport of your choice. I'm certain Alicia Rose and Lizzie will fare well enough."

Hythe, with its narrow, hilly streets, was one of England's port towns, and Olivia found its mellow jumble of old houses, inns, and shops exciting to view. It seemed that Trevor knew the history of every house in town and was able to expound knowledgeably on each one with great authority. He guided the curricle along the shore where fishermen sold their catch, each trying to outshout the other, saying that his fish was better than that of his neighbors. Suddenly a clean wind blew from the direction of the sea, and Olivia filled her lungs with it.

Offshore, ships were anchored, and Olivia found herself imagining they held smugglers. Of tea? Rum? A writer's mind, always imagining what could not be seen. She laughed, feeling gay and carefree, and for a long while she forgot that her husband was in London, doing whatever men did in London. She refused to let the thought worry her overmuch. Nor did she feel guilty from having come to Hythe with Trevor.

"Are you thinking of Fitz?" Trevor asked, looking into her gray-green eyes, pretending empathy. "When I was younger, death took my own beautiful love, just before we were to be married. If you are in love with Fitz, I pity you. I can feel your pain."

The lie sounded good to Trevor's own ears.

"I'm so sorry," said Olivia, and she wondered how she had ever thought Trevor's dark eyes sinister. Now they were filled with sympathy, and understanding, even slightly teary. "Why do you pity me should I be in love with my husband? Should a wife not be in love with her husband?"

"Not at all. Marriages among the *ton* are for convenience, to produce an heir to inherit, or to link large estates. Unless you are loaded with gold from the Colonies, gold his lordship does not need, I assume the reason Fitz married you was to give him a son. A daughter won't do. She can't inherit entailed estates, or his precious title."

Olivia heard the hardness that had crept into his voice, and she assumed it was because of his own loss of his beloved long ago. How dreadful it would be to lose in death someone one loved, and just before they were to be married. Laughing lightly, she gave a quick answer. "Lord Castleberry and I have only just married. An heir has not been discussed. Mayhap in time . . ."

She was not about to tell him that in time she would be put aside as his lordship's wife. No, it was none of Trevor Castleberry's business about Lord Castleberry's arrangement with his American wife, and when Trevor reached to take her hand, holding it in a possessive way, she felt something like a chill dance up and down her spine and quickly withdrew it. Was the chill a portent of something to come? she wondered.

"I hope I do not appear forward, and should I do so, I beg your forgiveness. 'Tis just that I feel such great sympathy for you. Fitz had no business leaving you so soon after you were married."

"He had business in London," Olivia said, again defensively, growing tired of making excuses for her husband.

Lyrical laughter spilled from Trevor. "Business with Lady Jacqueline, I am sure. But you need not be lonely while he's gone. I feel 'tis my duty to see that you are amused. I've been neglecting the big house lately, mostly because of old Fred's mistrust of me, but I shall make it a point to come to dinner more often. I have only to let the cook know."

"Is that not an odd arrangement? When you have such a complete household of your own."

"It started when I first came to Robinbrook. I lived at the big house then, until my house could be built, and the invitation to dinner has never been canceled."

They were quiet after that, and interesting sights passed before Olivia's eyes. England was so different from America, she thought, and then she heard laughter from the groom's seat, and this lifted her spirits. Alicia Rose was having a good time with Lizzie along. They stopped at an inn for a repast.

"We have two maids who will need to be placed with other servants," Trevor said to the proprietor of the inn.

But Olivia would have none of that. She wanted to be with Alicia Rose. "My abigails will sit with us," she told the man dressed like a penguin in dark tails and high collar points that stuck in his heavy jowls. His brow rose quizzically as he looked first at Olivia and then at Trevor, who was frowning ferociously.

Olivia thought for a moment he would refuse her wish and demand they sit separately from Alicia Rose and Lizzie; instead, an instant smile appeared, and his mood became jovial. "My wife is very fond of her ladies-in-waiting. Place them with us."

The man in the penguin suit bowed, then, turning, strode purposefully into the dimly lit dining room. "This way, your lordship."

"Why did you let him think you're Lord Castleberry, and why did you say Lady Castleberry is your wife?" Lizzie wanted to know as soon as they were seated at a white-clothed table which afforded, through a narrow window, a view of a trickling stream of blue-green water.

"I did not want on-dits to fly—"

"You could have called her Lady Castleberry, which she

is. Lady Olivia Castleberry, Lord Fitzgerald Castleberry's wife, not yours," the maid retorted.

Alicia Rose laughed.

"You girls behave yourselves or you shall be removed from our table," Olivia said, hardly able to contain her own laughter.

Plainly it was too much for Trevor. Anger laced his words. " 'Tis never good to have servants dine with upper orders, Olivia. I suppose that in America 'tis acceptable, but not in England." And then he turned his gaze on Lizzie. "When I am lord of Robinbrook, you will be the first servant dismissed, without references. That will teach you to keep a civil tongue in your head."

"I know you think you will be lord of Robinbrook, but you never will be. Lizzie can see into the future, and there's bad things in store for you. Just wait and see."

"Hush ,Alicia Rose" said Olivia, and she quickly changed the subject by asking Trevor if they could stop at one of the nice shops for a short time. "I would like to purchase new roses for Aunt Evaline's hair." Laughing, she added, "Those she wears are beyond enduring."

"Of course, Lady Castleberry, anything to bring you happiness," Trevor answered, his endearing charm instantly visible, making Olivia believe his threat to Lizzie had been in jest.

"But first," Trevor said, "I would like to show you the great medieval church dedicated to St. Leonard, the patron saint of prisoners, built, I think, in A.D., 1090. They say that in the vault beneath the church is a neatly stacked collection of skulls and bones."

"Ugh," said Alicia Rose. "I have no desire to see skulls and bones."

"But I would like to see the church," Olivia said. "Thank you, Cousin Trevor. for taking such good care that we see historical Hythe. England's history is fascinating."

He patted the back of her hand and smiled wryly. "I love

seeing your beautiful eyes light up. It seems to me that little wheels are always turning inside your head. I suppose that's true because of your creative mind. I do hope your manuscript sells. I'll see what I can do about an appointment for you with Miss Austen. I understand that you think she can be of help with a publisher."

"Oh, would you?" Olivia exclaimed. "I feel sure she can give me guidance."

"I promise," Trevor said, wondering how he could keep such a promise. He eyed Olivia narrowly. He had never heard of the famous writer until he was informed of Olivia's devotion to her.

Silence surrounded the table while they ate a delicious meal of stewed kidneys and boiled beef, and then it was off over the hillside to the church.

Lizzie refused to leave the carriage, and Alicia Rose decided to stay with her. Trevor was never far from Olivia's side as they viewed the high marble pillars, the carved ceiling, and Norman staircase. There were protesting creaks when they walked and a strong smell of must and old bones emanated from the basement. Eerie, thought Olivia, experiencing another small shiver, while Trevor seemed unaffected. Occasionally he touched her in a friendly fashion, and Olivia felt less fearful and thought herself foolish to have mistrusted him even for a moment.

If only her husband were so attentive.

The did not venture into the basement, and upon leaving the church they drove to the middle of the hillside town for Olivia to shop. Trevor waited at the equipage because there was not a boy in sight to hold the horses' reins. "You'll have to endure my absence," he said in a very light tone for all to hear, and then he whispered to Olivia, "I will be terribly lonely, so pray do hurry back to me."

Olivia did not reply to his tomfoolery. By now she was becoming used to it and took it with a grain of salt. This day, she determined, she would have a pleasant time and would not miss her husband overmuch. As she walked away, Alicia Rose and Lizzie walked three steps behind her, as good lady's maids were supposed to do. Talking over her shoulder, she complimented them effusively on their excellent behavior the last little while, but not at the inn. There was an ulterior motive for her effusiveness. Later, Alicia Rose, if she were so disposed, would tell her everything Lizzie had told her.

Inside the novelty shop, Olivia purchased three bloodred silk roses for Aunt Evaline, and a white linen handkerchief for her husband, quietly slipping it into her reticule. When he came from London loaded with gifts for her, she would have something to give to him. outside again, she noticed that dusk was settling over the busy little port city, and that day's light was fading in the west over the dark hills.

Sixteen

Lord Fitzgerald Castleberry left Lady Jersey and Almack's feeling well pleased with the plans for the grand affair he planned. The Season would be in full swing and London would be inundated with upper orders who had left their country estates to see and to be seen at balls, soirées, and smaller parties in grand homes.

Many a young thing would be cast by anxious mothers on the marriage mart, he thought, feeling sympathy for the husband searchers. He had never wanted to marry anyone except Lady Jacqueline, and now, seemingly, she was out of his reach. He felt abandoned and lonely.

Revenge by hurting her as she had hurt him had driven him to the extreme length of having this affair at Almack's. And he could not deny that he prayed his precious Lady Jacqueline would leave old Sappington and return to him. He dreamed for a moment about when he would again hold her in his arms, as he had done so many times, wanting her, but willing to wait until they were married.

His steps to the rented conveyance became lighter as thoughts took hold, and he began humming a lyric about love, while in his fomenting mind he made Lady Jacqueline his wife forever and ever, and he lost himself in the dream:

Her naked body was warm against his own burning desire.

Her arms were entwined around his neck—he could smell the soft white flesh of her freshly bathed body.

We'd Like to Invite You to Subscribe to Zebra's Regency Romance Book Club and Give You a Gift of 4 Free Books as Your Introduction! (Worth $18.49!)

If you're a Regency lover, imagine the joy of getting 4 FREE Zebra Regency Romances and then the chance to have these lovely stories delivered to your home each month at the lowest prices available! Well, that's our offer to you and here's how you benefit by becoming a Zebra Home Subscription Service subscriber:

- ✎ **4 FREE Introductory Regency Romances** are delivered to your doorstep

- ✎ **4 BRAND NEW Regencies** are then delivered each month (usually before they're available in bookstores)

- ✎ Subscribers **save almost $4.00** every month

- ✎ Home delivery is always **FREE**

- ✎ You also receive a **FREE** monthly newsletter, *Zebra/Pinnacle Romance News* which features author profiles, contests, subscriber benefits, book previews and more

- ✎ **No risks or obligations**...in other words you can cancel whenever you wish with no questions asked

Join the thousands of readers who enjoy the savings and convenience offered to Regency Romance subscribers. After your initial introductory shipment, you receive 4 brand-new Zebra Regency Romances each month to examine for 10 days. Then, if you decide to keep the books, you'll pay the preferred subscriber's price of just $3.65 per title. That's only $14.60 for all 4 books and there's never an extra charge for shipping and handling.

It's a no-lose proposition, so return the FREE BOOK CERTIFICATE today!

Say Yes to 4 Free Books!

Her warm, lovely rosebud lips opened to his tongue, letting him draw from the bottomless well of love.

In her sweet, little-girl voice, she was saying, "I will stay with you forever, my darling Fitzgerald."

Producing an heir never entered his lordship's wide-awake dreams as he bounded up into the hackney and to Id the driver to take him to White's. He would go to Hattie Marie later, before he returned to Robinbrook and to that woman who stirred him beyond endurance. He truly hoped Olivia held true to her threat to have a lock installed on the door of her bedchamber.

Love was not the driving force that made him want Olivia as it was with Lady Jacqueline—he could not bring himself to call her Lady Sappington. With his wife it was pure, unadulterated passion, a gift from God to all men if they were lucky. The gift of loving was much more rare. It happened only once in a lifetime. As it had happened with his mother.

At White's, disturbing news awaited his lordship. Only a short time after he had arrived, while playing whist with Nigel Avery, he was told that the king had taken a turn for the worst in his madness.

Even though he did not want to go, had never wanted to go, Lord Castleberry knew he had to leave immediately for Windsor Castle and, if unable to see His Majesty, leave words of encouragement and friendship from Fred. He had promised his dear grandfather, and a promise was to be kept. He placed an ace on his partner's trump trick and swore at himself. A dimwit was what he was. Avery laughed and assured him that it was only a game.

Whist was a four-handed card game where the dealer distributed thirteen cards to each player for that deal. The purpose was to win as many tricks as possible. Points were accumulated at the rate of one for each trick over six. Castleberry and Avery were winning big, and Avery groaned hugely when Lord Castleberry announced that he would be leaving after only one game. "Why?" he asked. "The mad old king will never know you came. I hear that his room is padded, and that the queen is afraid to go near him."

"His madness comes and goes, and, although he will never rule as king again, mayhap he will have lucid moments in which he will remember his old friend Fredrick Weatherby." He rose to go. "I gave my word to Fred, Avery, and I keep my word."

"I know you do, my friend, and if you will be so kind as to invite me, I shall accompany you to Windsor Castle."

"Have done, and we're on our way."

The other two men at the table, Lords Townsend and Gaylord, appeared not to notice when their money was collected by Avery and half handed over to Castleberry. They motioned for another set of partners and the game began again in earnest. Far be it for gamblers to let a small thing like a visit to a mad king interrupt their pleasure, thought Lord Castleberry.

"Glad to have seen you, Castleberry," Lord Townsend said without lifting his gaze from the cards he held in his hand.

"Don't stay away so long," said Lord Gaylord, "you're sorely missed, even if you do win our blunt."

Laughter followed, and, after collecting their black, high-crowned hats from the footman at the door, Castleberry and Avery were soon on their way to Windsor Castle in Avery's black and gold barouche.

The fold-back top, when in place, covered the half of the carriage where the two gentlemen sat, facing each other on plush squabs. A short, fat coachman sat on the box. "Put them to their bits," Avery called to him, and the cracking of a whip over the backs of the six sleek bays could be heard in the din of London's bustling streets.

Lord Castleberry was glad that Avery had invited himself along, and he was not surprised when his good friend looked at him, smiled, and said, "In your drunken stupor last night you mentioned more than once that you had gotten yourself leg-shackled to some American gel who was driving you to distraction. I thought you would be carrying the willow for Lady Jacqueline much longer than this. Mind explaining to an old friend, or is it none of my business?"

For a moment Lord Castleberry did not answer. He thought to say that one would say anything when one was foxed and should not be believed, but Avery was Avery, his good friend. "Had you not heard it before?" he asked of him.

"Not a peep. If you are truly married, why were banns not read, and why was it not puffed off in the newspapers? 'Twould make a great on-dit at the ladies' scandal broths they call teas, and I daresay that many a mama would cancel their daughters' come-out, for, as you know, you are the *ton's* greatest catch this Season. When Lady Jacqueline wed old Sapp, leaving you in the lurch, the mamas sat up and took notice."

"I've never wanted to marry anyone except Lady Jacqueline. Now, how about you? Has your situation changed?"

Avery sighed, and a look of sadness came over his countenance. "You know my situation. I'm trapped by honor. I foolishly let myself be caught in a compromising position and was forced to offer for the lady. The banns were read, and then she came down with some mysterious illness. Now I'm honor bound to the marriage contract. Remember the Duke of Wellington's plight? Not much different from mine, would you say?"

"Are you in love with her, or should I ask if you were ever truly in love with her?"

"I thought that I was. I thought the flame that was so suddenly ignited was love." He paused, and then, "I suppose it was love . . . puppy love, which never lasts."

"Why does she not release you from your promise? How long has it been?"

"A whole year. I've asked twice to be released, but she holds on to me as if we were already married. In truth, I think she rather enjoys reminding me that I cannot cry off. Since I've not fallen for any other chick, I would still marry her if she should recover. It would not be a bad marriage as *ton* marriages go. I'd very much like to have an heir."

Lord Castleberry had known of Lord Avery's sad lot for a long time, but they seldom spoke of it. As bosom bows, they had, during the Napoleonic wars, many times, talked deep into the night, when sleep eluded them, even though their bodies were battle weary to the point of exhaustion. Looking at Avery, he thought him a handsome man, rugged, for he loved the outdoors, and, even when speaking of his now-unwanted engagement, his blue eyes, under straight blond brows, held a twinkle. That he was an honorable man there was no doubt. Being the third son of a duke, he had chosen the academic world for vocation and had, after the war, began lecturing at King's College in London.

The two men fell silent; there did not seem to be overmuch to say. Lord Castleberry looked out at the countryside, bursting with April blooms and sprouting crops. He smelled the sweetness of the fresh air as they left smelly London behind, and the clopping of the horses' hooves against the hard road lulled him into a passive state. They passed Eton, where he had gone to school, as did Lord Avery. "Fond memories?" he asked.

Avery laughed. "Some. A few times I outsmarted the master."

"I don't think I ever did," Lord Castleberry said, chuckling. "I remember being terribly homesick, and then my parents died, leaving me to Fred."

"You love the old man, that's evident by your driving to Windsor to see a man who is as mad as a hatter. When you could be doing fun things in London, like winning hugely at whist."

"Or visiting Hattie Marie."

Avery sat forward on the squab. "I thought you pensioned her . . . and what about your wife? Or do you really have one? As you say, drunks do talk of outrageous things."

"I'm not a drunk, you know. I just let myself go a bit too much last night. If I told you I recently married, I spoke the truth. She's from America, a fine, bookwormish woman, interesting to talk with, but I'm not in love with her. I fear I did a foolish thing, and very unfair to her."

That was as much as Lord Castleberry wanted to tell his friend. How could he explain his desire to bed the woman to whom he was married in name only when he still so desperately loved Lady Jacqueline? How could he explain his foolish desire to see his ex-affianced's face when she learned he had married a homely American? Except Olivia was not homely. He had been tricked on that part. Avery would think him a scapeskull if he started talking in such a vein.

"When can I meet your new bride?" Avery asked, looking quizzically at Lord Castleberry.

"I met with Lady Jersey earlier today to plan for Olivia's introduction to London society. I expect to see you there. 'Twill be a grand ball," Lord Castleberry said, and then he abruptly changed the subject back to Lady Jacqueline. "Do you hear how her marriage to old Sapp is working out? Do on-dits have her happy with him?"

"I hate to tell you this for fear of spreading false tales, and for fear of building up your hopes that she'll return to you."

Castleberry gave a small, mirthless laugh. "You know me quite well, better than anyone."

"Drop the willow, Fitzgerald. She's not worth your love. She is cossetted and thoroughly spoiled. Rumors have it that she thought she was marrying a man of extreme means, when in truth her husband is a crusty fellow deep in dun territory. Keeping too many demanding mistresses. That's why at White's there's so many bets against the marriage lasting."

Lord Castleberry did not want to hear more. He would not rest easy until he again talked with Lady Jacqueline. He became most eager to get this visit to Windsor Castle over with. With luck he would be advised to leave a missive for the old king to read should he ever again become lucid.

And that is what happened. He was told by Queen Charlotte, who came immediately when told that Lord Fitzgerald Castleberry waited below stairs. The pitiful queen expressed great sorrow that most likely his majesty would never be receiving again.

"If you would like to pen a message, mayhaps . . ." Her voice broke.

"Yes, yes, that is what I would like to do," Lord Castleberry said, and the queen rang for a servant to bring paper and quill. Castleberry wrote quickly and then, bowing deeply, he left, even though her majesty issued an invitation for him to extend his visit. Many times the old king had hunted with Fred at Robinbrook, and many times Fredrick Weatherby had brought his grandson to court. "You're like family, Lord Castleberry," she had many times told him.

"I fear Fred will be sorely disappointed," said Lord Castleberry as the barouche tooled its way over the hard-packed country road. "Even though it is well known the king is mad, those who love him cannot bring themselves to believe it so. I should have talked with Fred, made him believe it, and then this trip would not have been necessary."

"Fustian, old friend, you've done your duty to the best of your ability. So cheer up, and let's think of something much gayer to do, like a trip to Bond Street, to Gentleman Jackson's for a bout with a pugilist. With your agility and your skill with your fists you'll make the poor devil wish he'd never been born." Taking a gold-encrusted snuffbox from his waistcoat pocket, Avery sniffed and then proffered it to Castleberry, who took it and breathed deeply of the brown powder.

"A capital idea," Lord Castleberry answered. "A bit of physical exercise will do me well, I am sure."

And get me in shape for my visit to Hattie Marie, he thought as he leaned back against the squab, with every notion of enjoying the noisy hush of the countryside during the jostling trip back into London.

Seventeen

Lord Castleberry awoke with the feeling something was wrong at Robinbrook and thought to return at once. He had been in London four days and had not yet visited Hattie Marie. He swore at himself for having postponed the visit, but after getting the sad and dreaded visit to Windsor Castle behind him, he and Lord Avery had gone a bout or two with pugilists at Gentleman Jim's. The exercise had lifted his spirits, and after that Avery had kept him busy doing things that made him gay and happy.

Between games of whist, they had raced their carriages down St. James's Street, betting hugely on themselves as winner, gone to the opera at King's Theatre, and had even danced a night away at Almack's. It reminded Lord Castleberry of the time after they had returned from the war when they had tried to cram all they had missed into one week.

Lord Castleberry opened his eyes just enough to see bright sunlight casting shadows across the high bed on which he slept. It must be nearing noon, he was certain. His lordship found himself chuckling. That rascal Avery had purposely kept him so busy that Hattie Marie, his former mistress, Lady Jacqueline, his beloved, and his AmerIcan wife back at Robinbrook could occupy his thoughts only fleetingly. It had been a wonderful respite.

Yawning, he turned and swung his long legs over the side of the bed. Last evening, after the fine time at Almack's, it had been suggested they spend this day at the gaming tables.

It seemed, or so Avery claimed, Castleberry had won all his blunt and he wanted a chance to recoup his loses.

After hurriedly finishing his toilette, he donned yellow pantaloons, an embroidered white waistcoat, a meticulously creased cravat, and a finely tailored blue coat that hugged his slender waist. Lastly, he pulled on black Wellingtons and then quit the room and descended the stairs into the lobby, where he found Lord Avery lounging in a chair, the morning paper resting in his lap.

"Demmet, Castleberry, you've slept most of the day."

"Why didn't you come up and wake me?"

"I encountered your valet, and he said you were sleeping. Gaming can wait. Your body needed the rest." Avery stood and slapped him on the shoulder. "I've known you a long time, Castleberry, and I've never seen you more weary than when you came into town. You needed the sleep. And your mind needed rest from whatever has been worrying you. You look your old self again."

"These past days have been good for me. I did sleep the sleep of the dead, and I've not done that in a long time."

"Are you still in the mood for White's?" Avery asked. "Or would you prefer the museum? I haven't seen Lord Elgin's marbles—"

"I prefer White's," Lord Castleberry said, and again the niggling feeling that something was wrong at Robinbrook surfaced. He was quiet for a moment. But at last he said, "I'm slightly worried about things at Robinbrook. Mayhap I should return today."

Avery laughed. "If something were wrong, someone would come for you. So pray do not start worrying. I give you leave to return to Robinbrook on the morrow. This day I shall win back my blunt."

"Do you mind if I have coffee before you start robbing me?"

They went into the hotel dining room, where Castleberry put away a huge breakfast of ham and eggs, jam and biscuits, plus a bowl of fresh berries. The aroma of roasting coffee beans curled from the spout of a silver pot placed on the white-clothed table, and more than once the waiter came to fill his cup with the hot coffee. "Are you sure you won't join me?" Castleberry asked.

"I ate hours ago. Besides, I gamble better on an empty stomach. Eat up. The only way I can beat a gamester like you is to fill him with food until he can't think."

Castleberry laughed, finished his breakfast in silence, and then, wiping his mouth with his serviette, rose from the table. Determinedly he pushed Robinbrook from his mind.

As if he could read his mind, Avery said, "I know there's something on your mind besides Robinbrook. You've got that certain look about you."

"You know me too demme well, my friend. I would like your opinion on something . . . if you promise to never tell a soul that I asked."

"You should know that I would never let it pass my lips. We've shared many secrets."

"This may seem quite ludicrous, but I have to know," Castleberry said, and then he blurted out, "Do you believe Lady Jacqueline and old Sapp have consummated their marriage? Do you think she could bear the old gaffer to touch her?"

If the look on Castleberry's face had not been one of utter seriousness, and pain, Avery would have laughed until he could be heard all the way to St. James's Street. Until now he had avoided answering this question, and even now he did not answer for a long while. A young groom brought his carriage, and the two men were about to board, when Castleberry, standing on the ground, pushed for an answer. "Do you? Or do you not?"

Avery could not lie to his friend. "I think old Sapp by now has her with the heir he wanted when he married her. Why else did he take her to Paris if not to get away from his mistresses? At fifty plus, I don't think he can take care of three women of a lusty nature, so he absented himself from London on purpose."

"Poor little Jacqueline," said Lord Castleberry. "Surely she did not know that Sapp wanted her only to bear an heir to his title. Did you not tell me that his fortune, all except that which is entailed, has been lost at the gaming tables?"

Instant anger, mixed with pity and with love for his friend, flew over Avery. How could a man be so besotted with a temptress such as Lady Jacqueline, who traded on her skin-deep beauty, whose heart, if she had one, was most certainly made of stone? Avery tried to control his voice. "Best you forget the doxy. She thought old Sapp was flush in the pockets, and she would be his darling. And, too, she was piqued with you for not doing her every bidding."

Lord Castleberry's hands curled into fists. "Don't call her a doxy. I'm sure Sapp pulled every trick in the trade to get her to marry him so he could show her off like a trophy. You'll have to admit there's never been a woman more beautiful. Not anywhere." He shook his head. "Her beauty is unmatched."

"Beauty is as beauty does, Castleberry, and I mean no offense, but 'tis time you take heed of the wife you have back at Robinbrook. I'll win back my blunt another time if you wish to return to Robinbrook. Never heard of a bride-groom leaving his bride practically on his wedding night. Take my advice and forget Lady Jacqueline."

Castleberry knew that Avery was right, but his good friend did not know the whole of it. Olivia was not truly his wife. Suddenly all desire to sit at the gaming tables at White's left him. He would go to Hattie Marie, pay her well, and then leave immediately for Robinbrook. Knowing the terrible temptation to bed Olivia would rear its head like a coiled serpent when he was again near her, he had to take care of *that* before he left London.

Regardless of how much Olivia stirred his bestial nature, she never meant to tempt him as he had accused her, he told himself. And he could hardly fault himself. To want an attractive woman in his bed was the nature of a man, a blessing, as well as, at times, a curse. In this instance a curse.

"I would like to beg off," he told Lord Avery. "Mayhap I should return home. If you don't mind."

"Of course I don't mind." Avery climbed into his equipage, this time a tilbury. Taking the ribbons, he gave Lord Castleberry a snappy salute. "Take care, Castleberry. Don't forget you owe me a chance to win back my blunt." A wide smile accompanied his words.

"I beg your forgiveness for disappointing you. I don't understand this sudden feeling about Robinbrook. But I shall see you at the ball at Almack's. If you hear about Lady Jacqueline's return from the Continent, please pen a missive. Or, if you have time, I would love having you come to Robinbrook for a visit."

"I would like that. It has been a long time since I've seen your grandfather. But I fear it's back to work for me. I asked leave for a few days to be with you. I hope you find Fred spry as ever."

Castleberry gave a small laugh. "I'm sure he's still able to express strong opinions on just about any subject."

They waved good-bye to each other, and Avery drove away, leaving Castleberry standing on the curb and looking after his friend, and when the tilbury was out of sight, he turned and gave the boy, whose name was Andrew, a sovereign. "Would you take a message to my driver? Tell him my carriage is needed. He should be near the stables."

Andrew, grinning broadly and squeezing the sovereign in his small hand before depositing it in his pocket, bowed deeply, almost losing his balance. "I'll be there in no time, your lordship. I know where to find him, drinking ale at the Hog's End with his doxy."

Lord Castleberry laughed at the street-smart boy. At that age he had not been familiar with the term *doxy*. Turning, he reentered the Clarendon and went to his rooms, where he penned a missive to his valet, suggesting he take public transport to Robinbrook. It did not bother him that his valet was not always underfoot. In truth, he rather liked doing for himself, and this day he wanted to travel alone. A short detour would take him to Hattie Marie's place in George Street.

Not that Henry would blab—a good valet always kept his employer's secrets—but Castleberry was slightly embarrassed. Having the coachman along could not be helped. He would swear him to secrecy and threaten him with the loss of his position if he so much as breathed a word of the visit.

Expecting a knock on the door by a footman telling him his carriage awaited, it was difficult for Castleberry to relax. He accomplished this by forcing his thought to center on Hattie Marie. He had met her at the courtesan ball held yearly in the beautiful Argyle Rooms, where gentlemen of the *ton* shopped for a new mistress, should his former one have left him for another protector. In Lord Castleberry's case it had been his first time to attend the ball, and he had spotted Hattie Marie at once. Her flaming red hair falling to her white shoulders had caught his eye. She had deep green eyes, and a beautiful smile that showed the most gorgeous white teeth he had ever seen. He would never forget bowing in front of her, then taking her hand and leading her to the dance floor, with not a word exchanged. She was his choice, and her green eyes and ready smile gave him the answer he sought. The night was one of the most memorable of his life, laughter, champagne, and physical satisfaction for both of them. It would never be more, they agreed, and when he went to her and apprised her of his situation, that he had fallen in love with Lady Jacqueline, she had released him with the same sweet smile she had welcomed him into her boudoir the night they had met. The pension was generous and would stop only after she had taken another protector. The house was hers to keep.

At first he could not afford a place for her, so she had

been generous and let him visit her at a small house she shared with another woman of her trade in a poor section of town. When Robinbrook's coffers were overflowing, he had bought the pretty little house in George Street.

Finding himself eager to taste again the sweetness of his former courtesan's lovemaking, his lordship left his writing desk and began pacing the parlor floor. Why did someone not come; why was the coachman taking so long? What if the boy Andrew could not find him? His lordship swore under his breath. He thought about his wife back at Robinbrook, feeling that he had abandoned her in a strange place. Poor girl, he thought, and he prayed that her writing was going well. He should have bought her a present, but he had selfishly forgotten to be that considerate. He would have his coachman stop at one of London's fashionable bookstores, and a book would be purchased for Olivia. Yes, that was what he would do, he planned, feeling better as he envisioned the look of rapture on her face when he handed it to her. He recalled her threat to have a lock installed on the door of her bedchamber.

Did she not know that he could break the door if he so chose? He was still smiling when he heard a forceful knock on the door. He opened it hurriedly, with intent to scold his coachman for the long delay in bringing his carriage. It was not his coachman, but a highly liveried footman holding a silver salver with a sealed missive out to him.

The footman bowed deeply. "Your lordship," he said, " 'tis an emergency."

Lord Castleberry took the missive and stared at the unfamiliar writing. "Who said it was an emergency?"

"The man on the horse, which looked as if it had been ridden to its last breath. The man, a groom, I suppose, didn't look much better. Fright was in his eyes."

As the footman stood on first one foot and then on the other, waiting to be dismissed, Lord Castleberry ripped open the missive and read, his gaze flying over Lady Patience's words: *Your grandfather has taken to his bed and desperately needs you. I fear for his life.*

Silently berating himself for not heeding the feeling that he was needed at Robinbrook, he thanked the footman and handed him three shillings. "I must return to my estate in the country at once . . . if my demme coachman ever brings the carriage."

"Your equipage is waiting out front," the footman said, bowing again. "Your coachman asked that I tell you." v

"Why didn't you tell me in the first place?"

Without offering an apology for the sharpness in his voice, Lord Castleberry closed the door behind him and started running down the hallway, taking the stairs at great speed, as he did the lobby of the hotel.

Out in the street, without so much as a greeting to the waiting coachman, he climbed into the carriage and ordered that the horses be put to their bits, which the coachman did with expediency, and they were halfway out of London before Lord Castleberry realized he'd left behind his top hat, and that he had not instructed the tired groom who had brought the missive on what to do. But the groom was no fool. He would engage a fresh horse from the stables and then give himself some rest and relaxation before starting back to Robinbrook.

Lord Castleberry heaved a deep sigh, not caring a whit about the hat, the groom, or anything else he might have forgotten. Settling himself for the long ride, tears came unbidden to his eyes. What would life be without Fred, who had already lived far past his time?

Just because he knew I needed him.

"Hold on, Fred," Lord Castleberry said into the silence that hovered inside the carriage. "I'll be there soon. I'll hold your hand . . . I won't let you go. Heaven doesn't need you half as much as I do."

* * *

"Do you see him coming, Lady Patience? He's had plenty of time to get here if that demme groom didn't stop on the way to drink the night away. You did tell him to ride the night out, did you not?"

"Yes, I did tell the rider that it was an emergency, and no, I don't see Fitzgerald's carriage. But that doesn't mean he's not near. One can't see too far in the moonlight."

She turned from the window and frowned at the man she loved as much as she had ever loved a man, and that was because they were both old and needed each other. Fred had been her lover since he had come to Robinbrook to raise Fitzgerald. She thought back. Why, it had been fifteen years now. "Get back in bed, Fred. If you're going to pretend to be on your deathbed, you must practice. I've never seen a dying man, but I hear his eyes roll back in his head, and a death rattle, whatever that means, settles in his chest."

"And his breathing becomes shallow," the old man said as he climbed back into the high bed and buried his head in a thick, downy pillow, shoving his white nightcap to an oblique angle.

His long white nightshirt looked as if he had slept in it for a month, Lady Patience noted, and smiled. He said his feet were cold, not because he was dying; they were always cold.

He took several shallow breaths, and then exclaimed, "I am near death with worry, else I wouldn't be trying to fool my smart grandson. That's not going to be easy. You remember, don't you, dear Patience, that you're to do the talking, you and the good doctor, who didn't even cringe when I handed him a fist of blunt. Where is the old gaffer anyway? He should be here trying to save me when Fitz arrives."

"He's only down the hall. I'll call for him when the time comes, so stop your worrying about that. You've enough on your mind. And do please keep you voice down, dearest. A servant might be listening."

She went to him and pulled the coverlet up to his chin. Bending, she kissed his forehead, which was cold and clammy to her lips. A fire had not been lit in the grate, and the room was purposely cold from the night sea air. A dying man was supposed to feel cold to the touch, so she had heard.

Lady Patience shook her head and went to sit in Fred's rocking chair near the fireplace. This was such a reckless thing he was doing, but she did agree that something had to be done to assure the Castleberry lineage. Fitz was off in London, panting after Lady Jacqueline, while Trevor, the scoundrel, was here at Robinbrook, taking care of Fitz's wife. There would never be an heir if that kept up, and should there be, it would most certainly be a bastard. Little wonder Fred was so worried, and his illness was not all pretense. She knew the old man well enough to know that his heart was breaking.

"And one can die from a broken heart," she murmured into the room's loud silence, into which the creaking of the rocking chair blended, as if she were not rocking at all. An occasional grunt, followed by a jerk of his long legs under the coverlet, told her that Fred had at last dozed off. A lone, flickering candle cast shadows across the bed, and on the mulberry walls that held pictures of her, the hounds, and of Fitzgerald. Pushing herself up from the chair, she went to look toward the tree-lined lane that wound toward Robinbrook. Surely Lord Castleberry would soon come to his grandfather. She prayed that the plan would work and that soon Lady Castleberry—Olivia from America—would be with child.

The law of averages spelled out quite plainly that Fred could not live forever. A smile stole across patience's wrinkled face as she turned to look fondly at the long frame under the coverlet. She loved the stubborn old man who would never die as long as there was a chance that Trevor Castleberry would inherit Robinbrook and the earldom. She had many times told Fred that he was being foolish, that Fitz had seen only thirty summers.

"A man can beget a child late in life," she had told him, but Fred was convinced that the wicked cousin would stop at nothing to gain what he coveted so much.

"When I'm dead and can't point an accusing finger at Trevor, Fitz won't live long. Even now, by courting Olivia in Fitz's absence, that demme Trevor's going to force Fitz to call him out, and the bastard, an expert marksman, will aim at my grandson's head. I'm sure of it, and something has to be done, and 'tis up to me. . . ."

Thus this drastic plan had been put into motion, and Lord Castleberry had been sent for.

Shuddering, and not from the cold sea air, Lady Patience prayed that Fred's plan would work. Again she went to the window to stare out. Trees lining the lane leading to the house rustled and whispered in the light breeze, and still no Fitzgerald. In the distance, below, the sea, marvelous, dark, and sedentary, waited, not for Lord Castleberry, as she waited, but for the red sun to rim the sky and shine down on it, as if it were its due.

The rumble of wheels moving over a hard road, the cracking of a whip, the jingling of harness, brought her out of her rumination, and then, blessedly, she saw lighted carriage lanterns dancing in the darkness.

Eighteen

When Robinbrook came into view, Lord Castleberry
leaned forward and stared at the magnificent, sprawling edifice glistening under the light of the full moon. His heart
lodged in his throat as he saw that light shone only faintly
through one narrow window in the far west corner, where
Fred's quarters were located. Surely if he had died, every
room in the house would be ablaze and mourning cries
would be heard. Even the chimney pots were silent of their
curling smoke. His gaze moved to the other side of the
manor house, where Olivia would be sleeping if all was
well, and saw only darkness. He heard a sharp crack of the
whip and felt the carriage list to the right as they careened
around a curve. The loyal coachman was doing the best he
could to get him home as quickly as possible.

They had not stopped to eat, but they had taken on fresh
horses at a posting inn. The delay had seemed interminable.
Now, in a strangled voice, his lordship said aloud, "Fred,
you can't die. You're all the family I have, unless you count
my wife." Then, after a pause, words came from somewhere
deep inside him. "And a cousin who can't wait for me to
die so he can inherit Robinbrook."

Has Cousin Trevor harmed Fred?

If that is true, I will kill him with my own bare hands,
threatened his lordship, feeling a tightening up and down
his spine as anger flooded his body. It was the first time
he had admitted that mayhap Fred had been right about the

cousin who was next in line to inherit Robinbrook. It was difficult to imagine anyone wishing another person dead for monetary gain and for the status of being of the nobility, but suddenly it became clear that truth lay in Fred's suspicions. It was not a figment of the old man's imagination.

"I now believe that it wasn't tainted meat that put me near death when Trevor served me the wine," mused Lord Castleberry as the carriage skidded to an abrupt halt in front of the dark manor house. Practically leaping from the carriage, he climbed the stone steps two at a time and found himself pounding on the huge front doors with the brass knocker, the sound ringing out into the night to join the waves that rhythmically pounded the shore.

The urgent pounding of the knocker soon brought the butler, who swung back the doors. Wearing a red nightshirt barely covering his bony knees, he bowed deeply from the waist. "Welcome home, your lordship. 'Tis always a pleasure to be awakened in the middle of the night."

"How is he?" Lord Castleberry asked.

"How is who?" the butler inquired in such a sleepy voice that his words were almost unintelligible.

"Fred, of course. My grandfather. I received word he was abed and desperately needed me. Don't you keep up with what's going on in the house, especially if someone is dying?"

"I have not been told that anyone is dying. The old doctor came and, as far as I know, has not left. Since they are bosom bows, I did not think it unusual. Lady Patience is with your grandfather, and that is not unusual. Only an hour ago I was awakened to bring tea, which she took at the door. I suppose one could call that unusual, but when a man is groggy from sleep . . ."

Before the plainly astounded butler could finish, Lord Castleberry was out of hearing distance, the stairs simply melting beneath his booted feet. When he reached the top of the winding stairs, his breath was labored and coming in short gasps.

Emotion more than being out of physical shape, he told himself, and when his quick steps had gained the door of the old man's quarters, Lord Castleberry entered without knocking. The room reeked of hartshorn, of burning incense, and of impending death. Lady Patience was wiping Fred's forehead with a crumpled wet cloth while wiping tears from her eyes with something white held in her other hand. The good doctor was bent over Fred, waving hartshorn in front of his nose. Lord Castleberry pushed him aside.

"Good God, if he's not dead already, that stuff will kill him."

Fred coughed and looked through slitted eyes just enough to see the fright on his grandson's face. "Glad you are here, my boy. I've been waiting to tell you—"

"Tell me what? Oh, what difference does it make. I only want to hear that you are going to live."

"I've outlived my time already, Fitz," Fred said in a low whisper. "Bend closer. I must tell you that it's imperative that you have an heir to Robinbrook. Promise me that you'll get your wife in the family way so I can die in peace."

"You're not going to die—"

"Oh, but he is," said the doctor.

There was nothing weak about Lord Castleberry's voice as his words boomed out into the room. "What's wrong with him? What medicine are you giving him? Have you tried leaches to suck the poison from his blood?"

" 'Twould do no good. His vital organs are slowly wearing out, and his being so sick with worry about an heir is not helping. Not a bit. Not a bit. See how pale he is, sign of lack of oxygen flowing through his tired veins. And there's tears seeping from his eyes. Poor, poor soul. See, even the hound knows his master is going to the great beyond. Surely, son, you can grant him his last wish."

By now Lady Patience was outwardly sobbing. It appeared to Lord Castleberry that she might reach the pearly gates before Fred. Gray hair, loose from its bun, fell in disarray around her kind, wrinkled face. As her red-rimmed eyes locked with Lord Castleberry's, she let out a little yelp of anguish, fell to her knees beside the bed, and began praying for Fred's soul.

As if on cue, Fred's breathing suddenly became more shallow, and something like a death rattle grated in his chest and gurgled up from his throat.

Lord Castleberry felt his grandfather's forehead—cold as ice. And then he noticed the open window, and no fire. His grandfather always had a fire in the grate at night to guard against the cold sea air. His lordship smiled to himself. They had staged their performance rather well. A little overdone mayhap, and he had been *almost* fooled.

"Why do the servants not know of his grave illness?" Lord Castleberry asked, a plan sending surges of pleasure through his tall frame and lifting his spirits considerably.

"Fred requested that we not alarm the servants," said Lady Patience. "The poor dear wanted to die in peace, but he refused to go until you arrived, so that you could grant his last wish."

"And what is that?" Lord Castleberry asked in a low, troubled voice. Knowing the answer, he smothered a smile.

Lady Patience sighed heavily. "That before morning you will have your wife *enceinte*. He cannot bear your cousin Trevor inheriting Robinbrook."

"Nor can I."

"Then do something about it," said the good doctor in a loud voice that filled the room. "You're the only one who can."

Lord Castleberry bent over his grandfather, even kissed his forehead, then affectionately rubbed his old cheek with the palm of his big hand. "Don't die, Fred. For you I will impregnate my wife before morning. But just for you," he lied.

"Do . . . do you promise, my boy? That bastard Trevor has been pursuing her in your absence."

"Just promise to hang on until first light. I want you to die happy."

Before another word could be said, Lord Castleberry whipped around and quit the room. As he walked down the long hall to his own quarters, a smile of delicious glee spread across his face, and he could hardly contain himself from whooping in the big old house and waking all the sleeping servants. He would satisfy his own desire for Olivia and make Fred happy at the same time. He could imagine laughter filling the room he had just left. Most likely Lady Patience and Fred were romping around the room, and the good doctor was counting the blunt Fred had paid him for his part in the splendid charade.

As his lordship's steps gained momentum, he prayed they had closed the window and lit a fire in the grate so that Fred would not catch his death and die before his grandson could slip into Lady Olivia Castleberry's bed and get her with child.

Lord Castleberry laughed aloud, and when he reached his quarters, he pushed the key into the lock, turned it, and then pushed the door open. The moon had shifted, disallowing its light into the room. Not even shimmering coals in the grate to afford a modicum of guidance. He fumbled in the darkness until he found a lucifer, with which he lighted a tall taper on the mantel. The hands on the clock registered near midnight.

This pleased his lordship immensely, for he needed time to gather himself and shift from being scared to death that Fred was dead, or dying, to planning on just how to go about getting into his wife's bed. As the taper caught and flickered, he noticed something drastically different in the room. His gaze went to the life-sized statue of Lady Jacqueline. He sat in a large, comfortable chair near the fireplace and laughed until his sides hurt.

Before he had left for London, Olivia had draped the body of Lady Jacqueline's likeness; now there was a large square of cloth over the head, with a rope securing it tightly around the throat, as if to cut off all breath if she dared to start breathing.

He looked for further mischief by his bookwormish wife and found the pink window coverings had been replaced by the faded green draperies, which were there before Lady Jacqueline had decided to decorate the parlor more to her liking.

And then his lordship realized he was sitting in his old chair, the one Lady Jacqueline had dispatched to the attic. It felt good and wonderful, and he sat there for a long while, just thinking about Olivia. He still could not concede that he was in love with the American, but he could not deny his desire to hold her, to feel her body against his, to make wonderful love to her.

It wasn't fair, he knew, for the agreement said "in only," but now he knew he would never marry Lady Jacqueline, for how could he when Avery had assured him that she was truly old Sapp's wife? His rationale toward Olivia was that after they had produced an heir together, she could take a lover if she wanted, and he would then take Lady Jacqueline as his courtesan. It was the way of the *ton*.

Something deep inside his lordship warned him that he should beget the child before he explained this new plan to Olivia. Her puritanical sensibilities would explode. Mayhap she would sleep through his lovemaking, thinking she was dreaming of some handsome prince coming to her bed. He laughed at that. Truly, he had lost his senses. And certainly this night he had no conscience.

He went to the sideboard and poured brandy into a glass but did not drink it. He wanted no dullness to his feelings when he took his wife. For nights now he had gone to sleep thinking of little else than holding her and kissing her and making her want him as he wanted her. The plan to see Hattie Marie had been a farce; it had been Olivia he had wanted.

"Thank you, Fred," he said aloud, not knowing for certain just why he was thanking Fred. Unless it was for pushing him over the edge and destroying his conscience. In his mind's eye he ripped the business agreement between himself and his wife into shreds and felt good for it. Where begetting an heir was concerned, one's conscience should never enter the picture. He held the brandy, not drinking it, but thinking it might prove useful if Olivia awoke and ordered him out of her bed. He would say that he had wanted only to share a glass of brandy with her.

Suddenly feeling the sweat and dust of the long day on his body, and wanting to go to his wife fresh and clean, his lordship decided a bath was in order. He looked at the clock; there was still plenty of time. In truth, he told himself, he was rather enjoying the anticipation of what was ahead.

In his dressing room he poured tepid water from a tankard into the brass tub, stripped naked, and, scrubbed his long frame until his skin tingled. He sang a bawdy song. He hummed a happy tune. He smiled into the flickering candlelight. Standing, he let water drip from his naked body and drain back into the tub, running in rivulets down his muscled thighs.

Hurriedly then, he rubbed himself with a thick white towel. His readiness was showing, hard and throbbing, pressed against his flat stomach. He was glad he'd left his valet in London.

"Olivia . . . oh, sweet Olivia," he whispered as he donned a blue silk dressing gown and combed his black hair with his long fingers. He really should shave, he thought, then decided to forego that part of his toilette. He had used up enough time in anticipation. If he did not know better, he would swear he had seen only sixteen summers and this was his first encounter.

Taking up the glass of brandy, he tiptoed through the parlor to the door that separated him from the woman he intended to impregnate with his child.

The door was locked.

Nineteen

Down on his knees, Lord Castleberry picked at the lock. "Demme the luck. I didn't think she would do it." He was amused. Having picked locks as long ago as Eton, he was confident there would be no problem. Or he could break the door and make a grand entrance. But that would preclude his seducing her while she slept. Turning back into the room, he thought to search for a long steel hairpin, the kind women used to hold their hair in place. The blade of his knife was too thick to be of use. For a moment he felt that his wife had outsmarted him, and then an ingenious idea popped into his head. Why had he not thought of it immediately?

The statue of Lady Jacqueline held a blond wig with more than one hairpin. Laughing quietly, he untied the rope from around the neck and took two of the longer pins, just in case he dropped one and could not retrieve it in the near darkness that was such a great hindrance to him. In his state of desire, giving up never entered his mind. Besides, he had promised Fred.

Picking the lock was not nearly as easy as he had thought it would be. Out of practice, he dropped both pins. But again down on his knees he went, crawling around and feeling on the thick carpet until both were in his hands again. Miraculously then, the job was done. The door opened without a creak, and another miracle hit him in the face, making him certain that God was on his side. A candle burned beside his wife's bed. He would not have to stumble around in the dark. Pushing his long frame up to its considerable height, and carrying the glass of brandy, he crept to the bed and looked down at his sleeping wife, who was lying—another miracle—in the middle of the bed.

A white nightcap covered her hair, and minuscule buttons closed the bodice of her white nightdress.

The buttons might be a problem when he undressed her, he mused, thinking Olivia's face lovely in the flickering candlelight. And he had ordered a homely American wife.

The good Lord must have had a hand in that too, he thought as he placed the brandy on the bedside table and then let his dressing gown slip to the floor, standing naked and looking down at her, savoring the peacefulness with which she slept. He slid his long frame under the coverlet and found that he was holding his breath. Leaning on his left elbow, he untied the ribbons of her nightcap and gingerly splayed her long, dark hair out onto the white pillow. He would start the seduction with feathery kisses on her cheeks.

And then something crackled beneath him. He swore into the room's quietness. The crackling sounded like a cannon being shot off in heat of battle. He prayed for patience.

It was a pad of paper and a feather quill. Plainly, Olivia had fallen asleep while writing on her manuscript. Thinking first to dispatch the paper to the bedside table, he changed his mind and, feeling no quilt whatsoever, began reading. He'd already admitted that this night he had no conscience, and to invade her privacy by reading her writing was inordinately insignificant compared to his planned seduction. By morning her beautiful body would be carrying the seed of Robinbrook's heir.

His body on fire, he kissed her cheeks, her neck, felt the warmth of her body, and the scent of rosewater wafted up to assault his nostrils in a most pleasant way. She turned, drew her knees up, and let out a little moan.

Letting go of his own breath and drawing away from her, he turned his attention back to the pad of paper and feather quill and felt his eyes literally pop out of his head. This writing in no way resembled *Sense and Sensibility* or *Pride and Prejudice*.

Incredulously, he read:

> *Lucifer's cold, penetrating eyes bore down on her, making her shudder with desire. But she felt no guilt; he was her husband. . . .*

His lordship would have read more, but feared he could not contain his laughter. Why, the little minx was writing about him. Once when she was angry, after one of their deep, stirring kisses, she had called him Lucifer, or the devil incarnate, he could not remember which.

He read again, *But she felt no guilt; he was her husband. . . .*

He let the pad and quill drop to the floor, turned back to her, and once again raised himself up onto his elbow and stared down into her lovely face. She did look rather innocent.

"Why has this woman stirred me as no other . . . when I'm not even in love with her?" he asked himself, lightly tracing the outline of her mouth with his finger and then spreading light kisses on her cheeks, tasting her flesh with the tip of his tongue. Oh, surely this was heaven.

He lingered longer over each kiss. And he was certain that he heard her whisper, "Lucifer, my love."

The intensity of his desire grew, and slowly, slowly, he began the process of unbuttoning her nightdress. It was awkward, his fingers so large, the buttons so small. Even in the dim darkness he could see through the thin cloth dark nipples needing to be sucked.

With the risk of awakening her—his confidence of success in the seduction having risen—he took a nipple between his teeth and began teasing it through the thin cloth with his tongue. He heard a deeper groan, and then her small hands pushed his big head away and began unbuttoning the small buttons herself.

His lordship could not believe his good fortune, for it was plain to him that his wife was fast asleep.

More sure of himself than ever, the seduction became more intense. Brazenly, he kissed her, and when she kissed him back, letting her tongue lock with his, all caution went out the window and his hands moved over her, caressing her warm flesh, squeezing and fondling her full, ripe breasts. Then he sucked them until her breath came in soft gasps and her body writhed in invitation for him to take her.

She wanted him, he was sure of that, as much as he wanted her. He kissed her throat and felt the pounding of her heart. Her little moans of pleasure filled his head.

How the hem of his wife's gown moved up around her waist, Lord Castleberry would later try to remember but never could, and how the coverlet ended up on the floor at the end of the bed would always be a mystery to him. But he would never forget the perfection of her shapely thighs in the shadow of the lone candle, or how she arched to meet his thrusts, or how he felt when he spilled his seed into her. Pure ecstasy screamed through his pulsating body, and the thought of begetting an heir to his fortune never once entered his mind.

Olivia lay for a long time, a willing prisoner in her husband's arms, feeling his warm breath on her cheek, and then hearing the soft snoring. She smiled to herself. He loved her as she loved him. They would have a wonderful life together. From this night forward, his desires, his needs, would take priority over her writing. She would be a good wife to him . . . satiated, she lay quietly in his arms, not moving, not wanting to awaken him from his peaceful sleep.

How wonderful their lovemaking had been. He had taken her before, in her dreams, but this was real, and he would always be beside her, and she could reach out in the night and touch him, mayhap arouse his passion when he had just finished practicing his art of seduction. Then their passion would last the night . . . until death did them part, as the vicar had said.

As the candle flickered its last flick and died into the room's darkness, sleep finally claimed her ladyship, a deep, satisfying sleep that lasted long past first light. The arms of the man she loved held her, and would hold her for the rest of her life. Never had she been so happy, so totally satisfied in every way. And it had taken her husband to prove the wonder of true love to her; no book she had ever read had spoken of such ecstasy.

Such were Lady Castleberry's thoughts, but when she became fully awake, warm sunlight streaming across her bed and thoughts of Lady Jacqueline as far away as the ocean was wide, the space beside her was empty. Her husband was gone. The coverlet was back on the bed, its satin edge tucked snugly under her chin. On the bedside table was a glass of brandy along with the notepad on which she had been writing last evening when she fell asleep.

She reached for the pad and read the unfamiliar script: "Please send for me when you awaken. We must talk."

The signature was a huge *F,* she supposed for Fitzgerald. How odd, she thought, how cold and impersonal after last night. Something was not right.

Straightening her nightdress, she bounded out of bed and went to pull the bell rope, twice, the second time to signify emergency. By the time the last button on her gown's bodice was buttoned, Lizzie was bobbing before her and looking as pleased as a cat who had just caught a mouse.

"At your service, Lady Castleberry. Do you need help

with a bath? And I can dress your hair. 'Tis a mess. I hear his lordship returned to Robinbrook in the middle of the night."

The maid's face was wreathed in a sly grin as her gaze moved to the tumbled bed holding two pillows, both obviously having been slept on. The white nightcap was in plain view.

"No, I don't need help with a bath, and never you mind about my hair," Olivia said, a sharpness in her voice she did not intend. The poor maid was not responsible for Lord Castleberry's actions. Imagine leaving his wife to greet the day alone after such a wonderful night of intimacy.

Lovemaking on her part; lust on his. No gentleman in love would leave his wife to awaken in a silent room . . . with stale brandy on the table beside her bed.

"Then what do you want?" asked Lizzie. "That good-for-nothing lady's maid of yours, that one from America, has gone into town again. She heard that supplies were being sent for, and she decided to ride along. If I was you, I'd send her packing and get me a good English maid."

"Oh, shut up, Lizzie. I don't need your advice. Would you find Lord Castleberry and tell him that I am in need of his company. I'll hurry and get dressed. Have coffee and breakfast brought—"

"For two?"

"I don't know whether he's had his breakfast or not. Most likely so, but have a pot of coffee brought. And an extra cup. The small dining room off the sitting room should be very pleasant at this time of morning."

Lizzie left quickly, and Olivia managed a smile when she thought of Alicia Rose, who was worthless as a servant, even a pretend one. Mayhap this morning she would tell Lord Castleberry that Alicia Rose was her sister and ask that she take her proper place in the household.

Olivia made short shrift of her bath, finishing the complete toilette in less than fifteen minutes. Lord Castleberry's note bothered her immensely. No, that was not the proper phraseology, she told herself. The note made her angry, and she wanted to hear its meaning from his own mouth.

Mayhap he wanted to talk with her about setting the business arrangement of their marriage aside, that they would from now on live a normal married life. Their marriage had been consummated, and an annulment was now impossible. But, even so, she could not imagine *wanting* to set the marriage aside after last night. As full recollection of their wonderful lovemaking hit her, she hugged herself and looked in the gold-framed mirror at her flushed face and sparkling eyes. Remembering made her breasts throb and the nipples harden. It was so wonderful to be in love.

I will tell his lordship that I prefer he wake me before he leaves my bed. 'Twas rather startling to wake and find him gone.

After rubbing her naked body dry as a powder puff with a thick towel, Olivia chose one of her prettiest morning dresses to wear on this special day, a green sprigged muslin with small puffed sleeves that barely cupped her shoulders. The skirt fell straight from its high waist under her bosom to the top of her half-boots. Lastly, she entwined into her red-brown hair an inch-wide green riband, leaving curly tendrils loose to frame her face. Pushing her anger aside, she entered the sitting room, now her and Lord Castleberry's parlor, walking lively and feeling rather spry. He would be there any moment, and she was most eager to see the satisfied look on his face. He might even open his arms in a bold fashion and embrace her, although she had heard that husbands were not quick to show affection. Well, that would not be true in her marriage.

"Oh, there you are," she heard him say as the door opened and he entered the room.

"Yes, and I've dressed especially for you. Once you said this was your favorite morning dress. When my new wardrobe is finished, I'm sure you'll have a favorite among those gowns as well."

He took her hand and kissed its palm, but there was no embrace. "I trust you slept well."

"I did, and I slept overlate." Smiling so that he would know she was teasing, she added, "And I'm piqued with you, your lordship, for leaving without greeting me in the appropriate fashion."

"What do you mean, appropriate fashion? I left you brandy."

Olivia frowned. Her husband was not acting at all like a new husband who had shared his wife's bed only hours earlier, and in a very romantic way. "You weren't drunk, were you?" she asked. "You do remember?"

"Remember what?"

"Surely you are funning. We consummated our marriage last night, and it can no longer be set aside."

"I thought you were asleep—"

Olivia gave an unbelieving laugh. "Do you think I could sleep through losing my virginity? I thought your prowess as a seducer quite extraordinary, certainly not something one could sleep through. I just did not feel the use for words."

He grinned wryly. "I take that as a compliment, but we must talk. I want to be perfectly honest with you about our arrangement. The plan has changed. We shall have a *ton* marriage."

"That sounds ominous to me. Are you going to tell me that you are still in love with Lady Jacqueline, that coming to my bed was merely physical release . . . a bestial act . . . like a rutting sheep in heat?"

"Olivia! You have such a way of expressing yourself. A lady of quality does not talk in such a manner. Sometimes I think those books you read tell you more than you need to know."

Olivia felt her voice break when she next spoke, and then

anger came forward to dull the pain. She lifted her small, obdurate chin. "Mayhap you should read a few books on the psychology of the human spirit. It can be crushed . . . if one will allow it."

He reached to take her arm. "I would never hurt you. You are very dear to me, in a way. Last evening something happened that caused *our* plan to change. I would like to explain."

"How could *our* plan change when I knew nothing about your intention of changing it?"

Just then a footman brought the breakfast tray laden with food, a silver pot of coffee, and two fine china cups and saucers. "You ordered breakfast, m'lady."

"Yes. Please place it on the table in the small dining room," Olivia said, and the footman carried the tray to the sunny room, then departed quickly, as if the atmosphere, which was so coldly thick that one could cut it with a knife, were too much for him to bear.

"I'd rather the servants did not know," said Lord Castleberry.

"Did not know what? That you took me when you did not love me . . . that . . . that you're still in love with that . . . that lightskirt?"

"Please, Olivia, be rational. Come, sit, and eat your breakfast. We can talk over our coffee. I see that you ordered two cups. I find you very thoughtful."

"Thoughtful indeed! I let a heartless, rutting jackanapes make love to me."

"I hope you are with child—"

"With child? Now I know you have windmills in your head. Our agreement does not mention a child."

"That's just it, Olivia. That agreement is null and void. We are truly husband and wife in the *ton*nish fashion. I would like to speak with you, if you will only settle down and listen. I think you will like what I have to say."

He guided her to the table, pulled out her chair, and carefully seated her. And then he poured two cups of coffee, steaming hot. Taking his place opposite her, he smiled at her over the cup's rim, waited a moment, and then began.

"When I was in town, making arrangements to introduce you into society, I received an urgent message to return to Robinbrook at once, which I did, almost killing my horses in the effort."

Lord Castleberry quickly decided not to tell his wife of Fred's, Lady Patience's, and the old doctor's charade of pretending his grandfather was dying. That Cousin Trevor had been practically paying his addresses to Olivia was of much more importance.

Olivia sat quietly, waiting, expressionless, seething with anger. And with pain. The scent of the food in front of her repulsed her sensibilities. As did the man across from her. The man she thought she loved. The man who had taken her in the night, praying she was asleep.

"I was quite concerned to learn that Cousin Trevor had been entertaining my wife in my absence," Lord Castleberry continued. "I forbid that to happen again. I have finally come to accept my grandfather's belief that Trevor has only one thought in mind, and that is to inherit my estate, along with the earldom. Right now . . . or until last night, he was the only heir."

Suddenly it all became perfectly clear to Olivia. Her husband had used her as if she were a dumb animal, for breeding purposes, without emotion and feeling. And she had loved him so much. When a tear crept to the corner of her eye, she angrily dashed it away. She would not be a simpering wife. She glared at the man across from her. Lucifer, a heartless, cold, calculating man. How could she have believed he cared for her? Any moment horns would sprout from his head. "My plan has changed as well. I plan to divorce you."

"Divorce me? Do you know how difficult a divorce is in England? A rarity. Parliament has to be petitioned—"

"Then I shall petition Parliament. I have grounds, for you're a despicable monster . . . a rutting sheep . . . a liar of the first water."

"You've already called me a rutting sheep," Lord Castleberry said. "And I've not tried to deceive you. From the start you have known that I'm very much in love with Lady Jacqueline, but that does not preclude our being married and having a child."

"I'd rather die than have a child by you, your lordship," she said so angrily that she, without realizing the consequences of what she was doing, or not caring a whit, flung the cup of hot coffee straight at those cold, penetrating blue eyes, regretting only that he ducked just in time to keep from being scalded. The fine china cup splintered into small pieces against the wall.

"I . . . I want you to have my heir," he said. "Won't you let me explain?"

"Let Lady Jacqueline have your heir. 'Tis not unheard of for a bastard to inherit. Just remember this, Lord Fitzgerald Castleberry, I will never be your broodmare."

Flinging herself from the room, Olivia stopped only long enough to take a silver candlestick and decapitate Lady Jacqueline's statue, and she laughed with mirthless glee as the blond wig departed from the head, which bounced across the room and hit the far wall with a loud thump.

Twenty

Back in her own rooms, Olivia grabbed the bell rope and pulled it twice, and Lizzie appeared almost before the rope settled. "Yes, m'lady." She bowed deeply.

"Where were you, hiding outside the door?" Olivia said. "And where is Alicia Rose? I want her to wait me." The sound of her waspish voice resounded in Olivia's own ears, and she was instantly sorry. Poor Lizzie could not help that she had married a cold-hearted, arrogant pretense of a man.

"Alicia Rose's not back, m'lady. I told you she's gone to the village for supplies."

"As soon as she returns, tell her I want to see her right away, and in the meantime, bring me a hammer and some nails. Twenty of them."

The maid's eyes grew big in her dark face. "Twenty hammers? M'lady, have you lost your senses?"

"No, I want one hammer and twenty nails. And yes, I did lose my senses, but only momentarily. I'm perfectly sane now."

Plainly Lizzie doubted that, and she left in such a hurry, rustling in her bombazine, she forgot to bob. "Be right back."

Olivia did not give a whit what Lizzie thought. Grabbing her pad of paper and feather quill from her writing desk, she began writing, and she wrote without letup, words flowing from the quill until she had filled five pages with her rage.

*The devil man wanted her to have his child, not be-
cause he loved her, but because it was imperative that
an heir to his great fortune be produced. A son to inherit his title. She could not imagine having a child by
a man who did not love her; a child should be conceived from love between two caring people. The ar-
rogance of his lordship, she thought as anger roiled
up inside her like a red mist . . .*

Olivia felt better when she was through, and she probably
would not have stopped the pouring-out of her soul had not
Lizzie returned with the hammer and nails. "I couldn't find
twenty. Will twelve do? Chester helped me look."

Chester was the backward boy who had come to Robinbrook, said he was hungry, was fed, and then had stayed
on. In Lord Castleberry's absence, Olivia had attempted to
teach the boy to read and do figures. Suspecting that a need
for eyeglasses was his problem, she had intended to speak
with his lordship about taking him into the village and having his eyes checked by a physician. Now she wasn't speaking to Lord Castleberry—ever again.

She wondered if mayhap Trevor would take Chester into
the village. She would ask him, she mused, smiling as she
remembered her husband's words regarding his cousin. How
ridiculous to think Trevor would harm anyone. He had
shown kindness to her only because he thought she might
be lonely with her husband gone.

"Now that you have the hammer and nails, m'lady, what
do you plan to do with them?" Lizzie asked.

"Never you mind, busybody. Go watch for Alicia Rose.
I need her badly."

"What can she do for you that I can't do?" Lizzie wanted
to know. "You know I can see your future, and what you're
going to do won't work. That big man can break down any
door he pleases."

"Out, out," Olivia said. "And don't come back until I

send for you, and I don't want to hear any more about your seeing into my future. No one can do that except God."

"My grandmother read palms."

"That doesn't mean you can. Now go."

"Yes, m'lady." Once more a contrite maid, Lizzie bobbed and left quietly.

"That girl has more curiosity than anyone I've ever known, unless it might be Alicia Rose," Olivia said to the room as she took up the hammer and nails and went into her bedchamber. There, even though she knew the lock was no deterrent to Lord Castleberry, she locked the door that separated her quarters from those of her husband and began hammering nails into the beautifully carved mahogany. His lordship would never again steal into her bed in the middle of the night and catch her unawares. Three nails, then four, went through the wood into the framing on the other side, without her smashing a finger. She was quite proud of herself. Before she had discovered books, her father had given her a block of wood along with a small hammer and a sack of nails for her birthday, and he had been pleased when she had learned so quickly to hit the nail square on its head without smashing a finger.

"Who taught you to use a hammer and nails? Ladies of quality know how to sew pretty stitches, not how to nail doors shut."

The voice came from behind, causing Olivia to whip around to confront the devil man who had taken advantage of her only a few hours earlier.

He *had* taken advantage of her, she fumed silently. By the time she was awake enough to know what was happening, she was so full of desire that she willingly gave herself to him, not only her body, but her heart. She was not really sure about her soul. She might have a smidgen of that left. For sure she had her American fighting spirit. Ignoring her visitor, she unceremoniously took up another nail and hammered it into the door.

His lordship's voice was stern. "Olivia, stop that hammering and listen to what I have to say."

"I care not a whit about being one of your simpering ladies of quality. Now that you say there can be no annulment, as our agreement clearly states, I want a divorce."

"A divorce in England is beyond the pale. You would be disgraced. As would I. I don't think either of us want our names bandied about in the press as being among the Great Unwashed—"

"Speak for yourself." Olivia raised the hammer for another blow at the nailhead, but his lordship's big hand grasped her wrist and held it in midair. "I said we must talk. Now, will you put down the silly hammer, or must I force you to sit and listen?"

A tear trickled down Olivia's cheek, and she silently swore at it. She did not want his lordship to know that she would shed one tear over him, so how could she wipe it without his seeing her.

With his free hand, using his long fingers, he took the tear away. "I'm not the devil man you think I am, Olivia, or the Lucifer you write about. And as far as last night—"

"Don't you dare mention last night to me again . . . ever. I was a fool. It did not happen. Do you hear?"

"I hear. But it did happen. A wonderful, lovely experience. 'Tis not your fault that my heart is committed to another. That does not preclude our having a child together."

"I wouldn't have a child by you if you were the last man on earth."

Olivia glared at him, and he smiled at her in his charming, wry manner. Taking the hammer from her, he laid it aside. "After last night, I'm sure that is beyond our control. A child has been started. I came to you last night especially to create an heir. I have no doubt—"

"I do. I shall will it not to happen. When and if I should have a child, it will be out of love, not to create an heir to your precious title."

"Willing yourself not to be *enceinte* is not the way it happens, Olivia. Once the seeds are joined, 'tis too late. Wishing, willing, praying, will not stop the child from growing inside you. I'm sure your mother explained that to you, or mayhap you've read about the reproduction process."

"My mother never told me anything about anything, especially having babies, but I have read medical books. And I know that I am not *enceinte.*"

They were by now in the sitting room of Olivia's quarters. Lord Castleberry had gently guided her to a chair, and he had taken a place on the deep plush sofa. He had thought to have her sit beside him, but he did not trust himself. Last night had not in any way diminished his desire to make love to her again and again. It was incredibly insane. Forcing his thoughts back to the business he wished to discuss so that he would not be distracted, he looked over her shoulder and stared through the window at the lapping sea, shimmering like undulating blue velvet under the bright morning sun. And then he began again: "Lady Castleberry—"

His words were cut off.

"Pray, do not call me that," she said with all the authority at her command. "I'm Olivia. I am not your wife."

Lord Castleberry could see that his wife was teetering on the edge of hysteria, and he could hardly blame her. He had been most unfair. Thinking it impossible to have a productive discussion with her in her present state, he went to pull the bell rope, and when a servant appeared, he ordered fresh coffee and scones with jelly. And then, leaning back on the sofa, he took his gold snuffbox from his waistcoat pocket and pulled in a deep sniff while taking note that the window coverings were old, faded, and blue. As in his own sitting room, Lady Jacqueline's pink had been replaced with the originals, and he had to admit the change made him feel quite comfortable. He tried another smile, his eyes seeking hers.

She did not smile back, and when he said, "I consider

you one of my best friends, Olivia. That is a great plus in a marriage," she retorted with utmost exasperation. "How thick is your skull, Lord Castleberry? I've already announced to you that it is my intent to divorce you as quickly as possible."

"Dear, dear Olivia, the most expensive commodity in England is a divorce, and you have no money. Unless your father can sell more of his first editions, and I doubt that he would consider a divorce for his daughter a just cause."

Olivia sat forward so quickly, she almost spilled from her chair. "How do you know about that?"

"My cousin. In a missive he wrote the day following your departure from the Colonies. He was very thorough in his investigation. By the bye, why did you not tell me that Alicia Rose is your sister, and that Mr. Pembroke sent her along to protect you." Trying for a little levity, he laughed heartily. "As if you, with your temper, would ever need protecting."

Olivia started to lie about her father's financial situation, but saw the futility of it. Lord Castleberry was right; she had little money . . . until her manuscript sold. So mayhap she should listen to the devil man's proposition. He'd said the plan had been changed. "Without asking me," she muttered through clenched teeth. So typical of a man, she thought. Now she knew why she had always preferred books to the evil creatures.

The tray holding tea, scones, and jelly was brought by a footman, who was dismissed by Lord Castleberry as soon as the tray was placed on a table beside Olivia's chair.

"Yes, your lordship," the footman said, bowing as he backed out of the room.

"I think I shall pour," Lord Castleberry said when he and his wife were alone. "I don't trust you not to try to scald me."

"You deserve to be scalded. Anyone can be truthful—"

"That is true, that is true. So why did you deceive my

cousin with iodine freckles, and with hair that looked like a bushel basket on your head?"

"Mr. Emry said you wanted a homely wife."

"And I do, or did. Now I find that of little importance. In truth, now that we will remain husband and wife, I appreciate your beauty." He poured two cups of coffee, handed one to Olivia, proffered the plate of scones smeared with jelly, then returned to his seat on the sofa, coffee cup in hand.

"Are you a liar along with all your other character flaws?" Olivia asked. "You purposely broke our business agreement."

"I'll admit, dear Olivia, the marriage was consummated on purpose. It is not unheard of for a man and woman to marry, produce an heir, and then go their separate ways."

"You mean you will have your mistress and I will have my lover. How utterly disgusting!"

His lordship determinedly plunged on: "Your allowance will be considerable; in fact, it will be unlimited. You may send blunt home to your parents. London society will be at your feet. Alicia Rose can have a grand come out. I shall purchase a handsome town house. You may visit the jewelers anytime you please. . . ."

And who will love me? Olivia remembered the linen handkerchief she had purchased for him, foolishly dreaming that he would come home loaded with thoughtful little gifts for her. She had told Cousin Trevor as much.

She thought about the book Trevor had bought for her, and how she loved it. But she would have loved it more had her husband bought it for her. She sipped her coffee and looked around the room. Anything not to look at *him*. At last she said, "I suppose Lady Jacqueline, when she tires of the old man, will become your mistress, and I'm fairly sure Cousin Trevor will become my lover. He seems more than willing, and he is kind and thoughtful. While you were gone, my happiness seemed to be all that mattered to him.

As a welcome gift to Robinbrook, he gave me Jane Austen's latest book."

Anger flamed Lord Castleberry. Cousin Trevor would *not* become his wife's lover. He slammed to his feet and stared down at her, his hands clenched at his sides as he fought between the desire to take her to his bed or her bed, since the door was now nailed shut between their quarters, or to strangle her.

He did neither.

Instead, realizing she was using Cousin Trevor to bait his anger, he informed her in a very authoritative way that she would listen to what he had to say, and then she could make any threat she wished to make.

"I'm not an unreasonable man, Olivia. It was never my intent to deceive you. Something beyond my control seemed to take over."

My desire to make love to you became stronger than my will, he silently admitted, cursing himself. The last thing he wanted was to hurt this sweet American girl who had trusted him enough to come all the way across the ocean to become his wife. And she had been an innocent; he'd learned that when he bathed after their lovemaking. Blood had been on his thighs. Yet, in the throes of their passionate coupling, she had not cried out in pain. What kind of cur was he?

But he really had intended her to be his wife in name only. Yes, things certainly had gotten out of hand.

"Olivia, don't ever think that last night was not wonderful for me. I pray that you are with child."

"I'm not," she said determinedly, still staring at an insignificant object across the room, seeing nothing.

Lord Castleberry sighed deeply. "A compromise can be reached, I am sure."

"The only compromise I'm willing to make is that I be granted an immediate divorce. I'll sue that you bear the expense—"

"Parliament would laugh at you, Olivia. I don't want a divorce."

He was right, of course, she thought. It was a man's world, and it seemed that a woman was allowed to live in it only for his pleasure. She turned her face away so he could not see the tears that blinded her gray-green eyes. The pain she felt was not because he would not allow her to divorce him, but because he did not love her.

Twenty-one

It was over—the conversation, the plan, all that Lord Castleberry had had to say had been said, and now Olivia was pacing the floor, waiting for Alicia Rose to return from her outing. An outing was all that it was, for she had no business traipsing off to the village with the household help going for supplies, Olivia complained. But moments later, when Alicia Rose burst into the room saying "You'll never guess where I've been," Olivia was so glad to see her that instead of scolding her, she ran and hugged her.

"I know where you've been. Right now I must talk with you. I've told Lord Castleberry that I plan to divorce him . . . but I have no money and will have to wait until my manuscript sells."

"A divorce! Have you gone addle-pated? Women of quality don't get divorced, not even in America," Alicia Rose said. She took Olivia by the arm and felt her trembling. "Oh, this is serious. Come sit, sister. I want to know the whole of it. I can see you are wretched. What happened? Talking will calm you down and make you feel better."

They sat on the sofa, Olivia demure and proper, red spots on her cheeks showing her anger, strangled words showing her pain. Alicia Rose took her hand and held it. "What happened, Olivia. I'm concerned about you."

Olivia began: "Our marriage has been consummated, there can be no annulment as the business agreement states. Divorce is all that is left. His lordship stole into my bed—

because his grandfather was pretending to be near death and saying he did not want to die until there was an heir to Robinbrook. My husband knew it was a hoax, but he acquiesced, he said, because it was so important to Fred."

"You could have kicked him out, Olivia. Surely he didn't take you against your will. His lordship is an honorable man. I'm certain of that."

"Alicia Rose, you're too practical. Of course I could have kicked him out of my bed . . . but, in truth, I did not want to." Olivia could feel her face flush hot with embarrassment.

"Olivia, this is perfect. You're in love with him, and of course you wanted him in your bed. And did I not tell you— let him make love to you and you would no longer be his wife in name only? Olivia! I don't take your meaning. You can't divorce Lord Castleberry; you love him, and besides that, you will be ostracized from society . . . you'll be disgraced."

Olivia gave a small laugh that failed to wipe away the pain. "He only wants me to have an heir to his fortune, and his title. His intent was to use me to make Lady Jacqueline jealous so that she would return to him and beg for forgiveness. He has this wonderful ball planned, and she is expected to be there. We, his lordship and I, are to act totally devoted to each other, and jealousy is *supposed* to bring her straight back into his arms. He will take her, of course, as his mistress, and they will live happily ever after. While I have the legitimate heir. And he said after that I could take a lover. But it can't be his cousin Trevor."

"I still think it's wonderful, Olivia. You're so much in love with him. I can see it in your eyes. It's even in your voice when you say his name. And I just believe that love will win out."

"I hate him, oh, I do, Alicia Rose. He's the devil incarnate. His plan is disgusting. It seems his heart is committed to Lady Jacqueline, his first love. His mother loved only once, so he feels the same destiny is his as well."

Olivia stopped for a moment before going on. "He still plans to have this wonderful ball, and he expects me to hide all this behind a facade of happiness. I will be sick, I know I will."

Alicia gave Olivia's hand a sisterly squeeze. "No, you won't. You'll pretend, just as he wants you to do. While we're in London—and I do plan to go with you as your abigail—we'll inquire about Jane Austen. She might even be invited to the ball. Better still, ask your husband to see that she's invited. See, Olivia, there might be some advantage to being married to nobility. It just might help you get your stories published. Until you can sell your manuscript and become rich in your own right, there's not much else you can do."

"I know you're right, Alicia Rose, but it will be so hard to pretend I'm happy, and I fear when I see this Lady Jacqueline, I shall be tempted to strangle her."

"I'll help you. Isn't that one of the duties of a faithful abigail?"

Olivia sat forward on the sofa. She was so glad their papa had insisted Alicia Rose go to England with her. What would she have done without her? "Oh, Alicia Rose, I forgot a most important part. Lord Castleberry knows you are my sister, has known it almost from the start. His cousin, Mr. Emry, the lawyer, even wrote about Papa selling his first editions to pay your way to England. Now, according to his lordship's plan, you are to take your rightful place in the household, have your own quarters, your own maid, a new wardrobe, and later you will be presented to London society, where you'll meet the *ton,* and all that rubbish."

"You mean I can go husband-hunting."

"Most likely so, one who will want you to produce an heir to inherit his estate, along with his title. And then you'll be free to take a lover." Olivia could not keep the sarcasm from her words.

"You may tell his lordship that I will choose my own husband, thank you," said Alicia Rose. "But I will take my own quarters, and my own maid. I think I shall rather enjoy being one of the upper orders."

This made Olivia laugh, and it felt good to laugh. Alicia Rose could always see the brighter side of things. Perchance they *would* meet Miss Austen in London. If her husband wanted her to pretend, then she would pretend, until she could get out of this bumble broth she had created for herself.

But there would be no more night rendezvous for the purpose of creating an heir. She would not be used. And she would stop loving the monster . . . and she would somehow stop her heart from breaking. Writing was the answer, she told herself. She would pour her heart into her writing.

Just then someone knocked on the door. Not Lizzie, Olivia quickly discerned, for Lizzie had a distinctive rap that almost ordered the door to open and let her in.

"Come in," Olivia said to the knocker.

It was Aunt Evaline, standing erect, with her head at that certain angle Olivia had recognized her first night at Robinbrook. In the old woman's graying hair were the red silk roses Olivia had bought for her when Trevor had taken her into Hythe. Before Olivia could invite the old woman to enter her sitting room, Aunt Evaline was walking down the long halls, reciting her pronouncement: "His lordship, my nephew, has instructed me to find quarters for Alicia Rose. It seems she's not your abigail after all, but your sister. I don't approve of subterfuge."

"Nor do I," Olivia said, "and I've found plenty since coming to Robinbrook. My father insisted that Alicia Rose come along to protect me." She gave a little laugh. "Mayhap he was wise."

Olivia heard a distinct giggle coming from Alicia Rose, and then her sister was saying, "I don't need my own quarters. Olivia and I have always shared a suite of rooms, and I think that will suit just fine here at Robinbrook. I'll just move across the hall, and Lizzie can have my maid's room."

Aunt Evaline's eyes looked as if they might pop out of her head. Her brow shot up, and her shoulders squared in a haughty manner. "I'm sure Lord Castleberry would take umbrage to sharing quarters with his wife's sister."

Alicia Rose stepped forward to stand beside Olivia. "Oh, but his lordship will not be sharing this suite of rooms. Olivia has nailed the door shut between her bedchamber and his quarters. And as soon as my sister's writings sell, she will be divorcing Lord Castleberry."

Olivia was tempted to kick Alicia Rose's shin. Instead, she reached out to steady Aunt Evaline, who let out a small gasp and looked as if she would faint dead away in a spell of the vapors. The word "divorce" came out in a whisper.

"Aunt Evaline, Alicia Rose and I are quite busy at the moment. Later Lizzie can show Alicia Rose different quarters. I'm sure there's one in Robinbrook's labyrinth of rooms that will suit."

"Lizzie," exclaimed the old woman. "She doesn't have the keys. They are in my keeping. When certain rooms need cleaning, I open the doors."

"Well, that will be changed," said Olivia. "I shall appoint a head housekeeper to take care of such menial chores so that you will have more time for your stitching. Opening doors to be cleaned should have never been put on your aristocratic shoulders. 'Tis not the thing, as I've heard you English say."

"Oh, but that is the way I want it."

"As I said, Aunt Evaline, that will be changed. Since I am Lord Castleberry's wife, I shall now be the mistress of Robinbrook. Now, if you will excuse me, I have many things to do. I have not yet written my pages for the day."

"There's never been a divorce in the Castleberry family, and why are you trying to take over if you plan to disgrace us all?"

The old woman rolled her eyes back in their sockets and tilted her head up, as if in supplication to a higher power.

"If only Lady Jacqueline had not acted so rashly, and then his lordship. He was a fool to marry an American. They would have never run off to that wild place had they wanted to conform to English ways."

"I agree, Aunt Evaline, but 'tis done. The colonists were a stubborn lot. I'll most likely remove the nails. You know new brides . . . in a moment of pique I threatened divorce."

The old woman sighed deeply. "No, I've never been a bride. If Mr. Appleby hadn't died . . . but angry words would have never been exchanged between us. Never. And I would have never nailed my bedchamber door closed. Not to my Mr. Appleby, I wouldn't. And I pray that you will think before you bring disgrace down on Robinbrook." Shaking her head worriedly, she repeated, "There's never been a divorce in the Castleberry family."

"Yes, I know. Now, as I said, Alicia Rose and I have some things to do before she goes looking for quarters. But there is one more thing—I will not tolerate Lady Jacqueline's name bandied about in my presence. The mere mention of her name makes me ill."

Aunt Evaline turned to leave, tottering down the hall, shaking her head. Olivia could hear her muttering to the empty hall, "I'll tell Fitzgerald right away. I can't believe . . . surely he can find a way to get rid of this American. . . ."

"Olivia, I can't believe you stood up to that old woman," Alicia Rose said as soon as the door was closed. She was laughing. "I'll write Papa today and tell him that you don't need me to protect you from the Castleberrys."

"I don't think that was what Papa had in mind. I'm certain it had something to do with why the Pembrokes left

England. This day I learned that our real name is Pemberton, not Pembroke. That's the name our ancestors took when they migrated to America."

"How did you learn that?" Olivia asked.

"When I went into Hythe, while Nelson was buying supplies for Cook, I inquired around, asking if anyone knew or had heard of the Pembrokes. It seems that one of our ancestors was hanged at Newgate. That's why Papa turned pale when he learned you were to marry an English lord."

"Won't the *ton* just love that juicy bit of gossip," Olivia said thoughtfully.

"I don't think they'll know, and that is one thing I will keep secret."

"I'm glad for that," retorted Olivia. "You should not have told Aunt Evaline about the divorce."

Alicia Rose giggled. "She should not have spoken so disdainfully about Americans. I happen to think the Pilgrims were a brave lot."

"I suppose, since we won our independence, 'tis only natural Aunt Evaline resents us. Or mayhap it's because she's so fond of Lady Jacqueline. And because the Pembrokes are not of the nobility."

"Oh, but the Pembertons were of the nobility. The old man on the bench in the park—that's where I got all this information—said so. And he was the only person with whom I talked who knew anything about the Pembertons going to America and changing their name to Pembroke. And he's as old as God and looked as if tomorrow would be his last day on earth. No one was about to hear our conversation. I didn't tell him my name was Pembroke. Now that I think back on it, he didn't ask. And I didn't ask him his name. I wish that I had."

"I strongly recommend you let the subject drop. Do no more inquiring, and pray don't mention the name Pemberton to anyone. Please. Papa would want the family secret kept. We are Pembrokes, not Pembertons."

* * *

"You girls know how to stir up a hornet's nest." The door had opened without Lizzie's loud rap. She did, in her haste, manage to give a quick bob. "Robinbrook is at sixes and sevens. The old man's in the Hunt Room, and, your ladyship, he wants to see you immediately, if not sooner." She was looking askance at Olivia. Then, turning to Alicia Rose, she added, "I'm to help you find quarters. I knew you weren't no lady's maid. I knew that the minute I laid eyes on you. I told you I can see your future as plain as day. I have the gift."

"You are going to be burned at the stake if you don't stop talking like that," Alicia Rose said. "Don't you know witches get burned."

"I ain't no witch."

"Hush," ordered Olivia. "I need to think. Why does Fred wish to see me? Is Lord Castleberry about?"

"How am I to know why he wants to talk with you? They don't tell servants anything. It's up to us to find out, and, to tell the truth, I just didn't have time to fool around. And no, I didn't see hair nor hide of his lordship. Lady Patience was there, sitting close to the old man and looking as if she hadn't slept a wink all night."

"Why didn't you call on your gift to tell you what was going on?" Alicia Rose asked teasingly.

"I just told you I didn't have time. I have to be real quiet before the visions come."

"Stop the tomfoolery," Olivia again ordered. "And be about your business of finding rooms for Alicia Rose, Lizzie. If you're going to be a lady's maid, you must learn to take orders."

"Oh, I will, your ladyship. Did I not come straightaway to tell you Mr. Fred wants to see you? If I was you, I'd go quickly. He seemed serious to me."

"I will, in a minute," said Olivia, and then she went to

the looking glass and pinched her pale cheeks to give them color. Only a short time ago they were flushed with anger at her husband. She could not understand why her anger had faded so quickly, and then she remembered the wonders of last night, when he'd held her in his arms and made wonderful love to her, and he knew there was no mystery as to why her anger had so quickly vanished.

Twenty-two

Fred beamed a huge smile at Olivia when she entered the Hunt Room. She returned his smile, then greeted Lady Patience, who was sitting on a stool at his knees, holding on to his hand. A white afghan was draped around the old man's shoulders.

Olivia found herself a chair in proximity. The nine black-and-white spotted hounds were stretched out lazily in various areas of the room. Through the great expanse of windows, she could see the hillocks bathed in the April sun.

Aunt Evaline was nowhere to be seen.

"Lizzie said you wished to see me," Olivia said, directing the statement to both of them, for, in truth, they looked as one, sitting as close together as two people could without one being on top of the other. Envy filled her. She wondered what it would be like to be that close to another person. Oh, she had Alicia Rose, but that was different.

Fred spoke first: "I did send the maid to get you, and I'm glad you're here, Countess. My grandson tells me that it is your desire to start a family right away. I want to express my congratulations. Robinbrook needs an heir."

Olivia was quite taken aback, but surprise was the stronger emotion. Before she could stop herself, she blurted out, "Does not anyone around here keep a secret?"

Lady Patience laughed. "Not where an heir is concerned. That has been Fred's paramount concern for a long time, and when it became apparent that Trevor Castleberry was paying too much attention to you in Fitzgerald's absence, Fred panicked. I feared we were going to lose him, and I had him send for Fitzgerald right away, declaring it an emergency that he return to Robinbrook at once." She patted Fred's age-spotted hand and smiled adoringly up at him.

Olivia was beginning to get the rest of the picture, the part that Lord Castleberry had not told her. So he had come home at Fred's urgent request, and then he had, at Fred's urgent request, come to her bed to plant seed for an heir to his demme fortune. That was the part that hurt the most. How could he hold her and make her feel so wonderful . . . when all he wanted was to order an heir?

She stared unblinkingly at Fred, and a long silence stretched between them. At their first meeting he had mentioned her having an heir to Robinbrook as if she were some sort of breeding stock.

Standing so quickly she almost lost her balance, she pulled her gaze away from the hillocks and said in her staid Bostonian voice, "I fear you've been misinformed. When I have a dear, sweet baby, it will be conceived from love, not to keep some supposedly scurrilous cousin—your opinion, not mine—from inheriting my husband's fortune and his title. A pox on his lordship's wealth, and on his title, and on him. I hope Lord Castleberry told you that I plan to petition Parliament for a divorce as soon as my manuscript sells and I can gather the blunt. That's all that is stopping me from traveling into town this very day and starting the procedures."

She looked at Fred, who had gone deathly pale. Since you could not look at one without looking at the other, she saw Lady Patience's hand fly to her gaped mouth. Without waiting for a reply from either of them, she whipped quickly around and left the huge Hunt Room, breaking the loud silence with the flapping of her blue morning dress's skirt swishing against her red half-boots. The hounds' heads went suddenly up, but not one made a sound or moved a paw.

In the hall she slowed her pace only long enough to take from her bosom a delicate handkerchief and wipe tears and blow her nose. She swore, "Demme that Fitzgerald. How can anyone have such a mean heart? I was right when I called him Lucifer."

So intent was Olivia on venting her anger that she did not hear the footsteps behind her. It was only when Lady Patience called to her that she realized she was being followed and turned to the voice. "Olivia, dear Olivia," the woman was saying, "wait for me. We must talk. You are being very foolish."

Olivia laughed a cold, cynical laugh that echoed throughout the long hall. "Lady Patience, how many children have you had for the sole purpose of producing an heir? How many men have come to your bed on the demand from a daft old man who is obsessed with wealth and title succession? What if I should have a daughter? Would we drown her? A female can't inherit. What if . . ."

Lady Patience drew Olivia into her arms. "Give Fitzgerald a chance. He will come to love you. This . . . this Lady Jacqueline is a fantasy, a figment of his imagination. He could not possibly love her."

Olivia pulled away. "And how would you know that? He's besotted with her."

"All men are besotted at least once in their lifetime. It's just that Fitzgerald's besotting came a little late. The title settling on his shoulders at such a tender age, and his taking the responsibility so seriously, he hadn't had time to fall in love."

She began walking slowly alongside Olivia, going in the direction of Olivia's quarters. For a long time they did not talk. It was not Olivia's intent to tell Lady Patience, whom she liked very much, the pain that ripped her heart. Lady Patience was a kind woman, caring and thoughtful of others. Alice Pembroke instantly came to Olivia's mind. How different her life might have been had her mother been con-

cerned for her feelings. Had her mother not constantly reminded her that her birth had been an accident, that she
had never wanted to bear a child.

Every child should be born from love, thought Olivia.
She had not been, and she would not have a child to be
used. Oh, how she, at this moment, longed for her mother.
She corrected her thoughts—she longed for her mother to
be loving and caring, like Lady Patience.

"I don't love Lord Castleberry," Olivia said, crossing her
fingers for the lie, and when Lady Patience did not answer
except with a kind pat on Olivia's shoulder, Olivia went on
to explain. "Lord Castleberry and I married for the wrong
reasons, his to get back at Lady Jacqueline, and I only
wanted to come to England to meet the lady who wrote
Sense and Sensibility and *Pride and Prejudice.* Isn't that
ridiculous?"

"Love grows out of kindness and understanding, Olivia,
" ' Lady Patience at last said. " 'Tis not this hot flash in
the pan young lovers make it out to be."

"Is that what happened to you and Fred? Did you grow
into love?"

Olivia was curious, that was all. She had no hopes of
Lord Castleberry growing to love her, and she had no notion
of being kind and caring to him while he acted like a love-
sick calf over Lady Jacqueline. If necessary, she would hold
onto her anger, which shielded her from the incredible pain
that pierced her heart like a poisoned arrow. She laughed
without mirth. Was she one of those young lovers who was
experiencing a hot flash in the pan? She thought not. What
she felt for her husband was real, else she would simply
pick up a book and begin reading, losing herself in someone
else's world. And she would add to her voluminous manuscript. After the divorce she would devote all her time to
her writing.

"Olivia," Lady Patience said, breaking into Olivia's ru-
minations. "Fred is my dearest friend as well as the love

of my life. I made many foolish mistakes before he came along. I didn't realize that being friends should come before love. I had lovers, but not marriage. I never wanted marriage. Fred is a wise man. He took what I had to give, gave me time, and, yes, I did grow into love with him. I would marry him, but we are too old."

"What are you suggesting, that I wait until Lord Castleberry is as old as Fred, and then mayhap, just mayhap, he will fall in love with me . . . and want me for something other than to bear an heir for his demme title?"

"Oh, my, no. You and Fitzgerald are much too young for that. He's as any man his age, virile and wanting, and he doesn't recognize what a jewel he has for a wife. It's like he's just now coming into majority, and Lady Jacqueline got there before you did.

"What I'm suggesting is that you act as his friend, give him understanding. I know that you two spend time talking about books and world events. He's said as much, and there's always a light in those wonderful blue eyes when he speaks of your time together. He laughs when he calls you a bookworm, but I hear happiness in the laughter. Olivia, you are in love with your husband. Don't throw it away by divorcing him. Give him time. Not your body, if you don't want to. *That* should never be forced. But be his friend. Continue your talks with him; he's a lonely man. Go to this grand affair he is planning and let him show you off to that scapescull Lady Jacqueline."

They had reached Olivia's quarters, and she stood with her hand on the doorknob, not knowing what to say but loving Lady Patience for her sage words. A mother's words. She would think on them when she was alone. She told the older woman so, proffering a small hand.

But Lady Patience would have none of that. Again she drew Olivia to her, and, sighing deeply, said in a low, soft voice, "My dear, Fitz is in love with you. He's just not aware of it yet."

* * *

Lord Fitzgerald Castleberry rode Becket—named for Thomas Becket—at a fast gait over the winding trail that led to the farm steward's house. He had told Fred about the old king's illness, and he'd watched his dear old grandfather cry for a bit, and then the conversation had turned to cousin Trevor. It had not been a good morning, and it was about to get worse, thought his lordship.

He regretted what he had to do, but there was no other course he could take. Cousin Trevor would have to leave the estate. An excellent farm steward, his cousin would not be easily replaced. But, hopefully, another man could be trained.

"A pension for three years, giving Trevor time to relocate, will be sufficient," Lord Castleberry said aloud, angry that his hand had been forced but relieved that he had finally faced the treacherousness of Trevor Castleberry. Not only had his cousin attempted to poison him, he was now trying to take his wife. And Olivia had threatened to take cousin Trevor as her lover.

"You know I could not abide that," he said to the midnight-black horse.

Becket threw his head up and snorted as if he understood every word his master had said. Lord Castleberry, chuckling lightly, patted the horse's long, sleek neck. The weather was pleasant, the air fresh and sweet. He drew in a deep breath. All around him corn and wheat grew in abundance. In the far distance, sheep grazed on the verdant hillsides.

His night with Olivia was much on his lordship's mind. He was sure she had conceived. Never had he experienced such completeness, such extreme ecstasy, as he had when she gave herself to him with so much feeling. Once he thought he had heard her murmur she loved him. He did not want that to be so, for he could not return the love. Passion was not love, he told himself for the hundredth time. And she *had* been a virgin. In a way he felt like a cad of the first water.

His lordship smiled when he thought about the door with nails hammered through it. How easily it would break against his one hundred eighty plus pounds, he thought, almost planning to do just that. Almost, but not quite. His wife could be standing there with a hammer in her hand.

Reaching the house, he tethered Becket's ribbons to a drooping tree limb, then climbed the steps to knock on the door with the brass knocker. Almost instantly a liveried butler swung the door open, and upon seeing who was calling, bowed deeply.

"Your lordship, welcome."

"Would you tell cousin Trevor that I would like a word with him? In complete privacy."

Lord Castleberry felt awkward. He was not wearing a beaver to hand to the butler. It was not a friendly call, and he could not act friendly. Dressed informally, with an open collar, he ran his fingers through his longish black hair, stood erect, and strove not to scowl.

The butler bowed again. "Yes, m'lord. Immediately. In the meantime, would you care to wait in the receiving room. 'Tis quite comfortable."

"I'll find my way. I do not have time to waste. This is a business call."

Lord Castleberry reminded himself not to let his anger show, to be a gentleman at all costs. He would say what he had come to say quickly and then leave at once.

Leaving the spacious and grand foyer, with its red Chinese-silk-covered walls and high scrolled ceiling, he went into a room furnished with Chippendale chairs and sofas and sat down. He remembered when he'd had the house built to his cousin's specifications. He'd thought then that it was ostentatious, but having had only Fred for family, he had been eager to please his newly found cousin.

Having a place like this to live should be an incentive

for a qualified man to come to Robinbrook as the new farm steward, his lordship thought, tapping his booted toe on the thick carpet while he waited, fearing his impatience showed. Time dragged interminably.

When at last the farm steward did show, his air of truculent bravado was obvious to Lord Castleberry. That he had taken an excessive amount of time with his valet was also obvious. Dressed to the nines, his navy-blue cravat was perfectly creased, and not one strand of his sun-streaked brown hair was out of place.

Lord Castleberry stared at him for a moment, and for the first time he saw in Trevor's eyes the hidden treachery Fred had so often spoken about. In his demeanor was the look of smug satisfaction from having made his employer wait.

In that instant, inside Lord Castleberry's head something snapped. The calm, businesslike words flew out the window as anger slammed through him in fiery waves. "Trevor, I demand that you absent yourself from my estate by nightfall. One year's salary will be afforded you by my man of business, and a recommendation of your expertise in farming will accompany your departure with a warning that the employer should keep his wife from your presence."

Trevor laughed while his face took on the color of a funeral shroud. "Why, Fitz, you must be funning. I was just on my way to welcome you back to Robinbrook. Your little bride was so lonely and missed you so much, I spent time reassuring her of your love, devotion, and loyalty. I felt that I was doing you a favor. I assure you my intent was honorable. I fear that despicable Fred has been spreading lies."

Involuntarily Lord Castleberry's big hands curled into fists. He longed to smash that smug look from Trevor's face, but caught himself before taking the first step forward.

"Fred is my grandfather. There's nothing despicable about the dear old man. In truth, he's the wisest man I've ever known. He warned me from the time you appeared at Robinbrook that no good would come from you . . . ever.

Now, I know 'tis true. My words stand. You have until nightfall to vacate."

"But . . . Robinbrook is my right. I'm the rightful heir. You can't do this."

"Robinbrook is not your right, not unless I die without issue. I don't intend for that to happen. In truth, I'm certain my wife is already *enceinte.*"

It was only then that the words seemed to soak into Trevor's mind. A frightened look, then anger such as Lord Castleberry had ever seen, spewed from his eyes. They became hooded, and dark, and his countenance became distorted. "I'll see that you regret this. Just because you can't keep your wife happy in bed, pray don't take it out on me—"

He did not finish, for Lord Castleberry's big fist slammed into his mouth, knocking him over a chair, which tumbled backward and crashed to the floor, with Trevor sprawled spread-eagle on top of it. As his lordship quickly turned to leave, he heard swear words, threats, then strangled mumbling coming from the farm steward's mouth. Foul words such as his lordship had never uttered in the whole of his life. And then silence as Lord Castleberry let himself out the door through which he had, only a short time earlier, entered with the greatest bent on behaving as a refined gentleman of the upper orders.

Trevor Castleberry was silent. His anger was gone—for one could not think straight when one was angry. He began planning, and before the door had closed behind his titled cousin, he knew what he had to do to assure that someday Robinbrook would be his. Cynical laughter spilled out into the room. Alone, still sprawled over the chair, he mimicked Lord Castleberry. "In truth, I'm certain my wife is already *enceinte. . . .*"

Twenty-three

Aunt Evaline had been in bed three days when Olivia, wearing a faded "Boston" morning dress and red half-boots, went to her apartment to tell her she could have the running of Robinbrook back. From Lizzie she had learned the old woman was quite inconsolable and would most likely die if something wasn't done . . . and right away. It seemed to Olivia there had been nothing but havoc since she had arrived at Robinbrook, all because of her. She felt terrible about Trevor's firing, and she did not believe the careless raillery with which he had entertained her had been calculated. Now Lord Castleberry had gone into London to hire a replacement. There was an employment agency there, he had told her.

She should not have threatened to take the farm steward as her lover, she thought now. She would never even consider such a thing, not even when Lady Jacqueline returned to her husband's arms. But mayhap her guilt was misplaced, she mused as she made her way down yet another long hall toward Aunt Evaline's quarters; Fred had said he thanked God that his grandson had finally come to realize that the present heir to Robinbrook was a dangerous man who would let nothing, not even murder, stand in his way of inheriting Robinbrook. Oh, what a coil, she thought, and she was no nearer getting her writings published than when she lived in America.

Her steps quick, she reached Aunt Evaline's quarters with

alacrity and was invited in by Gloria, a tiny woman with a wizened face and graying hair, wearing black bombazine.

"She's not well at all," the little maid said. "I felt her forehead, and 'tis quite hot. I've requested the doctor return at once. I understand that three nights ago he was here most of the night with Mr. Fred."

A pang of sympathy for the old woman passed through Olivia. Running of Robinbrook and her talk of what might have been had Mr. Appleby not died was all Aunt Evaline had, and her stitching, which Olivia understood filled dozens of drawers. Her hope chest, Lizzie had said.

"I don't think the doctor will be needed," Olivia told the maid as she swiftly passed through the sitting room and made her way to the bedchamber, which was decorated in lovely shades of green and salmon silk. The same colors had been used for the bed hangings, dark green brocade embedded with salmon-colored cabbage roses.

Aunt Evaline wore a white nightcap, her old, wrinkled face as pale as a ghost's. She lay snuggled between white sheets, and she truly did look to Olivia as if she might be dying. For a moment Olivia was taken aback, but only for a moment, and she thought that practice made perfect, and she was certain the old woman had had plenty of practice in falling ill just to get her way at Robinbrook.

"Aunt Evaline, 'tis Olivia. I've come to tell you that I've re-thought my decision to become mistress of Robinbrook, that is, if you will consent to keeping the position. I'm far too busy with my writing. When callers call, you may receive them . . . unless they ask specifically to see me."

Aunt Evaline's faded eyes opened to narrow slits. "Oh, Countess Castleberry. You've come to visit me. I think I must be ready to pass over to the other side . . . to Mr. Appleby."

"Stuff! You're not going anywhere. Now, I suggest you get out of bed, let your maid help you dress, and then come

below stairs for breakfast. I thought I smelled ham and eggs
cooking on my way to your rooms. You know scents rise."

"And I love ham, my favorite for breakfast. But I feel so
weak, I could never make it below stairs."

"Well, that is the only way you will be having breakfast."
Olivia turned to the maid. "Food is not to be brought to
her. She's weak only because she's been in bed too long."

The maid bobbed. "Yes, m'lady." Her eyes darted from
Aunt Evaline to Olivia.

Olivia stroked Aunt Evaline's cheek tenderly. "Three days
wasted, when you could have been stitching." She laughed,
hoping for levity. "Or opening doors to rooms for maids
to clean."

Aunt Evaline's eyes were now fully open, staring quizzically at Olivia. "Mayhap you Americans aren't so bad after
all," she said with great solemnity. "I'll tell Fitzgerald that
mayhap he should keep you. A divorce for a Castleberry is
beyond the pale."

"Oh, don't bother yourself with giving my husband advice. He gets plenty of that from Fred. And don't count on
us Americans giving in to every little thing. Or every big
thing." Olivia paused, and then: "There's one thing about
which I am adamant. I will not have Lady Jacqueline mentioned in my presence. She's no longer in my husband's
life."

Olivia knew this was not true, and she felt that hot arrow
of hurt again shoot through her heart. Turning away so that
the old woman and the little maid could not see the tears
that had suddenly sprung to her eyes, she left the room
quickly and went in search of Alicia Rose, who had settled
in a suite of rooms in the west wing, with a wonderful view
of rolling hills.

Alicia Rose knew everything about everybody, having
learned it from Lizzie. Mayhap she would know when Lord
Castleberry would return to Robinbrook. The big old house
seemed empty without his huge, booming presence.

She found Alicia Rose dressed and ready to go below stairs, and Olivia noted that the purple and green riding habit she wore was two inches too short for her. "You need new clothes," Olivia said, "there's a little left of the money we brought from home. I suggest you use it to purchase at least decent riding clothes, and a gown or two."

Alicia Rose twirled around the room, then stopped to look up into the gilt-framed mirror over the fireplace. "This does look rather antiquated in this beautifully appointed room, doesn't it?"

"That's why I suggested you purchase something new."

The room held soft sofas and chairs in various shades of blue silk embroidered with birds in deeper shades of blue. A plush Persian carpet covered the floor, and lovely fringed blue silk draperies framed the many windows that opened onto the verdant hillocks.

"Don't you just love it?" squealed Alicia Rose. " 'Tis the grandest room I've ever seen. I had no trouble at all in my choice. All rooms we looked at were absolutely divine, but these must have been prepared for Princess Caroline. The bedchamber is just as lovely, don't you think? The bed hangings of ivory and blue are too perfect to describe in words. I just suck in my breath. That's the best I can do, and a big lump comes to my throat. I just want to lie in bed and stare at the grandness of it all, Olivia."

Alicia Rose's enthusiasm was catching, and Olivia's spirits were immediately lifted. "I feel better now that your pretense of being a lady's maid is over. Mayhap we can go into Hythe on the morrow and talk with the modiste."

"That's a capital idea," Alicia Rose said. "Now, without further roundaboutation, let's go to the Hunt Room and breakfast with darling Fred. We're to ride afterward, so he said last evening when I left him."

"Pray, just don't mention my plans for a divorce, or the old man will take to his bed again. 'Tis a problem keeping the old ones up and about when they don't get their way."

* * *

"I've come to deliver Countess Castleberry's new wardrobe," Madame Hazlitt told the butler, who bowed, and then, in his stately tread, walked toward the wide stairs that would take them to Olivia's quarters. Behind them came two footmen, carrying as many boxes as they could hold in their long arms.

"Seems you need a cart," the butler said without changing his straight-ahead stare. Just then Lizzie appeared and offered her services, and later, when Olivia unwrapped one package after another, she gasped, squealed with delight, and clapped her hands with glee.

At last Olivia opened the box that held a gown of pale green satin covered with tiny pearls, so beautiful that she almost went into a spell of vapors.

"Have you ever seen anything so beautiful?" Lizzie asked.

"Never," Olivia said, fingering the satin.

Standing nearby, with a pleased-as-punch look on her face, was the modiste. "Lord Castleberry insisted that I bring out this gown as quickly as possible so that if you wanted changes, there would be time to make them. And he wanted me to take your sister's measurements so that I could quickly sew a wardrobe for her. I understand she'll be going to the grand ball also. I brought copies of *La Belle Assemblée,* and swatches of fabric from which to choose. I pray she can decide this day. There's not much time. Less than a fortnight."

"Lizzie, go fetch Alicia Rose while I open the other boxes," Olivia said.

"I want to see," complained Lizzie, who had not become more docile or obedient since becoming a lady's maid. If anything, thought Olivia, she had shown more insolence, but in a mysteriously charming way, always with a wide smile and a twinkle in her dark Gypsy eyes. It was plain she thought herself a cut above the other help in the household.

"Do as I say, Lizzie," Olivia ordered. "Alicia Rose will want to see along with you. I can't believe these wonderful gowns. In Boston, one new gown a season was the norm. Mama just did not see the necessity, even before money became scarce."

Olivia stopped, for she did not want an unpleasant memory to spoil the happiness of the moment. Quickly she slipped into the green satin gown, which swept the floor behind her. She stared into the looking glass in utter disbelief. Why . . . why . . . the gown made her beautiful, clinging in folds around her slender body, and the tantalizing décolletage, showing the white flesh of her bosom. Her rich chestnut hair fell to her white shoulders in appealingly, disordered waves.

She smiled at her own newly discovered vanity, and then she remembered the reason for the beautiful gown, the reason for the ball his lordship was giving—to bring Lady Jacqueline back into his waiting arms. It was only when she could push that hateful thought aside that she could find a modicum of happiness with her new wardrobe.

Twenty-four

Preparing for the move into town for the grand ball had turned the house into sixes and sevens. For the first time in Olivia's memory, she failed to write her allotted pages, and the manuscript remained in its black satchel beneath her high bed.

It was difficult to write with her mind so preoccupied. Lord Castleberry had not returned from his search for a new farm steward, and each day he was away seemed longer than the day before. And then the post delivered two missives, one written in feminine script and addressed to his lordship, the other addressed to Lady Olivia Castleberry. It was from Trevor.

"Mrs. Castleberry," she read. "I must see you at once. Only you can clear up this misunderstanding between your husband and me. I beg of you to meet me at the St. Leonard's Cathedral—the one where the skulls are kept—on Thursday this week, at twelve o'clock noon. Tell no one you are coming. I feel abandoned, as you felt when your husband left you at Robinbrook while he was in town panting after a certain woman. Pray, remember my kindness to you at that time. You are the only one who can help me. Kindest regards, Trevor Castleberry."

Olivia did not know what to do; cousin Trevor had been kind to her, and she was not sure that Fitzgerald had not acted rashly when he dismissed his cousin. True, Fred thought the heir to Robinbrook a scoundrel, but . . .

Those thoughts did not linger long in Olivia's mind. Of course she would not go. Had she not done enough damage by threatening, out of anger, to take Trevor as her lover? But there was a reason more important than that. She did not believe she should interfere in Lord Castleberry's and the farm steward's falling out. So she quickly penned a reply and sent it to Father Stephens at the church with an attached note asking that he give the missive to Trevor Castleberry. That was that, she thought, then turned back to her packing and planning for the ball.

She could not help but be excited, even though she knew the purpose of the ball. She wanted to see this Lady Jacqueline who had so captured her husband's heart. Madame Hazlitt had sent by footman the gowns she and her workers had managed, in the short time, to stitch for Alicia Rose.

"If more fitting is needed, Madame Hazlitt will come," one of the footman said as he turned to leave after depositing a dozen or more boxes at Alicia Rose's feet.

The gown fit perfectly, and Olivia deemed that the modiste was a genius. She watched Alicia Rose try on one pretty gown after another, one for every occasion. And two riding habits of startling purple and one of emerald green, which seemed to change the color of her eyes to a deeper shade of blue with specks of green.

Lizzie squealed and clapped her hands as she had done when Olivia modeled her more extensive wardrobe, and Alicia Rose simply beamed. Olivia had never seen her sister look more beautiful as she pranced around the room, showing off and laughing, especially when she donned a Regency cap made of white satin trimmed with ostrich plumage.

She has changed so much since we left Boston, Olivia thought as she looked at Alicia Rose's fully developed body, tiny waist, round, full breasts, not huge but adequate to fill the wonderful gowns, and slim hips. *Her body is now that of a woman's.*

And then came the dress she would wear to the grand

party at Almack's. It was made of blue silk and featured the new style, a flaring skirt with several rows of Brabant lace, above its hem.

The full sleeves reached her elbows and were tied with velvet ribands, giving the appearance of being youthful and flighty, which matched Alicia Rose's personality, Olivia mused, and the rich blue of the gown made her blue eyes seem bottomless.

The thoughtful modiste had made a Poland mantle, a wrap that fastened on the right shoulder, from the same deep blue silk, to wear over the gown should the night prove chilly, and April evenings usually were.

A note was attached to the mantel: *I pray you have an exquisite shoulder brooch.*

And there was a matching reticule, and matching slippers.

"That dress is going to bring you good luck," Lizzie said as Alicia Rose pranced around her exquisite rooms done in varying shades of blue. When neither Alicia Rose nor Olivia paid mind to her remark, the maid, frowning and having a strange look on her face, of which Olivia quickly took note, added: "But it will bring you sadness as well. Your heart will feel much pain."

"Oh, Lizzie, stop your tomfoolery," Olivia said. "Let Alicia Rose be happy about the gown. What is there about the dress that would bring sadness?"

Lizzie sidled closer to Olivia and whispered: " 'Tis not tomfoolery, Lady Castleberry, and 'tis not the gown. It is just something I see with my second sight, something I feel."

A chill danced up and down Olivia's spine, reminding her of the old saying "Someone just walked over my grave." She was glad Alicia Rose had not heard Lizzie's silly whispering.

Alicia Rose was laughing and saying, "I shall catch me a suitor. He'll think 'tis me which is attracting him, when it will be this beautiful gown. Oh, Olivia, isn't it of the first water?"

"The gown is beautiful, Alicia Rose, but you are of the first water."

Olivia hugged her sister with some trepidation creeping into the happy time.

Twenty-five

Lord Castleberry did not return to Robinbrook until the day before he, Olivia, Alicia Rose, and Lizzie were to leave for London, to attend the ball at Almack's. He had come directly to Olivia, apologized for his long absence, saying that he had gone as far north as Nottingham to interview a farm steward recommended to him by the London agency. But he was well pleased with the man, who had three children, a proper wife, and was well qualified for the job. His last employer, the Earl of Wiltshire, had died, and he had not cared to work for the new earl. They would be moving into Trevor's former home the latter part of the month.

Olivia was relieved that he was home. She had not heard anything more from Trevor and hoped that she would not. And she was most anxious to know who had written to Lord Castleberry. The missive, which she had taken to the sitting room between their bedchambers, had lain in the silver salver all this time, seemingly begging her to rip the seal. She smiled at the thought, for she would never do anything so reprehensible, but she did not deny the desire was constant. Now she watched his face as he sat in the chair on the other side of the fireplace and contemplated the handwriting on the parchment envelope.

"Aren't you going to open it?" she asked when the silence in the room grew heavy. His brow furrowed in a deep frown, and it seemed for a moment that he did not hear Olivia. Then he jumped with a start, as if it had taken her voice that long to travel the few feet between them, and began tearing away at the seal.

"It is from Lady Jacqueline. I recognize the writing, but I can't imagine her message. I thought she was in France. . . ."

Olivia fumed inwardly. "Most likely she is writing as an old friend."

She watched as he broke the seal on the missive and read the message quickly, then placed it in his coat pocket. Olivia waited for him to speak, and after awhile he did. "She only wanted to congratulate me on my marriage. . . ."

"How did she know about it . . . with her in France?"

"She's back in London."

"Then she will be at the ball. Your efforts will not have been in vain." In a derisive tone, she added, "You can show off your homely American wife to your beloved Lady Jacqueline."

"You're not homely, Olivia. Only that be the truth. 'Twould not be so hard—"

"I don't take your meaning." She did, but she wanted to hear it from his mouth.

"I think that you do. I could have kept our business arrangement and kept you chaste had you not been so appealing. Now, with the arrangement broken, we have a real marriage. Have you . . . do you think . . . has the curse come? I truly hope not. I do so need an heir."

"No, the curse has not come, and we do not have a real marriage. A *ton* marriage is what you are saying. I have told you that I intend to petition Parliament for a divorce as soon as my story sells. I'm not foolish. I will need money for Alicia Rose and me to live. Had the agreement not been broken, and I blame that completely on you for slipping into my bed unawares, I would have had the settlement you promised, after the marriage was set aside."

"I will still support you and Alicia Rose after you have my heir. You may live in London and continue your writing.

' Tis not unusual in a *ton* marriage for the husband and wife to have separate dwellings, and separate lives."

Olivia's temper flared openly. She sat forward in her chair. "You mean that I should take a lover. While you are bedding another man's wife. Of all the disgraceful proposals I've ever heard, this is the most outrageous."

"Pray, calm down, Olivia. The arrangement is not so strange by England's standards. And 'tis not new between us. We've discussed this before. I wish I could say that we would have a marriage of love, but I do not make promises I cannot keep. I love Lady Jacqueline . . . and I wish that I didn't. But I want you to be my wife, to have my heir."

"Indeed I have heard all this before. I will not have your heir, and I will not remain your wife while you keep Lady Jacqueline as your mistress. 'Twould be a sin against God, who says that a man and wife should keep one for the other, that marriage is a sacred trust."

With that, she practically leapt from her chair and headed toward the door, not the one she had nailed shut, but the one that led out into the hall. His lordship's big hand reached out and stayed her. "Please don't go, Olivia. We should discuss the ball, and other pertinent things. I've been gone, and I need to know what has happened in my absence."

Olivia could have sworn that he was reading her mind, for the next words out of his mouth were "Did cousin Trevor cause trouble while I was gone? Are you ready to leave on the morrow? Did the modiste sew Alicia Rose's wardrobe? And most important, did you like the ball gown Madame Hazlitt made for you?"

Between each question, he had taken a deep breath, giving Olivia time to think. She slapped his hand from her arm. "Yes, I am ready to leave on the morrow, yes, the modiste sewed Alicia Rose's wardrobe, and yes, I like my ball gown very much. I shall feel overdressed, but as an obedient wife, I shall do your bidding and wear it."

His eyes sought hers for a moment. "Did Trevor cause

trouble while I was gone? That's the one question you did not answer."

Olivia was not totally prepared to do so, but she knew she would not lie to him, not a whole lie anyway. "I received a missive from him asking that I intervene between the two of you. He called it a terrible misunderstanding."

"May I see the missive?"

Olivia did not have to think or plan what to say this time; her answer just came out, and quickly. "Yes, when you let me see the missive Lady Jacqueline wrote to you." She thought that fair.

His lordship reached into his pocket for the missive, and then handed it out to her.

"My dearest love," Olivia read with a sinking heart, and she castigated herself for having asked to see the demme thing. But she read on, for she could not have stopped had she tried.

"I have only learned of your marriage to an American, and, although I congratulate you, I feel totally responsible for your terrible fate. I should have never, in a moment of pique, told you that you deserved nothing better than a homely American for a wife. We received your invitation to the ball at Almack's and plan to be there. I pray 'tis not too painful for you. Remember that I will be near . . . for as long as you need me."

Olivia shoved the missive back to his lordship and in so doing poked him in the chest. "Isn't that just wonderful, she will be there as long as your need her, and she's so sorry for your terrible fate. Under the circumstances, I think you're demme lucky to have an American wife, even a homely one. If you had not deceived me . . ."

With his long arms Lord Castleberry reached out and pulled her to him, holding her and consoling her with gentle pats on the back, his chin resting on the top of her head. "We deceived each other. You're not homely, as you pretended to be, with all those freckles and terrible birthmark, and I deceived you by breaking our agreement that you would be my wife in name only."

"To please doddering old Fred, who has some insane notion that cousin Trevor is going to harm you."

More patting, and then he rubbed the palm of his hand up and down her back, and in so doing, pulled her yet closer to him.

"Olivia, it is not insane . . . what Fred thinks. I was foolish not to listen to him. While in London I had my man of business do some checking, and Trevor has a dark side, known only to a few. I'm surprised that it came to light, so deeply was it hidden. Please keep your distance from him."

Feeling the rising need in her husband's body, Olivia freed herself from his embrace and stepped back. It was growing late, and on the morrow they would be leaving early. The room was quiet as his lordship returned to sit in his comfortable chair. The fire threw out warmth, making for a homey ambiance. "I really must be early to bed," she said.

"Please stay for a while longer. We'll talk of more pleasant things. I promise to keep my distance."

Olivia returned to her chair, and there they were, she thought, she wearing a new gown of pale yellow stuff, her husband's booted feet stretched out in front of him. He had shed his coat and cravat. As she watched, he took his snuffbox from his waistcoat pocket and took a deep, satisfying sniff.

If I had Aunt Evaline's embroidery hoops and was sitting here stitching, 'twould made a picture of total happiness, of the perfect family.

"Oh, that we were," she murmured, and was quickly asked what she had said. Laughing lightly, she answered, "I was talking to myself."

"I did that while I was gone, especially on the long trip north. I wished for you . . . to talk with."

"Yes, 'tis nice to share one's thoughts."

"Are you looking forward to going into town? The ball? I pray it will be to your liking."

"I'm sure that it will. Every woman likes to wear a pretty gown. And I love to dance."

"Your hair, 'tis lovely tonight."

"I washed and brushed it today."

"It shines like freshly polished money."

Another light laugh. "Not like molasses?"

His lordship laughed with her. "Like burnt molasses."

And then they were quiet for a while, and his lordship felt the tenseness gradually seep from his body, leaving him filled with a satisfaction he could not explain. He would not let Lady Jacqueline intrude upon the feeling. He would think about her missive on the morrow. At last he said to Olivia, "I have a confession. I did something without asking your permission. It seems we both are always striving to deceive the other. I'm not sure that it is the right way—"

Olivia sat forward. "Oh, pray don't keep me on tenterhooks. I doubt that I would know you if you were always straightforward with me."

"I . . . I stole your black satchel that held your stories—"

"You what?" Olivia was immediately on her feet. "How dare you—"

"Please, Olivia. I'll explain if you will only calm down. 'Tis not like I destroyed it."

"Then what did you do with it? You had no right."

Lord Castleberry began to laugh. "You sound like I've just confessed to kidnapping your child."

"You have. Most likely the only child I will ever have."

"I pray not," he said sotto voce.

Before he could say more, Olivia had closed the distance between them and was on the verge, so it seemed to his lordship, of attacking him physically. "Calm down," he said, "and I will explain." Reaching up, he pulled her down onto his lap, but not without her resistance. However, his strength was victor. "I never meant to upset you this way."

"Well, you have. And I would thank you to stay out of my room. Does a person not have privacy around here?"

She thought fleetingly of Trevor's missive and vowed to hide it where *no one* could find it. She had never seen such a place. There were no secrets, absolutely none.

"I was fortunate to encounter Lord Mackleroy at White's. He seems to have an entree into the publishing business. He told me that Miss Austen is not well; in truth, he thinks *Emma* will be her last book. I had in mind to purchase a copy for you, and then the emergency message from Robinbrook came, saying Fred desperately needed me."

Olivia's voice was sharp. "Yes, I know all about that. That's when you stole into my bed and took advantage of me when I was asleep."

Lord Castleberry's laughter spilled out into the room. "You unbuttoned your gown . . . but let's not get on that subject. Now, let me see. We were talking of your black satchel, were we not?"

"Yes, and I want to know what you did with it."

"While in London I left it with the man Lord Mackleroy suggested I see, a Mr. Bates, in Fleet Street. He promised to read your writings and see if they had merit."

Olivia felt the blood drain from her face. "You didn't take all of them . . . not the pages since I came to Robinbrook. I never intended anyone to see the pages I wrote since . . . since . . . I left America."

"I took all, but don't worry. Your stories will be returned to you, and while I was about it, I told my man of business to have your writings, all of them, copyrighted. So they are safe, and nothing will be published without your permission. I thought you would be appreciative, since it is doubtful that Miss Austen can help you."

"I am appreciative, Fitzgerald. And I'm saddened to hear

of her illness. It's just that I did not want to show my work about Lucifer."

"Lucifer! Why, that's the devil. Why would you be writing about the devil?"

He was desperately trying not to laugh, but he did notice that she had called him Fitzgerald for the very first time, and that sobered him somewhat. Perchance they could become fast friends . . . if they ever stopped deceiving each other. He felt desire once again roiling its head. Scooting to one side of the chair, he was surprised to learn that with his arm around her shoulders and sitting a little lopsided, more on one hip than the other, it was large enough for both of them to sit relatively comfortably. He sighed deeply and pulled her to him so that he could rest his cheek on the top of her head. He smelled her freshly washed hair; the scent of rosewater wafted up to assault his nostrils, and he felt the warmth of her body.

He cupped her small chin into the palm of his big hand. "Are you still angry with me for stealing your black bag?" he asked in a low voice, and she answered, "No. You were only trying to help."

Meantime, the fire in the grate died a slow death, turning to gray ashes, and outside, the round yellow moon rose to its zenith while they sat cuddled in the big chair with its faded upholstery. And at last, they slept.

Twenty-six

When Olivia awoke the next morning, she was in her own bed, the white coverlet tucked under her chin. She sat up quickly and looked around, most specially at the extra pillow. It had not been slept on, and then she saw that she still wore her day dress. She laughed, the sound echoing eerily in the huge, silent room. Of course, Lord Castleberry could not have slept in the same bed with her without her knowing it. But she had been so tired. If she had dreamed, the dreams had left her.

The last thing Olivia remembered was sitting crowded down beside him in the big old chair in the sitting room. So he must have carried her to her bed . . . and not wanted to stay. He could have at least asked, she mused, but then remembered clearly Lady Jacqueline's missive. That was the reason. He'd returned to his own quarters to mull over the letter. It made her angry, and it hurt badly, but she admitted to being quite excited about going into town. The sooner she met this paragon of beauty whom her husband so loved, the sooner she could get on with her life.

That his lordship had taken her manuscript to a publisher came back to Olivia. There was no doubt that her manuscript would sell, but no one would publish what she had written about Lucifer. Her face burned when she thought of it. She shuddered. It simply did not bear thinking of the heroine's feelings of rapture when he touched her.

Surely, surely, the editor would not read those; there were

too many pages of her long manuscript to read, she reasoned almost prayerfully. While in London she would visit the publishing house and ask for *those* pages, explaining that they were for her eyes only. Hearing the clock on the mantel strike five times, she realized it was still quite early. But they were to leave at first light, his lordship had said, giving her a day to rest before the grand ball. "Stuff," she said aloud, "I don't need to rest. And he knows that . . . except he thinks I am *enceinte*. 'Tis his heir he is worried about."

Olivia had not at any time thought what she would do should she be with child. For it was impossible; a child was conceived of love. At least *her* child would be.

Leaving her bed and going to look out the window, she saw the fine mist rolling in from the sea, the first glimmer of sunlight dancing on its foamy tips, and she realized that she had fallen in love with Robinbrook. Just as she had fallen in love with its owner. Boston, her life there, seemed so far away. She turned back into the room and went to prepare for her toilette. A tankard of hot water had been left the previous evening, and now it was pleasantly warm, she noticed, as she washed her body from head to toe, using scented soap. Standing before the looking glass naked, she brushed her long chestnut hair one hundred strokes, and then slipped into a traveling dress with a modest neckline, and made of plain pale yellow stuff. In the next room were several boxes. One held the green satin gown, the one she would be wearing when she met her husband's precious Lady Jacqueline.

"Remember, you must act totally devoted to me," he had said. "And I shall pretend that my love for you is boundless."

Boundless!

Lady Olivia Castleberry wanted to spit. But she didn't; instead, tears pushed at her eyes.

In the next room Lord Castleberry mulled over Lady Jacqueline's missive. Mayhap he should think of her as Lady

Sappington, but he just could not. He wondered what she had meant by, "I will be near . . . for as long as you need me," and he cautioned himself not to read more into the missive than what was there. He read it again. Clearly, she wanted to be a friend, nothing more. Who had told her that he had married a woman from the Colonies, he wondered, and told himself that he would soon know. She had said in her missive that she would be at the ball.

With old Sapp.

He thought about Olivia then, smiling when he remembered putting her to bed last evening. He prayed that she slept well, for a woman in the family way needed lots of rest. At all costs he must protect the heir to Robinbrook, he mused, refusing to allow himself to think, even for one moment, of cousin Trevor Castleberry as the present heir. But it was true nonetheless, and it galled him that he had not paid heed earlier to Fred's deep concern about Trevor. If only his cousin in America could inherit, but, being part Indian, there was no record of his birth that he could use to lay claim to the entailed estate. And he was not a citizen of England. And mayhap Emry would not take to English life, Lord Castleberry thought, discarding any thought other than it was imperative that he produce an heir . . . as soon as possible.

Fully dressed, as he had been for over an hour, his lordship left the big comfortable chair and went down the back stairs into the kitchen. There, he found the servants eating breakfast, seated around a long table, and all talking at once. He stood in the doorway and listened.

" 'Tis said that our master whammed the jackanapes against his chin."

Laughter, and then, "Old Trevor deserved it, if anyone ever did. I tell ye, thet man's wicked, mean as the devil himself. They say in Hythe that 'e's fit to be tied, swearing vengeance all over the place. I wouldn't put it past him to come back here and burn this place to the ground."

"Don't be a scapescull, 'e won't burn Robinbrook, what 'e's due to inherit . . . unless the present owner gets busy with this new wife."

"If treacherous Trevor does inherit, all of us at this table here had better run fer cover. 'E'll have our heads."

"Turned out without one line of reference is what we have to look to . . . if thet jackanapes comes here," said one of the maids, a sorrowful look on her face.

Lord Castleberry stepped into the small room furnished with a plank-board table and straight-back chairs. At the far end, a fire burned in a smoke-blackened fireplace. It appeared to him that what they were feasting on was hot porridge, each from a big round bowl, hot coffee, milk, and big, round, puffy biscuits. suddenly he was hungry.

But the need to explain to his faithful workers that they should not fear having Trevor Castleberry return to Robinbrook was greater. Upon hearing his footsteps on the flagstone floor, they scrambled to their feet and the women bobbed, while the footmen bowed from the waist, saying in unison, "M'lord."

"Your worry is wasted," he told them. "Trevor Castleberry will not inherit Robinbrook; I shall see to that." Then, turning from their beaming faces and smiles of relief, he addressed Cook, who was fetching more porridge from a huge black pot that held a tin dipper with a long handle. "Would you please prepare a nourishing tray for Lady Castleberry and have one of the maids take it to her room. We shall be leaving shortly for London, and I fear she'll tire out if she does not eat well before leaving."

"And you, m'lord. Will you be eating with her?"

"No. I'll eat with Fred, in the Hunt Room." At the door he turned back, smiled, and said, "I beg of you not to worry. There'll be an heir to Robinbrook soon enough."

Still beaming and smiling, the servants bobbed and bowed to him again, mumbling thanks and congratulations.

His lordship believed what he had promised to be so. His

steps were light as he climbed the stairs to say good-bye to Fred, and to give his dear grandfather the same assurance. Silently, he planned: He would eat, but quickly, before the coach and four came. And then he began worrying about Olivia's health, and her welfare. Mayhap the ball should be canceled. Not for the world would he have her ladyship become too tired, not in her delicate state.

Olivia had never felt better in her life. The warm April sun bore down on the handsome town coach with the Castleberry heraldic arms on the doors of its enclosed body, and with squabs so plush she hardly felt the jostling at all as they tooled at a fast pace toward London. Six sleek black horses were at the tongue. Following was a coach carrying Henry, his lordship's valet, and the many boxes of clothes for the ladies, and for the maid as well.

Not completely happy with her choice of the yellow stuff traveling gown, Olivia had changed to one made of green muslin. Now she was thinking of how her husband's eyes lighted up when he saw her boarding the coach. "The color of your gown, Olivia, matches your extraordinary green eyes. I've often thought your eyes are like a cat's, changeable, and very expressive. At times they are gray, while other times they are green."

She had thanked him and let him help her up into the coach, smiling when he handled her as if she were a porcelain doll on the verge of breaking if not handled carefully. What a surprise he would be getting when he learned she was *not enceinte*. And not likely to be. Although her heart was not in it, in truth she felt such pain when she thought about it that she could hardly breathe, her resolve to petition Parliament for a divorce had not diminished. She decided to ask Lizzie, who was sitting on the opposite squab beside Alicia Rose, if a child was in her near future. "Lizzie, since you have the second sight, can you tell me if I'm with child?"

Lord Castleberry, sitting beside her, coughed, sputtered, gained his equilibrium, then lost it again. His words were barely audible. "Lady Castleberry, 'tis against propriety to speak on such a delicate matter with a servant."

Lizzie straightened, and her dark eyes twinkled. "I'm no servant. I'm a lady's maid for Lady Castleberry, as well as for her sister. That makes me two cuts above a plain servant, your lordship."

Olivia, smothering her laughter, found some excuse to open her reticule for a handkerchief to cover her mouth as she pretended to sneeze.

"Regardless of your cut, the subject should not be discussed in the presence of one's husband," said his lordship.

"I don't know why not, your lordship," Lizzie said in a most innocent manner. "If a woman's in the family way, let's pray that it was her husband who got her that way."

"I will not tolerate your obstinacy, Lizzie. When we return from London, I shall talk with you about going to another household, and mayhap they'll make you the chamber girl. That should humble you a little, though not much, I am sure."

"Oh, no," piped up Alicia Rose. "I could not bear not having Lizzie to wait me, though I admit she does very little waiting, but she does keep me from being lonely."

"Why, Alicia Rose," said Olivia, frowning. "You've not mentioned being lonely before. Has something happened and you haven't told me?"

"No, not that I can think of. It's just that I have these odd feelings occasionally, and when Lizzie's there, she can make me laugh."

Lizzie patted Alicia Rose's arm and looked at her with pity in her big brown eyes. "I know what happened, and I should be ashamed, and I am. I had no business whatsoever telling her that the blue gown, the one she's to wear to the ball, will bring her happiness as well as sadness. Mayhap someday I'll learn to keep my mouth shut, but when this feeling comes over me . . . that something's not right, I just blurt it out. 'Tis as if I can't help myself. This time I'm certain I was wrong."

But Lizzie was not sure she was wrong. When she saw Alicia Rose in that blue gown, the strangest force had invaded her body and told her that happiness as well as sadness was ahead for her mistress.

"I warn you, I won't believe you, but I'd still like an answer to my question," said Olivia. "A pox on propriety." She looked at her husband, and then back to the Gypsy maid. "Am I in the family way?"

For a moment Lizzie did not answer, and no one spoke. Olivia noted a strangeness in the maid's countenance, as if she were far away in her thoughts. She was frowning, her dark eyes growing darker, and appearing glazed. At last, she said. "No. But danger is ahead for you, your ladyship."

She addressed Lord Castleberry. "You'll have to protect her from that terrible Trevor. He has something bad in his mind."

Twenty-seven

Olivia was impressed by the Clarendon. It was late evening when they arrived, and a liveried footman came to let down the step. Lord Castleberry, alighting first, helped Olivia and Alicia Rose, leaving Lizzie for the footman. It was plain that he was angry with the maid. "I want that demme Gypsy replaced as soon as we return to Robinbrook," he said, when he and Olivia arrived in his suite of rooms on the fourth floor.

"Fitzgerald, you are being childish," she told him. "Lizzie entertains herself by pretending she can see into the future. What harm is there in that? And Alicia Rose is so fond of her."

" 'Tis dangerous, telling you that you are not with child. Such tomfoolery will cause you to be negligent and not take care of yourself."

"Her guess was right. I'm not *enceinte*. One coupling does not make a baby. I don't see why you insist—"

"I do insist. A man should know when he plants a baby. Our coupling was so complete—"

"No coupling is complete without love. Now, I would like to explore your apartment and learn where I am to sleep. Since you insist that we stay here together."

"For appearance's sake. It would be all over London that we have separate quarters, and us only recently leg-shackled. The ball would then be for naught."

"Oh, I see. Then your Lady Jacqueline's jealousy would

not be sufficiently riled. I keep forgetting the purpose of all this is to have her fling herself into your arms and ask forgiveness for marrying a man old enough to be her father. Could it be your ego which is suffering, your lordship, and not your heart?"

"I pray that it be my ego, and I pray that my heart would not hurt so—"

"Oh, save me, please," Olivia retorted, and then she turned from him and looked around the room. Plainly, Lady Jacqueline had not wreaked havoc on this room with her small baby-pink chairs and sofas. Red silk covered the walls, and moss-green velvet had been used in the window coverings, tied with variegated colors of fashion rope.

A chair large enough to hold his lordship's frame sat near the black marble fireplace, in which coals had been laid should a fire be needed.

Good English furniture filled the room, and there were bookcases filled with tomes with gold spines. A man's room, large and comfortable, she thought, and went to explore the other rooms, most especially *her* bedchamber.

She found five rooms, all large, spacious, and, like the drawing room, comfortably furnished, but only one bedchamber.

"There's only one bed," she said not too calmly. "If you think I'm to share that bed with you, you have windmills in your head."

There was a wry grin on his lordship's face, his big frame practically filling the doorway from which he watched. Olivia glared at him.

"The bed is large enough," he said, his smile widening.

"I shall go this minute and tell Alicia Rose that I will share her room. You are filled with trickery . . . and you take me for a fool."

Just then a knock on the door was heard, and when Lord Castleberry went to answer, a footman loaded with boxes stood there.

Olivia stepped forward. "Take those to my sister's room—"

Quickly, his lordship put Olivia behind him, and told the footman, "Take the boxes to the dressing room, Herbert."

Which the footman did and then made to leave with alacrity, but Lord Castleberry stopped him long enough to hand him a gold coin. And then another one. "For your silence."

The footman bowed twice. "Yes, your lordship. There's more boxes. I'll make sure the duty falls to me to deliver them." Smiling, he pretended to seal his lips with his long fingers. A small laugh followed, and then he was gone.

Olivia walked through the five rooms again, finding, incredulously, the second time through that there was still just one bedchamber. Returning to the drawing room, she found Fitzgerald languishing on a large leather sofa. With a hand on her hip she said, "I can't believe you expect me to stay here with you with only one bed."

"I explained that to you once, wife. 'Tis for appearance's sake."

On the way into town he had explained that when he was in London searching for a new farm steward, he had engaged rooms for Alicia Rose, and a separate maid's room for Lizzie.

Now she walked closer to him. At the advantage because he was sitting down, she glared down at him. "I will sleep with Alicia Rose. Or on a pallet on the floor . . . in the other room . . . with the door locked."

Lord Castleberry pulled her down beside him. "Are all Americans so hasty to jump to conclusions?" His voice was unruffled; in truth, Olivia thought it quite pleasant. "I plan to sleep in Henry's room, which is separated from my bedchamber by a short hall. He'll be staying in the hotel, and will come only if I send for him."

"I don't trust you."

He laughed. "Did you not bring your hammer and nails?"

Olivia felt her face flush. She had been quite silly, pushed by her anger. A door nailed shut would not stop her husband should he want to come to her room.

A silence settled over the room. Lord Castleberry held his wife's hand, and after a while he said, "After the ball, I plan for us to shop for a town house suitable for a family and for entertaining. I apologize for these accommodations. They've served me well, but I realize they are not suitable for a family. There must be an apartment for a nanny, a governess, and, for heaven's sake. servants who serve. Lizzie is almost useless as an abigail. You shall have a proper lady's maid."

In Olivia's mind's eye she could see the picture he was painting, the perfect *ton* marriage—a proper dwelling, a proper wife, proper servants, and an heir. And then there would be a place apart for Lady Jacqueline, if his lordship's plan worked and Lady Jacqueline had left her doddering husband.

"Have you not forgotten something?" she asked.

"I don't think so, but anything you desire you may have, dearest Olivia. So I don't take your meaning."

"When my manuscript sells, I shall petition Parliament for a divorce. So there will be no need for a town house, unless you wish to keep your mistress there."

"What about the child? What about the disgrace? And divorces are difficult, near impossible, in fact. You have no grounds . . ."

"Oh, but I do. I have the business agreement signed by both of us. I don't think you will stand before your peers and say that you stole into my bed and broke the agreement."

Lord Castleberry's heart dropped to the pit of his stomach. Why did his wife have to be so determined? His only hope of bringing his well-thought-out plan to fruition was for her to be with child . . . and that demme Lizzie had said there was no child on its way. But what did a crazy Gypsy know?

And Olivia was right; he had deliberately broken their business arrangement. Words, argument, reasoning, left him. Turning to his wife, he placed his long arm around her and hugged her to him, her head on his shoulder, his cheek resting in her sweet-smelling hair, and they sat thus for a long time, in the silent room, boxes unpacked, the fire unlit.

True to his word, Lord Castleberry slept in the valet's room. He ordered supper sent up from the hotel's kitchen, and they dined on fine fare in the small dining room, lighted by arms of flickering tapers. He purposely steered conversation away from anything that would cause an argument, and he purposely told Olivia he thought her lovely. He was not being untruthful, he told himself, for she was lovely with the light dancing on her rich red-brown hair, framing her face and falling to rest on her narrow shoulders. She had changed to a dinner dress of Devonshire brown silk, the color almost exact as her hair. The décolletage was low, as he had ordered the modiste to see to, but he kept his eyes, and his mind, more on her face. One false step, and his wife would refuse to attend the ball. He had seen expressions of her temper, and he could envision her ordering a hackney and returning to Robinbrook to await the publishing of her writings so that she could divorce him.

So when fatigue had overcome them, he had given her a chaste kiss and forced himself to go to the tiny room across the hall, the valet's room. There, he had tossed and turned most of the night, wanting to go to her, to make love to her, to reach the fulfillment he had experienced only once in his life—the night he had stolen into her bed.

When he finally did sleep, in his dreams he struggled with the difference between lust and love; he wanted Olivia, while his arms, his heart, reached out for elusive Lady Jacqueline. She danced through his dreams, laughing, looking back over her shoulder, flitting away from him, and when he awoke, nothing had changed. He absolutely knew it was Lady Jacqueline whom he truly loved. The painful memory of when she cried off, in truth, jilted him, once again engulfed him.

One could not turn love off any more than one could stop a raging river overflowing its banks, he told himself. This night he would see her. His heart hurt inside his chest with longing for the sight of her beauty, and tears blurred his vision. Willing them away, he donned a blue silk robe and went to have breakfast with his wife, and later that day he rushed out to purchase from Hamlet, the jeweler in Cranbourn Alley, jewelry for his wife to wear to the ball—a diamond necklace, a diamond tiara, and bracelets of rubies and emeralds.

His mother's jewelry, that which his father had given to her, his father's only love, would go to Lady Jacqueline even if she were never more than his *fille de joie*—his courtesan.

Twenty-eight

Olivia knew exactly what she would do, and it brought a huge smile to her face. As soon as Lord Castleberry left his suite of rooms, she hurried to ask that Alicia Rose and Lizzie go at once to a chemist.

"Why don't you go yourself," asked Alicia Rose, and Lizzie joined in by saying they did not know where to find a chemist and most likely they would get lost should they try.

"His lordship wants me to remain unseen in London until the ball. No doubt he's at his club right now, bragging about his American wife. He so wants to fool his peers, and most especially Lady Jacqueline."

Only recently had they talked of the "business arrangement" in front of Lizzie, but she was underfoot so much, it was difficult to keep secrets from her.

"That doxy," the maid exclaimed.

"Don't you dare say that, Lizzie. Someone might hear, and Lord Castleberry is quite put out of temper with you for saying that I'm not in the family way."

"You're not," retorted the maid. "I've got the gift, and I know."

"Oh, hush, Lizzie, about your second sight. No one believes such nonsense. Now, back to the chemist. I'm in the need of iodine."

Alicia Rose giggled. "Olivia, you would not dare. Did Lord Castleberry not tell you he had changed his mind about wanting a homely American wife, and did he not have that beautiful gown made for you? Why—"

"I have my reasons. Remember his original plan—to show Lady Jacqueline that looks did not count, that he could be totally devoted to an ugly American. Well, he shall have his chance to put on his charade."

Soon Alicia Rose and Lizzie became as excited about the turn of events as Olivia. A chemist was found not far from the hotel, the iodine bought, and then Lizzie pressed the green gown for Olivia and the blue one for Alicia Rose. The same feeling of impending happiness, and then sadness, came over the maid when the last wrinkle was gone from the blue gown. Something was going to happen this night, she told herself. She had no such feelings about when she pressed the green gown. His lordship loved Lady Castleberry; only he did not know it yet.

"I'm going to the ball, you know," she said when she brought the gowns from the abigail room and laid them on the bed.

"Oh, Fitzgerald will not allow that, Lizzie. You know perfectly well he is out of sorts with you."

"Every lady of quality takes her abigail to her social affairs. What if you should need your hair dressed? Some buck might muss it."

Olivia laughed. "Lizzie, now that you want to attend the ball, you want to tend *me,* when all along it has been Alicia Rose's welfare you've been interested in."

"I'd wait you if you wanted me to, but you like to do for yourself, and you are always writing. How can I wait you when you don't want me to wait you?" A petulant pout had replaced the maid's usual sunny smile. "If you say you want me, then his lordship will let me go, if you say you don't want me, then I don't have a chance. And I so want to watch. They tell me there's a room for the abigails who come to tend their ladies."

"Who told you that?"

"I've lived in England all my life; I know things."

"Oh, Olivia," piped up Alicia Rose, "what harm would there be in it?"

Olivia saw that she was outnumbered, and she really did not care if Lizzie came along, but Lord Castleberry was another matter. "I'll agree only if you promise that if his lordship gets in a pucker, you will not argue. As you usually do. I fear one more wrong step, and he'll carry through with his threat and send you to another household."

"It was not a wrong step to say that you're not *enceinte*. Just because his lordship wants an heir to take wicked Trevor's place in the line of succession does not make it so."

Olivia, grinning, shook her head. Sometimes the maid was too logical. "Anyway, Lizzie, should you go, I expect your best comportment. Do you know how an abigail should act at a social function?"

"I'm to walk three steps behind you, and then, upon entering the designated place, I'm to go to the room with the other ladies' maids and watch. If you should need my help, a footman will fetch me. I won't forget to bob properly. And while in London, you are not to appear in public unescorted. 'Twould disgrace you to walk on the streets alone. I shall be available for that service as well."

"It seems there are a lot of things which, according to the *ton* can bring disgrace to a woman." Olivia was thinking about the divorce she planned to seek, and then she added, "I don't give a fig about the *ton*. Let their tongues wag." She looked at her watch, suspended by a gold chain from her neck.

The time had passed rapidly, and she found that she was hungry. "We must eat lest we faint from the lack of nourishment." She pulled a bell rope to summon a footman, from whom she ordered tea and scones.

"With jellies . . . and small sandwiches," she added lastly.

Bowing with a flourish, the liveried footman said the customary "M'lady," and then quickly left, returning soon with a huge silver tray holding the tea and scones.

When they had eaten that, Olivia began thinking of meeting Lady Jacqueline. She had purposely, until now, pushed the thought from her mind. But she could no longer pretend she was going to a grand ball in her honor to dance, and to be loved by her husband. She could no longer ignore the pain in her heart or the reality of her place in her husband's scheme of things.

But she could keep her feelings hidden, she assured herself. During her years in Boston she had been adept at doing that.

She had no second thoughts about the freckles and birthmark, or the ridiculous way her hair would be piled atop her head, bouffant and resembling a chamber pot. By all means his lordship should have what he had ordered from America—a homely wife.

"Hurry, Alicia Rose, and apply the iodine, and dress my hair . . . before Lord Castleberry returns." She could not help but wonder if he had visited Lady Jacqueline and felt certain that he had. He had seemed eager to leave the hotel, telling her not to venture out.

The sisters helped each other with their gowns, as they had done when they were children, and then on into adulthood. When both were dressed, Alicia Rose began making the brown freckles and the horrendous birthmark, stepping back often to evaluate her work. "You look quite ridiculous, you know. If you don't mind my bragging on my artistry."

"A capital job," Olivia said, "and I thank you."

"You are utterly ugly, if that's what you mean," said Lizzie, after which she announced that she would now go don her new uniform she had made with her own hands just for this occasion. "I added ruffles and lace around the bottom of the skirt. I hope you don't mind, Lady Castleberry."

"Not at all, Lizzie. Just mind your manners and don't be

too bossy with Lord Castleberry. Out of temper, he's capable of making you walk back to the hotel."

Olivia stood before the mirror and looked, not at the freckles and bundle of hair on top of her head, but at the reflection of the green satin gown loaded with pearls. The low décolletage showed white bosom, but not embarrassingly so, she decided. The skirt, longer behind than in front, and weighted down with pearls to make it sweep the floor, she felt as grand as if she were Queen Charlotte herself. What would her husband think, she wondered, and just then she heard a knock on the door. Certain that it was her husband, her heart skipped a beat.

It was Herbert, the footman who had delivered the boxes of clothes to Lord Castleberry's suite of rooms. His sharp eyes bulged, and then he engaged in a spasm of small coughs. He covered his mouth with his hands.

Olivia, bemused, said, " 'Tis only a small joke, Herbert, which I'm playing on my husband. What did you want?"

"His lordship arrived back at the hotel not above a half hour ago, and just moments ago he rang for me. Of course I went straightaway. His valet had helped him dress in his evening clothes, so his lordship informed me, and then he asked that I come for his wife and bring her to his quarters."

"How did he know I was with my sister?"

"I don't know, your ladyship."

"Well, I shall come with you. I'm dressed for the ball as well. I want him to see my gown."

" 'Tis lovely, your ladyship," he answered. Keeping his gaze on the gown, he stepped back to let her walk in front of him. There was no further conversation, according to the strictures of the *ton*. It was not far, just in another wing on the same floor, and upon arriving at the door Olivia thanked the footman, and after he had bowed and taken quick leave, she opened the door and went in without knocking.

Lord Castleberry was standing by the window, looking out, his back to Olivia. He was wearing a black dress coat with long tails, knee breeches, clock stockings, and patent evening slippers. When he turned, Olivia thought she had never seen a more handsome man. Above his deeply cut waistcoat, a ruffled shirt, pristine white, protruded from the deep V, contrasting sharply with his sun-browned complexion. He was smiling.

But the smile quickly faded, and his blue eyes seemed to jump out of his head. "Olivia . . . what . . . why . . . what have you done to your face? And your hair, 'tis absolutely ugly."

"This is what your cousin Emry sent you, an ugly American wife. Remember at the church, you accused me of being an impostor because I didn't have freckles . . . or a birthmark? I'm certain your Lady Jacqueline will faint dead away when she sees me, and her guilt for having said an ugly American was what you deserved for a wife will send her flying back into your arms."

Suddenly his lordship was laughing. "You little minx." He came to her then and took her arm and began walking toward the door of the bedchamber.

"Where are you taking me?" Olivia asked. "Should we not be going to the ball?"

"Not with you looking like that. I've grown used to your lovely face, and no one shall see my wife looking as if she has spent the whole of her life under the hot sun."

"I'm your wife in name only."

"No. It is too late to claim that."

By now they were in the dressing room. With a wet soap-smeared cloth Lord Castleberry began scrubbing at the iodine freckles and the birthmark. "Demme! Stains are going to be left. I should beat you, you know."

His wry grin told Olivia that he did not mean that. In truth, he was in such a good humor, she found herself laughing. "You will admit that you deserve an ugly wife."

"That's exactly what Lady Jacqueline said, my dear wife,

and I disagree with both of you. My God, Olivia, your face will be red as a beet when I get through scrubbing."

"And you're hurting me." She took the cloth, wet it thoroughly, made suds by adding the soap, then began washing her face, using a circular motion. The freckles and birthmark disappeared, but still she could pass the ugly test, with her hair looking like a chamber pot on top of her head. She could barely stand to look in the mirror.

His lordship turned her to face him. Then, one by one, he removed the pins and let her long chestnut hair fall to her shoulders. Combing it with his fingers, he pushed it back from her face, his smile fading as his deep blue eyes searched her soul, as if looking for her secrets.

But he would not know them, Olivia resolved; he would never know the depth of the love her heart held for him, the pain she felt when she thought of his love for Lady Jacqueline. She wanted to turn away, to deny him the pleasure of her torture, but she could not, and in that instant she knew he was going to kiss her. And there was little she could do to stop him, for her body, hot and confused, began to melt into a languorous burn, the fire within her stronger than her trepidation and fear of total surrender. "Please," she said, fearing it came out as a mewling sound, and his mouth closing over hers stopped her plea for him to stop. His probing tongue demanded her all. She heard him whisper her name, heard him say that he wanted her as no man ever wanted a woman. But the words *I love you,* the words she so longed to hear, were left unsaid. He kissed her again with even more feeling. The muscles in his long arms throbbed as they held her against him, and her body trembled. It was difficult to think, to reason, to be logical, and then, by sheer willpower, the words *he wants me but he does not love me* pushed their way into her muddled thoughts.

Even then it was not easy for Olivia to relinquish the ecstasy of being in her husband's arms. Nonetheless, determinedly she pushed him away and said, "We must leave for the ball. We would not want to keep Lady Jacqueline waiting."

"First, I must give you the jewelry I bought for you," he said, and with that he took from a drawer a velvet box. On her head he placed the diamond tiara, and around her neck he fastened the diamond necklace, and lastly, the bracelets of emeralds and rubies. He then turned her where she could see her reflection in the looking glass. Olivia caught her breath, for now she truly did feel like a princess. Words would not come when she tried to thank him, but she tried, failing miserably as tears rimmed her eyes and she swallowed past the lump in her throat. Laughing, he kissed her soundly, saying that her warmth showed her appreciation splendidly.

And then he added, "As the mother to my heir, you deserve many more precious baubles than I can ever give you."

Twenty-nine

As they rode to Almack's Assembly Rooms in the same town coach they had traveled from Robinbrook, with the Castleberry heraldic arms painted on the doors of the enclosed body, Olivia's eyes darted from one great thing to another. Her curiosity made her forget for a short while what awaited her—the meeting with her nemesis. An amorphous haze circled the gaslights that lined the streets, and a silvery moon lent its light also.

Approaching their destination on King Street, St. James's, Olivia thought the building's exterior very plain, with simple and undistinguished brickwork. An Ionic doorcase framed a rather plain door. Nonetheless, regardless of its plainness, seemingly it was the place to be if one wanted to mingle with high society.

It is where Lady Jacqueline will be.

"There are six patronesses who run the Assembly Rooms with iron fists. No one is allowed beyond the hallowed door without their approval," said Lord Castleberry in way of relaying information. "And the dress code for men is very strict, knee breeches and white neckcloth required for the gentlemen. Without exception."

And then he told about the Duke of Wellington having once been turned away by Mr. Willis, owner of the building, and who stood at the foot of the staircase to inspect every gentleman's dress who passed before him.

"What did the Duke of Wellington do when he was

treated so shabbily?" asked Alicia Rose. She was sitting beside a silent Lizzie, opposite Olivia and his lordship.

"What could he do? Being military, he respected the house rule and left, and I'm told quite good-naturedly. He's an extraordinary man, self-disciplined and straightforward. Among men, the duke's a sort of god who sets excellent examples in all walks of life for others to follow. But not for him, we would still be at war with France."

"I hear he has a mistress," Alicia Rose said.

"That's acceptable," replied his lordship. "Because of his honor, he married a woman he did not love."

"Do English gentlemen all marry for honor and then take a mistress," Olivia asked.

"When the duke returned from the war after twelve years away, he learned that Miss Kitty Pakenham, the women to whom, in his youth, he had become affianced, was under the impression they would be married, even though they had not communicated in all that time. A man cannot cry off from a marriage contract. And even though his love for Miss Pakenham had long ago cooled, he married her, and it has worked out fairly well."

"And I suppose she took a lover . . . if her husband's bent was to take a ladybird."

His lordship reached to take her hand. "Lady Castleberry, one never mentions ladybirds in a real lady's presence, and one certainly never introduces one in polite society, lest the poor mortal rubs off, or is catching, like the measles. The proper wordage is, if one must mention it at all, it is that she is under his protection."

Olivia decided to let the subject drop. She had heard it too many times since coming to England. "If dress can keep a gentleman from entering this hallowed hall, what turns a lady from its door?" she asked, many thoughts going through her mind, which was unprepared for the explanation coming from Lord Castleberry.

"Divorce," he clearly stated. "Male or female. Both are

considered among the Great Unwashed, but disgrace for the woman is paramount. Total abandonment." He paused, and then continued. "Lady Holland is a prime example. Although erudite and well read, a wonderful hostess and conversationalist, she is shunned by the best circles of society. Almack's turned her away. . . ."

His lordship's inference was not wasted on Olivia. She knew perfectly well he was speaking directly to her, and this brought a small smile. How little she cared about the best circles of society. She would choose a well-read good conversationalist over almost anything society had to offer.

There was not time for further discussion about the Duke of Wellington, or of the six patronesses of Almack's, or the perils of a divorced lady in society for they were unloading with the help of a liveried footman, and a groom was taking the town coach away. Inside, Mr. Willis greeted them with a smile and a deep bow at the foot of the stairs, and at the top, Lady Jersey stood with an outstretched hand. "Lady Castleberry, 'tis with deepest pleasure I welcome you to Almack's."

Not feeling the least awkward, Olivia greeted Lady Jersey with cordiality and the good manners she had learned from her Boston socialite mother. Lord Castleberry introduced Miss Alicia Rose Pembroke as his wife's dear sister, and Lizzie, after taking Olivia's and Alicia Rose's mantles and reticules, was whisked away to wait for bidding should either of them need her. Things settled for a moment as quickly Olivia's eyes scanned the waiting crowd for the recipient of her husband's deepest love, and was quite surprised when Lady Jersey whispered, "She's the beauty in pink."

Olivia refused to look. She would not give the woman in pink the pleasure of her curiosity. The orchestra, which had remained silent until that moment, began playing a waltz, and Lord Castleberry, smiling down into his wife's face, led her out onto the floor and the dance began.

Forgetting her pain, Olivia felt like a princess and danced with such feeling, in perfect step with her husband, that she actually forgot *why* she was there. She reveled in her husband's smile, and the devotion that poured from his sparkling blue eyes. Not once, as she danced and danced, did she look at the lady in pink. She would play the part well, she told herself, and then she again made herself forget that she was playing a part. As in her fictional stories, she *was* the princess and her husband was the prince. She felt her long chestnut hair move against her bare shoulders as her body moved rhythmically with the music.

Olivia did not want the dance to end, but it did, and she heard her husband presenting her to the bejeweled ladies, with deeply cut décolletages, bosoms showing, and the *ton-nish* gentlemen, wearing skin-tight knee breeches, long tailcoats, and, without exception, white neckwear.

She thought of penguins as she glanced, unobtrusively she hoped, up at the six tall windows with round arches that graced the second-story ballroom. When the introduction, with great emphasis on her being recently from the Colonies, was over, she gave a courtly curtsy and smiled broadly when the ladies curtsied to her and the gentlemen bowed in unison.

Following the introduction, she danced with her husband, an English country dance, the minuet, contredanse, Scotch reel, and the Ecossaise, his lordship politely refusing all attempts of the other gentlemen to claim her for a dance, making the show of his possession, and of his total devotion. Laughing, he danced away with her, his eyes never leaving her face.

"Do you see Alicia Rose," Olivia asked, feeling she had abandoned her sister among these strangers.

It was only then that his lordship's gaze left her to scan the room. "She's with Lady Sefton, one of the patronesses, and reported the kindest of the six." He laughed. "Now she's dancing away with Lord Edgeworth . . . and there's a waiting line of young bucks. I would not worry if I were you; your sister is too pretty to go unnoticed. More than one *ton* gentleman will be asking to pay his addresses before the night has ended."

"And did you see Lady Jacqueline? I was told she's here."

"That she is, and she and old Sapp are headed in our direction."

"I don't want to dance with her doddering husband."

"And I don't want to dance with the lady in pink. Not yet."

They laughed together, and then he danced her into an arched alcove that led into a room where cards were being played.

"I fear we're practicing the worst of manners," she scolded.

"So we are, but at the moment I feel happy, and I don't want to lose that feeling by being in proximity with her . . . and her husband. It only brings an ache to my heart."

Olivia could no longer pretend. That awful hurt feeling returned, and she was angry with herself for forgetting, even for a moment, that her husband was in love with someone else.

"Do you play faro," she asked, going to a table and sitting down. Representations of thirteen cards were painted on the green baize, and the dealer, a tall, somewhat youngish man, seemed delighted that at last he had someone to whom he could draw against.

"I didn't know you indulged in gaming," said Lord Castleberry.

"In Boston we had a faro table in our basement. Father often played with his cronies, but never for very much money. What he did win, Mama insisted he give to some worthwhile charity."

Lord Castleberry smiled. "I'm wondering if there is anything you don't know something about, either by experience or by reading."

"There's lots I don't know. Life, for instance." There was a tinge of hardness to her words. "Would you like to play?"

They played for a while, placing small bets, coins furnished by his lordship, on chosen cards, laughing when they lost, or when they won. At last his lordship said, "I feel very selfish, keeping you all to myself. 'Tis the thing that we return and take up dancing again."

Olivia knew what this meant, and she braced herself for watching her husband dance with the lady in pink. But this did not happen, not right away. She found herself dancing with the Prince Regent, with Lord this and Lord that. She could not remember all their names. Lord Castleberry, smiling affably, changed partners as often as she, and included Alicia Rose, for which Olivia was thankful. He was taller than most of the other gentlemen, and far more handsome, she thought, as many times their eyes locked and he smiled across the crowded room at her.

Then her partner turned her and she could not see. When her husband was again in her vision, he was dancing with *her*.

If the sky had tumbled down onto her world, Olivia could not have felt more crushed. All the mental preparation she had practiced did not prepare her for the terrible pain she felt, and when the dance was over and her husband returned to her side, his words felled the final blow.

"She's very unhappy in her marriage," his lordship said.

"And I suppose she wants you to take her back . . . just as you planned." Her words were, with extreme effort, controlled, and then her temper flared. Through clenched teeth, and in an almost inaudible voice so that no one else could hear, she said, "She wants you back only because you are not available to her. So she thinks. When she again has you on her string, she will play you like a puppet. I thought you were smarter than that, Lord Castleberry."

"I told her that you are *enceinte*."

"You what? You have no right to share such information with that . . . that doxy, even if it were true. I've told you, and Lizzie has told you, that I am not with child. There'll be no heir other than Trevor, unless you wish to have a bastard by your beloved Lady Jacqueline."

"Please, Olivia, you will have tongues wagging."

"Let them wag. I should have never come here. I should have never come to England, I should have—"

"But you did all those things. And there's a good chance of getting your work published. That is what you wanted, is it not?" His tone was crisp, and Olivia realized that they were quarreling. "That is true," she said.

Olivia, fearing the silent tears might become real tears and show on her cheeks, gritted her teeth and forced a smile. Her small chin thrust upward, her eyes looking adoringly at her husband, she followed him out onto the dance floor, and the love charade began again: She smiled at him, he glazed down into her upturned face. Once he pushed a straying wisp of hair back from her face, and then traced the lines of her nose with his long finger before he whirled her out from him again.

Look, she wanted to say to all those who were watching, *can't all of you see that we're desperately in love?*

When Lord Sappington came to dance with her, giving a fancy leg, she refused politely, saying in her sweetest voice that she had not had enough dancing with her husband. And later, when Lord Castleberry wanted her to meet his lady love, she refused, saying she had had enough of Lady Jacqueline for one evening. She had glanced at her only once, when Lord Castleberry was dancing with her, and her beauty was truly shocking. Silvery blond hair framed a heart-shaped face, and her complexion was like the underbelly of a rose petal, and she danced like a fairy, so light on her feet was she.

"Olivia, you are acting childish," scolded Lord Castleberry. " 'Tis not like you haven't known how I felt about her . . . right from the start. My plan will work if you will only let it."

"Your plan is not my plan. You broke our agreement when you stole into my bed . . ."

"And you welcomed me."

"I was asleep."

"Olivia, the guests are watching. Let's dance. 'Tis almost time for the meal to be served."

And they danced again, but Olivia did not smile up into his face, or turn adoring eyes on him. A pox on what the people thought, especially Lady Jacqueline. Mayhap the morning paper would carry on its social pages news that Lord Castleberry and his *American* wife were at Almack's, quarreling of all things. And it might add: Could it be because the lovely Lady Sappington was present?

Then the populace would not be shocked when she petitioned for the divorce she planned to get, Olivia thought. Closing her eyes and blinking back the tears stubbornly trying to surface, she prayed that her manuscript would sell.

"And soon, Lord," she said sotto voce. "When I have moved to London and not in proximity with him, the pain will go away."

Across the room, unaware that his good friend Lord Castleberry and his new wife were quarreling, Lord Nigel Avery's eyes scanned the crowded ballroom. He was late. At the last moment a student had come for help with a project, and he could not refuse. His position as lecturer at King's College in London was top priority in his life, not a grand ball at Almack's Assembly Rooms. Were it not for his friend Fitzgerald Castleberry's invitation to come and meet his American wife, he would not be there.

Surrounded with laughter and dancing and gaiety, Avery suddenly felt alone, feeling for the first time ever the barren empty stretches that had composed his entire life. Suddenly, lecturing students was not enough.

He smiled in an attempt to lighten his mood. And then he saw her, a young girl with short blond hair. She was laughing with the others, and wearing a blue gown. Even from this distance he knew that her eyes were blue. Something stirred within him, a depth of feeling that threatened to overwhelm him, and he whispered, "Elizabeth," and began walking toward her, a force larger than himself propelling him.

As he neared, he saw that she was not wearing a blue dress, but an old-fashioned black mantle that swept the floor. She was taller than the laughing young girl in the blue dress; her silvery hair was long and unkempt, her face filled with pain. As he walked he heard nothing, not even the lively music of the orchestra, or the happy voices, or the laughter. He was alone, going to her, his heart thrumming, his hands trembling. And his heart was suddenly filled with an overpowering love. He felt alive. That vacuum in which he had for so long lived no longer existed. The long, barren stretches of emptiness that had composed his existence had at last come to an end, he told himself, adding a quickness to his steps.

Then the girl in the long black mantle was gone. The girl in the blue dress stood in her space. Avery shook his head and told himself that he had spent too much time bent over his history books, that he was becoming delusional. He thought about Lady Anne, whom he was honor bound to wed, and he almost stopped in his tracks. This behavior was totally beyond the pale for an engaged man. Even knowing this, nothing could stop him. Like a magnet drawn to steel, the force was stronger than his willpower.

Feeling foolish, he looked round for Lord Castleberry to ask who the girl in the blue gown might be, and to ask for an introduction, for he felt as drawn to her as he had the vision—he supposed he would call it that, certainly there was no one wearing an old-fashioned black mantle this night at fashionable Almack's.

Across the room, Lord Castleberry was talking animatedly to a pretty woman with long red-brown hair. No doubt his new wife, thought Avery. And then they were dancing and became lost in the crowd. Nigel proceeded on. He wanted to meet the girl, and he did not give a demme about propriety. He found himself smiling. Not in the whole of his twenty-six years had he broken the stringent rules by which he had been brought up. Living up to the expectations of his father, the Duke of Buckingworth, had not been easy. Now, his eyes glued to the girl across the room, he felt dowdy and wished he had paid more attention to his dress, even wished he'd purchased new tails, and mayhap a new cravat. He was tall and wore his clothes well, but seldom took the time away from his lectures to visit his tailor. He wanted to look striking for her, not for society as a whole.

She was standing near a tall white column, sort of leaning against it, as if she, too, did not give a demme about society. A lady of the upper orders did not slouch. Known for his ready smile and his ability to give the perfect leg, he brought both to fore and bowed in front of her, smiling broadly when he looked deeply into her blue eyes. "Pray, do not think me forward, but from the moment I laid eyes on you, I knew I had to meet you. At first I thought you were someone else . . . Elizabeth somebody, from my past, or mayhap from one of my history books. But there was such a resemblance. I looked for my friend Fitzgerald, but he was otherwise occupied, so here I am, breaking the rules of society."

Avery felt awkward, knew that he was coming across as a bumbling college lecturer, but he pushed his suit and brazenly reached to take her hand. "I'm Nigel Avery, professor of history at King's College, London."

She laughed, more of a giggle than a laugh, he thought, liking the sound it made, as if the music had influenced her response. Or was she laughing at him? "I'm Alicia Rose Pembroke from America," she said, "and we don't have such strictures as you English people do. At least I don't. I'm glad you wanted to meet me. Would you please kiss my hand. I've never had that happen before. But I understand 'tis done often in England."

Avery found himself laughing with her. Taking her hand, he did as she asked, feeling her pounding pulse as his lips passed lightly over the back of her hand. "And I wager, Miss Alicia Rose, you've never been kissed by a gentleman, not properly at least."

Dear God, I'm breaking all the rules . . .

"I shall not tell you my secrets," she said, and just then Lady Sefton fell upon them and made the proper introduction, as if Lord Avery had come to her and asked for the favor or an introduction, which would have been the proper thing for him to do. He knew that well enough, but tonight he felt daring.

"When I left, you were dancing with Lord Muchmore," Lady Sefton said, her eyes on Alicia Rose. "I should not have left you unattended."

"I apologize, Lady Sefton," Avery quickly said. "Pray, don't scold Miss Pembroke. I didn't wait for fear the dancing would be over and supper would be served, and I so wanted to partner her for a dance, and then escort her to the supper table."

A smile softened Lady Sefton's not-so-pretty face. "No harm done. I'll not tell the other patronesses, if you won't."

"My lips are sealed," he said, and he said he was so happy to be at Almack's and to have seen her, before leading Alicia Rose out onto the floor to dance a minuet.

And then into a curtained alcove, where he kissed her

properly, with all the feeling stored in his love-starved soul. A completeness came over him, and he reveled in it. No one existed except the two of them, melded together in an intimate embrace. It seemed so natural to Nigel. "Rose . . . may I call you Rose?" he asked.

Alicia Rose's answer came quickly. "Yes, and you may kiss me again if you like. . . ."

Thirty

Alicia Rose was ready for a set-down from her sister, who was obviously in a pucker. And several times during the fabulous supper Lord Castleberry had ordered, Olivia had cast disparaging looks in her direction. Now they were on their way back to the Clarendon, and silence in the coach was palatable.

Alicia Rose wanted to giggle, for happiness filled her from head to toe, and her heart felt as if it would burst inside her chest. When she could no longer bear the silence, she said, as nonchalantly as possible, "Lord Avery will call on you tomorrow, Lord Castleberry."

"He told me so," his lordship answered, then added, "Although I bear sympathy for his plight, my answer will be no. He cannot pay his addresses to you as long as he is engaged to be married."

"How do you know that he wants to pay his addresses to me?"

"I saw the way he looked at you all through supper."

As if she could stand it no longer, Olivia said in a scolding way, "And I saw you disappear behind that curtain. Even in Boston that would not be acceptable. And Lord Avery a stranger. You will never be asked to Almack's again."

"And I should care? I went this night only because my sister is Lady Castleberry. And Nigel is not a stranger to me, or did not seem so. I felt that I had known him all my life. That's why I let him kiss me—"

"You what?" Olivia's face flushed red under the lighted carriage lanterns.

"He kissed me twice, and I've never felt so complete, so . . . so one with another person. It was like I'd been waiting for him since the day I was born. Happiness just swept over me, without warning."

Suddenly Lizzie was sitting on the edge of the squab. "I told you that you would find happiness in that blue dress."

"Oh, dear merciful God," said Olivia. "Lizzie, we don't need your diatribe about what you told anybody. I'm totally out of temper with Alicia Rose."

"I think it is time we calm down," said Lord Castleberry, his resonant voice filling the coach. "I will have a talk with my good friend Nigel Avery and tell him to petition once again his release from the contract with Lady Anne. He knows the rules as well as I. I'm sure something can be worked out. I would like nothing better than to have him for a brother-in-law. We went through the war together. He would make you an excellent husband, Alicia Rose."

"And what if this woman doesn't release him?" asked Olivia.

"She must," piped up Alicia Rose. "She simply must."

That night Lord Nigel Avery danced through Alicia Rose's dreams. She relived the kisses, first gentle, as friends would kiss, and then with deep feeling. She smelled his masculine smell, basked in his wonderful smile, and when morning came she awoke knowing that someday she would be his wife. She looked at the red birds in her silk bed hangings and thought life was as beautiful as their spread wings.

But later it was Lizzie who, after ordering hot coffee and breakfast rolls brought up from the kitchen, then bringing the tray to Alicia Rose's bed, said, "Remember, dear one, I told you that sadness would follow the happiness."

"Oh, Lizzie, pray, don't say things like that. I like feeling happy."

The Gypsy maid looked at Alicia Rose worriedly. "Life has its valleys as well as its mountains. Right now you're on the mountaintop."

"How do you know that, Lizzie?" Alicia Rose asked, now sitting up in bed and sipping the hot coffee. The breakfast roll lay untouched on the silver tray. "How do you know the desponds will follow what I feel right now?"

"The blue dress told me so."

Thirty-one

Olivia did not worry overmuch about Alicia Rose's instant infatuation with Nigel Avery. Sweet, caring Alicia Rose, suspended between innocent youth and the full flower of womanhood, was experiencing her first crush, Olivia thought as she lay and stared at the ceiling of her husband's bedchamber. The curtains were drawn, and dimness hid in the corners. Her thoughts went to the grand ball. Lord Castleberry had displayed her as a trophy, elegant green gown, jewelry fit for a queen, and most of all, the bestowing of his wonderful smile that said he adored her, lying through his white, even teeth.

Adored her!

A show for Lady Jacqueline.

It was in that instant that Olivia knew she could no longer bear the charade. Plainly, her husband wanted to have his cake and to eat it too, as she had heard Cook back in Boston so often say. An heir, and Lady Jacqueline. That was his plan, and nothing she had said to him had seemed to register. Her plan of divorce had gone unheeded, as if she had not said it. Because she was a woman, she supposed. Over her objections he insisted that she was *enceinte,* and worst of all, had shared his belief with his precious Lady Jacqueline.

A child without love. It did not bear thinking on. Not for her. Last evening, after the ball, Lord Castleberry had seemed subdued, preoccupied, and when she had given him back the wonderful diamond tiara, the diamond necklace, and the bracelets of emeralds and rubies, he had not argued with her. He'd simply returned them to the velvet box and placed it in the drawer from which, earlier, he had taken it.

And then he had thanked her for playing her part at Almack's, not mentioning her getting out of temper with him. A chaste kiss before desultory steps had taken himself to the valet's room, where she was sure he had slept well, his perfect plan having worked perfectly.

Olivia had not fared as well, and she had awakened from the restless sleep knowing she would not be exposed to Lady Jacqueline again . . . ever. True, she had signed the agreement, but the agreement of wife in name only had been broken. And foolishly she had clung to the hope that he would come to love her and she had foolishly loved him. Now it was something of a relief to give way to her misery and face it head-on, pulling the impenetrable cloak of anger around her like a shroud.

Now that she had fulfilled what was expected of her at Almack's, she must leave Robinbrook, make her own plan.

With her head, not her heart, she told herself.

Throwing the satin-bound coverlet back, she sat upright on the side of the high bed, and when she scooted down and placed her feet to the floor and stood, the room began to spin.

This did not frighten Olivia. It was a familiar feeling, and when she felt a slight cramping in the bottom of her stomach, she knew that her monthly curse had come upon her, and that the pain would last only for a short time. Holding to the bed to steady herself, she waited a moment or so before she went to the dressing room to take care of herself, and then with great speed she finished her toilette. Tying her hair back with a riband, she then donned a simple morning dress of gray muslin. After last evening's extravagant display of finery, she felt comfortable in her scuffed half-boots and the plain dress. Later she would write, and mayhap go to the library to read.

Because she was pale, she took from the rouge pot a small amount of blush, applying it to her cheeks and lips, and then, adding a drop of oil to a brush, she stroked her thick, dark brows, and her long eyelashes, making them appear longer and darker than they actually were.

"That is that," she said, surprised at her calmness as she went to pull the bell rope to signal her wish for breakfast to be brought from the hotel's kitchen. Then on to the drawing room, with its crimson walls and lovely moss-green window hangings.

She pulled the curtains and, through the morning fog, dull sunlight shone through the best that it could, casting shadows. She looked out and saw other buildings. She missed Robinbrook, and the smell of the sea. And then she espied on the writing desk a missive bearing her name, written in her husband's masculine scrawl. It was not sealed, and she read it immediately, learning that he had left earlier to take care of business.

I hope that you can sleep until past noon. In your condition, much rest is needed, as you well know. I shall return as soon as I have finished. I plan to ride with you in Hyde Park at five o'clock, a very fashionable thing to do, for everyone will be there. And later, if you are agreeable, I would very much like to show you off to the opera crowd at King's Theater in the Haymarket. While I am gone, I think it a capital idea for you and Alicia Rose to shop on Bond Street. Fashionable stores are there, and I have an account . . .

Show you off . . .

"Well, I would not like, your lordship. And I have no desire to add to the finery you have already afforded me.

I have been *shown off* to your Lady Jacqueline as much as I can bear."

Olivia was surprised at her calm resolve, but after last evening, she painfully realized the sooner she could establish a place of her own and get on with her writing, the better it would be for her. Her pragmatic mind having accepted this, she told herself that the hurt she felt in her heart would diminish when she was out of proximity with him, and she reminded herself that she was twenty-three, old enough to stop loving a man who did not return that love. Relief that she was not *enceinte* washed over her. If that had been so, then she would have never been free of him. A child would have kept him in her life, and she would have grown old loving him. In time, memory of his seductive kisses, his wry smile, and the way he made her feel, warm and lovely and filled with desire, even confused at times, would go away. She was certain of that.

Breakfast came—ham, eggs, fluffy hot biscuits and various jellies, along with a pot of hot tea. She thanked the footman and then poured and drank heartily of the tea, almost scorching her throat but welcoming the heat into her stomach. When she was through eating, she would hire public transport and go to Fleet street and call on Mr. Bates. Hopefully he had read her manuscript, and hopefully he would return to her the pages she'd written since coming to England, pages about Lucifer and meant only for her eyes.

A knock on the door drew her attention. Thinking it was Alicia Rose, she invited the knocker to enter.

The door swung slowly open.

The cup returned to the saucer with a clatter, on its way spilling tea into the lap of Olivia's gray muslin dress. For standing in the doorway, as regal as the queen of England was Lady Sappington . . . Lady Jacqueline. She wore a handsome pink sprigged muslin morning dress that left nothing to one's imagination of hidden curves. The statue

Olivia had beheaded in her husband's quarters at Robin-brook came instantly to her mind. The round breasts, the tiny waist, and slender hips had not been exaggerated. But there was nothing cold and hard about the true Lady Jacqueline. She exuded elusive femininity, an inexplicable softness. Over a face of pale translucent, porcelainlike complexion, which looked soft to the touch, she wore a Gypsy hat of pink straw, tied under her chin with a pink riband. The curled plumage was of a darker shade of pink. Then Olivia looked into her blue eyes. They appeared cold, yet they were laughing. *Regal* flew from Olivia's thoughts, replaced by *goddess*. The object of her husband's love was too beautiful to be of this world. Little wonder he was besotted.

Olivia stood, visualizing the dark spot the tea had made in the lap of her gown and feeling terribly embarrassed and fiercely angry. Because she was well trained in good manners, she said to her visitor, "Lady Sappington, how nice of you to call. Pray, do come in."

"I shall not stay long," the unwelcome visitor said, sweeping into the room with the grace of a long, sleek tiger. I see that last evening must have worn you out. I had breakfast at first light."

"With your husband?"

"Oh, my, no. That old gaffer is still abed. Where is Fitzgerald? I pray he is out. I came to speak with you."

"Then, let's move to more comfortable space."

Leaving the chair in which she was sitting to partake of her breakfast, Olivia moved to occupy a capacious armchair near the marble fireplace, where coals of last evening still simmered, and motioned for Lady Jacqueline to take the matching chair on the opposite side, saying, "This is not a social call, then? I suppose that is why you are alone, without an abigail? I hear that strictures of the *ton* forbid a highborn lady from being on the streets without one."

"She's below stairs. I did not want her to hear what I

have to say. You know what big ears, and big mouths, servants have."

Olivia gave a polite laugh. "Since this is a business call, which precludes our talking chitchat and passing on on-dits, as I understand you English do over tea, I suggest that you say the whole of what you came to say and be done with it. I am quite busy. My husband will be returning shortly, and he has grand plans for our day."

"I saw him leave—"

"Oh, were you watching, waiting for him to be gone?"

Embarrassment and guilt showed on Lady Jacqueline's face, suddenly suffused with a deep flush. "Not . . . not exactly," she said. " 'Tis just that what I have to say is for our ears only."

"Then, get on with it," Olivia said, her anger growing. "I can't imagine discussing with you anything behind my husband's back, so don't be disappointed if I remain mum while you talk."

Lady Jacqueline took in a deep breath and sighed deeply. Olivia realized that her head was starting to ache. After a long pause, clasping her hands demurely together in her lap, Lady Jacqueline began. "I'm sure that Fitzgerald has told you that I am his only love, that, like his mother, he believes a man loves only once."

Olivia raised a dark eyebrow and remained silent.

"And I'm sure he has told you that it was I who goaded him into marrying an American. I specified ugly, and I see he did not satisfy that wish." She paused again. "I should have never, in a moment of pique, married Lord Sappington. I knew it was a mistake from the start, and last night at Almack's proved me right. Now, I am ready to rectify my mistake."

"Oh? And how is that?"

"I'm prepared to leave my husband and take up separate dwelling for Fitzgerald's convenience. But I felt, in all fairness, that I should tell you first, since you are in the family way. He imparted that bit of information to me last evening, and, desiring to be considerate, I feared the shock of *our* plan might cause you to lose his lordship's heir."

Olivia waited a moment before speaking, measuring her words. And then: "I take it that you do not plan to have children. And, oh, by the bye, since you have been apprised of my personal condition, might I ask if you and your husband have consummated your marriage, or has his advanced age prevented that from taking place?"

"Oh, my, no. Sapp is perfectly able to perform. Whatever gave you that idea? I've taken precaution, for the thought of bearing a child is repugnant to me. Can you imagine what it would do to my body? Blow it up like a barrel, I imagine, and then the baby's squalling would put windmills in my head. Even with a nanny." She gave a little laugh, which, to Olivia, sounded totally childish. The woman was fastly losing her charm, and Olivia waited, wanting to hear more, to get the whole of it, for she never wanted to encounter this calculating woman again for as along as she lived.

"I'm not foolish. I've not imparted my feelings about bearing children to darling Fitzgerald," Lady Jacqueline said. "I trust you won't tell. I'm perfectly willing for you to have his heir as long as I come first in his heart."

Olivia had had enough. She could no longer contain her anger; in truth, she told herself, an explosion would come at any moment if she did not rid herself of this jade. She remembered hearing Fred call Lady Jacqueline that, also a scapescull. This bolstered Olivia. It seemed that Lord Castleberry was the only one who could not see through this . . . this . . . doxy. Now on her feet, Olivia said in a stern, very unfriendly tone, "I'm most happy that you have apprised me of your and my husband's plan, Lady Sappington, no doubt made last evening when you were dancing. Now that I know, I will excuse you. I have much to do before he returns." She went to the door, opened it with a flourish, then stood back for the grand exit.

Lady Sappington swept across the room, her head held in a haughty tilt. "I do so hope we shall be friends, Olivia—"

"Lady Castleberry to you," retorted Olivia, and then she, restraining her desire to shove, assisted her visitor's departure by placing her hand to her back and helping her out into the hall, and as the door closed behind her husband's love, Olivia heard her mutter, "Such atrocious manners."

Alone, dry-eyed although stupid, hidden tears burned her eyes, Olivia swore under her breath and pounded the wall with her small fists, feeling the certainty of being loved beyond all else drain slowly from her heart. Time passed unnoticed, and then she sat at a small writing desk and penned a message to her husband:

> I have returned to Robinbrook. There is one thing I must do there, and then I shall return to London to find a place for Alicia Rose and myself. I fear I must accept your offer of financial assistance until my writing sells, and then I shall repay every cent. I have no desire to be beholden to you. I believe that last night at Almack's I satisfactorily fulfilled our business arrangement.

She signed her name, left it on the desk, and then went to yank the bell rope to summon a footman, from whom, when he appeared at the door, she calmly ordered the Castleberry town coach brought from the mews, where it was being kept. After he had bowed and left, quickly she packed her things and went to tell Alicia Rose she was leaving.

"But you can't leave his lordship to take public transport," argued Alicia Rose.

"Better he take it than I, and I am not of the notion to return to Robinbrook with him."

"Oh, sister, why are you so angry? I so wanted to stay in town. You know Lord Avery is supposed to call."

"He can find you at Robinbrook if he is so inclined. Or Fitzgerald can talk with him. I believe you have been told that this gentleman with whom you've suddenly become enamored is engaged to another woman."

"He is going to take care of that."

"And in the meantime?"

"I shall wait for him . . . forever, if it takes that long." Olivia let out a deep sigh. "I'm certain you will recover in time. But stay if you like. And where is Lizzie?"

"I'm here, your ladyship," the maid said, coming into the room from the bedchamber. "I heard it all, and I think we should go with you. It does not bear thinking on that you would travel alone, with knights of the road everywhere. You might get robbed, or worse yet, kidnapped."

After those words from Lizzie, Alicia Rose issued no further objections. "If you're determined, Olivia, but I don't see why you are in such a hurry to leave London."

"I had a morning caller, before I had finished breakfast. Lady Jacqueline. I am so angry that I don't think it would be safe for me to see Lord Castleberry at this time. Mayhaps not forever." Olivia turned to Lizzie. "If I so much as hear a peep out of you about this to the other servants, I shall help his lordship place you in another household. Or better yet, set you out without reference. Do you understand?"

Lizzie bobbed. "Oh, I do, your ladyship. I would never tell your secrets to anybody. I promise. I just wish I had seen that doxy. I would have told her what for, pushing herself on my mistress."

"Stop calling her a doxy, Lizzie. For your own good. Lord Castleberry might walk in and hear you. I've cautioned you of that before. Now, hurry and pack. I wish to be gone before his lordship returns."

Olivia turned to Alicia Rose, who was standing in the middle of the room, looking as if she were not sure of just where she was. "Dearest sister," Olivia said, hugging her. "I meant what I said. If you wish to stay and talk with your new friend, I will understand. It is so difficult for me to realize that you truly are a woman now. You've been my little sister for ever so long."

"I feel that I should go with you. You seem so strange, Olivia, so different. Are you sure it is your wont to run away from Lord Castleberry. He didn't send that . . . that woman to you, did he?"

"I don't know, Alicia Rose. I know only that she knew about his plan, which he has, more than once, imparted to me. 'Tis too dreadful to speak of. Now, please, if you are going, make ready. The coach will be at the door any moment. . . ."

Although the coach was pulled by four lively stepping horses, Olivia could not help wishing they were in less cumbersome equipage. She could not explain her hurry, except now that she had decided what she would do, she wanted to get on with it. She worried about what to tell Fred and hated very much to disappoint the old man. But he should know that if she had one ounce of decency about her, she would not agree to have Fitzgerald's heir while he kept Lady Jacqueline as his mistress.

She regretted that she had had to leave London before calling on Mr. Bates in regards to her writing, but she would send a missive, and he could send a reply to Robinbrook if she was still there, and if she had moved into town, then it would be forwarded.

A subdued Alicia Rose sat on the plush squab across from Olivia. Even Lizzie was quiet. Doom and gloom filled the coach, and, in an attempt to lighten the ambiance, Olivia, laughing lightly, said, "Can you imagine Lord Castleberry's surprise when he sees all those packed boxes? What a peagoose I was to forget that another coach transported our clothes when we came into town."

"At least his lordship won't have to use public transport,"

said Lizzie. "He can ride with the boxes." She laughed then. "As soon as he sees you're gone, he'll come tearing up the road to Robinbrook, covered in boxes. Poor Henry, most likely he'll be riding the boot."

The mood lightened somewhat after that, and the miles passed beneath the coach, the countryside unnoticed. At last, long after the coachman had stopped to light the lanterns, they arrived at Robinbrook, waking a grumbling butler.

Only Lizzie had noticed behind them the unlighted, two-wheeled curricle that had been following the Castleberry coach at a safe distance since they had left the posting inn, where they had stopped for fresh horses, and to hurriedly partake of a light repast. When the Castleberry coach turned from the main road, the curricle had continued on, as if going to Hythe.

Only now that they were safely inside the house did the maid breathe a sigh of relief. She told the butler, "Go to your bed before you totally wake up. I'll tend Lady Castleberry and Miss Alicia Rose."

"The devil take me," swore' Lord Castleberry when he returned to the Clarendon and found his apartment piled high with boxes and his wife gone. Disappointment rode him, for he had many times this day rehearsed his apology to her. Now she was gone and threatening in a missive to get a place of her own.

His first thought was to tear after her, but it was late, near the five o'clock hour, and his mind was going in a thousand directions. How could he rectify the wrongs he had done? He poured a brandy and lifted it to the portrait of his parents above the mantel. Tears clouded his eyes.

"You recognized true love. I was too blind to do so. In

truth, Papa, Mama, I'm pretty dumb where affairs of the heart are concerned, and I refused to listen to Fred. It took last night . . ."

He lowered his big frame into a chair, sat, and pondered, broodingly sipping the brandy. Now, at this moment, he should be riding in Hyde Park with his wife.

"My wife," he said aloud, and liked the sound of the words. He felt himself smile, thinking on the independent, erudite, stubborn woman he had married out of spite, and then, in the middle of his rumination, and his longing to hold her in his arms, to once again feel the completeness she had brought to him, a knock on the door caused him to pull himself upright. He knew better than to expect the knocker to be Olivia. Most likely he had lost her forever, and his heart told him that he had no one to blame but himself. Slowly, still holding the glass of brandy, he rose from his chair and went to answer the knock.

It was Lord Avery.

Lord Castleberry was never so glad to see anyone. He desperately needed a friend. "Avery, pray, come in. Gads wallop, I'm happy to see you."

"You look as if you need help," retorted Avery, his broad smile quickly fading. "What's wrong, Castleberry? Has your last friend just passed to the other side? And don't you think you should light a taper?"

He stepped into the room shrouded with day's last light and took his friend's hand and shook it. He noted with wonderment the boxes stacked neatly in the middle of the floor. Again he asked, this time his voice showing a much deeper concern, "What's wrong, friend? Why all the boxes?"

"Have a chair, Avery," Lord Castleberry said. "You're just what I need, someone to tell of my stupidity. Only a dear friend would listen."

Avery went to the sidebar and poured himself a drink, as always making himself at home in Castleberry's dwelling.

"Shoot away," he said, turning back into the room. "I'm a sitting duck."

"I love her," said Lord Castleberry.

A cynical laugh from Avery. "The whole town knows you love Lady Jacqueline, Castleberry. They know she's the reason you stayed away for six months, holed up God knows where. I just left White's, and your wife, whom you showed off so splendidly last evening at Almack's, is on everyone's tongue. They're calling you a fool."

"And they're right. I used her to make Lady Jacqueline jealous. And she allowed me to do this dastardly thing because of our business agreement. What a cad I've turned out to be."

"Did it work? Did the jade come running back to your arms?" Avery asked, and when Castleberry did not answer, just took a huge gulp of brandy and stared into the dead fire as if Avery had not spoken, Avery went on. "I can see that it did. Obviously your wife in name only has flown the coop. Back to Robinbrook, I suppose."

"She said in her missive that she planned to get a place of her own immediately, and she even conceded that she would need support from me until her manuscript sells. For Olivia, a woman who nailed the door shut between our chambers, that is quite a concession. A place of her own where I won't be welcome."

"Well, why the long face? 'Tis exactly what you want, is it not? Now all you have to do is purchase a dwelling for your Lady Jacqueline . . . or did she turn you down, and that's the reason for your deep desponds? You know, Fitzgerald, you said you needed a friend to listen, and so far you haven't made a lick of sense."

A deep silence fell, and after awhile Lord Castleberry got to his feet and stoked the fire and then went to pull the bell rope, ordering, when a footman came, a fire laid and supper for two sent up. When asked just what he wanted, he answered cryptically, "The specialty of the kitchen."

And then he closed the door on the astonished footman and went to the sidebar to pour more brandy for both of them, after which he returned to his chair.

"We could have gone out to eat," said Avery. "Might have done you good."

"No, I didn't want to go out. I really should order public transport and be off to Robinbrook. With good horses, I could be there by first light."

"I'll go with you. In your state, I wouldn't think of letting you off by yourself."

Castleberry lifted his glass and took a huge gulp. "I'm afraid, 'tis true, but not what you are thinking. I care not about Lady Jacqueline. I learned the whole of it last night when she practically fell all over me and begged me to take her as my mistress." He laughed, and the sound poured out into the room, mirthless and hollow even to his own ears. "Nigel, I believed with all my heart that I wanted just that. I spent the night tossing and turning and questioning myself. 'Tis not easy for a man to admit he has made a fool of himself, but by first light my head was clear, and I knew that I loved my wife, wholeheartedly, completely.

"I came to Olivia's bed, and she was sleeping so peacefully I did not wake her but went about making plans for our life together. But when I returned back here, she was gone, and her missive left no doubt that she was through with me. Coward that I am, I am afraid to go to Robinbrook, to face her. I believe she could have loved me . . . if I had not been such a cad. I often spoke of my desire for her, but I was careful to point out that a man could desire a woman and not love her. I even offered her a *ton* marriage. . . ."

Avery whistled through his teeth and then said, "I agree, you acted as a cad of the first water, but that does not mean you are a cad. In affairs of the heart, a man often acts foolishly. and most often he does not know he wants something until he has lost it. 'Tis the nature of the beast. We are born to be warriors; the heart has to teach us how to love."

"It all started when I lost my parents at fifteen. I reveled in the story of their love. Of different stations in life, yet Father defiantly married Mother. For a long time their love for each other was all I had to cling to, and the fact that I was born of that love, and that they both loved me. God had made my mother out of my father's rib. In the universe there was only one true love for a man. I believed that with all my heart, and until I met Lady Jacqueline, I held my heart in reserve, waiting.

"Her beauty overwhelmed me, and I was more than willing to give her my heart, I thought forever. Then when she married old Sapp, I would have done anything to win her back, and when I did, I did not want her. I couldn't understand the sudden turn of my feelings, and I pondered them into the night. And then it became clear. I was in love with love, not with Lady Jacqueline. Plainly, her beauty is only skin deep. Fred many times told me so, even called her a jade, but I would not listen."

A servant came to start the fire, and soon after that a footman, the same one who had delivered the boxes to the apartment, came with a huge silver tray laden with food. By then the fire was burning brightly and Avery had lighted a branch of candles. A servant did not speak until spoken to, and it was not until Lord Castleberry thanked him that the footman said, "Your lordship, I ordered the carriage brought for Lady Castleberry. She said she was returning to the country."

"She left me a missive, but thank you for telling me," Lord Castleberry said, but it was evident the footman wanted to say more, and his lordship asked, "Is there more?"

"Yes, your lordship. She left in quite a hurry . . . after her visitor—"

"Her visitor?"

"Yes, a very beautiful woman called. It being so soon after I had taken Lady Castleberry's breakfast, I'm certain the visitor was not expected."

Lord Castleberry held his composure until after the footman had left, a smug look on his face for having passed on the on-dit. Then a loud groan from Castleberry filled the room, and vitriolic swear words turned the air blue. "Demme, demme . . . that bit of muslin," he said, and Avery laughed.

"For so long I've wanted to hear you swear at your precious Lady Jacqueline. Thank God your eyes have been opened. Sit down, old friend, let's eat and plan your next move. After that I wish to speak with you about Miss Pembroke . . . Alicia Rose Pembroke."

They ate and the fire died, while the branch of tapers burned to the halfway mark in a room that had grown quiet and still, shadows dancing on the crimson walls. The bosom bows talked into the night, as they had done so many times when they were fighting alongside Wellington, and the next morning, long before first light, they set off for Robinbrook in the equipage that had, on its way into town, transported boxes of clothes and Henry, the valet.

This day Henry rode the boot, and the boxes of clothes all but inundated the two peers of the realm.

"Put them to their bits," Lord Castleberry said to the newly hired driver as he and Avery boarded and squeezed into the space left available. "I must arrive at Robinbrook as soon as possible."

A whip cracked and they were off, tooling fastly over cobbled streets clear of other carriages because of the early hour. Turning to Lord Avery, Lord Castleberry asked worriedly, "Do you think she will forgive me?"

A laugh followed, and then came Lord Avery's reassuring words, "I have no doubt. So stop your fretting."

Silently Lord Avery was praying that this would be so.

Thirty-two

Olivia was glad to be back in her temporary rooms at Robinbrook, where she could see through the open windows the unrelenting brightness of the blue sky, smell the fresh, sweet air, and hear the pounding of the waves as they climbed high to that blue sky, only to fall back down onto the craggy shore with a resounding swoosh. In the distance the sun danced on the blue-black water, turning its foamy tips to glittering diamonds. As she dressed in a simple day dress made of gray cotton twill, she would not allow her mind to dwell on her departure from this lovely place. This moment is all that counts, she told herself, savoring it, holding it for future memories.

Last evening, when she had arrived late from her hurried departure from London, she had not thought she could sleep, but she had, soundly, and now she had one thing to do, and she would dwell on that. Chester must have his eyes checked by a physician. She had promised the boy, and she could not break her promise. And there was Fred, dear Fred, who had meant well when he had tried to make things work that were not meant to work. What the aging man had done, insisting that right away she have an heir to replace cousin Trevor, was out of love for his grandson, and for Robinbrook. She would tell him what had transpired in London and apprise him of her decision to accept Lord Castleberry's generous offer of support for her and Alicia Rose until her manuscript sold.

But there was no need to upset the old man by mentioning the divorce, which would come later, she decided as she rummaged through her reticule for the name of the physician and the directions to his office, given to her by Lady Patience.

In so doing, she came upon the linen handkerchief she had purchased for her husband. That had been when she still had hope, she thought, laying the handkerchief aside, still in the soft white paper in which the salesclerk had obligingly wrapped it. She also took from her reticule a short essay on the medieval church dedicated to St. Leonard, the patron saint of prisoners, built in A.D. 1090. Why she had kept those two things in her reticule, she did not know. Except that she was like all women she knew, stuffing her reticule to capacity.

Dressed, she summoned a servant and asked that he find Chester and tell him to make ready to leave for Hythe right away, and to have a groom prepare an equipage, preferably something light. She would handle the ribbons. She then made her way through the maze of hallways to the stairs that led to the Hunt Room. There, she found Fred, thankfully alone. He seemed surprised to see her, and stood when she entered, coming to her and hugging her to his big, broad chest.

"Dear Olivia, I didn't know you had returned. How did things go in London? I'll wager you were the loveliest gel at the ball, and that Fitz was as proud as a peacock, showing you off. Come sit, and I'll serve you breakfast. 'Tis good to have you back."

The words *showing you off,* did not sit well with Olivia. She felt a coldness sweep over her as she went to a chair near the fireplace. The hounds were there, scattered in various places, their long, spotted bodies stretched to full-length, their heads resting on big paws. She envied them; they would be at Robinbrook forever, even after Fred was gone.

"I suppose Fitz will come as soon as he has finished his business in London," the old man said, his spiky white eyebrows raised quizzically. He placed the silver tray on a table beside her chair.

"I suppose so," Olivia answered. She lifted the cup of hot coffee to her lips, but suddenly the ham, eggs, and hot biscuits held no appeal to her palate. "I need to talk with you, Fred. I think it only fair to tell you that I know for sure that I am not *enceinte*. There will be no heir to Robinbrook by me. Mayhap by Lady Jacqueline . . ."

She told him, then, the whole of it, and she saw tears puddle in the wrinkles of his time-worn cheeks, and she felt horribly sorry for him. She even told him that she was as guilty as Lord Castleberry in the deception they had tried to pull off, each for his or her own selfish reason, but that she had come to love her husband, who was no longer her husband in name only.

And then she told him what had transpired in London, his lordship showing her off like a possession, pretending devotion to regain Lady Jacqueline's affection, and then she told him of the lady in question's visit on the morning after the ball. Was that only yesterday, she wondered, her own eyes suddenly hot from unshed tears. It seemed so long ago, and she felt changed somehow, a woman metamorphosed from a woman deeply in love into a woman determined to recover from such devastating pain.

"The devil take me," Fred said, and then apologized for swearing in the presence of a lady of the first water. "You're everything Fitz needs," he said. For a moment a silence lay between them, and then, sighing deeply, he added, "But I can't fault him for following his heart . . . as his mother did years ago when she fell in love with his father."

And then he added, "Olivia, I will not tell Fitz that you love him. That is up to you when the time is right."

Olivia rose from her chair and went to place the tray of cold food on the table where used trays were left and then came back to bend and kiss Fred on the cheek. "I promised Chester I would take him to a physician in Hythe to see about his vision. I've come to believe that is why he can't attend school with the other Robinbrook children. He may be a little slow in learning, but I believe his major problem is his eyes. His sculptures are wonderful, and he so much wants to read and write and cipher."

"Olivia," Fred said, his voice choked with emotion, "pray, be careful. Even if things have not worked out with you and my grandson, I will always feel they should have. I do not want harm to come to you because of us."

"I'll be careful, Fred," she said, and later she was to think of this as a portent of something to come. But at the moment she took it as concern from a caring old man. She left quickly and went to the stables, where a Stanhope gig had been made ready, one horse at its tongue. She smiled. When told that she would be handling the ribbons, she supposed the groom had chosen the simplest equipage the stables held, pulled by one horse.

Chester was already aboard, and she, after the groom had let down the step, climbed in and sat beside him, taking the ribbons and giving the black horse office to run. She smiled at Chester in an affable, reassuring manner, for she could feel his apprehension, and most of all, feel his hope.

"I'm ever so glad you are doing this for me," the boy said, and after that they were quiet, Olivia intent on her driving while drinking in the beauty of abundant crops growing in dark, loamy soil. She listened to the lowing of sheep on verdant hillocks, and occasionally a dog barked somewhere in the distance. The road neared the sea, and to the left, the deep water roiled, rolling outward with the tide, while the smell of clumps of red cherries ripening on heavily laden trees and sharp sea air filled her lungs.

The Stanhope moved swiftly, and in no time at all, so it seemed to Olivia, they were in Hythe, where narrow, hilly streets straddled a hillside, then sloped gently downward toward the seaport teeming with workers loading and unloading ships. She looked at Lady Patience's directions and went to the quaint clapboard building with a stoop at its entrance. Finding on the narrow street no place to tether the horse, she drove to the alley behind and left the equipage and horse there.

There was a back entrance and they took it, and after confirmation of what Olivia believed about Chester's eyesight, and thick quizzing lenses held together with thin wire rims and brought back to rest around his ears were supplied, taking considerable time, they emerged back into the alley.

"I can see you now, Lady Castleberry," Chester said, smiling widely. "Yer no longer just a blur."

They were in the Stanhope, and no sooner had the words left Chester's mouth, even before Olivia could reply she felt herself being dragged to the street by a man whom she had never seen. She quickly noted that he looked as if he might have slept on the docks—wrinkled coat, unkempt beard, long, straggly hair, and his breath smelled horribly like spirits. She heard herself scream, and in that instant she saw another man, another stranger, board the Stanhope, grab the ribbons, and tool fastly away. When Chester tried to jump from the equipage and come to her aid, he was harnessed by the man's long arm, and soon the Stanhope rounded the corner and was out of sight.

Olivia's only thought at the moment was for Chester's safety. "Poor boy," she murmured to herself, "he'll be frightened out of his wits." She prayed to God for his safety, and then, turning, faced her own captor, who was grinning at her insidiously, showing gums with missing teeth. Her voice was sharp. "What do you want? I have little money."

"Ain't money me wants," he said. "I'll get thet from another. I'm jest to hold you here till he comes. I suggest you don't try to run, fer I can outdistance a rabbit."

Olivia knew this was so and looked around for someone to come to her aid should she begin screaming, but saw no one. And then an open-top carriage came into sight, carrying a lone passenger, who was also the driver. The carriage slowed, and when it was alongside, Olivia felt herself being lifted and thrust onto the squab, and the two horses bolted into a fast run down the alley.

She demanded to know where she was being taken, and why, but met only hostile silence. It was not until they were climbing Church Hill that she realized where they were going, and it was then that she stole a look at her kidnapper, who had heretofore kept his head turned to the left, away from her. Now she saw that his eyes were masked, his chin twisted into an obdurate line. She knew instantly it was cousin Trevor Castleberry, and he was taking her to the medieval church dedicated to St. Leonard, the patron saint of prisoners. She prayed they would encounter Father Stephens.

"Why . . . why, Trevor, are you taking me to the church? Why are you kidnapping me? I thought we were friends?" She tried to keep the fright from her voice, but it was there, all through her body, screaming through her brain. The grinding of her teeth together did little to help, for she felt herself shivering uncontrollably, and she smelted the evil that seeped from the man on the squab beside her.

But the ominous silence of no answer was the worst to bear. She began to beat on him with her small fists, calling him names, and when she managed to scratch his face, bringing blood, he stopped the equipage and bound her hands. "You'll do as I say, cousin Olivia," he said.

Olivia soon realized that her hope they would encounter Father Stephens had been in vain. Trevor Castleberry was much too clever for that. Plainly his plan had been well formed long in advance, mayhap as long ago as their first visit to this church. She suspected that this time had been chosen because Father Stephens was on his knees somewhere in meditation. Still bound, she was led through a side entrance, a stone door to which Trevor had the key, and then down stone stairs that wound deep into the earth. The smell of molding bones came up to meet them. He was taking her to the crypt, which she had read about but had not seen, had never wanted to see. The thought was appalling to her. She would leave that to the pilgrims on their way to Canterbury years and years ago. Her research had told her the bones had been there since "time out of mind," shown to visitors by the parish chamberlain, who was paid the sum of one pound in addition to regular salary of four pounds. Well, where was the parish chamberlain now? she asked herself. Her fright had subsided, masked by a shield of anger.

Trevor Castleberry, for whatever reason he is doing this, will not hurt me.

And then they were inside the domed Golgotha, among piles of skulls and femurs. Her kidnapper had prepared a place for her. Hidden behind a pile of smelly bones, there was a blanket on the cobbled floor, a box on which to sit. He lighted a taper, then untied her hands.

"The parish chamberlain will find me," she said with bravado. "You can't get away with this, you know. . . ."

"The pit is closed for the sorting of bones. I've hired out to do the job, with this in mind. I can come and go and nothing will be thought of it. And you can scream your head off and not be heard."

"But why, Trevor? I've done nothing to you."

"Except get yourself with an heir to Robinbrook, which is rightfully mine. A physician will come soon to rid you of that burden."

"But, Trevor, I'm not *enceinte*—"

As if she had not spoken, he removed the mask from his eyes, and even in the dimness Olivia found herself looking into the glazed black eyes of a madman.

This was not the kind man who had brought her *Emma*, she thought. Or had he been play-acting when he was being so kind? Had thinking she was *enceinte* pushed him over the edge? A shiver passed through her, engulfing her whole cold body in an uncontrollable way.

Still, she refused to let him see her fright, or sense her unshed tears. Dry-eyed and looking defiantly up into his distorted face, she silently prayed, "Dear Lord, please let Fitzgerald find me . . . and soon."

Aloud, she said, "My husband will break every bone in your body," and cousin Trevor laughed, a dry, loud laugh that echoed off the piles and piles of bones and increased Olivia's belief that Trevor Castleberry was as mad as a hatter.

Thirty-three

Fitzgerald Castleberry was disappointed that when he arrived back at Robinbrook, Olivia had gone into Hythe with Chester, but he was not overly concerned. He spoke with Fred briefly and then went to the farm steward's house and told Zeke, Trevor's former valet, and the butler that he had managed to place them in another household, that the new farm steward had scoffed at the idea of having such luxury as a butler and a valet. This done with happy results, he returned to Robinbrook, fully expecting his wife to have returned home.

But she was not there, and it was growing late. He sought out Fred and was told that Lord Avery and Alicia Rose were walking along the seashore. Lord Castleberry had suggested to Avery that he apprise Alicia Rose of his feelings, and of his intent of breaking the engagement to Lady Anne as soon as it could possibly be done. Avery had asked for and had been given a short leave from King's College to come to Robinbrook and speak with Alicia Rose.

Lord Castleberry looked out and saw elongated shadows dancing under the trees, and he let himself become genuinely concerned about his wife. He'd had no doubt that she would buy Chester a sweet after the eye examination, and possibly drive him along the docks of Hythe, but, even at that, she should have been home long ago. He had rehearsed his declaration of love for her so much that he had found himself mumbling to himself about it.

"Fred, I've been a fool," he told his grandfather, and then the whole of his foolishness of thinking he was in love with Lady Jacqueline came out. "I realize now her shallowness.

"Not only have I been a fool, but a cad of the first water," he said, as he paced and re-paced the expanse of the huge Hunt Room, then returned to sit near his grandfather.

"I knew you would come to your senses," Fred told him, smiling proudly at his grandson. "Now all you have to do is beg, and I mean beg, for her forgiveness. Get down on your knees if you have to. She's not one to give in easily. She will have to know you mean it." He tapped his cane on the floor and gave a joyful little laugh. "I must say it serves you right, Fitz. You should have seen her wonderful attributes from the start. And, oh, by the bye, your wife informed me that she is not in the family way, but I'm sure that will be taken care of soon now that you are thinking straight." He grinned wryly. "If you can talk her into forgiving you for your foolishness."

Before Lord Castleberry could respond, or even think of the matter, Avery and Alicia Rose entered the Hunt Room, holding hands and smiling. " 'Tis all settled; we've declared our love for each other," Avery said. "I'm to go about getting my misalliance to Lady Anne set aside, and at your request, Castleberry, we've agreed not to see each other until that is done."

Alicia Rose spoke: "Nigel told me about your change of heart toward Lady Jacqueline, Lord Castleberry, so I feel comfortable in leaving Olivia in your care."

"What do you mean, leave her in my care?" he asked.

"I want to return to Boston for a short time. Nigel and I have agreed 'twould be impossible to stay apart with both of us in England." She felt herself blushing. Only young gels blushed, and she so wanted to be grown up . . . like Olivia. But that did not preclude her knowing love when she found it, she told herself. She looked at Nigel and smiled, and he smiled back, love brimming his wonderful blue eyes. Someday she would be his; she'd known it from the first time she had laid eyes on him, at Almack's assembly rooms. And he had felt the same way, so he had told her. Their short time on the beach had been wonderful. She could still taste his sweet kisses, which she knew would have to last her a dreadfully long time.

Even a month will seem forever, she thought, knowing that it did not matter. She would wait forever if she had to. She had said that from the start.

"Things will work out," Lord Castleberry assured them, and then his mind went back to Olivia. What could be keeping her? Taking a round watch from his waistcoat pocket and looking at it, he shook his head, his anxiety growing by leaps and bounds. As if the feeling had swept throughout the house, soon Lizzie, Aunt Evaline, Cook, and the butler joined the others, and only moments passed before Lady Patience and her hounds came through the door.

"I felt something was wrong," she said, her eyes immediately going to Fred. "Are you all right, Fred?"

"Yes, yes, I'm fine, dear. 'Tis Olivia who's giving us a fright. She left this morning, going into Hythe, and she hasn't returned. We're all becoming worried. If that Trevor has harmed her . . ."

"Now, don't start imagining things, Fred," said Lord Castleberry, but his heart was not in his words. Already he had considered Trevor as the culprit, and Lizzie's next words showed her to be of like mind. " 'Tis Trevor, Lord Castleberry. I can see it with my second sight."

His lordship did not have time to discuss with the silly Gypsy girl her second sight. Jumping to his feet, he declared he had waited long enough, that they would never learn anything sitting there waiting for Olivia to come home.

"Avery and I will go into Hythe and call on cousin Trevor . . . if we don't encounter the Stanhope on our way in. If he's so much as harmed a hair on her head, he will answer to me in a most formidable way."

And out the door he went, followed by Nigel Avery, both running at full capacity. At the stables a coach and four was made ready with great haste, and soon they were tooling down the curving road that led to the sea. At the main road they turned right and headed toward Hythe. They had not traveled far, when they saw a tall, gangly figure moving toward them, running in *U* spurts and then slowing, as if fatigue and shortness of breath would not allow him to move faster.

As they drew nearer, Lord Castleberry saw that it was Chester. His heart sank. Something was very wrong. The boy was carrying his shoes, and when they were upon him it was plain that he had been crying. Lord Castleberry jumped from the carriage.

"Chester, what is wrong? Where is Lady Castleberry . . . and the—"

" 'Twas a Stanhope we were traveling in, then a dirty man pulled her ladyship out of it and drove off with me. I tried to get loose, but another man jumped aboard and held me down. He pushed me out miles back, and I've been coming for help since." He began to cry. "I tried to help her, your lordship."

"I know you did, Chester. You did your best. Do you think you can make it on to Robinbrook while Avery and I go look for my wife? Can you tell me what the man looked like who dragged her from the carriage. Had you seen him before?"

"No, I'd not seen him. He was dirty, with missing teeth. That's all I know. I was so scared."

Lord Castleberry reached out and drew the boy to him and hugged him tightly. A lump formed in his throat, and he had trouble swallowing past it. "I like your glasses," he said, and watched a big grin form on the distraught face, and then he quickly regained the carriage, cracked the whip, and drove off, feeling guilty that he did not turn around and take the boy to Robinbrook. But Olivia was in danger, and he must find her. Praying with all his heart, and taking a big handkerchief from his pocket, he wiped at the tears that trickled from his eyes. "Avery, I don't think I can live if she is lost to me. I should have been here, taking Chester to Hythe myself."

"Don't be too hard on yourself, Castleberry. The mistake can be mended if we can find her in time. I worry that she, like Chester, is scared to death. First, let's get the Bow Street Runners involved. Because of the ships going in and out of Hythe, there's a cadre stationed there. They're good men, and smart. They'll help us. They'll find your cousin Trevor."

In Hythe, which was gained in much expediency, Lord Castleberry took Avery to the building that housed the Bow Street Runners and then proceeded on to the house where he had just recently learned Trevor had taken, in a better section of town. But his cousin was not home, nor was the Stanhope and black horse in sight. His lordship peered through the windows and saw only darkness. His heart pounded heavily in his chest, and his breathing came in spurts. Not even in the heat of battle had he been this scared. Scared for someone other than himself, he thought, liking the feeling of wanting his Olivia near, wanting to know that she was safe. *Dear God, I love her so,* he murmured in supplication to a higher power as, sadly, he turned away and went to search the streets of the town, driving at great speed, his eyes furtively searching for the Stanhope gig, and for a dirty man with missing teeth.

Thirty-four

The next three hours were the longest of Lord Castleberry's life. He searched the narrow, winding streets, the docks, collaring more than one man with missing teeth, only to let him go when he realized he knew nothing of Olivia's disappearance. He envisioned her dead, in an alley, or floating in the deep water out to sea. He cried, and prayed, and called to her.

At last, realizing he was going in circles, he returned to the headquarters of the Bow street Runners and there found Avery and two very alert young men standing beside the Stanhope gig. It had been found in Saltwood, a small village just over the brow from Hythe, they told him. The black horse had been tethered to an iron hitching post, and there was evidence that it had been there for several hours. But there was no sign of how the Stanhope and horse had arrived in Saltwood. No one who was questioned remembered having seen the driver, or any other occupant of the Stanhope.

And no sign had been seen of Trevor Castleberry.

The quiet was filled with moonlight as the four men stood contemplating what to do next. Each expressed a gut feeling that Olivia was in grave danger, that time was running out. Then an approaching carriage was heard, coming at breakneck speed. It carried Alicia Rose and Lizzie. Practically tumbling onto the ground before someone could help her, she thrust toward Lord Castleberry a folded paper. One il word spilled over another. "She's with the bones. I told you I could see—"

Lord Castleberry was ready to believe anything, even Lizzie and her gibberish. "Lizzie, what are you talking about?"

"She's in the church with the bones. I found this printing paper, talking about the skulls, and when I touched it, my hand became hot, like the paper was going to flame. Oh, pray, your lordship, you have to believe me. Her ladyship is there . . . with all those awful bones."

By now Alicia Rose was out of the carriage, looking harried and worried to death. Avery went to her and embraced her, and she put her head on his shoulder and sobbed. "What do we have to lose? Olivia has to be somewhere."

"She's right," said one of the Bow Street Runners. "We've nowhere else to look. I feel that when we find her ladyship, we will find Trevor Castleberry. On-dits have it that he's been acting queer in the head since he was forced to leave Robinbrook."

Lord Castleberry did not comment, for he was not in the mood to talk of his cousin being crazy. If he had done this dastardly deed, then the authorities could deal with him. He would not use his energy for doing harm. All he, Castleberry, wanted was to have his wife back, and then and there he promised God that he would love, cherish, and nourish her for as long as she lived if given a second chance.

They went hurriedly to the church, using three carriages, and all piled out at once, each racing to the big doors, only to find them steadfastly locked. Not a peep of light came under them, nor did a window show that a light burned on the inside. And it took several minutes of banging with the knocker to rouse the parish chamberlain, a not-too-happy parish chamberlain.

"What brings you here this time of the night?" he asked, holding high the taper in his hand. "The church is closed." And then his eyes fell on the Bow street Runners. His demeanor, Lord Castleberry noted, changed considerably. His lordship told him, "We have reason to believe my wife is in the crypt with the bones. She's been kidnapped—"

"No such thing has ever happened here. This is a place of God. Besides, no one goes to the crypt without my seeing them. I'm the one who conducts the trips down there. Or I did, before it was closed for work."

One of the Bow Street Runners stepped forward. He was a tall, burly young man with an authoritative voice. "I suggest you let us look for ourselves. Who's doing the work you speak of?"

"Why, Trevor Castleberry. A man with excessive knowledge of history. He's to restack and study the bones and give us his opinion of their origin. 'Tis suspected they go back to Saxon times."

"Is there another door through which a workman could enter the crypt?" asked the burly young officer.

"Why, yes, a small stone door on the south side, but there'd be no reason for Mr. Castleberry to go in that way when he can come through here. That door hasn't been used for years."

Lord Castleberry pushed past the parish chamberlain, taking, as he did so, the taper, for it was dark as pitch inside the church. Having never attended services at St. Leonard's, he was unfamiliar with its architecture, and checked several doors before he found one that opened onto a stairwell leading downward. Taking the stone steps two at a time, he practically fell over himself getting to the bottom. The smell was of death, and he almost wished that Olivia would be found somewhere else.

He heard a mewling sound and went to it, and there, on a pallet on the cold cobbles, he saw her, rolled into herself, crying softly. "Oh, Olivia, thank God you are alive," he said, kneeling quickly and taking her into his arms, kissing her cheeks, her brow, her lips, which were as cold as he imagined the pile of bones behind which she was hidden were, and she was trembling as she stared up at him as if he were a stranger.

The others were crowded around; Alicia Rose was crying softly, but only Lizzie spoke. "I guess now you will believe I have second sight, your lordship, and I know something else. Your Lady Castleberry will come through this, though not quickly."

During the next week Lord Castleberry hardly left Olivia's side. A physician was sent for, medicine was administered, and still she slept in a semiconscious state. Sometimes her gray-green eyes showed slight recognition, and then she would slip away to some unreachable place and hover there. The cold, and the trauma, had taken its toll. She burned with fever and would occasionally take a spoon or so of the soup Lord Castleberry fed her, while over and over he told her he loved her. To make it all bearable, and to keep his own sanity, he talked of their future, about the wonderful town house he had found in London in which they would raise their family.

"That's why I was late returning to the Clarendon, giving you time to take off for Robinbrook. I went to see Mr. Bates about your manuscript, and then house-hunting . . . I never loved her, Olivia; I was in love with love. I meant to give her my mother's jewels, but for some reason I never could. Now I know why. The love I thought was there was just not there. I was saving them until real love came along.

"I'm sorry she came to you with those lies. I never asked her to leave old Sapp. I thought that was what I wanted, but when the time came, when we were dancing, I knew how wrong I had been. The footman at the Clarendon told me about the visit, and then Alicia Rose informed me of what was said. Please, please, Olivia, my darling, wake up and tell me you forgive me. . . ."

Then one day, as Alicia Rose watched over her sister, she

saw a thin veil of perspiration form on Olivia's forehead. A smile formed on her wan face. Alicia Rose had never seen her more beautiful, her long hair framing her pale face and falling to rest on a lace-trimmed nightdress of fine, almost transparent lawn.

"Where's Fitzgerald?" Olivia asked, her voice weak and barely audible.

"He left only a moment ago to go to the library to search through more medical books. He has refused to let them bleed you, or to use leeches, and he's gone to read more about it. He's been worried sick about you, Olivia, and, oh, I have too. You can't imagine how it feels to see your wonderful sister so sick. The whole household has been paralyzed. Especially dear Fred."

"Trevor, what happened to him? Alicia Rose, he did not hurt me, just kept saying we were waiting for a doctor to come take care of my burden. I soon realized he was mad."

"The authorities have him. He will stand trial if he's sane. Lord Castleberry wants him to be analyzed by doctors in London. He even suggested that instead of prison, Trevor be sent to Australia . . . far out of proximity to Robinbrook."

"I don't ever want him near me again," Olivia said, again feeling fear pass over her. "But I do not want him sent to prison if he really is mad."

"You're not to worry about that. His lordship will see that the right thing is done. Your job is to get well."

"Oh, I will. I feel so much better." She rested for a while, then asked, "Fitzgerald said he went to see Mr. Bates. Did he like my writing?"

"Only that about Lucifer. Said the long manuscript had no life, no feeling. He's very interested in Lucifer."

"Well, I shall not write for him, then. Thinking on it makes my face flush. Someday, mayhap, I can write in that vein, but not now." She pushed herself up, and Alicia Rose told her of her plan to return to Boston for a short stay, until Nigel Avery would free himself of his alliance with Lady Anne. And then she told Olivia that she believed the apparition she had seen on the loggia was Nigel Avery in another life.

Olivia shook her head. "After Lizzie knowing I was with the bones at St. Leonard's, I can believe almost anything."

Alicia Rose laughed. "Lizzie's so full of herself now, she's hardly bearable."

A long silence fell between then, and then Olivia said, "I'll miss you while you're in Boston."

"I'll be back soon. I just feel that I want to see Mama and Papa, and I must put distance between Nigel and myself. Oh, Olivia, I love him so much."

Olivia reached to pat her sister's hand, understanding. She asked about Chester and was told that he had come often to inquire of her health. "Seemingly, the glasses have changed his whole personality," Alicia Rose said, and Olivia smiled, and a short time later she sat up and slid from the high bed to place her feet on the carpeted floor. "I want to go to the library where Fitzgerald is. And please, give me the handkerchief from the writing desk. I bought it for him when I had hope, and then I lost that hope. Now I believe in love again. 'Tis not much, but it's a symbol of my trust in him. Oh, Alicia Rose, I heard all the things he said to me when I was so far away. His words pulled me back, but I could not answer. I need to go to him. . . ."

"Peagoose! You're too weak to walk."

Olivia smiled. "Not if you'll help me."

And so, as when they were in Boston, one sister helping the other, they made their way down long, wide halls on whose walls horrid portraits of ancient ancestors hung, around corners, and then to the grand library, where the patina of the rich wood was like spun gold.

Lord Castleberry was standing by the window, looking out at the green hillocks, a leather-bound book in his hand. Plainly, he was in deep thought and did not hear them enter.

Alicia Rose, after depositing Olivia inside the door, stepped back and closed it softly behind her, leaving Olivia standing in her white nightdress, from under which two white feet protruded. She held the white linen handkerchief in her hand.

Her long chestnut hair hung loosely to touch her shoulders.

"Fitzgerald," she said softly, and he, turning pale as if he were seeing a ghost, came to her as quickly as his long strides could bring him. He was dressed casually, his collar open, showing twists of black chest hair. Reaching out, he took her into his long arms.

"Olivia, I've been so worried."

"I know. You talked to me, and I heard you. I just couldn't respond. I wanted so much to say that I love you too, that I want to have the heir to Robinbrook."

"A pox on an heir. 'Tis you I want, always, by my side. If it is in the scheme of things, then we shall have a whole gaggle of children. But that is no longer uppermost in my mind."

"What about Fred?"

He chuckled. "He's a wise old bird. Now that he knows I've come to my senses, he's very confident there will be heirs aplenty. I just want the completeness I felt when we made love. But more than anything, I want your forgiveness."

"That affords no problem," she answered with alacrity, smiling up at him and winding her arms around his neck.

She felt his arms tighten around her. Closing her eyes, she laid her head against his broad chest and felt wondrous strength seep from his body into hers. She leaned into him and heard from far off an ancient song of love, of strength, and of endurance. As she'd heard when her fever had taken her to another dimension, she thought. She loved him so very much, and she was where she wanted to be for the rest of her life.

He released her and picked her up into his arms. "You must not tax yourself. For a while, let me be your strength."

He gained a big leather chair, and they sat, her snuggled on his lap, her head on his shoulder, his face buried into her thick hair. He felt tears of happiness push at his eyes, and his heart pounded in his chest unmercifully.

"I love you," he whispered more than once, and the fire died to dull gray coals. Outside, beyond the windows, sheep lowed lazily on the undulating hillocks, and an owl hooted in the distance.

"I have a small gift for you," she said, "I bought it long before I knew how deeply one could love. . . ."

HISTORICAL ROMANCE FROM PINNACLE BOOKS

LOVE'S RAGING TIDE (381, $4.50)
by Patricia Matthews

Melissa stood on the veranda and looked over the sweeping acres of Great Oaks that had been her family's home for two generations, and her eyes burned with anger and humiliation. Today her home would go beneath the auctioneer's hammer and be lost to her forever. Two men eagerly awaited the auction: Simon Crouse and Luke Devereaux. Both would try to have her, but they would have to contend with the anger and pride of girl turned woman . . .

CASTLE OF DREAMS (334, $4.50)
by Flora M. Speer

Meredith would never forget the moment she first saw the baron of Afoncaer, with his armor glistening and blue eyes shining honest and true. Though she knew she should hate this Norman intruder, she could only admire the lean strength of his body, the golden hue of his face. And the innocent Welsh maiden realized that she had lost her heart to one she could only call enemy.

LOVE'S DARING DREAM (372, $4.50)
by Patricia Matthews

Maggie's escape from the poverty of her family's bleak existence gives fire to her dream of happiness in the arms of a true, loving man. But the men she encounters on her tempestuous journey are men of wealth, greed, and lust. To survive in their world she must control her newly awakened desires, as her beautiful body threatens to betray her at every turn.

Available wherever paperbacks are sold, or order direct from the Publisher. Send cover price plus 50¢ per copy for mailing and handling to Penguin USA, P.O. Box 999, c/o Dept. 17109, Bergenfield, NJ 07621. Residents of New York and Tennessee must include sales tax. DO NOT SEND CASH.

ZEBRA'S REGENCY ROMANCES DAZZLE AND DELIGHT

A BEGUILING INTRIGUE
(4441, $3.99)
by Olivia Sumner

Pretty as a picture Justine Riggs cared nothing for propriety. She dressed as a boy, sat on her horse like a jockey, and pondered the stars like a scientist. But when she tried to best the handsome Quenton Fletcher, Marquess of Devon, by proving that she was the better equestrian, he would try to prove Justine's antics were pure folly. The game he had in mind was seduction—never imagining that he might lose his heart in the process!

AN INCONVENIENT ENGAGEMENT
(4442, $3.99)
by Joy Reed

Rebecca Wentworth was furious when she saw her betrothed waltzing with another. So she decides to make him jealous by flirting with the handsomest man at the ball, John Collinwood, Earl of Stanford. The "wicked" nobleman knew exactly what the enticing miss was up to—and he was only too happy to play along. But as Rebecca gazed into his magnificent eyes, her errant fiancé was soon utterly forgotten.

SCANDAL'S LADY
(4472, $3.99)
by Mary Kingsley

Cassandra was shocked to learn that the new Earl of Litton was her childhood friend, Nicholas St. John. After years at sea and mixed feelings Nicholas had come home to take the family title. And although Cassandra knew her place as a governess, she could not help the thrill that went through her each time he was near. Nicholas was pleased to find that his old friend Cassandra was his new next door neighbor, but after being near her, he wondered if mere friendship would be enough . . .

HIS LORDSHIP'S REWARD
(4473, $3.99)
by Carola Dunn

As the daughter of a seasoned soldier, Fanny Ingram was accustomed to the vagaries of military life and cared not a whit about matters of rank and social standing. So she certainly never foresaw her *tendre* for handsome Viscount Roworth of Kent with whom she was forced to share lodgings, while he carried out his clandestine activities on behalf of the British Army. And though good sense told Roworth to keep his distance, he couldn't stop from taking Fanny in his arms for a kiss that made all hearts equal!